Passion's Fury

"I'll have you know I'm not a thing to be bartered, traded and sold to fit your fancy," Jamie cried in her fury. "I'll bed who I please. I ain't yer property and I ain't me father's!" Raising her hand high in the air, she brought it hard against Franco's cheek. For good measure, she moved to strike him once more but he caught her wrist in midair.

He pushed her down across the bed and gripped her wrists with one strong hand, holding them firmly above her head. "I won't fight you, Jamie," he said firmly as she struggled to escape him. "Perhaps I did roll the dice for you. Perhaps it is you I wanted." He leaned over and kissed her passionately until she moaned with reawakened desire. His lips explored the base of her throat, her ear, caressed her soft white shoulder.

Jamie's eyes closed as he nuzzled her ear deliciously. All of her anger had fled, spent in the rage she had unleashed on him. This was what she had come here to learn and she would not deprive herself of it. She would wait and see what the morrow might bring. For now, she wanted this man and she gave herself over to him completely . . .

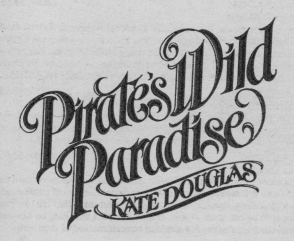

Pirate's Wild Paradise

KATE DOUGLAS

ZEBRA BOOKS
KENSINGTON PUBLISHING CORP.

To my mother, Camille Gilberto Fambrough,
for the gift of imagination.

ZEBRA BOOKS

are published by

Kensington Publishing Corp.
475 Park Avenue South
New York, NY 10016

Copyright © 1989 by Kate Douglas

First printing: February, 1989

Printed in the United States of America

Prologue

The minister read the rites in a rather unenthusiastic monotone. This was the third ceremony today he had been called upon to perform, but then, June was the month for weddings. The couple had chosen an inhospitable night to exchange their vows, with a hard driving storm battering the outer walls of the small wooden church.

The groom was nervous, the bride a bewitching, pretty little thing in a rose-patterned pink gown, clutching the young man's arm, holding a spray of violets in her dainty hand. The shade of the blossoms almost exactly matched the color of her eyes, the deepest, darkest blue Reverend Horvath had ever seen, with just a touch of lavender in them that considerably warmed what could have been an ice-cold hue without the purplish cast. Though she appeared to be into her twenties, she seemed a sweet and maidenly lass, when such a bride could have been very aware of her attractiveness and ability to beguile men. Black hair as smooth and dark as a raven's wing was swept up loosely onto the crown of her head, adorned with tiny sprigs of white and blue flowers.

Reverend Horvath had known Andrew Carmody since he was a boy. Lord and Lady Carmody only visited the Colonies every four or five years to check on young Andrew's progress with the family interests here in Virginia. The bride, he'd been told, had been orphaned. Neither of them had anyone to give them counsel or support in their matrimonial goal, so he discoursed at great length on the responsibilities of marriage, finally coming around to the formal portion of the ceremony.

"If there is any man present who knows just cause why this man and this woman should not be joined in matrimony, let him speak now or forever hold his peace . . ."

This part of the service seemed entirely unnecessary since there was no one in attendance but Reverend Horvath's wife and sister-in-law, who had been called upon to witness the ceremony, yet the reverend paused out of habit, never expecting the rest of his recitations to be interrupted by the hard, cracking slam of the church's front door being thrown open, followed by a powerful gust of wind from the late-spring storm raging outside. A deep roll of thunder heralded the appearance of a man who stood in the open entry, his hair and his cloak drenched from the downpour, a puddle of water quickly spreading across the floor at his feet. A brief burst of lightning streaked across the black night sky behind him, silhouetting his outline, and Horvath found himself wondering, aghast, if the devil himself might have come to call in the form of this stranger whose dark shape nearly filled the entry. He was tall, dark-haired and dark-eyed, and the hard, angry look on his face sent a shiver down the minister's back.

"This woman must not wed!" the apparition spoke, his tone low and full of menace.

Jamie Morgan's back stiffened as she spun about with the others at the sound of his voice.

The stranger stalked forward, his damp boots trailing wetness as he crossed the bare wood floor. Jamie saw Andrew out of the corner of her eye. He'd gone pale at the unexpected intrusion, whiter yet as Franco approached.

Franco DeCortega's slender frame was concealed beneath the great black cloak he wore, but not the height of him or

6

the width of his shoulders. He towered above poor Andrew, who had mustered all of the courage he possessed to marry Jamie without first seeking his parents' permission and had little left over for strange, dark men in the middle of the night. Andrew's frail nerves seemed close to shattered by the intrusion and he trembled slightly in the cool, rain-spattered wind that followed Franco up the aisle.

"This woman cannot marry this man." Franco stopped just in front of the minister, inserting himself forcefully between Jamie and her fiancé. "She is already wed, sir," he stated, addressing the minister. "She is my wife and therefore an unlikely candidate to become this man's bride."

"What . . . what did you say?" Jamie stammered, staring at him in astonishment. Reverend Horvath turned startled eyes upon her, horrified; Andrew looked at her, appalled; the two women behind the minister stared with their eyes threatening to pop out of their sockets. Jamie's state of mind quickly escalated from shock to outrage.

"Are you mad? What lies have you concocted?" she began, unable to believe even he could invent such an outrageous falsehood. "I most certainly am not his wife! It's untrue!" She turned from the minister's stern disapproval to Andrew's pale-faced shock. "Andrew, I promise you, the man is lying . . . I'm not his wife!"

Andrew's gaze wavered between them. "See here, sir, I . . ."

Franco gazed at her, the perfect portrait of the long suffering, infinitely patient husband, cuckolded and ill-used. " 'Tis bad enough to have left me, Jamie, but to deny our children . . ."

"Children!" she repeated, nearly shrieking the word out.

"Our poor, poor children." Franco shook his head sadly as he turned to the minister's wife standing just behind her husband, her round face etched with concern. "Babes, they are, madam . . . one just four and the other but two . . ."

"Oh, dear," the woman murmured.

7

"Stop this at once!" Jamie shouted, furious, astounded at his temerity. "Not a single word of this is true!"

" 'Tis no fault of yours, gentlemen." Franco glanced at Andrew who stood stock-still as if he had taken root in the floorboards. "You didn't know. Indeed, I don't know what comes over her at times, but," he sighed. " 'tis my cross to bear . . ."

Jamie's temper flared as if she'd been charged by the lightning raging outside, loosening her tongue, making her forget the behavior of well-bred young ladies. As the room swam red before her eyes, her diction reverted straight back to childhood's, deeper ingrained and closer to the surface than that which the good Lady Edwina had instilled in her charge. "You're a foul, scurvy liar!" Andrew's sweet young bride berated the stranger. "You cursed son of a sea snake, you'll stop lying now or I swear I'll see you pay for it!"

Franco clutched her wrist, wrapping his fingers around it in a tight hold that managed to cut her words off abruptly as he gave her arm a sharp tug. The black folds of his cloak hid his action from view so that her swallowed gasp might sound like the beginnings of a mad fit.

"You see what I must contend with? She loses her reason at times. When the moon's full." He kept his grip firm as Jamie struggled and tugged to free herself. "She can be a good wife, until the madness comes upon her . . ."

"Release my arm, damn you! You're breaking it!"

"Oh, am I, darling? I am sorry." Franco turned to her briefly, solicitously, the concerned husband who wouldn't harm her for all the world, but his hold hadn't loosened one whit. "She wanders off," he said calmly, as though nothing was happening on the far side of him where Jamie began prying at his fingers. "I never know where I may find her," he addressed the two women, "or in what circumstances."

"Foul liar!" Jamie kicked at him, missing his shin and striking the ankle of his boot, hardly fazing him. He gazed at her, his expression full of forbearance and sympathy.

8

"Truly, she is a good mother . . ." Franco shrugged help-lessly. "And, after all, we did vow in sickness as well as in health . . ."

Reverend Horvath had begun to nod in understanding of the poor man's plight.

"Andrew, he's lying," she cried. "I'm not his wife! The man is a liar! He's a pirate! A scurvy, thieving pirate! He couldn't tell the truth for the price of his own soul!" Franco gave her wrist another brisk downward tug. "Bastard!" she screamed at him.

Andrew stood silently watching it all, his expression tight with bafflement. The Jamie he had proposed marriage to wouldn't have known such curses, much less uttered them. Jamie realized her temper had again been her worst enemy and Franco well knew how to stoke it best. Even if Andrew were convinced of Franco's falsehoods, he would certainly never marry this shrew Franco had created for his sight.

"I'll kill you for this!" She turned to Franco, her ire flushing her cheeks. "I swear I'll carve your gizzard out for the crows . . ."

"Oh, my . . ." the two ladies clucked almost in unison.

"Poor child," Franco said sadly. "This really is one of her worst fits yet. I believe she truly doesn't remember me or her family, we who love her in spite of it all."

Jamie took a swing at him with a balled-up fist and missed as he stepped back out of reach.

"I think it best I take her home, gentlemen. The sight of the children often has a calming effect."

"Yes, of course," Reverend Horvath murmured.

"But . . ." Andrew leaned forward as if he intended to protest.

"Yes?" Franco glared at him.

" 'Tis true enough I can see that you know each other, but if she is your wife, surely you can prove your claim on her."

"I don't have any documents with me, if that is what you are asking for. I don't know how I can prove my claim

9

except perhaps with this . . ." Franco took a plain gold ring out of his pocket and let it lie in the palm of his hand. The gold shimmered and sparkled in the feeble lamplight. "She left it on the dressing table beside our daughter's bed."

"It's not mine!" Jamie protested. "I'll wager he's stolen it from some poor bride. The man is a pirate, I tell you . . ."

"I do have our children waiting at home to verify my claims. If you insist, I can fetch them from their beds . . ."

"Oh my, no!" Reverend Horvath's wife inserted. "On a night like this? Robert, you mustn't allow it!"

"Certainly not! Mr. Carmody, the man is obviously no pirate such as I've ever known them to be . . ."

"He is!" Jamie countered, furious that they were believing his wild tales of a wife who went mad at the full moon. "He's a Spanish privateer and makes his ill-gotten fortune out of raiding English ships." As soon as she'd said it, she realized how false it sounded. What would a Spanish privateer be doing on English colonial soil, risking his freedom and his life at the end of a hangman's rope?

"I am Italian, good sirs, ladies. My father had me taught King's English in hopes I might someday enter the diplomatic corps . . ."

The last part of his speech was the only truth he had yet uttered, Jamie thought, fuming. He was as Italian as she was, which was not at all! There was hardly a trace of any accent in Franco's speech, though it did contain a hint of foreign flavor in his pronunciations.

" . . . And there are times, good people, when she thinks me the King of France . . ."

Mrs. Horvath and her sister tittered quietly.

"Of course, there is one other way I can prove I am who I claim to be, but it shall entail the cooperation of your good wife, sir."

The rotund woman stepped forward, anxious to be of service.

"Sirs, ladies, if you will permit the indelicacy, my wife has

10

a small birthmark, just here . . ." While Jamie stared daggers at him, he pointed to the small of his back, just to the left of his spinal column, far too low for the most daringly cut gown to reveal. "And a mole here," he indicated a spot on his own chest that would correspond to just below Jamie's right breast. "If you would be so kind, madam, as to accompany her to a back room and ask her to disrobe . . ."

"Really!" Horvath muttered, blushing.

"Jamie, is it true?" Andrew asked her. "Do you have such marks?"

"It can easily be verified," Franco inserted.

"That will not be necessary." Jamie clipped the words out past seething anger. If she submitted to being stripped and searched, the evidence would be discovered. If she still refused to acknowledge him as her husband, it would be openly confessing that she had been his lover. "He knows damn well they're there."

"Jamie . . ." Andrew murmured, his handsome face anguished with the pain of betrayal.

"Young lady," Reverend Horvath admonished. "For the sake of your children, you must seek help for this condition before your illness carries you too far."

"I assure you, sir, I shall see to it immediately." Franco started to tow her behind him down the aisle. "Thank you, gentlemen, ladies. You've been so kind."

At the door, still open and blowing rain into the foyer, Franco paused to take her cloak from the hook and solicitously fasten it around her shoulders. "Take your hands off me! I can do it myself," she snarled at him.

Franco only smiled at her as he continued to lift the cowl over her head. "Come along, dear." He took her hand and pulled her firmly out the door into the sheeting rain.

"Will you never have enough of ruining my life?" she cried out in the street above the sounds of the crashing storm.

"I choose to think I've just saved it!" Franco returned, a flash of anger in his eyes now that his play-act was successfully ended. "For the second time, I've kept you from making a mistake you'd regret all the rest of your days!"

"Oh, and how's that?" she tossed back at him.

"Are you telling me you'd have married that . . . that whelp and been happy?" he shouted into her face.

"Indeed I would have! Andrew Carmody is rich and titled and . . ."

"Is that what you want? Is money and a title all that you care about?"

"And gaining my inheritance," she shouted back. If not for the crashing storm their volume would have awakened the entire vicinity. "Or did you think I'd forget about it?"

"Oh, no, my sweet. Not you. You certainly couldn't forget that! Then far be it for me to deprive you."

"You'll let me marry Andrew?" she asked suddenly, half afraid he might drag her right back inside. Though she had given thought to handling it kinder, she had been half prepared to bolt from marrying Andrew anyway, regretting the haste of her actions as the minister came ever closer to tying her to the young man forever. Only hope of gaining what was rightfully hers had kept her indecisive.

"Your Andrew won't spit in your eye now that I've had done with you. Or do you have an explanation you can offer him for how I've come to know the intimacies of your anatomy so well?"

"What then?"

"You'll see!" He spun about, taking her by the hand and nearly yanking her off her feet as he set off down the middle of the empty cobblestone street. The rain's steady downpour quickly drenched Jamie's light cloak and hood. The cool moisture against her skin make her shiver as Franco pulled her toward the docks.

"Where do you think you're taking me?" She hurried her

12

steps to keep pace with his long strides, fully certain that if she fell he would drag her along behind him. Her eyes stung from the mists of pounding rain while huge cracks of thunder rolled out of the pitch-black clouds. Her lightly clad feet, in low-cut slippers, were soaked through from sloshing into rain puddles. Her drenched skirt and cloak weighed her down and she was tiring rapidly, chilled to the bone.

"Franco, enough! Stop . . . please." She tugged back on his arm.

"I can't," she gasped, panting for breath. "Whatever you have in mind for me, have done with it here, for I can't walk another step."

He spun about on her, startling her with the intensity of the rage she saw blazing in the depths of his eyes. Only once before had he looked at her with such murderous fury and that time she had been sure his next move would be to kill her. "You're going to kill me," she murmured.

"Killing you is far from what I have on my mind," he seethed.

"What then?" Her eyes opened wide at him, the cowl falling back from her face. "What have I ever done to you to deserve such mistreatment?" Anger began to rise again. "I'm the one who should be angry. I'm the one who's been betrayed! The one who is owed reparations . . ."

"Indeed, and is that why you were going to go through with that . . . marriage, if you choose to call it such?" Franco watched her bristle. "You've had your attempts at revenge, and very successfully, too, my sweet, as you've cost me dearly chasing after you, but this is the end of it! You've gotten away from me twice on one scheme of yours after another, both times to see yourself wed to some fool with money and a 'sir' before his name who couldn't give you a moment's happiness . . ."

"Oh, and I suppose you could," she threw at him.

"Better than they ever will!" He tugged on her, drawing

13

her into his arms, locking her into his embrace before she could pull away. His lips came down on hers savagely, kissing her hard, almost snatching her breath away. At first, she struggled, pushing against his chest, then she began to slowly give way to her emotions, letting her arms slide around his neck, kissing him back with the intensity only Franco had ever stirred in her. Finally, she forced herself to pull away from him, but he refused to release her.

'Admit it," he smiled victoriously, as if he had proven his point. "You still belong to me."

"I'll say no such thing." She struggled against his holding her in his arms. Perhaps her senses had briefly betrayed her but she refused to give voice to her fear. "Let me go! I'll marry who I please, when I please, and I'll be as happy as it pleases me to be!"

"Really?" He raised one brow at her.

"Yes, really!" He finally allowed her to jerk free of his arms.

"Then I shall have to do something to prevent that, won't I?"

"Such as?" she began, but Franco suddenly leaned over and plucked her up off the ground, slinging her onto his broad shoulder. He walked off toward the docks with his burden kicking and screaming and pounding on his back.

"Put me down, damn you!" She beat on his back with balled-up fists, helpless to scream for aid from the sleeping houses with the rain muffling the sounds of her shouting. She felt as if her ribs were being crushed against his shoulder as he trod heavily down the street, letting her jostle over his back. They neared the port and Jamie saw the looming shape of the *Isabella* in the harbor outlined briefly against the black sky in a burst of gray lightning.

"Oh, no, you'll not get me aboard her," she shouted, renewing her attack on him, striking as hard as she could and only succeeding in bruising her own fists. "Put me down!" Her struggles had no effect on him as he walked surefootedly up the gangplank onto the swaying deck.

"Cast off!" he called out to the nearest seaman who gazed back at him blankly. "You heard me! Cast off!" he barked again, setting the man into motion.

The frigate began to pull away from the dock as Franco took his burden to the lower deck, into his cabin where he tossed her roughly onto the bed. Jamie glared at him in self-righteous indignation.

"You've no right to have done any of this," she sputtered, tossing her black mane of hair that had come loose of the pins that had held it, her eyes spewing sparks of rage. Even wet, disarrayed, and furious she was beautiful. Her cheeks were flushed and she shivered, perhaps as much from anger as from the exertions and the biting cold rain, but he well knew that, though she looked as delicate as a fragile orchid, her appearance was deceiving. She was a sturdy woman, of sterner stock than most. She'd survive. And she'd beg not one thing of him, neither towel nor blanket nor dry clothes with which to warm herself. As he watched her glare, he remembered Jamie as he had first met her. Barely more than a child then, she had brought out protective instincts in him he hadn't known he possessed. Franco looked back over the last four years with a poor assessment of himself as he had been then—vain, proud, too concerned over duty and propriety and, yes, even too prejudiced to see what had been right there under his nose, worth so much more than mere wealth and position. What a fool he had been, he chided himself. Twice now, he had almost lost her forever, for, content with her life or not, Jamie kept her vows. She'd remain faithful to the man she gave her oath to, whatever the cost to her own happiness.

"You can't keep me your prisoner forever!" she threatened, her eyes narrowing. "You have to dock sometime . . ."

"For what I intend for you, you shall never escape me again."

"What do you mean by that?"

15

"Dry yourself, my love." He tossed a towel to her from the rack beside his wash stand. "There are dry clothes in there." He pointed at a chest near the bed. "Do try to find something attractive."

"I'd rather stand naked than wear anything that would give you pleasure," she retorted.

"Now that, my dear, would pleasure me indeed." Franco smiled, turning for the door just in time to be missed by scant inches by the water pitcher she threw at his head.

Dawn broke over a calm sea in a burst of golden pink and orange. The sleek black frigate, her sails unfurled to the gentle wind at her back, rose and fell as softly as the breath of a sleeping dreamer on the lapping blue waters of the Atlantic.

Franco had spent the whole of the night on deck. His muscles ached from relieving the pilot during the worst of the passage through the storm and his eyes burned from the salt spray that had washed in his face. He wanted nothing more than a warm bath, a hot breakfast, and Jamie's arms around him as he dropped off into a blissful slumber, but all of that was denied him. The cook couldn't light a fire during the storm and was still busy swabbing out the galley, so there could be neither hot food or hot water, and as for Jamie's loving embrace, he'd consider himself well off if she didn't stick a knife in his ribs at her earliest opportunity. He had little doubt that her anger burned just as fiercely this morning. He had ruined her plans and she wouldn't forgive that easily.

"Not at all a bad passage for a lord's son, Conde DeCortega," Father Ramirez interrupted Franco's thoughts as he strode toward him. The fat, middle-aged priest had spent nearly all of the night sick as a dog in his bunk while the storm pitched and tossed the ship up and down and from port to starboard. "The DeCortegas I've known have always been land-loving men. Your father would have been proud of you."

"My father told me never to be a sailor or a merchant-man," Franco remarked, watching the horizon behind the priest's head. "He said the dangers were too high and the rewards too slender. And he was right."

"Oh?" The priest's smile faded. He was slightly afraid of this lean, handsome man before him. There was something in the young count's face, in the way he carried himself, that set a peace-loving man's nerves on edge, like standing near a leashed panther who might for the moment appear docile enough but was ever the wild animal at heart and could lash out without warning.

Although having learned the captain of this vessel was Conde Carlos DeCortega's son and heir had calmed the priest's initial misgivings about accepting the passage that had been offered to him, Father Ramirez still recalled that there had been rumors only a few years back about the youngest DeCortega turning pirate and rogue. Then again, free passage to his newly assigned mission in Havana was free passage after all and rumors were only tales for the idle tongued. Who knew how much truth or falsehood might be in them.

The old count's last remaining son had become an attractive man. Father Ramirez had last seen him when he was only a boy. Francisco Alonzo had grown taller than any other of the DeCortegas. The black waves of his hair, bound in back and held in place with a leather thong, had a reddish cast in the golden sunlight but his eyes were as black as inkpots, thickly lashed and slightly slanted to a downward turn that made them heavy lidded. He had the aristocratic profile of all the DeCortegas, and Isabella De-Cortega's thin, firm lips and wide, strong chin.

"Father, very shortly I will call upon you to perform that service I requested in return for your passage."

"Certainly, my son," Ramirez responded. "I was just

about to begin my daily offering of the Mass if your crew would care to assemble."

The count's face took on a strange half smile, one of the looks Father Ramirez found disconcerting. "It isn't a Mass I'm in need of, Father, though the crew may attend if they like. Later today, however I shall ask you to perform a ceremony for me."

"May I know the nature of the ceremony I am to perform?" the priest gazed at him, puzzled. No one was ill or had died aboard that he knew of. Perhaps a memorial service in the old count's name . . .

"You will be informed when the time comes," Franco answered him. He strolled past the brown-robed priest and down to the lower deck, selecting the pilot's cabin for a few hours of much needed sleep.

Aboard the *Isabella,* the captain's quarters were located astern with a full-size bed built flush against a broad expanse of windows that overlooked the foaming wake left by the vessel's passage through the sparkling blue waters. Jamie Morgan sat on the bed in Franco's cabin, the bay windows giving her an unrestricted view of the sea on three sides. There were heavy green velvet curtains with gold trim and the bed she was sitting on was firmly packed with goose feathers, spread with a dark green velvet to match the drapes. She had found a plain white muslin frock to dress in, determined to choose the dowdiest of the lot he had given her to select from. Still, the bodice was cut low and decorated with inexpensive lace; a kitchen maid's dress that was meant for chores and had no yardage left over for the frill of hoops and petticoats. If Franco would keep her prisoner, then a prisoner she would be and look the part.

She was no longer angry. Her temper, like her father's, might start out foul and tempestuous, but like the tropical gales of the Caribbean where she had grown up, the storms

18

quickly blew over and left calmer seas.

After a few solitary hours of reflection, she could better say she was extremely relieved. She hadn't loved Andrew Carmody and might have faltered trying to tell him so if Franco hadn't spared her the loathsome chore. As much as she hated to admit he could be right about anything, she would have been utterly miserable if she had gone through with it. She wasn't the kind for marriage. Lady Edwina had done her best, but beneath the polish that dear woman had applied, Jamie remained Morgan's offspring and always would. Unknown even to herself, she must have wanted Franco to learn of her plans and stop her from taking such a drastic, final step. Why else would she have confided them to Jocko, whom she knew would run straight away to Franco and tell him everything? Jocko would have thought he was saving her, too. Saving her from doing exactly what Franco had accused her of doing, marrying Andrew for spite. She might even have admitted it was spite, and that it was foolish, if he hadn't come in with all his lies and wild tales of a wife who went mad at the full moon.

Even after his behavior last night, though, she didn't hate him. She didn't hate him because she couldn't hate him. For as long as she lived, she would never be able to stop loving him. But what use was there in loving a man she could never trust? At least Andrew, if he wasn't even nearly as handsome or exciting, was still as faithful as a devoted lapdog. He would never betray her, or, if he did, she had to admit that she wouldn't particularly care.

When she had most needed Franco's love, where had she found him but in the arms of another woman? Morgan's trick, he'd said, but hadn't she seen the evidence with her own eyes? And how cunning to blame it all on the deceit of a dead man who couldn't defend himself against the accusations. If she had learned nothing else in her twenty-one years of life, she had learned that lesson well. She'd give her trust to no man again. And Franco DeCortega most of all!

19

Jamie heard the door open and glanced over her shoulder, making sure it was Franco before she turned back to her pensive view of the *Isabella*'s trail.

"Still angry, I see," he remarked, crossing the cabin toward her. She could hear his bootsteps across the wooden deck.

"I intend to remain angry until you set me free," she responded, gazing steadily out the window.

"Then that should very shortly be resolved." Franco's weight came down on the bed beside her. "We have a brief stop to make in Havana and, since you are as wanted there as I am in the English colonies, I suggest you remain below until we are underway again. We will then proceed to Port Royale where you may do as you please."

"I can leave the ship?" She turned to look at him as he leaned back against the pillows.

"If you wish," he answered easily—too easily, in Jamie's estimation.

"Why?" Her brows lowered into a suspicious frown.

"Tell me, did you ever tell your Andrew that you were a pirate, too?" His grin seemed mocking as he ignored her question, substituting one of his own.

"Certainly not!" She jerked herself farther into the corner, closer to the windows and away from him.

"I thought not. But then, you would have told the poor boy someday, wouldn't you?"

"That would be no concern of yours," she snapped, still miffed and determined to let him know it.

"Quite right." Franco sat up abruptly. "It's none of my concern," he smiled, thoroughly annoying her. "Couldn't you find a more becoming frock to wear?" He surveyed her plain white dress, obviously disapproving.

"It serves me well enough!" she retorted.

"Well, if it's your wish to be married in the attire of a scullery maid . . ." He stood up, towering above her.

"Married! Who says I'm to be married?"

20

"I say you are," he returned. "I promised you a husband of wealth and influence, and that you shall have."

Jamie sneered at his poor attempt at a joke. "And how do you intend to find a prospective bridegroom miles out to sea?"

"He's standing before you."

"You?" Her eyes widened as a smile crossed her lips. Whatever his game, he had to be teasing, perhaps punishing her for last night, taunting her over the foolishness she had almost committed.

"The same. It may interest you to know that, with my brother now deceased, I am Conde DeCortega. If you were willing to settle for a ladyship, then 'countess' should suit you rather well. It is what you've wanted, isn't it?"

"You're mad!" Her smile faded as she glared at him.

"Oh, yes, and wealth!" He snapped his fingers. "But that is solved for you as well. Since I am the only remaining heir, the entire fortune falls to me. Our revenues remain excellent, so that should keep you busy spending it or counting it, as you like."

"I won't be poor again! Ever!" She threw out at him, tears stinging her eyes from his mockery.

Franco's gaze softened. "I know . . ."

"Then stop taunting me!" She turned toward the windows to hide her tears.

"I'm not taunting you." He sat down on the bed beside her. "I promise you, you can be anything that you've ever dreamed of, everything that you've ever wanted. The fine house on the hill, the carriage all your own. If you still want them, Jamie . . ."

"Stop it! Just stop it!" Jamie choked. "The very moment this ship docks, I'm leaving it and I pray I shall never have to see you again!"

Franco stiffened, rising to his feet. "If that's the way you want it," he said, anger rising in him anew. "You may disembark at Port Royale or wherever else you like. You

21

may come and go as you please but there will be no more John Terrys or Andrew Carmodys, because I will be standing directly in your path. You may avoid my presence for the remainder of your life, but I promise you, you will never be free of me again!

"Now, will you come up on deck of your own accord, or must I carry you up there?"

"Why should I?" she asked, puzzling over all he had said. How could she be free and yet not free of him ever again?

Franco sighed with infinite patience. "There is a wedding party awaiting our presence on the forward deck. I intend to have a sufficient number of witnesses to the event to be certain you cannot claim it never took place."

Jamie smiled confidently, certain he was teasing her. "And who will perform the ceremony? Or will Captain DeCortega perform his own," she snidely remarked, determined to call his bluff. He was joking. Indulging in revenge himself in the cruelest way he knew.

"That has been seen to. Now, will you come?" He gazed down on her sternly, but she knew Franco was a wonderful actor when he chose to be, just as he had performed last night.

"If I, even for a moment believed you, I wouldn't have you," she returned to gazing out the window. "Not for all the wealth in the world."

"I am not presenting you with a choice."

Her head shot back to face him. "You couldn't make me!"

"No?" His eyes narrowed as he gazed down on her, sending a chill down her spine. "If a man can be made to marry a woman on the point of an irate father's sword, why then can a bride not be coerced into the same on the point of the groom's?"

"Hah!" Jamie folded her arms across her chest stubbornly.

"You will accompany me to the deck under your own power, or by God, it shall be by force!" He gripped her arm, pulling her off the bed in spite of her resistance.

"You can't make me marry you—I won't!" she said, stubborn and angry, trying vainly to yank her arm free. She was actually beginning to believe he meant this and the thought was terrifying. Of course she would never be free of him if she was his wife! She would be his wife wherever she went, wherever she hid. The fact would be there, an invisible chain that would bind her to him if she never looked on his face again.

"Wait a moment . . . Wait!" She pulled back as he started to drag her through the doorway. He stopped, glaring down at her.

"You've had your pleasure, now enough! If you want me to admit that I wouldn't have gone through with marrying Andrew, then I do admit it. I almost stopped the ceremony myself. I would have, if you hadn't burst in on us! You're right. I don't want a husband of wealth and influence. I don't want a husband at all! Not even for my inheritance. Last night gave me time to think and I realize I've been mistress of my own ship and mistress of my own life too long to let anyone become master of me . . ."

"That is unfortunate, darling, as you shall have one now." Franco tugged her through the door into the gangway.

"Franco, tell me what you want me to do? What do you want from me? I'll do whatever you ask if you'll just stop this nonsense at once." He started to pull her up the ladder. "I promise, I'll never marry anyone . . . I swear it!"

He jerked on her arm, propelling her out onto the sun-drenched deck, then paused for a moment, letting her take in the sight of the priest in his vestments, the *Isabella*'s crew gathered on the lower deck to witness the ceremony. Even the rigging was decorated in sprays of flowers and bedecked with white ribbons. He did mean it! She stared at the decorations through disbelieving eyes. The man had utterly lost his senses!

"No . . . Oh, no," Jamie began shaking her head. "I won't agree to this . . ."

"I've told you, you don't have a choice." Franco gripped her elbow to push her forward.

"I don't want to marry you, damn you!"

"Ah, but you'd wed Terry for your blasted money, wouldn't you?" Franco continued to tow her across the deck.

"That's different. 'Twas only business."

"And Carmody? Was he only business as well?"

"You're jealous," she suddenly stared at him through disbelieving eyes, her mind unable to grasp the full significance of the revelation. "You truly are . . . you're jealous." Never before had she suspected him capable of that emotion. Franco wanted what he couldn't have, coveted that which was denied him. The only reason he had ever pursued her was, in her estimation, because she was about to escape beyond his full possession of her adoration. Franco didn't love for love's sake.

"You said yourself that marriage is for simpletons and fools."

"I've changed my mind!" He stopped in front of the priest. "Father, you may begin."

"No!" she shouted, furious at him and at all his methods; his schemes, his lies, his forceful persuasion when all else failed him. "I won't do it! I won't have it! You can't make me! I'll wager he's not even a priest!"

"Now see here, young lady," the good father blustered.

"You wouldn't go through with it if he were a real priest!" she threw at Franco. "This is all a hoax to frighten me and you've succeeded but now I call your bluff. Go ahead, Father," she sneered. "It's all a sham, so go on with it."

"You heard the lady, Father." Franco briefly glared at her. "Do go on with it."

"But the young lady appears to be reluctant," the priest stammered, baffled by the woman's behavior. He had finally been told a wedding ceremony was to be his service paid in exchange for this voyage, but he hadn't been warned that the intended bride wanted no part of it.

"The bride is simply suffering from pre-nuptial apprehensions," Franco stated.

"The god-cursed *hell* I am!" she retorted, his comment reminding her of the embarrassment of last night. "The bride wants no part of you!"

"Father Ramirez . . ." Franco's gaze remained focused on the priest.

"But if she won't say the vows . . ."

"She'll say them."

"I will not!"

Keeping a grip on Jamie with his left hand, Franco drew his saber from his scabbard with his right, pointing the sharp tip of the weapon perilously close to the good father's abundant stomach. "Any tales you may have heard regarding my honor, or my *lack* of it, I assure you are true," Franco told him. "Do not think for a moment that I would hesitate to toss a man of the cloth overboard as easily as any other man."

Father Ramirez visibly swallowed, both of his chins quivering as a lump of saliva worked its way down his throat.

"You wouldn't," Jamie murmured, gazing at the gleaming swordpoint against the satin cloth of the priest's vestments. "Even you wouldn't do that." Her tone questioned, unsure of her own statement.

"I've learned from your own father, my love. I suggest you don't test me."

Confused for the moment, she stayed silent.

Father Ramirez opened the book to the marked-off pages and started to read the service, casting wary glances at the swordpoint that Franco had lowered only slightly.

"It won't be legal," Jamie inserted over the priest's intoned Latin. "You've forced the priest. You're forcing me. No court in any land will hold it binding."

"It's binding enough if the words are said."

"Binding for who?" she threw back at him. "Binding for me, perhaps, while you do as you please."

25

Father Ramirez stopped, watching the young lady.

"Father, continue." Franco paid no attention to her.

"The bride's name?" she heard the priest ask him. "I need the bride's name . . ."

"James Allison Morgan," Franco provided.

"James?" the priest inquired.

"James!" Franco snapped, turning Jamie's face red.

The priest cleared his throat. "James Allison Morgan, do you take this man, Francisco Alonzo Montenegro DeCortega to be your lawfully wedded husband . . ."

"No!"

". . . to have and to hold from this day forward . . ."

"I do not!"

". . . for richer, for poorer," he began to rush the words out, helter-skelter, fueled by Conde DeCortega's warning glare. ". . . in sickness and in health . . . for better, for worse, until death do you part?"

"She does!" Franco responded for her.

"I don't!" Jamie countered, yanking on his grip again. "I said I won't have it."

"Is it your wish to try me on whether or not I will take my vengeance for your refusal out on this poor innocent man or will you give the proper answer?"

"I do then, since I have no choice," Jamie said wrathfully.

"Do you Alonzo Francisco, ahem . . . Do you Francisco Alonzo DeCortega take this woman, James Allison Morgan, to be your wife . . . to have and to hold from this day forward . . ." Ramirez stammered his way to the bitter end.

"I do!"

"He can't!" Jamie inserted, bristling with anger. "He's never kept a vow in the whole of his life!"

Ramirez couldn't go on, staring from one to the other, troubled over how two people who seemed to despise each other could possibly be standing before him for this ceremony.

"Finish the rites, Priest," Franco ordered crisply.

26

Ramirez gave a start at the harsh note in the count's voice.

"I now pronounce you man and wife." He rushed the words out in a torrent. "In the name of the Father and of the Son and of the Holy Spirit. Amen." He almost choked on the last words, so great was his haste to be done with this and have the sword removed from the vicinity of his stomach.

The couple glared hatefully at each other as the priest quickly closed the book he had hardly read from anyway, then Ramirez remembered. He had forgotten the ring. "Ahem, Conde DeCortega," he inserted into the palpable silence. The sword had been removed but was still in the young man's hand. "We missed one thing . . . I forgot, you see . . . the ring . . ."

"The what?" Franco barked at him, startling the priest.

"The ring, sir. The bride's wedding ring."

Franco dug in the pocket of his waistcoat, removing the same ring he had displayed for Reverend Horvath and Jamie's intended fiancé. He expected more resistance, or at least another verbal onslaught, but Jamie mutely allowed him to lift her hand and place the ring on her finger. The plain gold band fit her finger perfectly.

"Are we legally wed then, in the eyes of God and man?" Franco asked in a tone of voice that sounded like a threat on the priest's life if he answered negatively.

"Well, yes, I suppose so . . . I mean, of course. Those were the proper rites and everything was in order . . . well, nearly everything. Yes, of course you are, provided, that is . . ." Father Ramirez stumbled over what he had been about to say.

"Providing what, Father?" Franco glared at him.

"Ahem, provided . . ." Ramirez glanced at the unwilling creature who had been forced into this marriage. "Um, provided it's consummated," he said softly.

"Speak up, man!"

"Provided it's consummated!" Ramirez forced the words out to a short burst of laughter from the crew witnessing the event.

Franco smiled tightly. "Thank you, Father, you have performed your service for me admirably."

Dismissed at last, the priest hastened below, wishing he could utter a word of consolation to the poor bride. The child's fright was likely to account for her behavior. He promised himself he would try, during the remainder of the journey, to speak with her and offer a sympathetic ear to her plight.

"Am I dismissed now?" Jamie asked sullenly.

"You may do as you like," Franco replied, turning away from her.

"Thank you so much." She curtsied abruptly, deliberately mocking him before she spun about on her heel and left.

The sun had finally set on a calm sea fanned by cool western breezes when Franco at last started down the gangway to his own cabin. He wasn't certain of what might be awaiting him there — a pot whistling past his ear, stubborn petulance, or even finding the door to his cabin firmly locked and blockaded with every stick of furniture the cabin possessed jammed against it, but the door opened inward easily and he stepped inside the cool, darkened interior.

Jamie had opened the windows to allow the brisk night air to circulate, and the heady scent of the sea filled the room, along with the sounds of gentle waves slapping against the hull.

Only a single lamp was lit, its wick turned low, and in the feeble light he saw Jamie lying in his bed, the covers tucked up to just below her bare shoulders, her arms resting on top of the dark green spread. She remained silent as he crossed the room, merely watching as he took off his frockcoat and waistcoat and laid them down over a chair.

28

"I must admit," he said finally, "I didn't expect to find you so : . . so . . ."

"So what?" she prodded, looking at him.

"I didn't expect to find you in my bed!" He felt uncomfortable admitting what he had been thinking. He had expected anything but this, to find her lying docilely and naked in his bed awaiting their wedding night.

"Would it give you greater pleasure to force me?"

Franco backed away from the question as if he'd been slapped. "No," he replied, feeling an edge of irritation. If she wanted to pick a quarrel, then do it — that was a reaction he could respond to.

He sat down on the edge of the bed and started to pull off his knee-high leather boots. The bed shifted under Jamie's movement, then he felt cool, strong hands caressing his shoulders through the thin material of his blouse, her fingers kneading the tired muscles in his neck. For a moment, he had stiffened, half believing she might be thinking of trying to strangle him, then he gave in to the comfort of the gentle massage.

"You used to say I had a soothing touch." She continued to work the muscles, pressing her thumbs in deeply and letting them trace a delicious course down his back.

"You still do," he admitted, dropping his boots to the floor. "Jamie . . ." He reached for her hand and gently squeezed it. "What are you about? What is this?"

"Nothing," she replied without rancor. "You have what you want. If I've learned nothing more from Morgan, grant me that I do know how to make the best of the situations in which I find myself."

"Are you comparing me to Morgan?" His grip on her fingers tightened.

"Do I need to?" she returned, throwing him off balance. Was she denying the comparison? Or saying there was no need to compare the obvious?

"How do you mean that?"

"How do you think?" she promptly replied.

"Enough!" Franco spun around and grabbed her by the shoulders forcing her down onto the mattress. "I could take it that you think of this marriage in the same manner by which you might regard a prison sentence . . ."

"Isn't it?" she retorted hotly. "You abducted me in the middle of the night, held that poor man hostage to the point of your sword, and then put the very words into my mouth . . ."

"You wouldn't have said them!"

"How would you know what I'd say or not? You never asked! You *never* ask!" She could see his anger evaporating, flowing out of him like mist in sunlight.

"If I had asked . . ." he posed, leaving the rest of the question silent.

"You'll never have an answer to that now, will you?" She gazed up at him, her eyes wide and beautiful in the lamplight. "This marriage is your doing, not mine. You can make what you will of it! If you think I will deny you my bed, you're wrong. My door will always be open to you. But you'll never know, will you, if you are there because I love you and want you or if it is only because of the vows you made me swear to."

"I'll know the difference . . ."

"Will you?" She played with the ties of his shirt, slowly unfastening them and as they came free, letting her fingers trail downward over his chest. When the last tie was unfastened, she lifted the garment over his head, then dropped it to the floor. Her arms reaching around his neck, she pulled him down toward her. She kissed his lips, finding them at first unresponsive and wary, then he kissed her back fiercely, as if by sheer force of will he would make her feel again every moment of lovemaking they had ever shared together. She couldn't deny that she wanted him, yearned for him, cherished the hard contours of his smooth, naked chest pressing against hers that did stir so many memories. He

30

reached down to tug the sheet away from between them, his gaze lingering on the naked flesh he revealed, then he anxiously removed the rest of his clothing and stretched out on the bed beside her.

"It will be as it was before between us," he promised in a husky, soft voiced whisper. "You loved me once and this time, I swear it, I shall do all in my power to remain worthy of it."

His statement, so earnestly uttered, brought tears to her eyes that she was reluctant to let him see and turned her face away. Was it possible that he could mean them? Could it be true? She wished it was so with every fiber of her being but too much pain lay in the path of her ability to utterly believe him.

He kissed her again with gentle, lingering passion, as if she was a fragile object of the most delicate beauty that he feared he might shatter with rougher handling. His lips left her mouth, and began to blaze a searing, damp trail against the skin of her throat, making her flesh prickle with anticipation even as she returned his light caresses, touching secret places they each had shared before. Her own desires sparking into flame, she felt the hard muscles of his back, his hips, his buttocks flinching with the effort of holding himself in check. He kissed each of her breasts in turn, then let his lips linger in the valley between them while his artful hands traced the contours of her excited flesh. Urging her legs to part for him, he teased and caressed her warm wetness. Jamie's soft moan told him she was ready for him and as he lifted himself up and came down upon her, she welcomed him with open limbs, arching her hips to meet his first thrust with a hunger that now raged as great as his own. Unable to help herself, Jamie whispered his name, her passions betraying her into answering his thrusts, desire sweeping her beyond all reason to the ecstasy that only he in all the world could fulfill in her. As he drove deeper and deeper inside her, her senses soared to the heavens to mingle with the stars and reeling planets. Unwillingly, she cried out as they reached the crescendo of their lovemaking in an explosion of fiery passion. Then, quietly, they settled back to the bonds of earth again in each other's arms. If only in that moment of tender satisfaction he repeated the simple words that might have banished her misgivings for all time, but he didn't.

"Tell me now that you didn't want me," he said near her ear, shattering Jamie's contentment completely. Her fingers tightened convulsively, her body stiffening beneath his as every cruelty of the heart he had ever visited upon her came back in full.

"It could as well be Andrew in your place, or any other man who offers me the means of gaining that which is rightfully mine."

Franco started as if she had pinched him, backing away just far enough to look into her eyes, certain he would find there the truth she refused to reveal. "You don't mean that," he stated.

"Don't I?" Jamie countered, forcing her tone to remain indifferent. "I told you, if it is your wish, I will keep the vows you answered. I did say that you should never know the difference. A small role, acting the part of the contented lover, is the least I can do. I expect only that you, in turn, will keep the promise you made to me, that when we dock in Jamaica I may leave this ship and never have to look at you again."

For a moment as she watched his face, she was almost impelled to relent. Was it a flicker of genuine regret and sorrow she'd seen there? But if he could take Polly without a moment's caring, how then couldn't he do the same to her? Why had he forced this marriage upon her? Why had he whispered such words to her only to turn about and offer her such a large helping of humble pie to swallow? Was all he wanted the ultimate prize won out of his private war with Morgan? Jamie fervently wished she could make herself

32

believe it wasn't so.

Say it, her mind pleaded with his silence. Tell me once more that nothing happened that night. Tell me that I am the one you care for and that revenge on Morgan means nothing to you. Simply say it and I'll make myself believe once more.

Instead, his look hardened into anger. "As you wish," he spat, moving away from her. "Go if you will. It matters not to me what you do!"

Jamie spun away from him, turning her back on him. She could feel his movements as he did the same. Hot, bitter tears burned her eyes but she refused to give in to the pent-up sobs that threatened to wrack her body if she dropped her guard and gave in to them. She wept silently, letting the tears course down her face, feeling anger at herself for once more letting him break her heart.

If only he would say, "I love you. I've always loved you. I always will," but the words would surely catch in his throat to choke him. Why couldn't he say what she so eagerly and so often had told him? She loved him still. She always would. She always had. Quite likely she had loved him from the first time she laid eyes on him, even as he stood above her with the point of his sword at her throat.

Chapter One

Tiny puffs of white clouds, like the speckled skin of a mackerel, dotted the bright azure, sun-drenched sky as the *Lady Morgan,* her canvas sails furled, waited at anchor within the refuge of the bay. There was little activity on the deck this summer morning in 1693, because of both the midafternoon heat and the lack of need to accomplish anything other than bearing the hours of idleness waiting for the Spanish galleon, laden with cargo of gold, to sail past their hiding place.

In the storage hold of the three-masted pirate ship, the air was only slightly cooler than above, on deck, but confined and stale. In the stuffy atmosphere below, Jamie Morgan was anxious to be done with her task, impatient to reach the fresh island breeze on the quarterdeck. There was no time for foolishness while there was work to be about. She soundly slapped at the hand she caught slyly reaching around her waist, striking hard, with a sharp, loud crack that left Rory McGregor shaking the offending hand in the air.

"Ye doan have to hit so hard," Rory complained in his thick Scottish brogue. "I did'na mean nothin' by it."

Jamie gave him a disapproving scowl. "Are ye going to help me with this keg o' powder or not? If not, I'll do it myself." Jamie spoke in the mixed dialects of the sea, tutored by sailors who had taken ship from ports in Liverpool to Edinburgh to wherever chance had flung them from. Theirs made up a musical language all their own, consisting of flat monotones interspersed with unexpected lilts in the strangest places and generously strewn with colorful curses.

"Aye," Rory grumbled, helping her lift the keg onto its rim and between them struggling the heavy barrel over the deck of the dimly lit hold. " 'Tis a lovely lass ye are, Jamie," he remarked, equally pushing his own weight into the rolling of the keg across the slanted deck. Rory, at eighteen, wasn't very much larger or stronger than the girl who helped him with the task. She was dressed as he was, in dark blue, buttoned breeches that ended at midcalf and flapping white shirts sizes too big for either of them. Of late, though, Rory had become all too aware of the fact that Jamie had been selecting larger shirts yet from the clothing booty taken. Yesterday he had deliberately let himself lose his footing with a roll of the ship to fall against her only long enough to assure himself that the breasts he suspected were truly and wonderfully there beneath the rough-spun cotton blouse. The brief contact had been sufficient to cause Rory a sleepless, restless night.

Jamie had ignored his remark, concentrating on shifting the barrel along to the ladder. If she'd let him, he'd waste their time with nonsense while the galleon sailed past without so much as a shot fired across her bow because Ned didn't have his gunpowder for the cannon. And who'd be blamed for the delay that cost them the gold? Why, she would, of course, while her gallant Rory hid himself below decks until the captain's wrath subsided. *Thank ye very much,* but she could do without the flattery.

"You go first," Rory decided when they had reached the nearly vertical ladder to the deck. "Pull it from above while I push from below it."

"And if it slips, ye'll be killed!" Jamie exclaimed, opening her blue-lavender eyes wide at him.

Rory felt like his heart just might burst. Jamie had the most beautiful eyes, dark blue with just a hint of lavender in them, and lush black lashes so long and thick he wondered how she kept them open. For a long while Rory McGregor had been carefully observing every detail of Jamie's approach to womanhood. She was seventeen and her once boyishly flat and shapelessly trim figure had, over the past few years, taken on gentle curves and angles that had never been there before. Her rounded face had lost its girlishness, her cheeks narrowing to display fine, high cheekbones, a small, firm nose and wide, sensuously inviting lips tinged a natural shade of dark pink. The long waves of raven hair Rory had seen only a few times in the last few months since she had taken to concealing the abundant, unruly curls beneath a red bandanna and a tri-corner hat.

Rory was sure he was in love. Now it only remained to convince Jamie of it as well. So far, his every effort at revealing himself had been met with rebuffs of irritation and confusion by his beloved. But he knew he wasn't the only one watching the emergence of the new Jamie in spite of the boy's clothing and the over-sized hats she hid beneath. Beyond the crew, who missed few of the details if chance brought them their way, there was Captain Morgan himself, and he would be the most dangerous part of young Rory's pursuit. Just this past summer, Captain Morgan had watched Jamie dive, naked and graceful as a sea bird, off the starboard deck into the blue, fathomless Caribbean. Until then, Rory and Jamie had grown up together and always swam naked, side by side, but after that awakening incident, the captain brought their companionship to an abrupt end, ever after ordering all crew hands, including Rory, to be engaged on the other side of the ship while Jamie swam. The captain kept lookout for sharks himself, and Lord help the curious soul who tried to watch with him. Jamie was the captain's only child, a girl who had been presented to him strictly out of her mother's spite. After she died when the girl was four, Captain Morgan hadn't known what to do with a daughter so he had raised her like a son for as long as childhood disguised the differences between the sexes. Even Rory had thought her a lad when he first came and carried that misconception through the whole of the first winter season.

"What are ye two pups about down there so long?" The question drifted in from the opening over their heads where a huge shadow blocked the light. "Where's Ned's powder?"

The voice belonged to Jocko Chalks and the pair gazed upward at his towering form on the upper deck. Jocko was as large, solid, and brown as a banyan tree that had suddenly grown legs, arms, and a head to walk off from its spot in the soil. Six feet and nine inches tall, every inch of his beefy black frame was pure muscle. Once an escaped slave from Jamaica, Jocko was now Captain Morgan's first mate and second in command of the vessel.

"The keg's too heavy," Jamie called up to him. "Rory wants to take the bottom, but if it slips, he'll be squashed flat sure."

"I can do it!" Rory complained, anxious to display his muscles for Jamie's benefit. To prove himself, he nudged the barrel over, wedging his foot beneath the rim, then tried to lift the heavy weight—hopelessly. The barrel wavered as he struggled with its mass, then his arms gave out and it landed on the deck with a loud thud.

Jocko's bellowing laughter sounded from above, mixing with Jamie's muffled giggles, and Rory's freckled face flushed as red as his flaming hair.

"Ye two stand back now." Jocko came down the ladder, the gold chains about his thick neck rattling with every step. Like most of the pirates, he sported a wealth of booty about his person: a double pierced ear on the left side adorned with two gold hoop earrings, bracelets tight about his wrists, and chains of gold hung around his neck. Since he rarely found a frockcoat or a waistcoat that would fit him, he sported color-ful shirts and silk sashes into which he tucked two or more pistols, his cutlass, and at least one dagger. "I'll take it up afore ye breaks a bone tryin'."

"I can do it!" Rory protested, his flushed cheeks burning with embarrassment.

"Give it a few more years, lad." Jocko pushed him aside to lift the keg effortlessly onto his broad shoulders. "The two of ye get on up to the deck afore me. Jamie, yer father wants ye on the for'castle, hear now?"

"Aye, Jocko." She called out nimbly scampering up the vertical steps.

"Rory, yer to help Ned with the cannon. That galleon should be by now near any time."

Rory scowled at Jocko, bristling from his shame in front of Jamie.

"Git!" Jocko stomped a heavy-booted foot on the planks.

"I'm not a boy no longer!" Rory shouted.

"Ye're a pup till I tells ye dif'rent!" Jocko snarled. "Now move yer arse!"

Rory's fists clenched but he took the steps, hearing Jocko's heavy tread just behind him.

"Ye mind a warning, lad," Jocko said when he had emerged on deck. "And be sure the captain don't never catch ye over long alone with Jamie."

"Why?" Rory drew himself up to his full height which still fell considerably short of Jocko's, better than a foot below the first mate's.

"Ye're not babes like ye was. It won't do to have him thinking ye harbor notions about the lass."

"And what if I do?" Rory returned.

"Ye best not, boy," Jocko's fierce dark eyes glowered in warning. "Jamie ain't for the likes of no cabin boy and ye'll be best served to remember it!"

"I'll not be a cabin boy forever!"

"Aye, that's true . . . Ye'll be an all-too-common pirate and that's worse!" Jocko started walking toward Ned who was impatiently waiting for his barrel. The squat Ned Shanks sported a beard that nearly concealed the features of his face behind gray-speckled bristles. He was short and foul-tempered, and already had his hands on his hips as he tapped a booted toe on the deck.

"So's Morgan a pirate," Rory grumbled, walking beside Jocko.

39

Jocko pulled up short in his tracks, turning to glare down on Rory. "It's such as that ye best not be remembering," the hulk warned. "Ye're only alive 'cause Jamie took a fancy to having herself a playmate and ye ain't that no more! Captain can take a notion to rid himself of ye now ye're growed, especially if he thinks ye have a loose tongue. Ye go wagging it as ye're doing where he can hear, and the least he'll do is cut it clean outa yer mouth! Ye keep shut of that kind of talk, ye hear, boy?"

"Aye, Jocko," Rory responded, his temper cooling in spite of the resentment he still felt burning in his chest as he realized Jocko was only trying to warn him. Rory was the only living witness, beyond the pirates themselves, to an unprovoked attack Captain Morgan had made on an English merchant vessel bound for home with a cargo of spices from the Colonies. Rory had been newly apprenticed as a cabin boy on the merchant ship and only his tender age had moved Morgan to spare him—that and the entreaties of the seven-year-old Jamie who wanted a companion. Where Morgan stood, as privateer or pirate, had never been clearly defined, even to England who had granted him his Letter of Marque. Licensed by the crown to prey on enemy vessels for their cargoes, he was suspected of taking no pains to avoid an English ship if profits were slim on his legitimate ventures, yet no witnesses existed to prove it. Either they joined the buccaneers willingly and swore loyalty to Morgan, or they made their peace instead with the Almighty.

"Get on with ye, lad, afore I lose me patience," Jocko scolded, striding forward to set the keg down beside the squirrely Ned busily engaged in readying the cannon. "Here's yer powder and yer boy," Jocko told him.

"Aye," Ned mumbled through blackened teeth that might never have been cleaned since he left his mother. "It's about time ye showed up," he barked at the boy. "Let's get this keg open now." The pair set to their labors while Jocko strolled across the deck to rejoin his captain.

Morgan wanted nothing more than Jamie's presence nearby. From experience, she knew she was to wait and serve as messenger whenever he wanted instructions sent to any of the crew. As long as she kept an ear cocked for the sound of an order, she was free to let her own thoughts stray.

She was wondering what the devil had been coming over Rory of late. He was acting damned odd, not at all the carefree companion he used to be. Instead of the laughing, freckled face she had known, she was frequently as not met with a serious, intent expression from him that seemed to bore right through her like a harpoon straining for the deepest flesh. The looks gave her the shivers and made her wish to be anywhere else but near her old childhood friend.

It seemed that now there was hardly anything they could do without someone deciding there was a task for one or the other to be about, but Rory himself was changing so much she was frequently relieved when someone did disturb them. All the games he conceived of seemed to have touching involved. When they played their own game of dice and no one was looking on, Rory wanted a kiss put up as the wager instead of the trinkets they used to play for. Jamie didn't really mind the kisses. Slippery wet and puckered though they were, they were also rather warm and tingly, not unlike how it felt to be up in the crow's nest when a lightning storm was approaching, the way the charged air made your scalp prickle and raised the fine hairs on your arms.

Rory's secrecy about the touching games told her there was an element of danger about them, adding spice to the activity. But sometimes he tried to slip his hand beneath her blouse, or he grabbed her leg and squeezed almost painfully. She didn't care for those games and slapped him soundly for them or strode off and stayed away until he promised he wouldn't do them again. And he had become so clumsy of late, tripping and falling, his body pressing against hers just a bit longer than an accident provided for. He was becoming damned odd, she frowned, her eyes locked on the horizon past the reef.

She could see nothing beyond the island's tip, the outcrop of rock hiding their ship from view, when O'Brien called down from the crow's nest, "Ship ahoy! Here she comes!"

The deck became a flurry of activity while Jamie lent her own slight weight into the hoisting of the sails. The wind blew out the canvas and the *Lady Morgan,* waving the red battle flag of the buccaneers, jolted forward, picking up speed as it took a direct course to intercept the galleon, firing warning shots across the bow.

Jamie caught sight of her father watching the Spanish ship, his ice-blue eyes locked on his target as a hawk sights his prey. Lightly protected by two sleek frigates in escort, the slow, clumsy galleon was going to be an easy mark for the privateer.

Morgan began shouting orders, and, under Ned's direction, eight of the sixteen guns aboard the *Lady* cracked the air with loud, shattering booms, the acrid scent of burned gunpowder rapidly fouling the air and stinging Jamie's eyes. As she finished rubbing them, a large white streak in vaguely feline form raced across her line of vision and dived headlong into a stack of boxes lashed to the deck.

McGee! Jamie's mind screamed, fearful that a return fire from the escort vessels or the galleon might find the boxes an excellent target. In the confusion of Rory's puzzling behavior, she had utterly forgotten to lock McGee below in his case for the coming battle. The *Terrible McGee,* a twenty-pound, solid-white tomcat with battle scars to prove his prowess, feared no one and nothing with the exception of a cannon's bellow. Named after a sailor who had drowned in a storm, the meanest ship's mascot on the seas now mewed plaintively from inside his hiding place as she searched frantically through the crates. Finally she saw McGee's bright, slanted yellow eyes in the shadows beseeching her to explain the jarring sounds that set his feline nerves on edge. She yanked him out, bearing the claws dug fretfully into the skin of her shoulder as she lifted him up to carry him to the storage hold.

"Don't ye worry, McGee, I'll have ye safe inside yer box," she told him, finding the crate Ned had converted to a cage for her and disconnecting McGee's claws to place him inside it. The cat jammed himself into the back, hiding behind the pile of rags Jamie had stuffed in for him.

Jamie slammed the cage door shut and bolted it before hurriedly scrambling back up on deck. In the time it had taken her to fetch McGee and safely stow him below, the pirate ship had disabled both escort vessels. The fires on their decks lit the daytime sky with a brighter glow than daylight's, black billows of smoke rising like towers into the sky. The *Lady Morgan* threw grappling hooks over the galleon's rail and the pirates lashed the lines fast before scrambling up the sides of the larger ship.

For someone his size, nearly as tall and broad as Jocko, Morgan surefootedly led the charge up the ropes to the galleon's deck, grabbing a sailor who tried to stop him and tossing the man over the side to land on the planks of the deck below at Jamie's feet. There was a sickening crack as the man's neck broke on the wooden deck.

Jamie spared the body no more than a glance before she took the grappling rope in her hands and pulled herself up, hand over hand, toward the galleon's deck. Unarmed except for the dagger in her sash, Jamie's function was to circulate in and out among the melee of Spanish crew and pirates, lending a hand to her own side where she could. To her knowledge, she had never killed anyone, but she had stopped the fighting for a few unlucky enough to encounter her slashing dagger. She aimed for legs and arms, not quite able to bring herself to stab at a man's body.

She raised herself over the rail to stand on the galleon's deck, her eyes casting about at the frantic pitch of the battle for where she could best help out. Aboard the *Lady*, cooks

43

and cabin boys alike took part in the fighting if they wanted a share of the booty taken, and Jamie unsheathed her dagger, preparing to give Bob Layton a hand with a hard-fighting Spaniard. As she started forward, she felt a hand grab her shoulder in a biting grip and spin her about so hard she toppled, sprawling onto her back. Jamie jabbed with the knife, feeling the blade slice cleanly into flesh. The man screamed in pain and released her just in time to receive a death-dealing blow from Layton's cutlass. He gaped, his mouth opening to emit a low gurgle, then he pitched forward, catching her unaware and taking her down with him, her back striking the planking painfully as his full weight pinned her down.

In sudden, superstitious fear of all things dead, Jamie grappled with the body as if life still impelled it into holding her down. A sob escaped from her lips as the Spaniard's blood poured out of the wound, gushing over her chest. In near-panic, she fought to free herself, pushing against the dead man.

An arm descended, throwing the body off her and to one side, and she felt a moment of relief that was allowed to last for barely the space of a single breath. She looked up, expecting to see a pirate's familiar face above her but instead there were dark, blazing eyes boring into hers with a look of malevolent hatred that chilled her into paralysis.

"Curse your pirate's soul to eternal hellfire!" the man seethed, taking her by the front of her soiled shirt and in one swift motion, jerking her to her feet. "Defend yourself!"

A saber's point glinted in a blinding silver arc before her eyes and Jamie reflexively dropped the dagger, hearing it clatter to the deck. She winced, waiting for the searing pain of the sword.

"Damnation, you're but a child! A mere boy."

A hard shove tossed her roughly aside, sending her flying against the rail. The man, clothed in a fine black suit of Spanish cut and design, returned to the fighting, selecting

44

Jim Taylor as his next opponent. The man was good, very good, with the thin-bladed saber that slashed around Jim's cutlass, drawing a small spurt of blood from the pirate's sword arm.

In pain and surprise at seeing his blood spilled, Jim lost the cutlass, in the same instant groping instead for the pistol in his sash. Jamie rushed forward, smashing her weight against the man who had spared her, knocking him off balance before he could thrust the saber into Taylor's chest.

"Curse you, brat!" The Spaniard spun about, his saber pointing straight between her eyes, his blazing gaze seeming to weigh the wisdom of repeating his previous mistake in letting her live, until Taylor managed to free his pistol, taking aim at his distracted foe.

"No!" Jamie sprang forward, putting herself in front of Taylor's target, watching confusion contort the pirate's face.

"Jamie, stand aside!" Taylor continued to aim, but he couldn't fire without hitting Jamie. "Move away from him!"

"Stand away, brat!" the Spaniard said in perfect English. "I don't hide behind children." He pushed her away from him, but Jamie moved back to her position as his shield, blocking Taylor's aim. She had been duty-bound to help Taylor, but the other man had spared her life when he could as easily have taken it. Even now, he could take her hostage but he hadn't. "I'll not let ye kill him," she told Taylor.

"Have ye gone daft? Stand away."

"What's this?" She heard her father's voice from the sidelines, then saw him step into the ring of spectators quickly surrounding them. The battle was over, the galleon won by the privateers. Morgan's waistcoat and the front of his ruffled shirt were spattered with Spanish blood. Henry Morgan was a big man, though not quite of Jocko Chalk's dimensions. He sported a heavy mustache that added a sneer of cruelty to the thin lines of his lips. His nose was long and narrow, and the eyes glaring at Franco DeCortega were the deepest, darkest, most intense shade of sapphire blue the Spanish nobleman

45

had ever looked into.

"I'd prefer to meet my death with my sword in my hand," the young lord told the tall, broad-shouldered man in the spattered waistcoat, who had to be the leader of this band of cutthroats and thieves, "but this whelp of a cabin boy won't get out of my way!"

The dark sapphire eyes lowered to focus on the cabin boy still standing in front of the Spaniard. The privateer's thin lips pulled back into the semblance of a smile.

"So, the whelp won't move, eh? Seems bound to protect ye. What do ye think o' that?" He laughed, prompting the motley crew of pirates to chuckle with him.

Franco could see the boy's thin shoulders trembling but the lad stood his ground, barring the pistol's line of fire.

"Move away, boy," Franco tried to step around the lad, not doubting for a moment that the captain of this band might order the boy shot to remove him.

"Jamie, step aside!" Morgan jerked his thumb, ordering her away, his gaze locked on the doomed Spaniard.

Franco watched the boy shudder, inclined to obey but not doing so, as if the muscles had decided for themselves to mutiny against the captain's order. The lad couldn't be more than fourteen, his cheeks as cleanly peach-fuzzed as a girl's, his frame small and slender.

"Ye heard me! Move!" The captain bellowed with an unexpected roar that might have set Franco's own feet into motion, but the boy remained firm, standing stock-still, blocking Taylor's target. Murder blazed in the captain's eyes as he glared at the mutinous cabin boy. It was the huge hulk standing beside the captain who finally broke the charged atmosphere by grabbing the boy's arm and roughly jerking him away.

The captain seemed passably pacified, folding his arms across his barrel chest as he focused on the Spaniard. "There . . . ye have yer saber against Jimbo's pistol. Go on with what ye were doin' afore the whelp stepped in."

There were snickers and grins from the circle of pirates. Morgan leaned back on his heels to watch while Jim Taylor readied his pistol, taking great pains with his task to torture the Spaniard.

Jamie broke away from Jocko and pulled on her father's lace-frilled blouse sleeve. "Papa," she whispered.

"Not now." Morgan waved her off absently, his irritation at her already forgotten in light of the entertainment about to be presented.

She saw Taylor begin to sight down the pistol. "Papa . . ." Jamie plucked at his sleeve again but he paid her no more heed than he would a fly buzzing his ears.

"I won't have it!" Jamie shouted into the pregnant silence that waited to be broken by the pistol shot, then was appalled at herself for the outburst. All eyes had turned on her, including the Spaniard's. She looked up at her father. She didn't know why she was placing herself against the crew for the sake of this stranger in the fine black suit. Perhaps because she had expected to die and he'd let her live when Jamie wasn't at all experienced with the concept of mercy.

But he was Morgan's captive now, and most often he killed the crews, either leaving them aboard a fire-ravaged hull quickly sinking into the briny deep or he saved them for better sport later. Facing Jim Taylor's pistol might be an easier end than the one that could await him if they took him prisoner. Morgan was known to use captured seamen for target practice, stringing them up on the yardarm and letting the crew practice with their pistols, the object being to see how long their victim could live and making bets on the outcome. Sometimes he preferred to chum for sharks, then toss the captives in. Though she had grown up among them, Jamie had never been able to stand the sight of the games that even Rory participated in. She always hid below with McGee, cuddling the cat for comfort, sometimes burying her head under a pillow to muffle the screams of the dying men.

"At least let him die like a gentleman, Papa," she said softly.

47

"He could've killed me, but he didn't." For several moments, she didn't know if Morgan had heard her or not.

"Aye," Morgan murmured, his grin returning, confirming Jamie's regret at having interfered. The look on her father's face warned her she had given him an idea regarding the disposal of their prisoner. "Oh Lor', Papa, no," she whispered barely loud enough to be heard by him if he had been listening, but he was obviously beyond hearing any pleas she could present.

Her face tightened in mental anguish as she squeezed back tears that started to well in her eyes. The brave young man didn't deserve what was coming to him — none of them did, but least of all one who would spare what he thought was a child in the midst of heated battle.

"Aye," Morgan said again, his thoughts still forming. "Ye can fight the man even, can't ye, Taylor? Or ain't ye got the stomach for it?"

"Me arm's wounded!" Taylor complained, earning a round of guffaws from the men, for the wound was barely more than a scratch on his forearm. But he had already faced that swiftly flashing sword that had proven the man's skill with the weapon was exceptional and had no desire to try his luck again on even terms. "I can't fight with a wounded arm, can I?"

"The man is right," the Spaniard inserted. "I won't fight a wounded man, but I will any able-bodied man who cares to try me." The man stared straight at Morgan, daring him to take up the challenge any leader of men would have responded to in Franco's estimation. Jamie saw the dare thrown down, knew the stranger was trying to goad Morgan, but what the young nobleman wouldn't know was that Morgan was no gentleman at all. He played by other rules.

"Ye won't fight, eh?" Morgan's smile turned malevolent. "Ye'll fight for yer life, won't ye?" he asked, leveling his gaze at the man.

"Not unfairly. Not even for my life . . . and certainly not

48

for your entertainment." The Spaniard's black eyes blazed, his grip on the hilt of the saber tightening.

"Quite the proper gentleman, ain't ye?" Morgan poked fun at the man, producing more laughter. "Then if ye won't fight for yer own life, would ye fight for the whelp's?" In a sudden, swift movement that caught her off guard, Morgan's arm snaked around Jamie's throat, grabbing her head up into the crook of his arm. She let out a gasp of surprise, her eyes bulging as he cut off her air. She knew Morgan wouldn't kill her but his grip hurt terribly and he had put the edge of his cutlass against her throat, the bloodstained blade only scant inches away. Morgan's gaze remained locked on the Spaniard. "The whelp was willing to save yer life. How 'bout you? Do ye return the favor?"

Jamie struggled, trying to let her father know he was choking her. Morgan's threat was only part of the game, to prod the Spaniard to fight. The man gazed at her, his fury at Morgan vying with pity for her plight. If not for the hold Morgan had on her, Jamie was certain the Spaniard would have attacked him, but the young man was quickly learning Morgan's rules of foul play.

"Very well, I'll fight. Let the boy go."

Morgan loosened his grip, the cutlass removed from her neck, but he didn't release her. Jamie gasped for breath, gulping in huge swallows of sorely needed air.

"But now we did say 'twould be a fair fight, didn't we? And poor Jimbo here is sore wounded," Morgan sneered. He inched closer to the prisoner, dragging Jamie with him in one arm, the cutlass in the other. "Put out yer arm," he ordered.

The Spaniard stared at him until Morgan tightened his hold and the "boy" gasped again as her breath was cut off.

Franco produced his sword arm, staring into the pirate captain's deep blue eyes, as lovely as any woman's but cold as glacial ice. The pirate captain grinned as he slashed down with a wicked stroke that bit through the material of Franco's coat sleeve and sliced cleanly into flesh. A crimson river of

49

blood immediately gushed out of the rent in the garment and Franco nearly lost his grip on the hilt of the sword as a wave of searing pain washed over him.

"Well, look here." The captain turned to the crew. "This blueblood has red blood like the rest of us."

Jamie gazed at the man with pity while the crew laughed at Morgan's jest. She tried to tell him with her eyes that she was sorry, sorry she had gotten him into this, sorry she had been used to force him into Morgan's game. The man looked back at her as if he heard her thoughts, smiling faintly as if to assure her that the incident was not her fault. He flexed his fingers, his wrist, and more blood spurted down his hand, but he still had the mobility of his arm.

"Now, Jimbo, me boy, is that fair enough for ye?"

Taylor, grinning, liking the odds now since Morgan's saber had carved a wound much deeper than his own small cut, took the cutlass Ned Shanks offered him.

The combatants squared off on the galleon's deck, facing each other as the circle around them widened. The Spaniard was bleeding heavily, the black material of his coat glistening with moisture, red droplets staining the polished oak deck of the galleon.

The pirate's cutlass, much thicker and heavier than Franco's thin-bladed saber, could easily snap the lighter blade in two if the weapons collided. Franco avoided contact with the broader blade, swerving out of the way as the pirate began to swish the cutlass through the air, aiming for his midsection. He leapt backward, avoiding the slashing strokes, reserving his rapier for just one good thrust.

The one they called Jimbo began to chuckle with confidence at Franco's backward leaps, swiping the air back and forth as he followed the Spaniard's retreat. The pirates began jeering and laughing, urging their companion to be done with the cowardly cur who wouldn't stand and fight.

"Hey, you've missed him again, Jimbo. Get him!" members of the crew taunted. "Cut him in half an' be done wi' him," a toothless mouth shouted.

Jimbo's expression sobered into anger as Franco dodged another swipe, leaping well back from the path of the blade.

"Got away from ye again, bucko," a voice called out. Jimbo's next swing swooshed through the air heavily, inches from Franco's chest. "He ain't got much fight in him, but the lad's spry now, ain't he?" someone else called out. "Stick him! Run him through!" the catcalls continued.

Angry, Jimbo slashed again and missed, snarling in rage as Franco leapt backward out of reach, but this time his boot slipped in the widening pool of his own blood. He started to fall. The crowd surged hungrily forward to witness the kill, and, with an enraged growl, Jimbo charged, the cutlass raised high, certain of his success in bringing the sharp weapon down on his opponent to cut him in half.

Jamie wanted to turn away, not wishing to see the finish of the man she had risked her father's wrath for, but her eyes were frozen on the scene in horror. The glinting blade of the cutlass began its downward arc when suddenly the saber appeared out of nowhere, even as the Spaniard was falling backward. His back barely touched the deck before he darted upward, thrusting the steel-tipped point between two of Jim Taylor's ribs.

Taylor gasped, bulge-eyed, choking with a gurgling sound deep in his throat. Blood started to gush out of his open mouth and the cutlass dropped to the deck with a clatter, Jim's body sprawled on top of it.

In the utter silence that followed, Franco regained his feet. There was no victory in having won, nor any in pitting his skill against the clumsy, sword-wielding oaf he had killed. Franco turned to Morgan and defiantly tossed the bloodied saber to the deck at the man's feet.

A flash of simmering anger glinted in the captain's dark blue eyes. "Take him aboard the *Lady*," Morgan grumbled. "Put him in the hold."

Chapter Two

What Morgan referred to as the hold was a cell built into the hold on the lower deck. There were firm iron bars, deck to ceiling, to keep him confined on one side of the dim, but at least dry, storage area. While the hatchway remained open he could see something of his surroundings, which consisted only of assorted crates and boxes stacked so that their weight was evenly distributed and leaving narrow aisles between them.

After the pirates left him, Franco peeled off his blood-soaked coat and shirt to assess the damage to his forearm. The wound throbbed, bleeding profusely, and Franco tried to use his shirt to wrap around the deep cut hoping to staunch the flow of blood. The white linen became soaked through in seconds. He needed someone to help him fashion a tourniquet until the wound had time to close. If he couldn't stop the bleeding soon, he might very well remove the problem of his disposal from the pirates by bleeding to death here in the cell.

The privateers were still aboard the galleon, retrieving the gold stowed in her hull. They would have a good haul for their efforts, part of it DeCortega gold Franco was accompanying back to Madrid for his family.

The youngest of the DeCortegas was twenty-seven years old, idealistic, arrogant, and hot-tempered—and it was exactly those traits that had brought him into this predicament. Almost a year ago, now, he had overheard a quip that he decided to take as a slur against his family and challenged the offender to a duel.

When his elder brother, Lorenzo, in another room of the salon, heard of the duel his hotheaded brother was instigating, he quickly sought Franco out to ask him if he had lost his mind. He well knew Franco was one of the finest swordsmen and pistol shots in Madrid, quite possibly in all of Spain. He had proven his skill both in gentlemen's practice matches and a few earnest duels his volcanic temper had already gotten him involved in. Lorenzo didn't fear that Franco might lose — he feared he might win! And if he did, that might very well spell an end to the DeCortega fortunes!

Any fool knew Alamonda was a distant relative and very close friend of the king's, and courting the king's displeasure was tantamount to begging for the DeCortega holdings in the New World to be confiscated by the Crown.

Since Franco adamantly refused to apologize to Alamonda, even after his father ordered him to, the count chose to send Franco away until he learned to cool his temper and amend his ideas of what constituted pride. After all, his father explained, Alamonda had only been jesting. Had Franco no sense of humor at all? Since the answer seemed affirmative, he was shipped out the very next morning, ostensibly to oversee the family holdings in the New World in the hopes that months at sea and new surroundings might give him a fresh outlook on life.

The plan partially succeeded, as Franco found an entirely new cause with which to plunge himself back into trouble. What Franco discovered in the new land sickened the constitution of a young man with very strong ideas about conduct and conscience. Raping the land of its resources for the benefit of Spanish coffers was bad enough, but he found it appalling that the mines were being worked with native slave labor, beaten and starved into submission, kept like condemned prisoners in chains. The DeCortegas owned slaves. Their bondage had never troubled his conscience, but the DeCortega slaves were well fed and fairly treated—not whipped like horses in harness to a cruel master. His outspoken views fouled him with the governor, his host, and Franco was sent home again to see if his family could teach him manners as well as the economic realities of life before they again let him out of their sight.

It was his homeward-bound journey that had been way-laid here, or was it to come to a conclusion on this foul-stenched ship a few miles out to sea? His blood had soaked through the bandage he had wrapped around the wound and now dripped steadily onto the floor between his feet.

He heard a scratching sound coming from an area of the hold stacked with crates, kegs, and boxes lashed down to the gently rolling lower deck, then a low and plaintive "mew" came from the same direction. A moment later he heard a light tread on the steps and looked up to see a form descending. The boy!

Franco watched the lad enter the hold, glance for a moment in his direction, then seek out the sound of the mewing.

"Here, McGee, I'm coming." The boy made his way to a darkened corner of the hold and Franco could hear a latch being drawn back. He had his first good look at him as the boy stepped back into the light streaming down through the open hatch. Again he guessed fourteen as the boy's age, perhaps younger and simply tall for his age. He seemed reed-thin in the baggy folds of the overlarge white blouse hanging loosely about his hips. Tight breeches hugged slim legs to the buttoned knees. His calves were enclosed in black stockings but seemed better fleshed out than the rest of him. The lad was carrying a burden in his arms like a mother carries a newborn babe, holding the large white cat on its back and cuddling it closely against him as a girl might snuggle her doll.

"Here, boy!" Franco called out to him. The boy looked up, startled, as if he had forgotten Franco's presence in the hold. DeCortega had never gotten so good a look at the lad's face until now, as the child met his gaze for a moment of surprise. Beneath the tri-corner hat that effectively shaded his features, the boy had wide oval eyes fringed with lush lashes that a beautiful woman would surely envy. Franco recalled that at fourteen, his own face was taking on the leaner, harder look of a man, his forehead heightening, his cheeks narrowing, the peach fuzz on his chin slowly turning to black bristles he was proud to begin shaving once or twice a month. This boy didn't appear to have that pleasure yet, his face softly rounded and delicately featured. "Here, boy, would you help me?" Franco beckoned to the lad to come closer.

The wide-eyed gaze traveled up the hatchway, seeking shadows across the blue sky, then, when none appeared, turned back to the prisoner. The young fellow stepped hesitantly closer but stayed out of arm's reach.

"Here, would you help me?" He displayed the blood-soaked bandage. "I need a tight binding to stop the bleeding. I can't tie one by myself."

Idly scratching the cat's pink ear, the boy gazed at the bloody bandage and the blood-soaked floor.

"Please," Franco added.

"Ye'll need more than that," the boy spoke at last. "It'll bear stitching." The lad met his gaze as if asking for permission.

Franco nodded his assent. "Please . . ."

The boy put the cat down and climbed up the hatch as nimble as a monkey. In a few minutes he was back with clean strips of cloth bundled in his arms and what looked to be fresh clothing. The boy put the bundles on the floor, selecting a strip of white muslin from the pile. "Put yer arm through," the boy said.

Franco complied with relief, sticking his arm through the bars. While the boy was gone he had harbored the notion that he might not come back at all. He thought he might have to lend instructions, but the lad appeared to know what he had to do. He tied the strip tightly just above Franco's elbow before he gently began to unwrap the blood-soaked rag of Franco's shirt.

"Your captain has a foul sense of humor," Franco remarked as the boy worked, watching the lad's downturned face bent over his labors. He doubted the cabin boy could have much love or respect for the vessel's chief officer, not after the way he had seen the child treated to a cutlass across his neck.

"Aye, he does that," the boy agreed after a pause during which the old bandage came free. Blood seeped from the deep cut that looked even more gaping and raw than before. The boy winced as the gash was revealed. "I'm sorry for that."

"It isn't your fault." Franco smiled at the boy's sympathy. "Your captain did it, not you."

"It does need sewing. I thought it would, so I brung these." He drew out a long needle and catgut from the pocket of his tight breeches. "And this, so ye don't have to look so a'scared," the boy gave him a slight smile as he drew out a silver brandy flask from the folds of his garment.

"I am not 'a'scared'." Franco repeated the boy's vernacular.

"If ye ain't, ye ought to be . . . I ain't never done this before." This time the boy smiled shyly, revealing even white teeth and becoming dimples on the soft smooth cheeks. "I helped Cookie a time or two, but I ain't never done it myself."

"That's comforting." Franco accepted the flask the boy slipped through the bars for him. The boy unstoppered the top for him and Franco swigged deeply of the fiery liquid, feeling the warmth spread quickly through his chilled body.

"Ye best be half drunk before I start," the lad warned.

"I agree." Franco stared for a moment at the sharp-tipped needle the boy was threading, then took another deep swallow from the flask. "Are you certain you know how to do this?" he asked.

"It can't be much different from sewin' my breeches, can it?" The boy gazed at him, and from this close Franco could not only see the color of his eyes but their sparkle and realized he was being teased.

"Do the patches in your britches hold?" he returned.

The boy grinned again. "Well enough, I reckon. Take another I'm going to start."

The boy carefully scrubbed much of the stale blood away while Franco downed more of the brandy. "It won't hurt as much if ye don't look," he warned. "I never like to look when Cookie's treating my wounds. I think of something else."

"Such as?" Franco prompted, wanting the boy to keep talking to keep his mind occupied as the lad had suggested. The boy took the first stitch and Franco felt pressure more than pain, the damaged skin numbed by the tourniquet.

"I don't know." The boy shrugged, concentrating on his work. "Different things, I reckon. Like being rich enough to go where I like and to do as I please without nobody to tell me otherwise. And to buy me a fine house on a hillside with fine things all around me. And a carriage, a fine black carriage drawn by coal-black horses all alike, so's all who see me pass will be green with envy . . ."

Franco smiled at the lad's grandiose schemes. Suddenly the boy looked up, puzzled by a thought. "But ye'er already rich. What do ye find to dream about?" he queried, making Franco's smile broaden.

"I suppose I dream of other things." He really wasn't certain of what he had dreamed about when he was the boy's age. He had wanted for nothing. His father's demands on his sons had been slight, his expectations for his off-spring to simply raise strong, healthy sons who wouldn't gamble their fortunes away or lose them in foolhardy ventures. "For a while I dreamed of being a soldier and of discovering new lands like the conquistadores had done. I dreamed of doing wonderful things that would leave my

57

mark on history."

"There ain't no profit in the likes of that," the boy returned.

"True." Franco laughed at the lad's pragmatism.

"I won't be remembered by nobody, I reckon, except maybe by the hangman who pulls the rope taut. But I'll figure my life well spent if I spend at least some of it rich as the devil and free to do as I please."

The boy had perhaps meant the remark lightly, but it had a sobering effect on Franco. He didn't seem to be at all like the others, not even like the red-haired cabin boy who had watched Franco's peril with the rest, a look hungry for the sight of blood in his eyes.

"How did you come to be here?" he asked, but the lad tied the last knot off and ignored the question as he began wrapping the wound with shreds of pink muslin undoubtedly ripped from some lady's stolen garment. The boy was good at his nursing task, his touch gentle and soothing, especially the cool hands that came in contact with Franco's skin.

"Your name is Jamie, isn't it?"

"Aye." The boy's gaze lifted momentarily.

"Jamie what?"

There was another long pause that left Franco wondering if this question too might be ignored. "Allison . . ." he responded. " 'Tis Jamie Allison."

Not for all the world did she want him to learn her last name. If he didn't know already, he would soon find out that the captain who had treated him so harshly was none other than Henry Morgan, the same who had already garnered an infamous reputation throughout the Caribbean and all points from the new world to the old. Her name was James Allison Morgan, her father having decided his unborn child would be named after his grandfather, be the babe boy or girl. Of course, he hadn't really expected the child to be born a girl and keep him to his word. She didn't

58

want this man to know who she was, or how she came to be here, and if he thought her male—a boy—then better yet, for she would also rather he remained ignorant of her true sex.

She finished tying the bandage and released the tourniquet, atoning in some small measure for what her father had done.

"Thank you, Jamie," the stranger said kindly, his dark eyes focused entirely on hers. She felt her heart skip a beat before her pulse began racing. He had the blackest eyes, like liquid pools of ink, and heavy, arched brows above them.

"That was very kind of you. My name is Franco DeCortega." He smiled, offering his unbandaged arm out through the bars to shake hands.

Jamie hesitantly accepted the gesture. His hand was warm, strong, the long fingers wrapping lightly about her palm so firmly that she knew he could crush her small hand if he chose to. She jerked her hand away. "I have to go," she murmured, confused by the emotions this strange man was inspiring in her. Like her father and the rest of the crew, she convinced herself she hated "Spanish dogs," not for anything they had ever done to her, personally or impersonally, but simply because such an attitude made it so much easier to prey on them. The politics between Spain and England were none of her concern. She only knew Spanish galleons had hulls full of gold for the taking and she had her own hoarded store of booty plundered from the Spanish ships but no genuine enmity toward England's foes. Besides, for a rich cargo, Morgan would plunder an English ship as easily. Or French. Or Dutch.

"Will you come again?" he asked her, of course not knowing she was not a boy. "To change the bandage," he added, smiling. "Providing your captain decides to let me live that long."

"Aye . . . I'll come." Jamie picked up the bundle and

pushed it through the bars at him—a change of bandage, two shirts in varying sizes, a waistcoat, and a frockcoat stolen from the ship's stores. Then she quickly darted for the ladder before he could see her face unaccountably turning red.

"Papa?"

Morgan grunted in acknowledgment while picking his teeth with the point of a dagger. He was at the end of what he would consider an excellent day. The galleon had been seized with only minor damage to the *Lady* and only two men lost, one the scoundrelly Taylor, whom he had never liked anyway—the man had shifty eyes. Morgan had dined heartily on Spanish food and good red Spanish wine and was ending his repast with Spanish cigars and brandy. He had five prisoners from the plundered ship to provide the evening's entertainment and was looking forward to that when his meal digested. In all, he was in excellent humor and had completely forgotten Jamie's earlier transgressions. There wouldn't be a more opportune time to discuss the issue foremost in her mind.

"Papa, what are ye going to do with the other prisoner? The one in the hold."

Henry Morgan cast a frowning glance at Jamie sitting across the table from him. Sometimes he ate alone in his cabin. Other times, in better humor, he insisted Jamie eat with him. "Why do ye want to know? Ye done gone soft on him, have ye? If ye have, I'll box yer ears for being a little twit!"

"Of course not!" Jamie denied the accusation vehemently. "With a Spanish dog? I would be a twit, then, wouldn't I? I was just thinking is all," she plunged in quickly. "He weren't no sailor, nor part of the crew, 'cause he was wearing that fine black suit and all, so I was wondering why he'd have been on that ship at all, unless he was a passenger, and if he was, well then, ye reckon he might be rich?"

Morgan chose another tooth to plunder while dwelling on the thought she had implanted. "Could be, lass . . . Could be."

"Well, he sounds rich, the way he talks and all. And he told me his name . . ."

"When did he do that?" Morgan snapped crossly.

Jamie felt her face draining to pasty white. She would have to hope Morgan would accept her excuse. "I went down to the hold to bandage his arm . . ." Morgan scowled deeply so she talked faster. "I did because you was busy and I couldn't find ye to ask if ye wanted it done or no, so I had to figure it out for myself and I figured as how he prob'ly was rich. And if he was, then ye sure would want to hold him for ransom. Well, it ain't likely ye could ransom a dead man if he went and bled to death and all, so I grabbed up Cookie's bandages and I tended to him. He's awright now and even grateful." She giggled to sound out her father's mood. She couldn't read his expression. "Well, I did figure ye'd be madder than hell if I let him bleed to death when ye wanted to hold him for ransom."

For several seconds she wasn't certain her idea had taken proper seed in Morgan's head. If she didn't somehow convince him the Spanish prisoner was worth holding on to, the man would shortly be executed like his condemned companions. Sometimes, occasionally, Morgan spared one if he thought the man's family might pay for his return. If not, prisoners were too treacherous to hold and too bothersome to keep. Jamie didn't quite understand what she was feeling for the dark-eyed stranger with the velvet-soft voice, but she did know she liked him and she didn't want him to die. She had taken his supper from Rory, making an excuse that she had to go that way anyway, and had gone down to visit him again, just to see if those odd emotions he had stirred in her would surface again. They had. She experienced all over again the warm flush he brought to her cheeks, the heart-thumping racing of her pulse when she stood near him, all of it sharp, sharper than before.

"I'm thinking ye might be right," Morgan said at last, intruding into her thoughts. "I'm thinking we might have us a look at that ship's log and see."

"I done that, Papa, on account of I figured ye'd want to know."

"And?" Morgan's scowl briefly returned.

"Over fifty boxes of the gold in the hold was his . . . well, his family's, I expect. I can't read Spanish but figures is figures all the same and it was next to his name."

"That so?"

"Aye," she answered, nodding.

Morgan's face suddenly broke into a broad smile. "It's good thinking ye did, patching him up. Ye're a sly minx, ain't ye?"

"Gold's gold," she shrugged, greatly relieved, "however ye come by it."

Franco assessed what little remained of possessions he could still call his own. He had lost ownership of the contents of his cabin and the purseful of money he had locked in his trunk. There remained only what he had on him when the ship was attacked: a few sovereigns, the gold watch and chain his grandfather had bequeathed to him, and the DeCortega family signet ring, though he knew he could lose those as well if the pirates noticed them on his person. They were all he had left with which to bribe the boy.

Morgan had told him what his status was to be. The pirate had asked for much less than the DeCortega family could easily afford, but Franco did not avail Morgan of that fact. He simply cooperated, writing the letter Morgan dictated but using his own phrases instead of the pleading tone the pirate was suggesting. The money was to be delivered to a certain inn on Port Royale by a particular date that left sufficient time for the ransom note to reach Spain and the ransom itself to sail back. His loathsome task accomplished, Franco had been escorted back to his cell.

The coins he had removed from his ruined suitcoat might buy him extra comforts from whomever brought him his meals. Sometimes it was Jamie and sometimes the red-haired boy who sullenly dropped the tray just outside Franco's cell. By doling the money out, he might purchase a flask of brandy now and then, an extra blanket, for the nights were cool, and perhaps, if fortune chose to smile on him, a deaf ear and a blind eye to a bid for an escape. To even contemplate one, though, he needed a friend—a truly bought, handsomely rewarded friend from among this cut-throat crew. The other cabin boy, as yet a nameless entity to him, might be bought but Franco wouldn't trust him to live up to his part of any bargain struck. But the other boy, young James Allison, seemed to be cut of a different fabric. He had already proven himself to have a kind and sympathetic heart and had a sense of fair play that these pirates, as yet, hadn't managed to cull out of him. If young Jamie accepted the gifts Franco offered, he could be as assured as he ever would be among this group that if the chance came, the boy would help.

As he had promised he would after dinner, the lad returned just before sunset, bearing an oil lantern in one hand and a fresh bundle of strips of clean cloth in the other.

"I found ointment to put on it," the lad said as he put his parcels down on top of a keg. "And another flask of this . . ." He smiled, drawing a container out of the voluminous folds of his shirt. "More brandy to keep yerself company with." The lad smiled broadly and the look was one that could not be called anything but . . . well, attractive. Franco never had much opportunity to look into the boy's eyes, as he nearly always kept them cast downward and the light in the hold was feeble, but the child's black lashes were

63

thick and long, lightly brushing the edge of his brows. There was something almost femininely graceful and gentle in the boy's movements as he carefully removed the old bandage, rubbed the ointment into the mending wound, then tenderly wrapped it again, taking great pains with his ministrations to his patient.

"Thank you, Jamie. You've again been most kind," Franco told him as the knot in the clean bandage was fastened.

"We'd best change it often to keep the cut clean as I've only seen the dirty ones infect," the boy said, blushing solidly as he met Franco's gaze for a moment.

"Yes, I expect we'd better," Franco said, watching the pink color tinge the boy's cheeks. Was he that painfully shy?

"I got to go." Jamie gathered his ointment and soiled bandages. "Rory will come with yer supper."

"Wait, can't you stay and talk for a short while? It's dreadfully lonely down here and you're my only friend."

The boy looked up at him for a moment, then his gaze darted toward the open hatch.

"Jamie, tell me if you would, are you under the captain's instructions to see to my care or were you forbidden to tend me . . ." Several times Franco had seen Jamie check the hatchway opening, and his movements when he came down often seemed furtive, as though fearful of being caught.

"Oh, the captain wants ye tended. How else would he get his ransom?"

"Then he will set me free when he has it?"

"Aye," the lad responded. "He has to. He knows if he was to break his word, wouldn't nobody pay a ransom to him as he couldn't be trusted. He does some things right. Like keeping his word if he'll give it, and paying his debts and the like. If he owes ye, ye'll get it. If he vows he'll do it, he will. It's just about other things he ain't so fair," Jamie gazed down at the wooden planks.

"You've known the captain for some time then, haven't

you?" Franco again wondered how long the boy had been among the pirates and how he had come to be there. Jamie was a good boy and not like the others.

"Aye, I been here some time," the lad replied. "When he gets his gold, he'll set ye free."

"I see, but you didn't answer my first question. Does the captain send you down here to tend me?"

"Aye, I'm to see to yer wound."

"And what about the other things?" Franco smiled at him. "The brandy? The ointment? The lantern and the blankets?"

The boy didn't answer for a moment, then said in a hushed tone, "It might be best if ye didn't let nobody know ye had them."

"I felt they might have been your own idea," he said as the boy shrugged, making light of the chance he was probably taking in presenting the extra articles. "I owe you a great deal, Jamie."

"Ain't nothing." The boy blushed again solidly, from his collar to his cheeks. Trying to avoid Franco's gaze, the boy turned his head so that the golden glow of the lantern-light caught his profile. *Franco, my man, you've been too long at sea and deprived of the opposite sex* . . . He hastily brought to an end his study of the lad's delicate face, one that could only be described as, not attractive as Franco had first shame-facedly confessed, but more as exceptionally pretty. "Look," he quickly found a topic of conversation. "Your cat seems to have taken to me. He's been sleeping on my bed all afternoon." Franco pointed out the curled feline napping on his cot.

The boy smiled at the sleeping cat. "McGee don't usually take to strangers. He don't usually like men at all."

"He likes you, doesn't he?"

Jamie looked at the man, startled. She had very nearly given herself away and she wasn't sure she wanted to yet. This man, this stranger, stirred excitement in her that she hadn't yet been able to fathom. His mere presence made her feel ill, like the first flush of a coming sickness. She felt feverish around him, her stomach tied in knots, her heart leaping in her chest each time he spoke to her. He made her feel dizzy sometimes, and weak, like her legs had just turned into jellyfish tentacles.

"Your McGee must make some exceptions then, hmm?" the Spaniard said to her.

"I . . . I suppose he does." She turned quickly away, her gaze on the hatch as she heard her name called from above. "I got to go."

"Jamie, one moment more," Franco reached through the bars to grasp her arm. His fingers seemed to sear her flesh and she paused, waiting.

"I'd like to give you something for all the trouble I've been to you . . ."

She shook her head, denying wanting payment. She could hear Jocko calling her.

"Just a minute. Take this." Franco thrust a gold watch and chain into her palm and closed her fingers around it when she tried to pull free without it. "Please, take it. Not as payment but as a gift."

Her brows furrowed. "I done nothing to deserve it."

Franco had chosen right—the lad wasn't yet corrupted. "It's for being my friend when I sorely needed one. I want you to have it." He released the boy's hand but it stayed closed over the watch and he still looked at Franco, baffled. "If your companions find it on me, they'll take it anyway. I'd rather know you had it," Franco explained.

The boy started to move slowly toward the ladder.

"Jamie . . ."

The lad stopped.

"Perhaps someday, if an opportunity presents itself, if I need it, you might help a friend?" Now was the moment of truth—if the boy would or would not accept the watch as a bribe.

"Ye want me to help ye escape?" The wide eyes studied him intently and Franco felt like a man who had just betrayed his best friend.

"I will if I can," Jamie said, affronted. "I don't need yer watch!"

The lad tried to give the piece back to him. "No, I do want you to keep it," Franco answered quickly. "I'd rather know you had it than to think of one of the others taking possession of it. Please, Jamie, keep it. As a gift and nothing more."

The boy seemed to ponder the thought for a moment. "I'll hold it in safekeeping till ye're free."

"That isn't necessary . . ."

"I will!" the boy stated abruptly.

"Just as you say, Jamie."

"There ye are!" Jocko bellowed, halfway down the ladder already. "I been searching the whole ship for ye. What are ye doing down here, ye scalawag?" The mate glowered at Franco as he came down to the bottom of the steps.

"I've been changing his bandage." The boy moved toward the ladder, jamming the watch and chain into a back hip pocket.

"Well, if ye're done, come along. Ye're wanted on deck."

"Aye, yer worship." The boy mocked the pirate with a grand sweeping bow that made Franco as well as the pirate smile but also distracted the mate's eye from her action as she pulled her shirt down over the bulge in her pocket.

"Get on up there, ye scamp." The mate tapped the lad's bottom as the boy squirreled past him and up the ladder. The pirate paused to glare at Franco one last time, his gaze obviously questioning what had been going on down here, but after a second's more hesitation, he followed the boy up to the deck.

Chapter Three

"I'm filthy from a week in that cage. Do you have any objections to my having a swim while your men are about their tasks?"

Franco DeCortega had a way of asking for a favor as if he was issuing a royal decree instead. The trait irritated Morgan, but the buccaneer also respected pluck in a man, and the Spaniard had that in abundance. Only today he had let him out to have the cell cleaned. Jamie had reminded him that without fresh air and sunlight, his prisoner might sicken and die on him, forever cheating Morgan out of his ransom, so they took him along to the beach of a tropical island where the pirates were gathering fruits, hunting for meat, and storing fresh water from one of the island's lagoons.

"I suppose there's naught wrong with it," Morgan agreed sullenly. "But see ye don't drown yerself. Yer people won't pay for a dead hostage."

"For your sake then, Captain, I shall employ extreme caution." Franco bowed grandly to peals of Morgan's loud laughter. The ship had weighed anchor in a lonely cove where soft-tipped waves lapped the white sand beaches. While the men drew fresh water from the inshore pools and collected what fruits and vegetables could be found on the tiny island, Franco had been given his freedom to walk about as he liked, there being nowhere he could escape to.

"Jamie!" Morgan called out, cocking his thumb toward the prisoner. "Take the dinghy and go with him. His lordship has a mind to bathe." Of the crewmen he had taken ashore, only one of the two cabin "boys" might be spared and Jamie, Captain Morgan knew, was the far better sailor. McGregor he wouldn't trust to navigate a dinghy across a washtub.

"Aye, Captain," Jamie answered him.

"I hardly think I need an escort," Franco scowled. "I have no intention of trying to swim to the nearest Spanish port."

"I doubt I'd put even that notion beyond ye," Henry Morgan returned. "But the dinghy's to be sure ye don't swim out too far. And somebody has to watch for sharks. Yer precious life ain't worth a farthing if I've nothing but a drowned rat to present them when they come with the ransom. Jamie will take the dinghy and row beside ye, or ye don't take a swim. Have yer pick."

"I'll take the dinghy." Franco sighed his displeasure heavily. "Come along." He beckoned to the boy to follow him.

"I'll take it." Rory McGregor started to spring forward anxiously.

"You'll do as I told ye and carry the muskets for the hunting party!" Morgan snapped at him. "Off with ye! Now!"

Franco watched the red-haired young man look disconsolately over his shoulder as he slowly returned to the beach, the uncomfortable truth written all over the McGregor boy's freckled face. He had heard such things happened aboard ships that were out of port for months at a time, especially in crews' quarters where conditions were closely packed and privacy a luxury unheard of. The McGregor boy was in love, dreadfully, hopelessly in love with his fellow cabin boy. The young Scot was looking after them, gazing at Jamie as the dinghy was readied to be cast off the shoreline, his yearning emanating out of him as if he wished he could pull his fellow crewman back to his side by sheer force of will. And poor Jamie seemed innocently unaware.

"You may as well row me out past the sandbars." He spoke sharply to the boy, taking out his anger at McGregor on the lad. Franco calmed himself as he sat down in the bow of the dinghy, watching Jamie ready the oars.

"That's far enough," he said, seeing the beads of perspiration on the young man's red and straining face. He had purposely let him row farther out than he had originally intended. Rowing developed the chest and shoulder muscles and Jamie needed both if he would ever escape the God-cursed fate he seemed destined for if ones like Rory and the others managed to have their way.

They were a good five hundred yards out to sea and the current had taken them southwest of the landing party. Jamie was not only a weak oarsman but one with a poor sense of direction. The boy's straight-out line from the beach should have taken them nearer to where the *Lady Morgan* was anchored. Instead Jamie's course had taken them away from the ship, close to the point of the island, and the tide was bound to sweep them past the jutting rocks to the farther side before long. Well, that would give the fellow a good row back to either shore or shipside, Franco decided as he loosened the ties of his white muslin shirt and then pulled the garment over his head. He began to unfasten his trousers and Jamie suddenly turned away, blushing solidly.

"What's wrong? Have you never seen a naked man before?" Franco pulled the trousers off, one leg at a time, amused at the lad's obvious discomfort. "Do you mean to tell me that sleeping with a shipful of men, you've never seen one as God made him?"

Jamie was turned completely away from him, even the lad's ears were pink where they poked out of the red bandanna.

"Well, you'd best have an eye on one now. I don't intend

to be carried out to sea or serve as dinner for the sharks while you keep your eye on the sea gulls!" Franco stood up and dove gracefully over the side, cutting the water cleanly. The crisp saltwater stung his hot skin with icy tendrils of blessed coolness. He dove deep, kicking his way to the sandy bottom. In the crystal clear blue water he could see the coral reefs to his left, well under the water line beneath the *Lady Morgan*'s hull. Apparently, Jamie's sense of direction wasn't as poor as he had thought. Had he been taken there, he might have dived onto sharp coral rocks that he might not have seen with the sun's glare on the water. Perhaps the lad was worth the time and trouble it would take to salvage him. An idea began to form that if he ever got out of this, it might be worth an effort to save Jamie as well from a life that was bound to end as the lad himself had said, at the end of a hangman's rope. He had no doubt whatever that Morgan would sell his own grandmother if the price was right, and Franco could easily arrange to buy the pirate off from any claims he had on the boy. He could take Jamie on as a servant first, then, if he proved tractable enough as Franco was sure he would, he might even adopt him, though provisions would have to be made for natural sons he might have someday.

Franco stayed down in the cool depths until his lungs were ready to burst, then kicked off the bottom, slicing through the water and breaking above the surface. His eyes stung for a moment, blurring his vision. When he could see again, the dinghy was some fifteen yards away and Jamie was looking frantically for him on the far side of the craft, scanning the azure depths from horizon to horizon.

"Franco, please come up," the lad pleaded with the empty sea. Franco smiled at the concern in his tone.

"Jamie! Over here!" he called out.

The boy spun about, relief flooding over the beautifully feminine face. "Thank God! Ye worried me sick to death." Jamie rubbed at eyes that were red and luminous. It could

71

have been the glare and the spray of the saltwater, or could Jamie have been frightened enough for his safety to be crying?

"Don't ye never do that again!" the boy scolded, and Franco was not only amused, he was touched. He truly had frightened him with his overlong stay below.

"Very well, I won't." He smiled, breaststroking his way through the water toward the dinghy. "You look hot up there, Jamie boy. Why don't you peel off and come in. Join me."

The lad was quickly flustered, his fair smooth cheeks turning pink over the delicately chiseled cheekbones. "I . . . I can't. Who'd be here to watch for the sharks?"

"I was teasing about the sharks." Franco swam lightly to keep up with the slow westward drift of the unanchored dinghy. "Shuck down, lad. Come in."

Jamie's face flushed solidly to crimson and his head shook slowly from side to side.

"What are you afraid of? Can't you swim?"

"I can swim well enough!" Jamie returned defensively.

"Well, what then?" Franco came close enough to push himself up on the low siding of the small, flat-bottomed boat, leaning on the rim.

"I ain't a'feard neither!" Jamie added, a bit offended.

"I think you are." Franco decided to torment him and see how the boy reacted. "I think you're afraid to shuck down in front of another man and I also think I know why." Jamie looked at him sharply. "Jamie, at your age it's only natural for certain urges to be stirring. And since you've never been around a woman before, well, that presents certain difficulties in your development."

Jamie's arched brows furrowed deeply. Perhaps he didn't like what he was hearing but it needed to be brought out in the open. The tiny craft had rounded the point of the island and still drifted on unnoticed.

"Tell me, Jamie, do you trust me?"

72

Jamie thought for a moment, then nodded.

"Good," Franco said, smiling. "Then do as I tell you. Take off your clothes and jump in."

The violet-blue eyes opened wider. "I can't . . ."

"Yes, you can, Jamie! Nothing will happen to you. Take them off and come into the water."

"I can't do that."

"Jamie, do as I say!" he said sharply. "You must learn that there is nothing wrong with two men swimming naked together. I'm not Rory and you're perfectly safe!"

"Rory?" Jamie questioned, puzzled.

"Yes, Rory!" Franco snapped impatiently. "And some of the others as well! Don't you think I've noticed the way they look at you, and I understand how uncomfortable they make you — with excellent cause — but you can't hide as you're doing. You have to make a conscious effort to overcome these temptations."

"Oh," Jamie murmured, looking as though he might be finally comprehending what Franco was trying to tell him. "Yer thinking Rory might want to make love to me, is that it?"

"Well . . . well, yes." Now Franco could feel a flush of warmth on his own face not caused by the heat of the sun.

"Ye might be right on that," Jamie nodded solemnly.

"Then you haven't yet given in to his persuasions?"

Jamie's head shook vigorously.

"Nor will you . . ."

Again a vigorous, negative shake.

"Good, I'm very glad to hear it." Franco pushed off the edge of the dinghy, treading through the water away from the boat. "Now do you think you might be able to go for a swim?"

"If ye think it might help my development . . ." A sly smile crept over the lad's face, puzzling Franco.

"I know it will." He answered the boy with conviction.

"Then I reckon I'll do it!" Jamie plucked off his boots, one

73

by one, then yanked his shirt out of his trousers and began to unfasten the button-down breeches.

Franco was glad he had reached the boy in time. He watched the lad stand up and turn his back to him before pulling down the trousers. Franco sighed and looked away—even the poor fellow's buttocks were soft white mounds of shapely rounded flesh. He looked back just in time to see Jamie, still standing in the boat with his back turned, remove the tri-corner hat and loosen the red bandanna. A flood of ebony waves descended, falling in a black cloud down his . . . *His? Her* back!

The arms that gathered the waist-length raven mass and fastened it at the nape of her neck with the bandanna couldn't be any less than lusciously feminine, the curve of her hips that rested on one leg alone, the succulent alabaster thighs revealed beneath the hem of the long muslin shirt, could be nothing but female. Jamie wasn't a lad at all, but a woman! A very beautiful, very desirable woman!

Franco straightened up in the water, his arms treading to keep himself afloat, staring in amazement at the transformation. She reached for the hem of the shirt, drawing it slowly upward. "Ahm, Jamie," he called out, but his voice had suddenly lost its volume.

The unveiling reached her waist.

"Jamie," he tried again but did no better, almost swallowing a mouthful of saltwater as a wave splashed into his face. She drew the garment over her head and this time Franco did swallow a wave as the white body was utterly revealed to his gaze. She tossed the garment to the bottom of the boat, then turned around. Franco saw full, pink-tipped breasts and an enticing mound of thick black hair between the pearly thighs before she spread her arms wide and arched free of the boat, knifing into the water.

She broke to the surface a few feet farther on, then swam with clean sure strokes toward him.

"You're . . . you're a woman!" he finally managed to

74

stammer when she stopped near him. He saw unmistakable mischief sparkling in the violet eyes he was no longer afraid to gaze into.

"Aye," she replied. "I know."

Looking at him playfully, she suddenly somersaulted in the water, her buttocks briefly breaking the surface as she dove for the bottom. Still appalled by the revelation, Franco smiled to himself, admitting a great sense of relief. If the truth were told, he had found the lad unaccountably attractive. Now, he was immensely relieved to learn his loins had only responded to what his other senses had failed to discover. In retrospect, it was all so clear any fool could see it. Jamie had never admitted she was a male, she had merely never disagreed with his assumptions. He knew no man could stir him as she had even in her boy's disguise. Inside, somehow, he had known . . . And that opened ground for another question. Did the others aboard the pirate ship also know of Jamie's true sex? Did Morgan? Perhaps there was no more amiss with Rory's sense of direction than Franco's; the young Scot only knew what was hidden beneath the disguise.

"Franco, you idiot," he chided himself, smiling broadly now as he jackknifed in the water and followed her down into the depths. He found her gliding along the bottom in shallower water than when he first dove off the boat. Apparently, the tide was sweeping them gradually closer to shore. Swimming above her, he feasted his eyes on the curves of her body as it swayed against the gentle motions of the tide. She turned her head to look at him, then broke to the surface for air. He came up beside her.

"Why didn't you tell me before?" he asked, gazing deeply and without hesitation into those lovely eyes. She only smiled her answer, gulped a lungful of air, and cut beneath the waves again. Franco followed her under the surface, reaching for her hand as she swam for the bottom, grasping her fingertips and drawing her around toward him.

A sudden sharp, stinging pain startled him into releasing his air in a gurgle of air bubbles. Something burned his back and his left side like fire. He gasped, inhaling saltwater into his lungs, then began to choke on the water, his body reflexively wanting to sputter it out and at the same time drawing more in. Flailing desperately for the surface, he felt Jamie's sleek, naked body come up on his left side, supporting him upward. They broke through and Franco coughed, spitting seawater out, gulping huge swallows of moist sea air.

"Ye swam into a school of men-o-war," Jamie told him between his fits of coughing. "They're heavy round here this time of year. Can ye swim?"

Franco nodded, the pain from the jellyfish stings growing sharper and more intense.

"Swim for shore. It ain't far." She swam just beside him, helping him along when another spasm of pain or coughing caught him. They finally reached shallow water and Jamie offered herself for him to lean on as they waded ashore. They were beyond the promontory of rock that divided the island, hidden from the landing party in an isolated alcove sheltered by tall pines and thick-fronded palm trees that lent cool shade to the sugar like sand.

Jamie helped him lie down, then ran off into a thicket of brush just beyond the tideline. Franco could feel the stings like a branding iron circling his back. Red tendrils of poisoned flesh snaked across his stomach. In a moment, she was back with thick spurs from a cactuslike plant clutched in her hands. "Turn over," she ordered, "yer back's the worst."

Franco had found the cool sand comforting and hated leaving it but he complied with her wishes, turning over onto his stomach. Gently, Jamie brushed off the sand that had clung to him, then began applying the torn edge of the plant to the damaged tissue. Immediately, he began to feel relief from the stinging-hot pain. He turned his head to see what she was using that offered such prompt respite. It was a dark green spike with thorny edges and a sharp-tipped point.

"It's a plant the natives use," she replied to his questioning gaze. "It works wondrous well on stings and such. The pain will go in a minute." Her fingers deftly rubbed the plant's soothing medicine into his skin, across his back, and working her way to his side. "Turn over," she said, and he moved onto his side. He could hardly feel the stings at all now and could easily have done the remainder himself but he enjoyed her touch too much to relinquish the gentle massage of her fingers.

"Now yer front." Jamie stayed with her task as he turned onto his back. Her fingers worked the plant's lotion into his skin, arousing more than she realized as she concentrated on applying the medicine to the last of the red welts.

While she labored, her face etched with concern, Franco studied every detail of the magnificent body revealed to his gaze. *Madre de Dios*, she was beautiful! How ever could he have been so mistaken. So blind. Her damp hair had come loose, the scarf lost in the water, or was that what she had used to brush the clinging sand from his body? The long dark tresses fell forward to her waist, covering her breasts. The gentle swell of her abdomen rose and fell with each breath she took. Her calves tucked beneath her, she knelt beside him, administering her wondrous lotion, having completely forgotten her nakedness just as she had forgotten his.

"Have I missed any?" She leaned back, gazing at him, innocent of any knowledge of what the sight of her was doing to him. It had been so long since he had had a woman—any woman—and to have this exquisite creature so close . . .

"No, you haven't missed any," he said, his voice husky with desire.

Jamie stared at him, startled, suddenly remembering her

nakedness and flushing solidly. In the water, the sea itself seemed to be a cloak, their swimming together side by side a natural act she had engaged in so many times with Rory while they were growing up. But it was not so with Franco DeCortega from the moment when he reached for her hand and began to draw her closer, the simple action sending a warm flush through the timber of her soul as he pulled her to him in the water. When she revealed herself as female, she had had no further thought in mind than wanting to watch his expression as he learned the truth. Or did she . . . ?

If that was all she had wanted, she didn't have to purposely expose herself by such slow degrees, catching his admiration and surprise out of the corner of her eye, reveling in the interest she saw there. No, she had wanted him to want her, feel the desire she had heard so much about, this wonderful, unknown thing that was supposed to happen between a man and a woman who loved him.

Loved him? Did she? Was that it? Was this warm sensation she felt throughout her body as he boldly gazed at her now, was that love?

She didn't know—wasn't sure. She only knew she didn't want to run as she had always wanted to turn from Rory when his eyes took on a very similar, heavy-lidded look that, on Rory, chilled her thoroughly. Now, the same expression in Franco's eyes kept her rooted in the soft sand, forever the statue for as long as he chose to gaze upon her.

Franco reached up and touched her cheek with his open palm, the contact like a shock that found every corner of her being and startled each cell awake. He pushed the waves of her hair back behind her shoulder, exposing her breast to his view, then he let his eyes slowly roam over her bare skin that was suddenly tingling with anticipation and apprehension. Jamie had heard the good and the bad about what happened between men and women when they made love. Some, like her father's whore Polly said it was better than

78

the most wonderful thing one could imagine. Others said it was fun for the man, but mostly uncomfortable for the woman. Rape was awful, that she was sure of. Her mother had killed herself rather than bear another child out of Morgan's advances. But what was it like when two people cared for each other? Was it like this? Like the emotions surging through her now as Franco's fingers locked in her hair, pulling her down to meet him as he propped himself up on his elbow and leaned upward to softly brush her lips with his own. In Jamie's limited experience, she had never felt anything so gentle, yet so stirring. It wasn't truly a kiss, like those Rory occasionally bestowed when she would allow it, but rather a bare touching of flesh, his lips brushing against hers as softly as a feather might stir against her skin. He kissed her cheek just the same way, then trailed a course downward to caress the edge of her throat.

Jamie closed her eyes, reveling in the new sensations. She moaned as his lips moved farther down across her shoulder, the tip of his tongue barely tasting her flesh until he found her breast and gently suckled her nipple into his mouth. Another moan escaped her as the pert nipple swelled and hardened under his ministrations. He pulled her down to lie beside him in the soft cool sand. He let his lips touch her mouth again, gently nibbled her lower lip, urging her mouth to open with a probing tongue, then, as though impelled by a sudden change of mood, he kissed her fiercely, hungrily, his mouth moving hard against hers, his tongue darting deeply into her mouth. Instead of fearing the sudden onslaught, Jamie felt a flush that made her dizzy with its intensity. She tried to match his passion equally, doing just as he did during the soul-searing kiss, wanting only to convey how very much she wanted this to go on forever. If this was love and desire, it was indeed wonderful, more than she had ever imagined. But, if it was love, how did one ever survive it, she thought as she finally yanked herself away from him and gasped for air.

Franco gazed at her in concern. "What's wrong?"

"I . . . I couldn't breathe!" she panted.

Franco's look changed from puzzled to smiling amusement, then he laid back down against the sand and laughed.

"What's funny?" she asked him, a bit miffed by his laughter.

"Darling," he chuckled, his dark eyes bright with merriment. "You don't have to hold your breath."

"I don't?" she puzzled.

"Certainly not." He continued to smile. "You merely breathe through your nose."

"How?" she queried.

"Come here and I'll show you," he beckoned with a crooked finger.

At Franco's prodding, she laid back down beside him. There was a heavy, crackling sound in the brush behind them, then harsh men's voices.

Jamie jumped to a sitting position with a start. "Oh, Lord!" she murmured, her eyes suddenly wide with fear. "It's Morgan with the hunting party! He'll kill me sure . . ." She started to leap to her feet to dart off like a startled doe but Franco held her back.

"Doesn't Morgan know you're a woman?"

"Aye, of course he does!"

"Well then why should he care? If you're nothing more than a cabin boy to him . . ."

The crackling brush sounds came closer. "Sweet Jesus," she murmured, watching the thicket. She looked down at Franco, her face suddenly drained pale. "Morgan's me father!" she blurted.

"Your *what?*" It was Franco's turn to sit up with a start. He felt every inch of his nakedness and as vulnerable as a newborn babe with his clothes on the dinghy out to sea. And Jamie's as well. *"Madre de Dios!"* he muttered under his breath, tempted to spring to his feet and run, dragging Jamie behind him, but there was nowhere to escape to with the footsteps so close and they couldn't flee back to the water as naked as Adam and Eve without Morgan spying them when he emerged from the thicket. He had seen all he cared to of Morgan's foul temper. And finding them here? Like this? Franco had little doubt that Jamie's fears were justified. For her sake more than for his own, he had to think fast and perhaps save both of them.

"Push on my back as if I've drowned and you're trying to save me," he spun over onto his stomach, pretending unconsciousness as Jamie grasped the hastily conceived plan and began to shove against his shoulders just as Morgan and the band of five pirates pushed their way past the thicket into the beachside clearing.

"What's this?" Morgan roared above the sound of the surf.

"He was drowning, Papa," Jamie explained hastily. "I pulled him out!"

Franco pretended to be aroused by Morgan's loud shout. "Yes, yes," he said weakly, adding a few strangled coughs for good measure. "I was nearly done for and your ransom with me if this brave child hadn't risked her life to save me."

Morgan's blue-eyed gaze roamed over the both of them. Until this moment, as he strained his neck to study Henry Morgan's features to see how much of their tale might be accepted, he had never noticed the icy blue of the buccaneer's strangely hued eyes and how very close they were to Jamie's deep blue shade. Hers had a touch of lavender in them that added warmth and softness that was missing in Morgan's glacier-shaded gaze, but now that he had the missing pieces in the form of his newly acquired knowledge, there were no remaining doubts in his mind—Jamie was indeed Morgan's daughter—his natural child and not a foundling the pirate had chosen to raise and adopt as his own as Franco had been half hoping since she made the remark. Though age and rum and extremes of weather had left their marks on Morgan, in his youth he had undoubtedly been an extremely handsome man. Even now he retained a certain comeliness about his features, an attractiveness of face that his daughter had inherited. She had Morgan's eyes, and his lush, heavy lashes. She had her father's coloring, the exact same shade and wave of hair, though Morgan's was salted with gray. Seeing the two together, there was no mistaking her as Morgan's own now that he knew what he had learned.

Franco, you have an extreme talent for placing yourself in jeopardy, he told himself silently as Morgan stared from one to the other, studying their nakedness with a slowly simmering rage beneath the surface of exterior calm.

"And will you tell me then, why the both of you are as naked as jaybirds?" At just that moment, Morgan noticed his crewmen eyeing Jamie's nakedness barely concealed beneath the long black tresses that covered her shapely form. She saw their attention as well and jumped back, hunching even farther behind the waves of her hair. Franco sat up to give her another shelter to hide behind and she quickly took it but Morgan had already spun about on the men. "Get out of here, ye scurvy louts!" he shouted. "I catch ye ogling her ever again and I'll run ye through sure as I'm standing here!"

The men scattered, tripping over the underbrush in their haste to get back the way they had come, Rory McGregor the slowest and the last to disappear back into the thicket. Franco considered his chances thread-slender of coming out of this alive.

"It's my fault." He said, acting weary to coincide with his story of nearly drowning. "I always swim nude to keep my clothes dry . . ."

"Then what's *she* doing naked?" Morgan gestured toward Jamie with the point of his drawn cutlass that he had used to chop his way through the mangrove.

Franco thought frantically for a believable lie. Nothing seemed even remotely plausible. Had he been on his own soil and discovered in such a predicament with a gentleman's daughter, he would have been honor-bound to marry the girl, regardless of whether anything had happened. But how would Morgan view the situation? And what would he demand by way of satisfaction? What could Franco possibly say that would convince Morgan of their innocence?

"To keep my clothes safe like ye told me!" Jamie inserted into the silence, a hint of righteous indignation in her tone, apparently a faster thinker than Franco was. He almost visibly sighed with relief while keeping up his hopes that Morgan would believe the tale she wove.

"Ye told me, didn't ye, that if I ruined one more set of clothes, ye'd skin me? Well, I was on the dinghy and I saw Franco diving and he dove straight into a school of men-o'-war and ye know damn well what them things can do," she explained evenly, apparently allowed to curse in her father's presence. "Sure enough, they stung him, and he gulped a gallon or more of seawater, so there weren't nothing to do but go in after him. But I remembered as how ye told me not to go ruining my clothes as they're hard to come by and I didn't want to make ye mad but I didn't want yer ransom to drown neither, so I just peeled them off and I dove in after him."

"Is that so?" Morgan glared at Franco, who acknowledged the look with a nod since he could think of no further embellishments that might lend credence to her story. It was pitifully weak at best, and he knew by the pirate's stare that he didn't believe them.

"Get yer clothes off that dinghy," Morgan ordered her crisply. "And his too while yer about it. Then ye get yerself back to the ship!"

"Aye, Papa." Jamie scurried off to the shoreline where the tide had deposited the small wooden boat. Franco didn't dare look after her, gazing instead at Morgan standing above him with the cutlass waving idly back and forth at his side as if the pirate captain hadn't yet decided whether or not to cut the offender in two for the outrage.

"I'm no fool to be believing the likes of a tale like that," Morgan said finally when the girl was out of earshot. "Ye mind what I say, yer lordship." The pirate's voice lowered as his eyes narrowed dangerously. "Jamie's me only daughter, though to you, she ain't nothing more than a wench to serve ye pleasure . . ."

"That is not true, Morgan," Franco protested, but Morgan spoke right over his denial.

"Ye mind what I say," he repeated. "Jamie ain't for the likes of any man who hasn't so much as a farthing to his name. I mean her for better things. She ain't for no sailor and she sure as hell ain't for the likes of that red whelp, Rory, and she ain't a plaything for the likes of you to use to pass the time of day. She ain't for no man at all till I say so. Ye got that firmly set in yer mind, Spaniard?" The cold blue eyes stared at him harshly.

"I do, Morgan," Franco replied evenly, weaponless and uncomfortable with his disadvantage. "I assure you, I had no intention . . ."

"I know damn right well what yer intentions were!" Morgan snapped, his low-timbred voice growling. "Just remember this . . . If ever I catch ye again messing about with me girl, ransom or no, I'll feed ye to the sharks while she watches!"

Chapter Four

After they came back to the ship, Franco found his few belongings removed from his cell in the hold. He was given a closet-sized space next to the captain's cabin where a few minutes of inspection revealed that the room previously had belonged to Jamie. Not an article in it would hint of a woman's presence: there were cabin boy's clothes in the chests, boots, floppy white shirts, and buttoned-down breeches but he doubted private quarters would have been accorded to Rory. He didn't think either that conscience had instigated the captain's sudden change of heart regarding the comfort of his prisoner. He wanted Franco on deck where he could keep an eye on him. If granting his hostage freedom about the ship was the price for his peace of mind, then the captain would pay it. Undoubtedly, Jamie now slept in the captain's own quarters and Morgan kept her busy with tasks throughout the day so they couldn't speak to each other in passing.

Franco knew also that Jamie had paid heavily for the incident on the beach when she appeared the next day with her left cheek swollen and a large red welt across her face. If there had been no other reason, he hated Morgan for that alone and vowed to himself that someday, somehow, he'd kill him.

* * *

Tortuga Bay, in the Leeward Islands of the Caribbean, was as an independent country unto itself. Located on a portion of the island that was set well into a bay, the place was protected on all sides from surprise invasion.

Massive cannons set up at either end of the bay's entrance forbid penetration by any ship not flying the skull and crossbones of the pirates. There was always one, and usually more, pirate vessels patrolling the outward shore of the settlement that could be reached on its undefended side only by treading through impenetrable mangrove and putrid, treacherous swamp.

Unlike Port Royale, Morgan's landbase on Jamaica, where merchants came to purchase wares at hefty discounts, Tortuga Bay was entirely populated by the Brethren of the Coast and their families. Each ship that entered went about its own business, minding its own affairs, and only the captains came together for informal council meetings as a situation might call for it, to judge by vote the righteousness of a cause or the guilt and punishment of an offender. They had drawn up rules to live by and articles of government that included a welfare program for aged or infirm buccaneers. Morgan, as the colony's founder, held an informal governorship of his own over the island.

The dockside edge of the town, at first appearance, looked like any other port except for being smaller and even more ramshackle than the average New World port. The buildings were all flimsily constructed. A few more successful efforts by the navies of countries most heavily preyed upon by the pirates, had tried to penetrate the bay's defenses and supposedly destroyed the colony only to later discover that their efforts had been in vain. At the first sign of trouble that could not be fended off, the pirates and their kin fled into the swamps at the back of the island. How so many could disappear so quickly God only knew to the bewilderment of the navies who never managed to figure it out. The buildings could be reduced to rubble only to reappear in a few days, hastily constructed and ready to be knocked down all over again.

Most of the businesses were run by retired pirates, many bearing scars or crippled from the action they had seen in their prime. Everyone knew everyone else by name and there were many who called out greetings as Franco's guards escorted him down a dusty path through the narrow main thoroughfare of the dockside shops. Gray, wizened heads peered out of the several taverns along the way, calling out invitations to stop in for a tankard of ale or rum, a hearty meal, or a hearty wench to satisfy any appetite.

"Ye keep moving along now, yer lordship." Jocko walked along behind him. "There ain't help to be found for ye here. They'd as soon keep ye themselves for the ransom as help ye get free, and many of them I wouldn't swear would turn ye loose alive."

"I have no intention of trying to escape under the present circumstances," Franco said. Jocko caught his emphasis on the word "present" and laughed.

Beyond the docks and taverns were family dwellings as fully haphazard in construction as the shops. With the sunny climate they lived in, they did not seem to require sturdy construction to ward off winter cold, of which there was none. Most of the shanties were windowless, with only wide gaps between boards for ventilation. Several dwellings had roofs made only of thatch. Franco imagined that following each violent tropical storm, entire buildings had to be remade practically from scratch. As they passed by, pirate wives tossed out water from the morning's cleanup and hung wash out to dry on lines while pirate children played naked in the dusty streets.

Jocko led the way through the maze of houses then out a small trail that led directly into tropical jungle. They followed a winding path that, to Franco, seemed hardly visible in the tangle of overgrowth, until they finally emerged into a small courtyard set before the side entrance of a magnificent three-story mansion.

Franco could not have been more surprised if he had suddenly come upon a king's palace in the midst of this tropical jungle. The house was of white stucco, with a porticoed entry in front. The roof was constructed of red tiles. Obviously, the place had cost a goodly fortune to build here on this isle where most of the material would have had to have been transported at great expense. Franco doubted the tiles, stone, wood, and the stucco to cover it with could have been stolen in the course of the buccaneer's usual adventures.

While not quite as large as many fine homes Franco had seen in other ports, and considerably smaller than the De-Cortega ancestral manor house, still, for where it was, the mansion's very existence in this wasteland was astonishing. The home's presence was hidden from the shoreline by broad-leafed vines that had been encouraged to grow up and over the structure to aid it in blending in with the foliage that was its backdrop.

"This place belongs to Morgan?" Franco queried of the man beside him.

"Aye, 'cept we all use it when we're into port — all the captains and their first mates, that is, if they have a mind to." Jocko answered, pointing the way through a tangled path of tropical flowers and verdantly green brush being tended to by an old man wearing an eyepatch. The gardener revealed a smile full of black broken teeth as he waved a greeting at Jocko.

"That there is Sheltie," Jocko explained to his prisoner. "He was Morgan's first mate a'fore me. Morgan lets him live in back of the mansion on account of he owes him for putting out his eye."

"Why did he do that?" Franco asked to keep the conversation going more than for any genuine interest in how the mate had lost his eye. Nothing Captain Morgan did would surprise him, but during the course of their journey here, few of the pirates aboard the ship would converse with their Spanish captive, either through preference to avoid his company or out of fear of earning their captain's distrust and suspicion if they became too friendly with the hostage. Franco, ordinarily an outgoing sort and now denied even the "lad's" company, had found the ostracism boring to the point of starvation for human companionship.

"Accident," the mahoghany mountain stated in answer to Franco's question. "Captain was drunk and he put it out with his bare hands in a rage a'fore he even thunk of the reason. When he sobered up, he was awful sorry."

Franco turned in midstride to gaze at the pirate. "I'm sure the captain's regret was a great comfort to Sheltie."

"Aye," Jocko laughed. " 'Deed it was."

Franco was thinking instead of Jamie, wondering how she had grown up amid all this filth and corruption. "Jocko, where is Jamie's mother?" he asked as the guards escorting them dropped off and the hulk alone led him toward the front door half concealed amid the greenery.

"Jamie's mother?"

"Yes, Jamie's mother," Franco repeated impatiently. "Morgan's wife. Where is she?"

"Morgan ain't never had a wife. He's married to the sea, he says. Reckon it's so."

"But Jamie does have a mother, doesn't she?"

"Oh, aye, that she does. Least, she did. She were a pretty li'l thing too. Much like Jamie, but kind of small and delicate, like one of them flowers." He pointed at a beautiful purple-and-white blossom Franco couldn't identify as it was of a tropical nature. "Captain caught the lass off a French ship." The pirate scratched his clean-shaven, glistening scalp. "Like with you, he was going to hold her ransom, but the temptations come to be too great, if ye knows what I mean," Jocko winked.

"Yes, I think I know what you mean," Franco frowned.

"She was set to marry some lordship or other on Martinique, but by the time the ransom come, the lass was with child and Captain wouldn't give her up then — not carrying his babe and all." They had stopped just outside the front door of the mansion. "There weren't nothing to do but send the ransom back."

"He returned the money?"

"Aye." Jocko nodded, wiping beads of perspiration from his shiny skull with a soiled rag he had drawn from his pocket. "Captain keeps to his word, even if its killing him to do it. Ain't never knowed him to welsh on a bargain he struck nor a debt he owed."

Franco recalled Jamie saying something very similar regarding her father's sense of honor. "Then what happened to the young lady?" He prodded for the rest of the story.

"Oh, well, Jamie was born — a girl, when Captain wanted hisself a boy. But it weren't meant to be. He kept the lass after Jamie come, hoping what happened onc't could happen again. He built this here fine house for her too, to try and keep her happy. Another babe come, and a boy he was too, but he died not a week after. Weak, sickly li'l thing he was. Captain wanted to go on trying to have hisself a son, but the lass couldn't bear no more of it, house or no, being naught but a breeder for a pirate, she must have felt like, so she up and shot herself with Captain's own pistol."

"She killed herself?" Franco asked, appalled.

"Aye. Jamie weren't but four or so, I reckon. The lass never could stand the sight of Jamie no ways, as she took so much after Morgan. See, she was blonde and fair herself. Some French ladyship," the pirate explained. "Duvalier, I think her name was. Aye, that was it! Antoinette Duvalier. I ain't thought of that in years." The first mate seemed proud of himself for producing the information.

Duvalier! Franco recalled having heard the name before. If his memory served correctly, the Duvalier family was French aristocracy, vaguely related to Louise XIV, the

90

present king. Franco had once been introduced to an envoy from the court of France whose name had been Duvalier—Bertrand Duvalier. He remembered having liked the man.

Could Jamie truly be the daughter of this cutthroat Welsh pirate on one side of her parentage and a gentle, French aristocrat on the other, one who had found her status so unbearable that she had sought release from her deplorable fate in death?

"Then who raised Jamie?" Franco inquired as they stepped inside the front foyer that was sparsely furnished but boasted a magnificently curved winding staircase to the upper story.

"Morgan did! And I did!" he added proudly. "And Polly some, I reckon. She's Morgan's woman. And then there's Mary. She was Jamie's wet nurse when the French lass up and refused to nurse the babe she'd borne. Mary belongs to Tully. Ye met him on the ship. Or Tully belongs to Mary, might be more fitting," the mate chuckled. "Mary keeps this fine house for the captain and sees to the cooking and the like. Jamie is Mary's girl more than she ever was her mother's." The giant led the way up the staircase then down a hall to a bedroom on the far end. He threw the door open with a flourish to reveal an adequately comfortable room with a four-poster bed, a simple chest and wardrobe, and two small settees placed before the fireplace. There was a rocking chair near the wide expanse of windows that overlooked the bay in the distance.

"Mary says this be yer room. Ye behave and Morgan says ye can come and go as ye like. He thinks ye have sense enough to know there ain't escape to be found for ye here."

Franco glared at the man for the information, not in the least intimidated by the pirate's size. Franco had a certain amount of insecurity about his possible fate at the hands of these ruffians, but he wasn't afraid of them. He understood that if he ever allowed one of them to back him down and humiliate him, he would lose the edge his bravado had

91

earned for him. What's more, cowering wasn't in his nature, no matter the odds. "You may assure your captain, as well as yourself, that I have no intention of attempting any escape until I am absolutely assured of success in such a venture. I see that would not be forthcoming here — yet. Do give me credit for bearing some common sense," he snapped crossly.

To his surprise, the massive pirate laughed uproariously. "I best take care or I might come to like ye!" he bellowed, chuckling loudly. He clapped Franco on the back with a huge black paw, a blow that nearly felled him though Franco was over six feet tall himself and no weakling. "Ye're awright, ye are!" Jocko passed judgment as he strode from the room, still chuckling merrily.

The pirate's reaction left Franco deep in thought as he watched the mate leave. He was certain that he had made no error in earning Jocko's approval. The mate's good will might prove useful someday. He decided to go on cultivating associations of friendship, not only with Jocko but with the rest of the buccaneers as well, including, if he could, Morgan himself. It couldn't harm his position. And he might have need of their respect, even their liking, sometime in the future. Morgan, whom he despised, would be hardest of all to win over, but what harm could it do to try?

Perhaps his father's efforts in sending him to sea had, after all, resulted in a new outlook. The Franco who had left Spain a year ago wouldn't have harbored such a thought as befriending his captors. He would have challenged them all — one at a time or en masse, even if the conflict cost him his life. There would have been honor in dying nobly for a just cause, however stupid the action might be deemed by the more cautiously minded. Now he looked at his circumstances in a different light, wiser he hoped, and more mature than he had been.

In the days that followed, Franco further discovered another advantage to be had in cultivating their friendship, as it helped to pass the time. Here on the island and associating with other ship's captains staying in Morgan's mansion, he found less restraint in befriending him than that employed by the common sailors aboard Morgan's ship. He soon learned that the favorite sport of the buccaneers while ashore, besides drinking and wenching, was gambling, winning and losing vast fortunes on a turn of the cards or a roll of the dice. A pirate might be wealthy from the results of his ill-gotten gain in one minute and as poor as a slave the very next, having lost all he had on a single hand at cards or a badly thrown toss. For men whose lives overflowed with adventure, stakes had to be high just to gain their interest.

Franco had gambled before at court, as cards and dice were a gentleman's pastime as well, but he had never allowed the ventures to fill his hours as he was doing now. There was little else to do on the island, though as Morgan had promised, he was permitted to come and go as he pleased. At least once daily, he swam in the clear, inland lagoons and frequently went for long walks along the white sand beaches, but the remainder of his time passed slowly, the days stretching endlessly before him, the nights warm, sweet-fragranced, and moonlit, but devoid of companionship.

Once he had gone down to the docks to see what the taverns offered, but the wenches were rough, foul-mouthed, and dirty. He had no desire to ease his boredom with the likes of them and, ignoring their advances, he drank a full tankard of rum then staggered back to the mansion to lose his frustration in sleep.

As for Jamie, he hardly ever saw her since the ship docked. He caught fleeting glimpses of her, but she rarely dared to catch his gaze before she disappeared into the recesses of the mansion or into the brush of one of the island's many trails. If he wasn't flattering himself, the girl had developed an infatuation for him. He saw it in the sad-eyed looks she gave him in the brief moments before she fled up a path or down a hallway. He recalled it in bringing back the memory of how she had cared for him aboard the ship in the days before he knew she was not a boy. Franco realized Morgan's threat was the reason she avoided him. The captain had undoubtedly warned her with the same advice he'd given Franco—that if he caught them alone, even Franco's hostage status wouldn't save him. She had already suffered a bruise on her cheek because of him, and Franco had no wish to place her again in such jeopardy, though his desire for her burned as sharply as ever. He couldn't help but remember her as she had been that day, naked and innocent, openly curious to whatever he wanted to teach her, so willing to surrender that Franco's loins ached with the thought.

But Morgan was the cruelest man Franco had ever met and there was no way to judge how far his wrath might take him.

His observations resulted in one more discovery he would never have suspected. In his own foul way, Morgan, the blustering, vile-tempered pirate, truly did seem fond of the girl who was his daughter. He had deduced that it was sheer terror of Morgan that held ones like Rory and O'Brien and others in check. Men who would hardly have hesitated in mercilessly taking any woman they seized on the high seas, wouldn't dare look Jamie's way with open lust in their eyes. Not in Morgan's sight. And not in Jocko's, or in the presence of Ned Shanks either. Shanks was small and squat, but as deadly as a viper. Franco had witnessed the ship's chief gunner catch a man cheating at cards and toss a dagger across a crowded, smoke-heavy room to strike a fatal target dead center in the middle of the fleeing man's back. Both mates seemed to look on Jamie as the daughter his seafarer's life had denied him. Any man who would try to force her to submit to his will and face all that wrath for his trouble had to possess a death wish.

Since he had no impulse toward ending his life prematurely, and already cared more deeply than he would like to admit for the girl who had befriended him when no one else would, he stilled his impulses with the thought of what his lust might bring down on both of them.

In the days aboard ship, Franco had observed Morgan on many occasions, and in pleasanter moods, treat the girl to rib-cracking affection, throwing his powerful arms around her and giving her brief hugs that had to be as painful as the blows he also dealt when she displeased him, twice sending her sprawling for one offense or another. Each time, Jamie accepted the harsher treatment as she absorbed the affection, with equal nonresponsiveness. She didn't hug back and she didn't offer resistance, simply getting out of Morgan's way in either of his moods as quickly as possible. He had never seen her cry.

For himself, he had to stifle his impulses to thrash Morgan soundly for his blows to the girl by realizing that, weaponless except for his fists, he'd simply be killed for his trouble and Jamie no better off than if he had never interfered.

Finally, though, the day had come when he could watch in silence no longer. He walked inside the mansion's entry to find Morgan, having cornered Jamie against the lowest steps, ready to administer another slap like the one he had obviously just given her. Jamie's hand was at her cheek where a fiery red welt had appeared.

"Morgan!" he shouted before the huge palm could descend a second time. "Leave her alone or so help me you'll have me to deal with for it!"

Henry Morgan stopped, turning slowly around. "And who are you to be giving me orders?" he said, his tone filled with threat. "She's my daughter and I'll do as I please."

Franco was too angry this time to care about his precarious position as a hostage. His hands clenched into fists at his sides, anxious to pummel the bully senseless. "Not while I'm here, you won't!" Franco glared at him through hate-

95

filled eyes. "If you touch her again in that manner, I promise you, you'll have me to contend with."

To Franco's surprise, Morgan grinned, showing large white, even teeth. "Ye think ye can take me then? Hand to hand?"

"No!" Jamie sprang up to look at Franco fearfully.

"Any way you like," Franco returned, determined to give a good account of himself. Morgan stared at him through glacier-hued eyes, then threw back his head and laughed.

"Bless me now, if I don't think ye might!" he roared, and laughingly drew Polly, Shanks, and a few of the others out of the dining hall into the entryway. Morgan was large enough to break him in half in hand-to-hand combat, and the man was no coward. Franco had seen him fight aboard the galleon when the pirates bested the Spanish ship. He had watched Morgan crack two sailors' heads together like he was splitting coconuts. He had no wish to fight him on such uneven terms but he couldn't, and wouldn't, back down.

"Put a sword in my hands and I'll show you how willing I am to fight," Franco returned.

This produced only renewed guffaws out of the man Franco had promised himself to at least try to win over in some semblance of friendship. "Oh, now," Morgan said between bursts of laughter, "Not me." He pretended fright. "I've seen ye with a saber in yer hands. I'll be no Jimbo Taylor and have meself skewered!"

Following Morgan's example, the others began to laugh with him, making Franco itch to launch himself at the mocking pirate.

"Aye." Morgan wiped tears of mirth from his eyes. "It's right good ye are with that weapon, and it ain't in me nature to bet on poor odds. Ye'd have me liver on the end of that weapon 'ere long, I'd wager." To Franco's further astonishment, Morgan clapped him on the back in a friendly gesture, just as Jocko Chalks had. "If ye ever decide

96

ye've had enough of being a dandy and want to turn pirate instead, ye let me know it and I'll stake ye with a ship of yer own any day. Ye've got guts, man, and I like that!" A thoroughly bewildered Franco was shoved toward the dining hall with a heavy, friendly paw on his shoulder. "Even if ye be a Spaniard, yer the kind of man I like. Let's split a keg of rum between us and see if yer gullet's as big as yer mouth."

"Jocko, have ye ever been in love?" Jamie asked, watching him whittle a form out of a piece of pine wood. She couldn't tell what it would be yet and realized she might not even when he'd finished the sculpture. Jocko was not an artist.

Franco and Morgan were inside, playing a game of dice and swilling rum as the sun set. Seeing Jocko on the veranda, she had been drawn out to talk with him.

"Aye, that I have, onc't," he replied, keeping to his idle labor.

"You were in love?" Jamie, though she had asked, was surprised by his answer. She sat down beside him on the step. The evening was warm, fragrant with the scent of a gentle sea breeze. There was a soft glow in the west from the setting sun that lit the horizon with muted shades of purple, orange, and pink. "Who was she? What was she like?"

"Her name was Winona. She was the prettiest thing I ever laid my eyes on. She belonged to a family that lived on Royale. A fine lady's maid, she was. I met her one Saturday in the market square, shopping for the people what owned her. I was going to buy her, ye see, all right and proper. Me being a free man, she'd be mine then, and not stolen property. She liked the idea well enough to be saving her own coin when she could get it, working extra sewing for others when her mistress would let her."

"What happened then?" Jamie prodded when the ex-slave fell silent to ponder the carving in his hands, his thoughts perhaps centered on a dusky maiden he'd known long ago.

"Her massa had himself a bad turn of fortune. He sold her whilst I was at sea. Sent her to some plantation in the So' Seas, so I never see'd her again."

"Oh," Jamie murmured, saddened by his tale. In sympathy, she laid her head down on his beefy bicep. For several minutes they listened to the sounds of the birds nestling in the branches and the hum of the dragonflies catching their evening's repast on the island's ever-abundant mosquito population. "How did ye know it when ye were in love?" Jamie asked him at last, her head resting on his shoulder.

"I don't rightly know how ye knows it," he replied. "It's just something ye feel coming on inside ye."

"Like an ache?" she queried, raising her head to look up at him. "Like ye hurt inside, but there's nothing wrong?"

"Aye," Jocko chuckled. "Sometimes it's like that. Ye've done gone soft on the Spaniard, ain't ye?"

"Morgan says I've gone daft in me head," she grumbled. "He whacked me a good one for it, but Franco made him stop it."

"Did he?" Jocko glanced up, apparently approving of Franco's action.

"Aye, only Morgan made a joke of it all and now he has him in there." She cocked a thumb toward the mansion's interior. "Being all friendly like, drinking and gambling."

"How much liberty did ye allow the Spaniard that day on the beach?"

"Ye heard about that?" Jamie's face reddened.

"Aye, ever'body did."

"Not that much," Jamie replied, shamefacedly. "But I wanted to."

"Aye, then, ye're in love." Jocko chuckled and returned to carving the figure in his hand.

"Papa says he'll skin him if he catches us," Jamie furthered.

"Aye, and he might at that, so ye best not give him

cause," Jocko advised her. "It's yer own interest yer papa's looking out for, girl."

"But Franco'd never hurt me . . ."

"Mebbe not like yer papa will, with a smack or a slap to set yer head right, but the Spaniard has it in him to hurt ye other ways, not by meaning to, but hurting ye nonetheless. Yer papa don't want to see that happen to ye and neither do I, so ye mind what we tell ye when we say ye best stay away from him." Jocko, too, often defended her from Morgan's anger, not defying the captain, as Franco had, but often setting himself up as a brick wall between them. It was Jamie's own temperament that often resulted in stoking the captain's ire. While Franco had seen the stoic, silent Jamie in the captain's presence, and might presume her to be a meek little mouse in need of a champion, Jocko knew her better. He knew the slaps did little to change Jamie's mind, often making her more rebellious and stubborn. He also knew Morgan wouldn't go any farther. If he couldn't smack his ideas of good sense into her, he'd spin about on his heel and stomp away in a rage, muttering that she was as mule-headed as ever her mother had been before her. At times, Jamie could twist the wily Morgan around her little finger. When he'd listen to no one else, he might weigh the wisdom of her advice. She knew how to talk him into a good many things Morgan would never have thought of on his own. Like keeping the Spaniard for ransom.

To Jocko's mind, the captive might prove too dangerous to hold on to and the better he came to know the Spaniard, the firmer his convictions became. If ever turned to vengeance, he'd make a deadly enemy. Though young yet, the hostage had the qualities of a leader—one who might be partnered an equal but who would take second place to no man.

Just before the ship docked, Jocko had suggested, carefully so as not to rule him, that the captain consider freeing his captive ahead of the ransom's arrival. To Jocko's thinking, there were two ways to deal with a man like DeCortega—kill him while the opportunity was available or make a partner of him before the situation might turn to give the prisoner an advantage.

If they simply let him go when the ransom came, the man wouldn't rest until he had vengeance on his captors. He would seek them out whatever the cost, and even the score with his foes if revenge took him the remainder of his life. However, if his captors were to turn the tables themselves, befriend their hostage, release him without waiting for the kidnap ransom to arrive, perhaps even lured him into joining them in a venture or two, he might be turned away from a thought toward hunting them down. There might be even more profit, Jocko had offered for his captain's contemplation, if they could turn the Spanish nobleman into an ally. He could bring in more revenues in six months than ten times the ransom price. Give him a ship of his own and reliable men to sail with him. Send him after cargoes the Colonies were shipping back to Mother England, let him keep enough to make him happy and turn a percentage over to them and Morgan would be richer and perfectly innocent of any involvement in piracy against the English Crown.

Morgan had laughed heartily at his first mate's suggestion, but then Jocko saw the wheels turn in the captain's head.

"Aye, it might have merit if he has something to keep him here . . ."

The captain had said no more about it, dismissing Jocko from his cabin aboard the ship, but Jocko knew he was still pondering how to put such a plan into motion. He didn't want the Spaniard on the wrong side of Morgan before his idea had time to be put into effect.

"Ye mind me words, girl," he explained to Jamie, still sitting close beside him. "The Spaniard might just come to be right fond of ye, even love ye, in a way, but men, most of

100

us, don't think on it the way young girls do. Ye'd let yer heart rule yer head, and that's plain foolish. Franco, he's a man. He has things to do, and places to see afore he's ready to settle down. And when he does wed, don't ye know, girl, it's going to be to a female of his own station?"

"But I'm half Duvalier," Jamie protested, her vehement tone overwhelming her own lack of certainty. Deep inside she knew what Jocko said was true. Franco belonged to an old and noble house, the son of a count. Perhaps half her bloodline was above reproach but the other side was undeniably tainted.

"Ye stay away from him now, afore he breaks yer heart," Jocko advised solemnly.

"Why are ye so sure he will?" Jamie pulled away from him to stare at him in a huff. "Mebbe he won't care about things like that. Maybe he'll take me with him when he's free. He was going to, I know that . . ."

"Aye, afore he knew Jamie the lad was a lass instead, but it's a whole different thing now, ain't it?" Jocko put his arm about her, hugging her gently in spite of her miffed resistance. "Lass, what can I tell ye? Mebbe he would, girl." He hadn't the heart to disappoint her further. "Mebbe he would."

Some three hours had passed since his defiance of Morgan, and Franco's head was reeling from matching the pirate drink for drink. The one man Franco had felt he truly would never win over was now his bosom friend and all for the fact that he had defied him. Would he never have done with being confounded by these people?

Jamie had vanished shortly after Franco dared Morgan to combat, her shouted protest the last he had seen or heard of her. He had spent the time since that episode being challenged to games of dice with Morgan and three other ship's captains. For some reason that only fate could answer, he

101

was winning regularly and had propelled the few sovereigns in his pockets into a hefty pile of gold and silver that lay on the table before him. Night had fallen solidly and the scenery was black as pitch outside the windows. Candles had been lit around the room and a blazing fire stoked in the fireplace warded off the evening's damp chill.

Morgan too had been winning; the pots rather evenly shared between them. That and the rum had put the pirate captain in a jovial frame of mind as Jocko, Morgan's first mate, walked into the room.

"What do ye think, Jocko," Morgan said as the mate strode over to the fireplace. "Should we keep this Spanish dog and make a pirate of him?"

Jocko looked at his leader in some surprise that Morgan would bring up the scheme here, now, in front of the others. "Aye, captain, we could give him our own letter o' marque to make him legal." The first mate tried to make a jest of the captain's remark, recognizing that Captain Morgan right now was sailing into rough seas on an ocean of rum he'd imbibed during the past few hours. It was not the time to initiate such a plan as the mate had conceived of. The captain was always the worst off for any bargain he struck while strong brew clouded his judgment.

Morgan bellowed with laughter at Jocko's comment, taking up the dice, ready for his next roll. "We'd be our own country then, wouldn't we? The land of Tortuga Bay, a sovereignty under King Henry Morgan, the First."

"Ohh, ain't that grand now," Polly tittered from beside him, and Morgan slapped her trim backside good-naturedly, then pulled the woman down onto his lap.

"That would make Jamie a princess of the new country then, wouldn't it? What would ye think of that, Spaniard? Me Jamie a royal princess. She'd be a fine catch then for any man, wouldn't she?"

Just then, Franco noticed that Jamie had entered the room sometime during the conversation, her presence undoubtedly prompting the remark. She had come to stand near the first mate by the blazing hearth, and the fire lent her face a soft, golden glow in the yellow light. She had removed the bandanna to let her raven hair fall heavily down her back like a glistening veil. By God, she was beautiful, even in the baggy boy's clothing she always wore. He only too well recalled what she looked like without them.

"She's a fine catch now," he answered Morgan's question, mesmerized once more by the sight of her. Jamie possessed a beautifully elegant face and a body that set his blood on fire. It was difficult to believe she could be Morgan's daughter, yet he had to remind himself that she was. He recalled as well Morgan's threat, and not for anything would he risk putting her in danger.

"Ye keep gazing at her like that, man, and I might come to believe ye might marry her yerself," Morgan returned, watching him carefully.

"She's a prize worthy of a king's ransom," Franco stated.

"Is she now," Morgan's eyes narrowed. "But yer only fooling, ain't ye? Ye wouldn't take up with the likes of her. Not a fine lord such as yerself." The pirate's voice lowered but could still be heard in the sudden silence that had descended into the room.

"Morgan!" Polly complained, poking him hard in the ribs.

"Well, 'tis true, ain't it?" Morgan persisted. "Would ye take up with the likes of her and take her home to yer fam'ly? Or would ye be ashamed to be seen in her company 'mongst yer own."

Franco watched Jamie's cheeks flaming red, but she managed to spare her father a furious glare. "You underestimate her worth, Morgan," he said, letting his gaze roam back to the table laden with the piles of gold and silver in front of his place and Morgan's. The other three captains playing with them had only a few scattered coins in front of them now.

"Do I?" Morgan glowered, suddenly turned to a foul change of mood. "Ah, she'd be a fine one to bed, but not the kind a man could take to wife. Not for a fine lord such as yerself. Ain't that more like it? She's a good one to roll with 'neath the sheets, I expect, . . ."

"Damn you, Morgan, stop it!" Polly jabbed him in the ribs with her elbow again, then jumped up from his lap to go toward Jamie. The woman reached out for her but Jamie pulled free, jerking away from her.

"Well, ain't it so?" Morgan goaded, his eyes never once leaving Franco's face.

"No, it's not so!" He seethed with anger at what the vile pirate was putting the girl through. "How the girl was raised is not her fault," Franco responded, the rum clouding his judgment. He hadn't realized how his statement might be taken until the words had escaped and then it was too late to take them back. One glance in her direction revealed the full impact of his speech had struck exactly where he had never intended to aim, at Jamie, and not at Morgan, where he had wanted his thrust to strike.

"Aye, I thought so!" Morgan slapped an empty tankard on the tabletop.

Franco heard a strangled cry from Jamie's side of the room, then saw her start to flee out of the corner of his eye.

"Stay, girl!" Morgan bellowed. Jamie's footsteps across the wooden floor immediately stopped. "Stay right where ye are and I'll show ye what yer fine Spanish lordship thinks of ye! I'll make ye a wager, Spaniard." He gathered up the dice he had discarded. "All or nothing on one toss each, highest score wins all."

Franco was glad the ordeal was over. He pushed his pile of coins into the center of the table. "Good enough," he said, expecting Morgan to take the first roll. It would be worth it to lose and put Morgan into a better frame of mind for the girl's sake.

"It ain't gold we toss for."

"What then?" Franco looked at him.

Morgan took on an evil grin. "I said all or nothing. I wager ye yer freedom, Spaniard, if ye win. And if I lose the toss, ye get . . . Jamie." The pirate let his voice purr over her name.

Franco could only stare at him, dumbfounded. "You can't possibly be serious."

Morgan sat back, smiling. "If ye lose the toss, I double me ransom. Ye work for me till a like amount is paid in full."

"Work for you?"

"Aye, I think ye have it in ye, I do. I stake ye with a ship of yer own and ye work for me for one year, pirating where I tell ye, when I tell ye, and against who I tell ye. Ye keeps a percentage for yerself and the rest goes to me till yer debt's paid off. What do ye say?"

"How would you know you could trust me with a ship of my own?"

"Ye're a man of yer word, ain't ye? Most gentlemen are, and lordships most of all. 'Sides, Jocko here would first mate ye. He'd cut ye in half first notion he got ye weren't doing as ye were told."

"That is a great deal to risk on a single throw."

Morgan's gaze narrowed again. "So's mine, or don't ye think so?" He leaned closer over the table. "Ye know well enough Jamie's been with no man before. She's yers, if ye win, and yer freedom with her."

Franco knew he must be playing him along for a fool. "Morgan, even you wouldn't wager your own daughter," he laughed.

"Then accept me bet and we'll see," Morgan dared him. "Ye best me and my girl is yours. Yer freedom too. Ye can leave whenever ye like."

"With a knife in my back, I presume."

"I don't welch on me bets!" Morgan's fist slammed onto

the table, rattling the contents. "I'll take ye to Royale myself! From there ye can take ship to anywheres ye like."

"And Jamie?"

"I said she's yers and I'll keep to me word! Only one thing ye'll vow to me first. When she's naught but trouble to ye, ye'll send her home. Give me that much and ye'll see that I keep to me word."

Franco still couldn't believe the man meant it — unless that was part of Morgan's game, hoping to win either way the dice fell. Win the toss and he had Franco as his slave for a year as well as the ransom. Lose and he hoped he might someday have a rich son-in-law if Franco's sense of honor impelled him to marry the girl, which it would if he took her with him. The way he yearned for her now, she'd be with child before long and no child of his would be born a bastard. Perhaps Morgan had already sensed that out of him as well. That the pirate captain seemed to have him so well figured out irritated Franco.

"Very well, Morgan. You have my vow and I accept your wager. You roll first."

Grinning slyly, Morgan shook the dice in his hand, then tossed. A score of nine rolled onto the table, a five and a four. Satisfied, he handed the dice to Franco.

Franco shook them thoroughly in his cupped hand. Morgan already seemed certain he'd won, a self-satisfied grin on the weathered clean-shaven face. Franco released and the ivory cubes danced across the table. The first cube landed, exposing a six. The second stopped rolling on a four, a score of ten.

The room was deathly silent as Franco looked up from his winning score to Morgan's face. The pirate's cheeks had gone livid while he continued to stare, bug-eyed, at the traitorous dice. Franco was about to say that he considered the entire wager to be in jest anyway, when Morgan suddenly sprang to his feet, one huge arm upending the table, sending the piece of furniture and its contents flying across

106

the room. "Damn yer soul, ye black-hearted Spaniard!" Morgan shouted, then turned and stalked from the room.

Franco's gaze sought out Jamie's. She was standing stock-still, just where Morgan's crisp order had left her. Tears rolled freely down her cheeks as she looked back at him with anguished betrayal in her eyes. He had allowed her to be used as part of the wager, a thing to be bartered and traded, won or lost. He had let too much rum and Morgan goad him into a bet he should never have struck. He could have said, *should* have said, that Jamie was to be left out of the bargain.

"I'm sorry, Jamie," he murmured, but she was already past him, her hand covering her mouth as she fled for the stairs to the upper story.

"Bastard!" Polly glared at him. "Ye're as bad a one as he is!" She stormed from the room, her heels clicking heavily as she crossed the floor.

Even in defeat, Morgan had won, Franco thought as, one by one, the spectators left him. He had managed to prove to Jamie, and to all of them, including himself, that there was only a very thin line between a Franco DeCortega and the likes of a Henry Morgan.

Chapter Five

"Where do ye think ye're going?" Morgan roared, meeting her in the hallway as Jamie tread barefoot in her nightdress toward the Spaniard's room.

Jamie spun about on him, anger and outrage flashing sparks of fury at him. "Where should I be going but to pay your damned debt!" she returned, drowning out his next intended shout and bringing Morgan up abruptly. " 'Twas *you* put me up as the wager! 'Twas *you* that lost!"

"The Spaniard would never hold ye to it," Morgan said, having utterly lost his bluster while he faced his daughter's wrath.

"Maybe not, but I'm going to him just the same," she stated. " 'Twas you, wasn't it, asking me this very afternoon how I thought Franco might be convinced to stay on Tortuga? Is this what ye had in mind? Offering me to bribe him?"

"No." Morgan answered shaking his burly head. "I thought I'd win the cursed toss." Jamie gazed at him in a manner he had never seen from her before. At this moment she looked every inch the woman grown. The Spaniard had done that, Morgan realized. Not only stolen his daughter's loyalty from him but sparked the change from child into mature woman. Now it would be different eyes that watched him, different words chosen to speak to him,

108

a different person he would ever after be addressing. Jamie was not a child anymore and with her girlhood, his last firm hold on his daughter had vanished.

He hadn't thought of the consequences of his actions until now. Jamie had always been his shadow, following him about, eager to know all he could teach of the sea and sailing. In her, he had deposited his hopes for a better future that he could live vicariously, through her good fortunes and successes. The turn of events in his own life had denied him fulfillment of his aspirations, but Jamie's was still full of promise. He did love her and had raised her as close to him as he would have a son, but Jamie was not his son, she was his daughter, and a daughter left her father's house to join with the man she had chosen.

Seeing the pair on the beach that day and then listening to Jocko's suggestion of making an ally out of their hostage, Morgan had wanted a plot whereby he could not lose either his daughter or his captive. To his mind, a man couldn't know how much he wanted a thing unless it passed, even fleetingly, into his possession. Until he sampled the sweet charms of Antoinette Duvalier, marriage had remained far from his thoughts, but when she carried his child, his own flesh and blood growing within her body, the idea of making her permanently his obsessed him day and night. He had tried every threat and every bribery within his power, yet she remained willful and stubborn, only making him want what was denied him even more desperately. Finally she took his pistol and forever removed herself from his captivity and Morgan mourned her as the only woman he had ever loved. To his reasoning then, it was only logical that the young Spaniard would not be tempted to wed beneath his station unless he had similar inducement.

Henry hadn't intended to lose the bet but now that he had, Jamie would be the only chance left to keep the Spaniard here and working for him as Jocko had suggested. The idea that she might go with Franco had not entered his rum-fogged mind until this moment.

"Do you truly think I can keep Franco here if he wants to go?" she asked him. "Sometimes, Papa, you're a fool." She turned away from him, walking toward DeCortega's door.

"Jamie . . ." her father called out to her, but she pushed Franco's door open and went inside, closing it firmly behind her.

Jamie found the room empty and sat down in the rocking chair near the window to wait, her spirits lower than she ever remembered them being. It wasn't only that her father had used her as a bauble to dangle in front of Franco, it was that Franco had accepted the bribe that cut deeply into her heart. She had suffered her father's punishment this morning because she had insisted Franco could never be coerced into becoming a pirate. He was too fine, too noble. He would never stoop to piracy whatever Morgan offered him. She had said Franco was a gentleman, but then, what would Morgan know about that, and that was when he struck her for her sass. She had known when she said it, that nothing could provoke Morgan to violence faster than reminding him of what he was, no more than a highwayman of the open seas, a plain and common thief.

Henry Morgan had been born poor on a small farm in Llanrhymney, Glamorgan, Wales, in 1635. Through his boyhood, he watched fine lords and gentlemen ride past in their elegant clothes and fancy carriages or astride their prancing steeds and, rather than resent that they were highborn and he was not, Henry envied them with a will that decided if he could not be reborn to title and position, why then, he would earn them for himself and all his descendants. Taking to the sea seemed the easiest way to accomplish his purpose. Others had won titles and rewards by serving the king as privateers. He could do the same and work for what his lowly birth had denied him. He set sail for the West Indies under Captain William Penn in 1654 and sailed with Captain Christopher Myngs against Cuba in 1662. In 1668, he was appointed colonel of troops at Jamaica, given command of an expedition that captured Puerto Principe in Cuba and won him considerable renown, but the position of prestige he longed for had been denied him thus far. He was no more than plain Henry Morgan, Captain Morgan, but a commoner as untitled as he'd been born.

Antoinette Duvalier had baited him constantly with reminders of how unworthy he was. She was a lady. Successful ventures or not, what was Morgan but a pirate and a rogue? Though few knew it, Morgan had offered to marry her, but "the French lass" refused, preferring her "shame," as she called it, to ever accepting the man as her husband. He had built this house for her and spent a fortune furnishing it, showered her with silks and jewels, but her affection could not be bought at any price.

Jamie's own memories of her mother were of a beautiful but remote woman who hated the child she gave birth to as much as she despised the father. Though she was barely more than a toddler, Jamie recalled as if it was yesterday how she had once crept into her mother's room, even though Mary, who tended to Jamie, had warned her never to go in there. "Your *maman* is ill, *ma petite*," the nurse would tell her. "You must not disturb her." But Jamie had gone inside anyway, determined to see her, curious and confused about this person who, as long as Jamie could remember, had always been too "ill" to receive her. Her mother had been sitting at the dressing table, combing her long locks of beautiful blond hair that fell in a long cascade down her back. She spied Jamie's form in the looking glass and her mother's lovely face crumbled before Jamie's eyes into an ugly mask of grief and rage. Her mother's mouth opened in a mad shriek as she screamed, "Marie, come and get her OUT OF HERE!"

Mary had come in and whisked her away, and not many weeks after that Jamie had been awakened from her nap by the sound of a pistol shot, the scurrying of many feet on the upstairs hallway, a great commotion near her mother's room. Forgotten in the excitement, Jamie stood, sucking her thumb, something she wasn't supposed to do anymore, and watching as her mother's blood-spattered body was carried down the hallway, her long golden hair trailing on the carpet.

Mary had told her it wasn't her fault, that her *maman*'s illness was responsible, but the mad shriek caused by her presence in the room that day had stayed with Jamie, haunting the years of her adolescence.

Perhaps Jocko was right and she was no more worthy of Franco's love than her father had been of Antoinette's, but, if Franco wouldn't take her with him, or stay in the Caribbean on her account, then at least she would take something for herself out of the foul arrangement the two of them had cast over the gaming table.

She hadn't forgotten the beach incident either. DeCortega had stirred emotions in her that she hadn't suspected existed, and her curiosity had not yet been appeased. Well, now it would be and with Morgan's own sanction. Her own burning questions would be solved this very night.

Franco wished he was capable of becoming uproariously drunk. The rum imbibed in the past hour added to what he had previously absorbed, had only made him more somber yet, depressed and self-examining, finding naught but fault at this moment inside himself.

He was a free man, if Morgan's word was good, but the

112

cost to his self-esteem had been much greater than if he had rolled below Morgan's score and lost. Jamie Morgan was a beautiful, sweet, and gentle young woman, not an object to be placed on a gaming table. Good God, how had he ever allowed Morgan to goad him to that?

Certain in his own assessment that he was too vile for even such as they to associate with, the pirates had left him to his own company in the dining hall and he now sat in an armchair before the cooling hearth in the fireplace, despising himself thoroughly for his part in the bargain.

Franco knew no other future for himself but to go home again. He was the second born son of Conde Carlos DeCortega. His elder brother, Lorenzo, was a greedy man but not a cautious one. Franco might be the more hot-blooded of the two, but in business he was cool, sensible, and logical. Carlos depended on Franco's judgment in business matters to counter his brother's extravagances. He had made provisions for that in his will that left half of the family holdings to Franco so that he would have equal say in any venture his brother might be tempted into. Lorenzo had been furious when he learned of the will's contents, incensed that their father would not bequeath everything to him as the eldest, but Carlos knew Lorenzo too well for that. Left unhampered, Lorenzo would spend the inheritance until nothing was left, not even the dowries of their two sisters.

Other DeCortegas also depended on them for their livelihood—Franco's mother, his widowed aunt, dependent cousins, the servants and slaves who served the household, the farmers and craftsmen who lived on DeCortega land and looked to the family for their future security. Rich or penniless, Franco knew he could make his own way in life, but who would look out for them if he shirked his responsibility? What would become of them if Lorenzo squandered everything?

No, there was no choice in the matter. Franco had to go

113

home again. Then could he take Jamie back to Spain with him? Certainly not in the manner he had intended for Jamie, the boy—as a servant and later, perhaps, an adopted son. She was not child enough for anyone to consider his ward. He could take her away from here. He could make her his wife, and what then? He knew the answer only too well. The court life of Spain was notoriously straitlaced and intolerant. He had seen foreign princesses reduced to tears by the Spanish nobility that looked upon all other Europeans as heretics and barbarians. Even among their own nobility, as illogical as such reasoning was, distinctions had been made between those who were born in the New World colonies and those born on Spanish soil—the homeland born of course, having the higher standing, even though both might come from excellent houses and bear old and distinguished names. How could he, in good conscience, expose Jamie to the abuse that she would certainly experience if he took her home with him? He wasn't entirely certain of how his own mother and father might react to his wedding a girl of English and French descent, not even a Catholic, and more, the daughter of Henry Morgan, the pirate. For himself, he might be able to weather the trouble, but could she? Or would his selfish act ruin all of the beauty that was inside Morgan's daughter, removing her every chance of eventual happiness? However he examined the problem, no satisfactory answers presented themselves.

Pulling himself out of his dark thoughts, Franco got to his feet, the alcohol blurring his focus as he dragged himself up the stairs using the carved ebony handrail for support. The mansion was silent as he pushed open the door of his bedchamber and spied Jamie, asleep in the rocking chair beside the open window. A faint night breeze ruffled the lace curtains. She had lit neither the fire in the grate nor a candle, her head resting on her shoulder, looking so much like a young woman who had nodded off prematurely after her first ball that, overcome by affection, he was impelled to lean over and bestow a gentle kiss on her forehead. She was wearing a softly diaphanous nightdress that covered her from her neck to her toes while her hair, unbound, hung loosely down her back. Bending over her, he could smell the faint lemon scent of the rinse she used to wash her hair.

As his lips finished brushing her brow, Jamie's eyelids fluttered open and she looked up at him, her eyes growing big and round and uncertain.

"I fell asleep," she murmured softly.

"Jamie, you needn't stay." He knelt in front of her, grasping both her hands in his. He couldn't resist being moved by the sight of her—waiting here to pay her father's wager. "We were only joking. We never meant the bet in earnest."

"Morgan meant it," she stated somberly. "And so did you."

"I apologize for that. I never intended to let it go so far. You deserve better than the treatment we've offered you."

"Then why did you accept it?"

He could see anger simmering beneath the surface, roiling like an angry sea in the depths of the lavender eyes that watched him accusingly.

"I was thinking . . . I . . ." Franco realized what he had been about to say and stopped abruptly.

"You were thinking about your freedom and nothing else!" she said harshly, hurt and angry. She had tried to keep her temper checked, to follow through on her plot of learning everything that only he could satisfactorily teach her, but having him in front of her, an available target, the outrage was too much to bear without striking back. "That I came with it meant nothing to you one way or the other!"

"No, not entirely," he denied, shaking his head. He wasn't sober enough for this situation and her anger had

115

taken him by surprise, though she had every right to be. The Jamie he had known aboard the ship was a quiet, gentle girl, brave enough to defy Morgan and the pirates . . . but perhaps there was more to her than he had previously imagined. In truth, he had been thinking of his freedom, and of besting Morgan, and Jamie had fallen somewhere behind those other considerations. "I wanted you . . . I . . ."

"Papa was right!" she shouted over his denial, suddenly furious. "You're just like he said you were! It was never *me* that you cared about!"

"That isn't true!" he shouted back, growing angry at the accusations she wouldn't let him refute, but she had already pushed past him to stand up, spinning about in a rage he hadn't known she could possess, her eyes aflame.

"Damn you!" she swore furiously. "You're as big a liar as he is when it suits your purpose! You used me and that's all you ever had in mind."

"That is not so . . ."

"Isn't it? Isn't it just what you were thinking when you thought Jamie was a cabin boy you could bribe to help you?"

"It may have begun like that, but . . ."

"And it's the same now. Well, I'll have you know I'm not a thing to be bartered about, traded and sold to fit yer fancy. I'll bed with who I please. I ain't yer property and I ain't Morgan's."

"I know that," Franco countered. "I said I was sorry and I am. Will you listen to me . . ." Jamie had started to turn away from him, Franco catching her by the arm to turn her back, but she yanked herself free, recoiling as if she'd been touched by something disgusting and filthy.

"Don't come near me again! Ever!" she raged. Raising her freed hand high in the air she brought it down hard across his cheek. The stinging slap brought him abruptly back to sobriety.

"And don't think ye can treat me like this again!" For good measure, she raised her hand to strike him once more but Franco caught her wrist in midair.

"I won't let you do that," he warned, holding his own growing anger in check. No man had ever slapped his face and lived to tell about it. No woman had ever had cause to do so.

"Try and stop me," she seethed through clenched teeth, raising the other hand and trying to bring it across his face, but Franco caught that one too and wrapped his fingers tightly about both her wrists. "Stop it!" he shouted as she jerked and tugged to free herself. "I don't want to fight you."

"Let me go!" She tried to kick his shin but only succeeded in hurting her bare foot against his boot. Her wince of pain gave him the chance he was seeking to yank her forward and, while she remained off balance, push her down across the bed. "I won't fight you, do you hear?" he warned, stretching her arms above her head to keep her immobile. Her chest heaved from her recent exertions, her luscious breasts only inches away from his face, barely concealed beneath the filmy material, turning his anger into wanton desire.

Jamie saw where his gaze was traveling. "Let me up," she demanded, squirming to free her wrists from his grip.

"No," Franco continued to let his eyes rest on the firm, full breasts that rose and fell with each respiration as she caught her breath. "I'm bigger than you are, and I'm stronger, so for now, I'll do as I please." He gripped both wrists with one hand, holding them tightly together above her head, leaving his other hand free for exploration. "How do you know it wasn't for you that I rolled those dice?"

Franco propped himself up on his elbow, letting his gaze travel the length of her body, then following with the palm of his hand, caressing her up and down the length of her as far as his arm could reach until, in spite of herself, she began to relax under the tender administrations. "Perhaps it is you I wanted," he murmured, then leaned over and kissed her passionately, his tongue darting deeply into her mouth, gently demanding, until Jamie moaned with reawakened excitement. His grip on her wrists slowly loosened, cautiously, aware of one more legacy she had inherited from her sire—a volcanic and unpredictable temper. Though he was surprised to uncover it, he found it stimulating, a bit like daring to play games with a loaded pistol. Would she allow his advances, or was she only awaiting an opportunity to renew her attack? He didn't know and the insecurity of it added spice to the adventure. There was, indeed, more to Morgan's daughter than he had thought.

His lips explored the base of her throat, her ear, caressed her soft white shoulder. He reached down to lift the hem of her nightdress above her knees then slowly, teasing himself with the unveiling, pulling it higher and higher, to reveal the tantalizing bare flesh. When he reached her shoulders, he waited to see if Jamie would lift her arms to help him remove it. With only a moment's hesitation, Jamie cooperated, stretching her arms out while he removed the garment.

He twisted his body, then came down on top of her, urging her legs to part with his knee as he leaned his full weight on her, startling her with the abruptness of his action, but then he was again exploring the curves of her body with eager fingers and experienced hands, her moment of fright soothed by the gentleness of his touch. She could feel his hardness pressing against her through his trousers and her flesh prickled with anticipation mingled with uncertainty. They had not come close enough before for her to know if it might hurt or not. All she remembered was the tingling excitement he had stirred in her then and now had restimulated inside her. She found herself tensing, her muscles flinching warily.

118

"I promise you, I won't hurt you," he said softly, letting his lips linger against her throat.

Her eyes had closed and she opened them again as she felt him move away from her to undress. In a few minutes he was back, lying beside her, his lips nuzzling her ear deliciously. All of her anger had fled, spent in the fury she had unleashed on him. This is what she had come here to learn, and she would not deprive herself of it. Her feelings remained piqued over the wager, but she would wait and see what the morrow might bring. For now, she wanted this experience and gave herself over to it completely.

He smelled too strongly of rum, reminding her of all the times Morgan had hugged her fiercely until her ribs cracked, all because strong brew had fouled his senses, and she wondered what pain might be in store for her, but Franco found the lobe of her ear and delicately nibbled it. His warm breath sent a delicious shiver through her as gentle hands explored her, tracing the minute details of her with infinitely slow delight.

Jamie lay perfectly still, yet her muscles quivered beneath his massage. He tasted her skin with the tip of his tongue, drawing a damp trail downward to the hardened nipple he then sucked into his mouth. Jamie frowned in puzzlement.

"I don't understand," she said aloud.

"You don't understand what, darling?" he said, pausing.

"Why that feels so good. I wouldn't have thought it would."

Franco raised himself up to gaze at her. "It becomes much better than this," he replied. His hands caressed her stomach, her hip, her thigh, then reached between her legs. Jamie gasped, this time in pleasure, as he softly urged her legs to part for him. She hesitated only a moment, then complied.

"I won't hurt you. You have my promise," he whispered huskily before raising himself up to trail a path of caress-

119

ing kisses over her abdomen. He intended to take infinite pains with Jamie, reminding himself of her inexperience. She was exquisite in every detail, a beauty who would have few rivals to compare. She was also a paradox to him, still so young and yet so very much a woman. Her innocence charmed him, her womanhood inflamed him, and he felt at this moment that he could spend the rest of his life exploring her many facets.

He felt the rush of heat throbbing in his loins but held himself in check, bending over her, prolonging his own agony, knowing how much more enjoyable his pleasure would be when he had awakened it in her.

He kissed the soft black mound and Jamie sucked in her breath, arching her back in pleasure as he tasted her womanhood. He breathed in the musky scent of her, intoxicating himself with the fragrance until he could no longer deny himself reaching his goal.

This time she didn't feel the weight of him as he came down on top of her, aware of nothing but the fulfillment of the need he had stimulated inside her. Her senses reeled with passion as he urged her legs apart again and slowly entered her, taking infinite care not to startle or harm her. He pushed, and at first she felt pressure more than pain, overwhelmed by the hunger she was experiencing. "Easy, my love." He whispered gentling words to soothe her. He pushed again, driving deeper, and Jamie felt a fiery burst of pain that popped her eyes open as she gasped.

"That is all," his whisper promised. "It shall never hurt again."

He began to move inside her, slowly, and though she still felt a twinge of pain as her soft flesh was parted, she welcomed it, responded to it, beginning to meet his thrusts as he drove ever deeper and faster within her. Every nerve and muscle she possessed became taut as she reveled in the ecstasy he provided. Her nails racked his back unmindfully. She called out his name in a husky, breathless whisper. There was yet something more she needed and she didn't know what it was until she reached it, shuddering, her senses exploding into fragments as he drove deep, then released, fulfilling her completely.

After this wondrous torture, he relaxed on top of her and Jamie relished the sweat-dampened weight of him, content to hold him, lightly massaging the firm, hard muscles of his smooth back.

"Which is it?" she wanted to know a short while later as she lay beside him, her head nestled against his shoulder.

Franco was half asleep when her question brought him up out of his utter contentment. "Which is what, my love?" he asked, perplexed.

"You said before that you never meant for me to be part of the wager. Then later, you said you did."

Franco opened his eyes, knowing he was not going to be allowed to relish this moment and realizing he was treading on treacherous ground. Which answer, he wondered, did she want to hear? He might be damned in her eyes for either. "Both," he finally decided.

Jamie lifted her head from his chest to peer at him.

"I do believe we had no right to place you on the table as part of the wager," he explained. "That was wrong of us, and for my part in it, I humbly apologize, but, if you are wondering whether it induced me to play, it did indeed, for I could think of no grander prize than you, my sweet." He kissed her forehead, congratulating himself when he saw her pleased smile.

"Ye're probably lying, but I love you for saying it," she settled down again on his chest.

Franco thought of protesting but chose, rather, to let the topic drop. "Does Morgan know you're in here?" he asked when she seemed content, cuddled beside him.

"Aye, of course he knows."

"I can't believe he allowed you to come."

"You won the wager. What could he say?"

"Still, I would have expected something."

"He told me I didn't have to come. He said you'd never hold me to it. But I wanted to. I'm glad I did." She smiled, kissing the firm muscles of his chest with the light scattering of curling black hairs across it. "I'm glad you don't have a lot of hair on your chest like some men do," she commented, letting her fingers casually play in the sparse matting.

"Oh, really." He peered down at the top of her head. "And how many naked men's chests have you seen, my girl?"

"A few," she admitted, looking up at the pretended disapproval on his face. "I'm not blind, ye know. The sailors mostly work with their shirts off. I can't walk about with my eyes closed, can I?"

"Perhaps I'd better see that you start."

"You're not worried about the likes of them, are you?"

"I'm beginning to worry about the likes of *you*." He pulled her up until her face was even with his. "You're a hot-blooded wench, and now that I've awakened you to the pleasures to be found there, perhaps I should keep you under lock and key."

She smiled, thinking he was teasing, but he was staring into her eyes intently. Then he gripped her neck and kissed her passionately, his lips moving against hers, his tongue seeking out the secret mysteries of her mouth. Jamie molded herself against him, relishing the feel of his naked skin against hers. The hairs on his chest tickled her breasts erotically. It was true. Now that she did know the pleasure, she would never have enough of him.

His lips left her mouth, igniting blazing conflagrations as they trailed down over her throat. "I love you," she murmured as he pulled her closer yet. He stopped, his arms locked about her but unmoving.

"Jamie . . ." he said.

"I know," she burst in before he could go on. "I won't ask you to stay for my sake. I know you can't. Only let me tell you while you're here. I love you. You don't owe me anything because of it."

"Jamie, my sweet, wonderful girl, how can I ever bear to part with you?" He wrapped her in his warm embrace, making love to her again, slowly, deliciously, bringing her to even greater heights of wonder as he searched out new territories on her body and caressed them with his hands, his lips, tasting them with the tip of his tongue as though to commit them to memory. Jamie followed his example, exploring every part of his being, returning pleasure for pleasure, touching, tasting, filling her senses with the essence of him.

This time, as he had promised, there was only a small twinge of pain as he pressed into her and Jamie found herself soaring even higher, throbbing with excitement and satisfaction, answering his thrusts as her urgency overwhelmed her until, in a burst of explosive energy that joined them as one, they both came down again, untensing, relaxing, fulfilled and spent, falling asleep in each other's arms.

Chapter Six

As dawn rose, sweet and clear, Jamie burst into the wide, busy kitchen of Morgan's mansion, her sudden presence startling Mary Lambert as the girl entered with a broad, happy smile on her face.

"Mary, where are me . . . *my* mother's trunks?" Jamie asked, correcting herself in midsentence. The fact that Jamie had been trying to improve her language lately had not been missed by the housekeeper who had raised her since the day she was born, but the question surprised Mary, who turned abruptly around from the porridge she was stirring at the large cast iron stove. Her given name was Marie, but the pirates had always called her Mary. Marie Lambert had been Antoinette Duvalier's personal maid when the French noblewoman set sail for Martinique to meet her contracted fiancé. She had boarded the ship as a young woman of barely twenty, with high hopes of meeting a decent man in the New World, one who would marry her, provide for her, and give her several children to love.

When the French ship was taken, she was brought to Tortuga Bay along with Morgan's hostage. She had been raped by the pirates before the French ship they had raided had finished sinking into the deep and she had no idea which of them fathered the stillborn son she had borne nine months later.

Antoinette had given birth to Jamie only a few days later, and when the noblewoman refused to nurse the child, Mary had taken Jamie to her own full breast.

Mary had taken a different point of view than her mistress about her captivity, making the best of the situation in which she found herself. She had tried to instill the same kind of outlook in Jamie. "Circumstances always change, *ma petite*," she would tell her charge, "And usually for the better if you only let your mind change with them. Bitterness leaves naught but a sour taste in your mouth."

Robbed of the life she had hoped for, she had been far more cruelly abused than Antoinette, who had always been Morgan's possession alone. She was used by one pirate after another until her pregnant belly swelled sufficiently to cool their lusts. She had borne a child who hadn't lived. The birth had been difficult and no other babes had ever come. Yet out of it all, she had survived. She made a life for herself here. She had been given Jamie to nurse and to raise as her own. She had found Tully Seevers, who liked her fat and complained if she didn't fill his hands wherever he chanced to grab her. She had made herself learn to be happy with her niche.

While Morgan ruled the colony, Mary ruled the house he had built. She had brushed his feet off tabletops more times than she could count. She had heard about Morgan's dastardly wager with the hostage and was so infuriated, she almost charged up the back staircase to defend her girl from the blackhearted Spaniard, but Tully had held her back, convincing her it was too late now to change whatever had already happened.

Never before had Mary heard Jamie ask to see anything that had once belonged to her mother. As young as she had been when her mother died, Jamie had been fully aware of Antoinette's rejection. Perhaps in retaliation for that pain, Jamie seemed to have driven her mother's very existence out of her mind as if Antoinette had never lived. Until this moment, the housekeeper hadn't known Jamie recalled the trunk full of clothes that had rested at the foot of her mother's bed.

"I truly do not know what has become of your *maman*'s trunks," Mary answered her, moving aside to let one of the servants under her direction remove a kettle from the stovetop. The kitchen was bustling with early-morning routine, fetching water, stirring pots, and baking bread while soiled dishes, pots, and pans were being washed in a corner away from the pattern of heaviest traffic. "Perhaps they are in the attic. Shall I have Tully look for them?"

"No, I'll look." Jamie started toward the stairs that led to the attic.

"Are you well, *ma petite?*" Mary puzzled over Jamie's condition this morning. The girl seemed in high spirits, her step light and brisk as she moved across the kitchen.

"*Oui, très bien,*" Jamie pertly replied. Mary had considered it her duty to teach the girl French. The language was part of her heritage. After all, she was half Duvalier. Jamie, a bright young woman, soaked up her lessons like a thirsty sponge. She read and wrote in both English and French. Morgan had once found himself deeply disappointed to discover that the cartons and crates taken off a sinking ship were filled with nothing but books meant for some fine gentleman's library. Jamie asked for them and had read most of them. She understood a sea chart as well as Morgan himself and had learned navigation by pestering Morgan's pilots for the knowledge, plotting reliable courses herself since she was fourteen. Jamie spoke in the dialect of the sea only in an effort to be more like the pirates she sailed with and to avoid setting herself apart. The girl had loved the sea ever since she was old enough to ask Morgan to take her with him. It was by her own choice that she sailed with them.

"What of your breakfast, pet?"

"Oh, later, Mary, please," she complained as Mary set her hands on her ample hips, expecting the resistance.

"Cold porridge is fit for nothing but as plaster to seal the holes in the walls." Mary returned to the girl's petulant frown, not amused when Jamie mouthed the words back to her in her familiar speech. "You are not too big yet not to need your breakfast," she finished as Jamie grumblingly complied, shuffling to the table and plunking down into a chair before the place Mary had set for her. The housekeeper dished up a bowl of steaming porridge and placed it in front of her, then sat her bulk down in the closest chair.

"You truly are all right, my pet?" Mary gazed at her in concern but could see nothing in Jamie's countenance that would lead her to think she might be hiding her feelings.

"Why shouldn't I be?" Jamie smiled, realizing Mary referred to the wager and its aftermath.

Jamie had left Franco asleep, too excited to stay in bed any longer, fired with purpose to carry out a new plan she had formulated in the night. She understood why he could not stay in the Caribbean. He had a family, a place to return to. As she had promised him, she would never ask him to stay. But last night had given her hope that he would ask her to go with him and when he did she would gladly, joyfully, say aye.

"Don't I look all right to ye, Mary?"

"Oui, ma chère," Mary agreed. "You do. The Spaniard was not unkind to you then?"

"His name is Franco!" Jamie corrected abruptly, tired of people referring to her beloved as *The* Spaniard. He was the man she might very well wed soon. "May I go now?" she complained, having hardly touched the porridge.

"Oui, ma petite, you can go," Mary answered absently.

Jocko and Ned Shanks, having spent the night in their own rooms in Morgan's mansion, came into the kitchen, Chalks stretching his enormous frame and Shanks yawning loudly.

"Good morning, Jocko." Jamie let her high spirits spill over to encompass everyone. She hopped up onto the chair she had just vacated to bestow a kiss on the top of the shaved, bald head of the first mate, then jumped to the floor again. "Good morning, Neddy, me own best love," she teased, tugging Shank's beard and using the expression she had tortured him with ever since a brazen, golden-haired harlot met the *Lady Morgan* at dockside one day and called exactly those words out to him in front of the entire crew. Jamie had used it on him mercilessly ever since she had overheard the remark.

She had begun to scamper for the back stairs to the attic just as Morgan walked in, his face puffy and his eyes bleary from last night's drink. "Good morning, Papa." She dove into his arms for a moment, hugging him fiercely, forgiving him entirely in the aftermath of her happiness. She spun about to skip up the stairs to the upper story and out of sight.

"What the devil has gotten into her?" Morgan grumbled, still half asleep and foggy.

Mary glared at him. "Have your breakfast!" She slammed a plate of ham, eggs, and sliced bread on the table before him.

"Truly, Mary, how do I look?" Jamie surveyed her image in the mirror with a critical eye but one that did not possess a great deal of knowledge in the subject. She hadn't donned a dress since she was five and though she had seen other women wearing gowns, in truth, she had never paid attention to their fashions.

The gown Jamie had selected out of her mother's trunks was woefully out of date. Mary knew styles must have changed in the eighteen years she had been away from Paris, but she couldn't know and had no way of learning what fashion demanded now in women's apparel. Mary never left Tortuga, and Polly was the only one who visited between the buccaneer's island and Port Royale on a regular basis. Polly was flamboyant in her own selections, and thus was not a reliable model.

"Truly, *ma petite*, you look wonderful," Mary assured the girl. After breakfast was served to the household and the servants were set to their tasks, Mary had pulled her vast bulk up the back staircase to the attic to find Jamie, having located her mother's trunks, busily engaged in sorting through the contents. Jamie told her she wanted a dress, an exquisite dress, the very finest of those her mother had taken with her from France. Mary didn't need to question why, after a dozen years of refusal to wear anything but boys' clothing, her charge was now looking for a gown. Jamie was in love with the Spanish captive. Mary remembered her own first infatuation fondly, as well as the wild joys and intense heartbreak such a first love often brought with it. There was no other course available, as the buccaneers might put it, but to see it through all the gales of emotion and weather the storms as they came.

Jamie finally selected a light blue silk gown from the several that had rested in the trunk these past years. The contents of the chest had been Antoinette's trousseau and it was packed to overflowing with gowns, petticoats, muffs, and jewelry. The trunk was cedar-lined and, having lain in a cool, dry attic, the materials inside it were undamaged by either mildew or insect invasion. They took Jamie's choice downstairs, to Jamie's room, where Mary had the dress aired and brushed, then tried to fit it to Jamie's frame. The gown was woefully short and small, and the best of Mary's efforts could do little about the fact that there was not enough material to work with. Antoinette had been almost petite. Her daughter, though trim and slender, was taller as well as larger in the hips and bosom.

Mary repaired the bosom's scantness by tucking lace around the edges and let the skirt's hem out as far as it would go, but the gown still only reached to her ankles, leaving her slippered feet exposed.

Every day she was in port, Jamie bathed in the inland lagoons of the island and washed her hair with the soap mixture Mary scented with lemon oil. She had done both with extreme care before working her way into the still-tight-fitting garment.

"It hurts," Jamie complained about the stays Mary had fastened, trying to force the daughter into the slender waist of the mother's gown. She succeeded, but Jamie looked as if she was being strangled, her face red under the strain.

"Pain is the price a woman pays for beauty, *ma chère*," Mary assured her, smiling as she surveyed her handiwork while Jamie began to turn and pose before the mirror. Though the garment was inadequate, it did look lovely on her, the light blue color accentuating the depth of the lavender in her eyes. Polly had volunteered her efforts into the transformation by offering to fix Jamie's hair, fastening the raven tresses into an elegant, upswept style held in place with Jamie's mother's gold hair combs. Mary sorted through the jewelry box until she found a simple necklace of gold filigree with earbobs to match, fastening them on Jamie to complete the effect.

"You could be the belle of Paris," Polly assessed, gazing at Jamie's reflection when the makeover was complete. "I never saw a lady on Royale that could best you the way you look this minute. Myself included in that, by the way."

"That's sweet of you, Polly. Thank you." Jamie impulsively hugged the woman. "And you too, Mary," she turned to her foster mother to embrace her. Mary Lambert had tears in her eyes as Jamie backed away again to preen in front of her image, examining her reflection from every side, pleased with the effect. "Just wait until Franco

130

sees me. Will he like it, do you think?"

"He will, else he's blind!" Polly stated. "Ohh, and isn't he the handsome one, though. I wish I had seen him first."

Mary poked Polly's ribs with her elbow, reminding the woman that Jamie didn't need to feel she had to compete with a possible rival. Polly usually reserved her affection for Morgan alone, but when he was away she felt no compulsion to remain faithful, plying the trade she had engaged in since she was fifteen, usually for money, sometimes simply because she felt like bestowing her favors free of charge. She was an attractive woman of twenty-five, amply proportioned and seductive.

Mary's reprimand seemed needless as Jamie appeared to have missed Polly's remark entirely, swaying her skirts in front of the mirror, enjoying the effect of the shimmering silk.

"We had best go down, pet, as supper must be ready and the men will be waiting," Mary reminded her.

"You really are certain I look all right?" Concern crossed the girl's features once more.

"Indeed, pet, you do," Mary put her arm about Jamie's waist, turning her toward the doorway.

Jamie entered the dining hall, watching nervously as all eyes turned on her, including Morgan's, but, most of all, she saw Franco's gaze alight on her with surprise and admiration. She felt slightly embarrassed by so much attention being drawn to her, but she looked ravishing, she knew she did when she saw the approval in Franco's eyes. The primping, the fixing, even the pain of the corset was worth the discomfort to see such a look from him.

He abruptly stood up from the table and approached her, extending his arm for her to accept. "Miss Morgan," he said, smiling. "May I be the first to tell you how

131

ravishing you look tonight?"

"Thank you, kind sir," Jamie replied, carefully pronouncing her words and curtsying just as Mary had shown her. Franco led her to her place at the supper table, seating her between himself and Ned.

"Ye look grand tonight, Jamie," Ned murmured in open astonishment. Even Morgan was staring at her as if he had never seen her before.

Rory McGregor, who was acting as serving boy at the table, stood by the buffet board, chewing on his lower lip, smoldering with resentment and jealousy.

When supper was over, Franco escorted her out into the garden where the silver moon lit the pathway with soft light. Jamie breathed in the scent of fragrant blossoms. The evening breeze stirred the short curls at her neck and tickled deliciously. She felt wonderful, strolling arm in arm by Franco's side.

"Jamie, I wanted an opportunity to speak with you alone," Franco said, walking slowly, his hand over hers where it rested on his arm. "I have arranged passage to Royale with one of the ship's captains. He's leaving in the morning. From there, I can book passage home."

A quick "yes" was ready on her lips the very moment he asked her to go with him. She didn't care if he didn't marry her before they left. He would want to introduce her to his family first. That's the way such things were done. After all that had happened between them last night — and today, seeing the approval on his face when she appeared in the dining room — she couldn't imagine his wanting to leave without her. Hadn't he said as much when he murmured that he didn't know how he could ever part from her?

Franco stopped along the path and pulled her around to face him. He lightly touched her chin and she looked up at him. "You really do look stunningly beautiful tonight. You're always lovely to look at, but tonight you're exceptional."

Jamie smiled, hoping she appeared coy enough to encourage him to speak the words she so desperately wanted to hear.

"I'll never forget how you look at this moment with the moonlight on your hair. I feel that we have become fast friends over the last few weeks and I hope that never changes . . ."

Changes, Jamie's attention caught on the word. Why should things change between them? They were much more than friends now.

"You are a wonderful girl and I know, someday, you'll find great happiness . . ."

What was he saying? Jamie felt a lump straining in her throat, hurting, aching there like something that couldn't be swallowed.

"You do mean a great deal to me," Franco continued, holding both her hands in his. "I can never tell you how much . . ."

"You're not taking me, are you?" Jamie wanted to hear it all said clearly, straight out and not hidden beneath the gentle gibberish that she realized was only being uttered to lighten the blow. "You're leaving and you don't want to take me with you."

"It isn't that I don't want to, sweetheart . . ."

"No!" Jamie jerked free of his hold. "Tell me the truth! You don't want me anymore, do you?"

"Jamie . . ."

"Don't tell lies to me! It's true!" she threw out at him, crushed and straining to keep her voice under control. "I'm not good enough for the likes of you! I'm not smart and grand, like the ladies you're used to. Just as Papa said, Jamie's fine to bed when there's nothing better, but she's not good enough to take home!" Tears started to roll

133

down her cheeks but she wouldn't let him touch her. "No, leave me be!" she cried out as he tried to soothe her. "Just go then! Go home to your fine family and your fancy, proper ladies! I wouldn't have gone with you anyway! I wouldn't want to go! Go on! Go! I hope your damn ship sinks with you on it!"

She spun about on her heel and ran, blazing her own path through the foliage blindly. Tears misted her sight so that she couldn't see where she was going. She ran wildly, letting the hem of her gown catch on thorns and ripping it free to plunge recklessly on into the brush. She heard him running behind her, then his steps fell off as he lost her in the darkness.

Jamie ran until she could run no farther, finally dropping heavily onto a soft carpet of grass, her chest heaving from her exertions. She had no idea how long she lay sobbing on the ground, pouring out all the hurt and frustration into the soft earth with her fountain of salty tears. After a while, she cried herself out from sheer exhaustion. When she at last sat up again, her gown was damp with the night moisture. Torn and shredded, smudged with grass stains, the dress was ruined, but she didn't care. She would never wear a dress again as long as she lived, she promised herself. She'd done nothing but make a fool of herself, an utter, complete ninny in Franco's estimation, just as Morgan had warned her she would.

Jamie pulled herself up, her tired muscles aching. Sniffling, she wiped her nose with a torn piece of the sleeve, then dabbed at her wet eyes with another edge of the remnant. Donning a dress had not made a lady out of her. She was not a boy and she was no longer a girl. Jamie didn't know what she was anymore.

Chapter Seven

If there was one trait Franco possessed that ran as deeply as his arrogance, it was his conscience. He continued to see Jamie's huge eyes brimming with tears long after he lost sight of her in the darkness. He had known he would hurt her with what he said, but he had bungled the matter of saying it kindly and made a mess of things. He had wanted to explain how deeply he cared for her—yes, damn it, his fists clenched. He loved her. This rough-edged girl had won his heart. But, for her sake, he couldn't take her with him.

If he remained here on Tortuga and became the pirate Morgan wanted him to be, he would never see his family again. His father's heart would be broken. And if he took Jamie with him? Perhaps he could tolerate the abuse, the ostracism and humiliation that would be heaped upon her by the Spanish court, but how could she?

What to do? Where to go where the two of them could live in peace? He had no answers. He couldn't stay. She couldn't come with him. The Colonies? Where? He would be as unwelcome in British colonies as she would be in Spanish settlements, especially if it were ever learned that her father was Henry Morgan, the scourge of the Caribbean, the same wily Morgan who sank their ships and raided their less adequately defended towns.

Franco had not wanted to marry just yet, having always felt that the proper woman would present herself when the time came. He knew Jamie would not ask for marriage if he never offered it, yet what else was he to do with the girl if they were to remain together?

Conflicting thoughts swirled around in his head, making his temples throb. He wanted Jamie with him, yet a small part of himself actually shrank from the image of presenting her to his family as his wife and he despised that nagging voice inside him that asked, Can you take her home with you and let society be damned? Can you? Are you brave enough to take her to a place where the two of you would be unknown? Can you make your fortune on your own merit? Can you support her, take care of her, without your family's fortune?

All his life, Franco had had whatever he wanted the moment he desired it. With the exception of his temper, which had always been difficult to control, he had considered himself to be a good son, a dutiful son, one who loved and respected his parents. What would it do to them if he threw everything away for the sake of this slip of a girl he had unexpectedly found here on this foul island?

Yet the picture of Jamie, the lad, shyly but courageously tending him refused to leave his memory. Jamie on the beach, revealed as a woman. Jamie in his bed last night, warm and loving, as eager and tender a lover as he'd ever known. Even Jamie tonight, wearing the first gown she had quite likely ever worn in her life, donned for his sake, filled him with an overpowering urge to spirit her away from here, away from this island and the influence of the pirates. How could he, he asked himself, desert her here either?

He couldn't, he decided with the very next thought that entered. Leave her with Morgan and the other pirates? Jamie had thus far developed, not with their help, but in spite of it. She was beautiful and sweet, with an unaffected charm that, he knew, would soon enough win over both his parents. Her rough speech, her manners, and the lack of proper apparel, would be easy enough to overcome with the proper tutors and dressmakers. Marriage was not what he had sought for himself yet, but what difference would it make if it was now or several years from now if he had found the woman he wanted? If society damned them for it, then he would have to find enough strength inside himself to carry both of them.

While he was lost in his troubled thoughts, a short, muffled scream suddenly intruded, bringing his senses around to the present moment. He listened, his ears tuned to the sounds of the jungle beyond the veranda where he was waiting for Jamie to run herself out and come back to him so he could tell her of his decision. Even the busy insects had been hushed, so the scream couldn't have been his imagination. Had Jamie fallen and hurt herself? Was she in trouble? He started toward the steps that led down to the path they had walked on just a half hour before. The trail, he knew, led toward the lagoon where he frequently swam. As his foot touched the dirt path, he heard voices, subdued but arguing. He couldn't make out the words but one voice sounded like Jamie's, angry yet with an odd tone of fear in it that he had never heard before. Then the words clearly reached him. "Stop it this instant! Let me go!"

Franco's momentary image of Morgan having cornered her changed to a picture of her battling an unknown assailant. He walked faster, trying to locate the place where the voices came from.

"Jamie?" he called out, hearing a tremor in his own voice that feared for her safety. "Jamie, answer me! Where are you?"

He heard a shout cut short, as if a hard hand had

smothered it. He began to run, plunging off the path and into the thicket, pushing his way through tangled vines and overgrowth, past broad-leafed plants and thorny spines that pulled at his clothing. As he came closer, he could make out the noise of a struggle taking place, but the direction was difficult to discover.

"Let me go!" he heard her demand, obviously wrestling for her freedom. "Don't! You're hurting me!"

Franco broke into a faster pace, annoyed by the tangled jungle growth that slowed his progress. He was near enough now to hear her assailant. "Ye give it to him. Ye kin give it to me now!" a man said to her, a voice he thought he might recognize if the tone wasn't so slurred and ugly.

"Jamie, where are you?" he called, hearing a crashing through the brush near him. It was Ned Shanks who burst out into the path Franco was blazing through the verdant forest. "It ain't you?" Shanks muttered quickly. "Then where is she?" Shanks held a machete in his hand that Franco belatedly realized would have been used on him if he was the one causing Jamie's distress.

"This way." Franco led the plunge into the thicket toward the place he last heard her call from. The sounds of the struggle continued, giving them a beacon to head for, but Jamie's attempts at calling out to him were being smothered by a hand or a gag that prevented her from answering him. Rushing forward, Franco finally broke into the meadow just in time to see Morgan, Chalks, and two other men emerge into the clearing from the other side. Jamie was being held on her back on the ground, struggling fiercely against her assailant's attempts to hold her immobile. Franco had almost reached her before he recognized Rory. The boy heard him, sensed his presence, and abruptly pulled away, his face suddenly filling with terror at being discovered. While Franco was still reaching out to grab the offender by his collar, a

138

pistol shot rang out, the rapport echoing off the trees. Rory grasped for his chest, then dropped like a stone, face-first, across Jamie's legs.

Franco turned around, appalled, staring at Morgan who still had the smoking pistol in his hand when suddenly Jamie began to scream hysterically, over and over again in an endless stream. She was sitting up, staring at Rory's corpse, the skirt of her gown spattered with the boy's blood. Her hands raised to her cheeks as she continued to scream mindlessly.

Franco immediately knelt by her side, grabbing her in his arms, pulling her out from under the boy's body and she fell silent. "There was no need for that, Morgan." Franco glared at him as he held Jamie tightly against him. "You didn't have to kill him." Though Franco had intended to give the boy a thrashing he would not soon forget, the deed hadn't yet warranted a death penalty, though it could have come to that had McGregor succeeded at his goal.

Morgan stalked toward them, his gaze leveled narrowly at Franco. "This is yer fault, Spaniard," the pirate threw at him. "Ye had to have her and now look what we're left with. She never wore a dress before and McGregor knew he'd have me to deal with until he believed it wouldn't matter. I knowed it since ye come. I should have thrown ye to the fishes. Ye've caused her nothing but trouble from here on."

"Then there will be no more, Morgan. When I leave tomorrow, I'm taking Jamie with me."

"No, I don't think ye will." Morgan drew a crumpled piece of paper out of his surcoat pocket and threw it on the ground beside Franco. "This come just after supper. Read it when ye find the time for it," he said harshly. "Ye're not the match for me Jamie now. Yer father is dead!" he threw out at him cruelly. "Yer lovin' brother holds the family fortune now and it seems yer precious

139

life ain't worth a farthin' to him. We can dispose of ye however we like as far as he's concerned. He'll pay not a penny of yer ransom. 'Tis too bad ye won yer freedom else I'd be laying ye out beside him."

After the others had walked away, Franco picked up the letter like a man in a daze and tucked it inside his pocket. He didn't have time to think of what the letter said, his own troubles pushed into the background in his immediate concern for Jamie. She had sunk into a fearfully lifeless shock, her eyes open but unseeing, her breathing regular but shallow. Her skin was deathly pale in the moonlight and felt cold to his touch. Morgan hadn't noticed her state while Franco held her in his arms, but she appeared almost catatonic, not responding when he called her name. Lifting her to her feet, he found he would have to carry her as her legs refused to support her. He picked her up, cradling her in his arms as he walked into the house. Her head fell against his shoulder, her arms hanging limply at her sides.

Morgan met him at the bottom of the stairs, too intent on Franco to notice his daughter's condition. "Ye're not taking her anywheres tomorrow," he warned. "I won't have her a penniless begger."

"Get out of my way," Franco ordered, moving past the pirate to carry Jamie up the stairs. He put her down on the bed and loosened her bodice, releasing the stays until she could breathe freely, then he poured a small amount of brandy into a goblet and, holding it to her lips, he forced some of it down her throat. The fiery liquid seemed to restore some life to her as she backed away from the cup, coughing and resisting any more of it. Sensing a male presence near her, she began to fight, flailing as if he was Rory. Franco put the cup down and gently stopped her aggressions. "You're safe now, sweetheart. It's only me," he murmured.

Her eyes focused as she looked at him, then the memory rushed back and her face crumpled into a mask of grief. "Why did Papa kill him?" she asked in a small, tight voice filled with pain, beginning to cry. "He didn't have to kill him. Rory was always my friend. I don't understand."

"Morgan thought he was protecting you, sweetheart."

"But Rory was my friend. He was always my friend before . . ."

"I know, darling," he soothed her, stroking her lightly.

"He didn't mean to hurt me. I know he didn't. Papa didn't have to kill him." She started to weep and Franco held her, stroking her, petting her softly until she fell asleep. Only then did he have the opportunity to ponder what Morgan had told him, relaying the news like a slap in the face. Carlos DeCortega was dead. During the many months Franco had been away, his father had died. He had loved Carlos. He would sorely miss him.

He tucked Jamie under the covers of his bed, then lit a lamp to read the letter. Lorenzo had not even bothered to pen the missive himself. It wasn't his brother's handwriting. The message said only that Conde Lorenzo De-Cortega felt it would be foolish to give in to the demands for a ransom, as such an effort would only succeed in encouraging kidnapping on the high seas. To his mind, Francisco was already dead, since he knew that giving in to the demand of the pirates would not result in his brother being returned alive.

Franco read it through twice, then crumpled the paper with a clenching fist. He knew Lorenzo resented the fact that the younger son had been included in the will and had been their father's favorite. Never, though, would he have believed Lorenzo would go as far as this. Franco made up his mind firmly now that he wouldn't desert Jamie. Morgan wouldn't allow her to leave with him and he didn't know what he might be facing when he reached home, so he couldn't take her with him yet, but he would come back for her—that he vowed to himself as he would swear to her tomorrow. He didn't know how long it might take him, or what circumstances the future might hold, but he would return for her someday. Only first, he had a deep score to settle with Lorenzo.

Jamie awoke to a feeling of utter despondency, unable to discover its cause in the first few moments of gathering awareness until the events of last night bore into her mind in a maelstrom of sudden memory. Rory was dead and Franco was leaving. She sat up abruptly, with a convulsive sob, tears springing to her eyes as she recalled her childhood friend lying dead across her legs, his life's blood seeping into the material of her garment. As another sob escaped, Franco's arms came around her, pulling her close to him in the bed, whispering soothing words in her ear as he urged her to lie down again and let her weep while he stroked her with a comforting hand.

"Rory . . . Rory," she mourned for the boy who had once been her closest companion.

"I know, darling," Franco murmured. He let her cry, knowing she needed to release her grief. Only tears could wash away the pain of all she had been through. For himself, he was holding his emotions locked away, accepting his father's death stoically, since tears, in his case, would avail him nothing. They couldn't bring Carlos De-Cortega back, nor could they lighten the burden in his heart. All he could do now was vow to himself that he would see his father's last wishes carried out, as he had left them in his will. Lorenzo would not get away with this. Franco would not be so easily dismissed, pushed aside and forgotten. Obviously, his brother had hoped he would be killed by the pirates and thus believed he could do as he pleased. Franco would prove otherwise to him. When he returned to Spain, Lorenzo would have no choice but to honor the contents of the will. Then, when he had reclaimed his rightful place, he would send for Jamie. Regarding that question at least, his mind was settled. He would not leave her in the hands of that vile scoundrel Morgan any longer than he had to.

When she had cried herself to sleep again, Franco continued to hold her wrapped snugly against his warmth. She had slept soundly through the night, at times so deeply that he had to sit up in bed and watch the rise and fall of her chest to assure himself she still breathed. Exhaustion from the emotional turmoil had taken its toll, sapping her strength completely, and she needed this rest. For him, sleep had been an elusive shadow and he had remained awake, silent and unmoving for fear of disturbing her slumber but his mind active, recalling every word of his brother's answer to the pirates, imagining the great glee with which Lorenzo was undoubtedly planning his future as sole inheritor of the family's wealth and position. At least he hoped Maria and Theresa, his sisters, would be safe until he could return to look after their interests. And what of their mother? he wondered. How was she feeling, believing she had lost her husband and her son? Was she aware of Lorenzo's treachery? Or, more likely, had Lorenzo lied to her, told her Franco had been killed or lost at sea? Isabella was a strong, forceful woman. She would never have allowed Lorenzo to pen such a message, would have taken her case to any authority at her disposal to have the ransom for her missing son paid—had she been given the truth of Franco's circumstances. For that matter, Franco had to wonder if his father had been lied to. The note gave no details of when Carlos had died. Was he deceased long before the ransom letter's arrival? Or was he cruelly informed of his son's peril, hoping the shock might stun and overburden an already weak heart, since Carlos had not been in good health when Franco bid him farewell before this fateful journey? Perhaps his father too had been offered a lie, since Lorenzo opened the daily mail and tended to much of the ordinary business. A simple task, then, to tell him that Franco's ship was sunk with all hands and passengers lost. Perhaps these were only wild imaginings on his part regarding Lorenzo playing a role in their father's death, but if he learned there was any truth in it, Lorenzo would pay heavily for the sin of patricide if he had that to add to those already lying on his remorseless conscience.

Anxious to be on his way home again, Franco had still let the first ship he arranged passage on depart without him. He couldn't let Jamie awaken to find him gone. In a few days, when she had regained her strength, he would explain to her why he had to leave and could not take her with him and he would give her his solemn vow to return for her as well as extract from her a promise that she would wait for him.

"I understand," Jamie said sorrowfully. "You needn't explain to me. And I'm very sorry about your papa." Everything in Jamie's being cried out to beg him to stay, or to take her with him, but she had given her promise that she wouldn't do either and she was determined to keep that vow. They stood on the deck of the *Lady Morgan*, watching Port Royale grow bigger over the ship's bow. Soon they would be docking and Franco would be gone. Terrified that she would never see him again, still she would not let his last sight of her be that of a tear-streaked face. There would be time for crying after he left.

"You don't believe me," Franco stated, gazing down at

her dry-eyed but sad face, holding both her hands between his own. At his urging, and to please him, Jamie had chosen another of her mother's dresses from the chest and wore it for him. It was a coffee-brown brocade and felt heavy on a form that was used to light cabin boy's clothing, yet she bore the weight of it and the discomfort of the corset and underthings for his sake, without complaint.

Her hair was unbound, held back by her mother's gold haircombs, but descending in a black wave down to the small of her back. Franco had said, in spite of fashion, he liked it best in this style. There was no fear of any pirate getting ideas into his head after what had happened to Rory. She had even managed, in some measure, to forgive her father for her friend's murder, realizing it was Morgan's way of protecting her. She had bruises on her wrists and on her ribs and thighs from her battle that night, and on her cheeks from where he had smothered her cries with his hand. She realized now that he might have turned to even more forceful measures had help not come to her rescue. Everything in her life seemed to be turning around too quickly for her to keep pace with. She couldn't pretend to be happy, or offer the barest ghost of a smile as their moment of separation became ever more imminent with each mile the ship sailed over.

"I do believe you mean what you say," Jamie answered him, knowing she did believe he meant what he was saying, but such a long journey lay ahead of him and when he was back among his own . . .

"You do believe me, but you think I am fooling myself, is that it?" he finished her thought for her. He took a step closer and brushed his lips across the tip of her brow. "I promise you, you're wrong. I will come back for you or I will send for you when this matter is settled with my brother. I'd take you with me this very moment if my father still lived and this situation did not exist, but I can't jeopardize your well-being by letting you risk your safety with me. Jocko says he thinks my brother, having gone as far as this, will have no choice but to engage in further infamy against me if only to protect his interests. He may be right, though I doubt Lorenzo has the courage to try such tricks in my presence. In any case, we shall see, but I can't let him learn of you. He could try to use you as a weapon against me. You do understand that, don't you?"

"I do," Jamie said, lowering her head to fight the tears that stubbornly tried to well in her eyes in spite of her efforts to hold them back. "I understand, and I'll wait for you forever. You know that. I love you with all my heart, Franco, and I always will."

"My sweet girl," he murmured, drawing her into his embrace. "You will remember your promise to wait for me here on Royale, or back at your home on Tortuga, won't you? You will keep your promise not to sail with Morgan on any more ventures? You've sworn it to me, and remember, you belong to me now." He backed up enough to let her see his smile, lifting her head to make her look at him, moved by the moisture in her eyes. "Please don't weep, my love. Not even when I am gone from you, for I won't have tears marring your beauty even when I am not here to revel in it. You must think, instead, that it will not be so very long before I come back for you and we'll never be parted again. I do wish my father could have come to know you. Your beauty and your sweet disposition would have quickly won his heart, just as you've won mine. But you will see, my mother and my sisters will love you. When we are at last reunited, my darling girl, I'll give you so many children you won't have time to regret the decision you made to be with me."

"I could never regret it," Jamie stated, laying her head

against his chest, wanting to believe in this dream and make it her own. There were so many months ahead of them, and the lovely, charming ladies of the Spanish court would be there to tempt him into forgetting her. And the problem of his nationality, and hers, still stood between them. Logic might yet prevail to convince him that love between them was impossible without one or the other giving up all ties to the land of their birth. She was still English and he remained Spanish, and the peace between those countries was always uneasy. At present, King William was waiting to see who the old and ailing but childless King Carlos would leave his country to. He had even made peace with Louis of France, his archenemy, while the question was unresolved. But if Spain was bequeathed to a son of France, William would certainly take up arms against both Spain and France. All that could happen while Franco was away and then what would happen to their love, separated by years of war?

While she could yet savor the feel of his strong arms around her, Jamie nestled against him, her heart palpitating with the fear that, once he was gone, she might never see him again.

"Jamie, come in here and sit down," Morgan told her. McGee, cuddled in her arms as she walked into her father's cabin, hissed at Morgan so Jamie put the cat down on the floor. Tied at dockside at Port Royale, the ship was rocked slowly from side to side by the gentle waves lapping against the hull. "Ye ain't going to wear that frown for the rest of yer life, are ye?" Morgan questioned as she complied with his wishes and sat down at the table across from him. "Ain't it time ye come to yerself again?"

Jamie shrugged morosely. Morgan seemed intent on conversation, something he did now and again when the mood struck him. Most of their talks in the past had consisted of his wanting to know what she thought about various schemes he had in the making. As long as she agreed with him, the discussions proceeded without difficulty.

"Ye didn't make yerself believe all that fine talk he spouted afore he left, did ye? That he'd come back for ye and spirit ye away from yer papa?" Her father mocked Franco's promise with the tone of his voice.

Jamie said nothing. Not for anything would she give him the opportunity to heap more scorn on the dream she convinced herself to carry until only time itself proved it false.

"Aye, I hope not, but I'm a'feared ye do. Then I think ye must know too . . . No, I think ye need to be made to know that it ain't no fault of yers things worked out as they done."

"Aye," she mumbled, annoyed, wishing he might find another topic. Franco had left two weeks ago, setting out from Port Royale aboard a ship bound for Spain. She had managed to wave farewell with her eyes dry as the ship set sail. She had been too crushed by utter despair in those final moments of parting for tears to avail her any relief. She stood, pale and sick, forcing her hand into the air to answer his good-bye wave, making herself smile only so that he could carry it back to his homeland as his last memory of her.

Every night before he left she had spent with him in his cabin—the same one that had been hers and would be again now that he was gone. They had made love each night and she had those memories to sustain her through the long, lonely nights ahead. But when he was gone, she had taken off her dresses and the trappings of femininity, donning her old clothes and her old way of life. She would refrain from joining in any ventures with the pirates if only because she had sworn to him she would, but not until he came back was there any reason to dress as a woman again.

Whether they stayed on in Jamaica or returned to the pirate base made little difference to Jamie, but Polly had come with them and she wanted to remain in the bustling port for a while, so Morgan was staying with her.

On Royale, no one looked at the color of a flag a ship was waving—only the glitter of their gold and silver caught the eye. The Jamaican port was an English colony but had never had a governor, or law and order imposed by the Crown. The town contained a jail and a gallows and both were used infrequently for the few punishments ordained by a council of pirate captains. Taverns and whorehouses abounded near the docks and trade in stolen wares was brisk and profitable to both parties in the transaction. The port, where any pleasure or vice was catered to for the right price, had often been referred to as Henry Morgan's City of Sin, a modern-day Sodom and Gomorrah. Good Christians living near the Caribbean port were convinced that a day would come when an avenging God would strike the evil city asunder. Royale had been rocked by several earthquakes over the years and each one renewed belief that the Lord was watching, briefly doubling attendance in the city's churches for the weeks following each minor disaster.

To Jamie, Royale was home as much as Tortuga Bay was. There was very little she hadn't seen or heard about, though her education in such matters had come mainly from witnessing and overhearing most of the rougher facts of life.

"Girl, I expect ye don't quite grasp what it is I'm trying to say to ye," Morgan stated. He sat at the table with his forearms resting on the rough surface, his fingers, for once, interlocked instead of busily engaged in fidgeting with something. Her father was a man who rarely stayed still, impelled by nervous energy that kept

149

him constantly in some form of motion and made him twitch with nervous spasms if he couldn't disburse his movements elsewhere. Jamie stared at him, wondering what he was trying to explain to her.

"I'm trying to tell ye that it ain't no fault of yers that I raised ye like I done." Morgan's bushy brows creased. "The fault is mine and I take full responsibility for it."

"What are you talking about, Papa?"

Morgan leaned back in the chair, his hands digging into the deep pockets of his brown velvet frockcoat. "I made a mistake raising ye as I done. Look at ye! I raised ye to be a son and ye ain't that! Ye're a girl. No, ye're a woman growed now, I reckon, or near so. Ye should be looking like a woman, dressing like one and acting like one. Ye could have been as fine a lady as any what the Spaniard has ever met at home."

Jamie sighed, wishing he would drop the subject. She didn't need to be reminded of her shortcomings. If he was trying to lift her solemn mood, this was not the way to accomplish it. She had never heard Morgan talk this way. He had always seemed satisfied with her the way she was. And never before had she known him to admit his guilt over anything.

" 'Tis the real reason he found ye lacking, pet." Morgan only called her that when he was in his jolliest moods, or at a certain point of being in his cups, yet at the moment he seemed cold stone sober. "It weren't that ye done something wrong. It's that I let ye grow up not knowing anything a woman needs to know to catch a man's fancy. I didn't mean to do it to ye, pet. I just forgot, is all." He shrugged his massive shoulders. "And now I find ye're grown and I done nothing to see to yer future."

"My future's here, Papa. With you." Until Franco returns, she added silently.

"No, it ain't," Morgan barked crisply. "Ye're a female,

curse it all! And it's high time ye learned how to be one!"

"I'll learn when I'm ready," Jamie promptly replied.

"No, ye won't. Ye'll learn it now." Morgan's gaze narrowed, a portent that he meant what he said. "I made up my mind to it! I booked passage with Captain Bonner, who is setting sail come dawn and ye're going with him!"

"Where?"

"To England, of course! London! Ye're going to a fine girl's school he knows about. They take young women from most any walk of life providing they can pay for it. I'm buying ye two years there up in advance, on condition they keep ye and try their damndest to make a lady of ye!"

"I'm not going anywhere, especially not to a 'girl's' school." Her lips curled unpleasantly over the word. "I'm too old for that. What's more, who would take me?"

"Ye damn well will go like I tell ye!" Morgan emphasized his statement with a heavy, calloused palm striking the tabletop, rattling the contents. "I took care of all that."

"My home is here and I'm not leaving!" Jamie defied him hotly, the same temper that matched her sire's and had earned her slaps in the past. "You may think me foolish all you like, but I promised Franco I'd wait for him here."

"Aha! So ye do carry silly notions about in yer head. I thought so. Still, ye're my daughter and ye're going to do as I tell ye to do," Morgan retorted. "And I ain't going to hear no more sass from ye! Ain't no man going to find ye lacking the graces of being a fine lady! Ye'll go and ye'll learn, and ye'll do as they tell ye to do, or ye'll answer to me for it!"

There was little point in trying to argue with Morgan when he was like this, but Jamie had her own deeply ingrained stubborn streak.

"Franco doesn't care about that," she stated. "He loves me as I am."

Morgan leaned toward her with a smile he usually reserved for dangerous occasions. "Then why ain't he here? Or why ain't ye with him?" he goaded.

"You know why!" Jamie shouted.

"Aye, I know what he told ye but, if it 'twas me, I'd not let a woman I wanted for my own out of my sight, let alone leave her far away from me for damn near a year if it takes so long. Well, maybe yer Spaniard has a different way of thinking and I can't fault him for it if it's yer welfare he's concerned about. But, if he does come sailing back for ye after all, just what is it he's to find?" he goaded. "A girl still wearing boy's clothes, her manners no better than the lowest sailor's, or a fine lady he can be proud to call his own?"

Jamie stared at her father, left speechless by his comment. Of course he was right. She could be using this time to better herself, to make Franco proud of her, but that the idea had come from Morgan surprised her. McGee further startled her by jumping into her lap. "Who will take care of McGee if I go? He only knows how to live on the *Lady Morgan*."

"Shanks will take care of him. Ye know he's right fond of that feline."

Jamie began to struggle with her feeling. She had never thought of leaving home before unless it was to be at Franco's side, and before she had met him, it had never entered her mind. "I don't want to leave you, Papa." She had never been away before, had accompanied Morgan everywhere for as long as she could remember. In the past, her common sense had talked him out of a good many of his more foolhardy ventures. Who would look after Papa if she went away? Life with Papa was a bit like living under the shadow of an active volcano, but, in spite of his many and varied faults, his was the only parental affection she had ever known. "I'd miss you," she admitted.

"I'll be missing ye too, pet," Morgan said gently, then drew her, cat and all, onto his lap. "But ye'll see it's for the best. Ye'll come back a grand lady any man will be proud of. Think of how yer Spaniard will look upon that. Ye have it in ye, I know. And if yer Franco don't come back for ye, then some other man will come along for ye, and ye'll make him right proud to have ye."

Jamie wanted no one but Franco, certain her feelings could never change. "When he comes," she scratched McGee's ears. "*If* he comes, you'll tell him where I've gone?"

"I'll tell him, pet, I promise ye. But don't ye count on it overmuch. Young men say things they don't always mean. I did when I was younger. Don't hold it against him if he don't keep his word. Nor against yerself either. 'Tis my fault ye come up as ye've done and I mean to set it right."

"I love you, Papa," Jamie admitted, one of the few times, perhaps the very first time she had ever said those words to him, but she was thinking that two years was such a long time and she might never see him again. His cruelties and abuses aside, intentional or otherwise, unlike Antoinette, he had loved her in his own tumultuous fashion and had given her his own brand of affection and security.

Morgan pulled her head down onto his broad shoulder. "I love ye too, pet," he murmured, patting her shoulder. "Ye've had a damned poor example of fatherhood to guide ye, but ye'll come out of it right enough."

Chapter Eight

As they stood in the entry, dressed in their finest for the afternoon's planned outing, Lady Edwina Westcott surveyed the lineup of prettily dressed and dainty young women with a critical eye open for any defects of dress or deportment. Of the twenty girls between fifteen and twenty, all were in their first blush of young womanhood, spirited, inquisitive, and bright. Though all ranged from moderately attractive to extremely so, Jamie Morgan managed to stand apart from the rest of them as a red rose in a bouquet of daisies. In the mere two years of her attendance here at Lady Westcott's School for Young Women in London, Mistress Morgan had had the longest route to travel and had succeeded in going the farthest. For that accomplishment, Edwina felt herself to be in no small way responsible.

Edwina Westcott had been born into the aristocracy. She had grown up amid all the benefits her class had to offer, but when, ten years ago, her brother had squandered her inheritance along with his own at the gaming tables of London, Edwina found herself noble still of birth, owner of the title "Lady" Edwina, but penniless just the same. Without a proper dowry as befitted her station and without land or property to support herself on revenues, she quickly decided to take her bleak future

154

into her own hands. She offered a business pact to the man who had won their three-story London townhouse in a game of cards and offered to share the profits with him if he would allow her to open a finishing school for the growing number of daughters belonging to the new and increasingly wealthier middle class.

Lady Westcott knew the refinements. These girls needed to learn them to attract husbands worthy of their new stations in life. Coming from diverse backgrounds from all over England and the Colonies, the young women who attended the Westcott School were instructed in manners, proper speech, the arts, and academics considered appropriate for females. They were taught house-managing skills, from keeping a small household with the aid of only a few helpers to the supervising of the large staffs required to run an estate or even a palace. While a few of her students came from the lower echelons of the nobility, most were the offspring of the nouveau riche, with fathers who had made fortunes that bought their way into the upper classes. All the girls, and the parents who had sent them here, expected the young women to marry well, into wealth, or a title, or both. Edwina enjoyed watching, and feeling a part of, turning girls from such humble, neglected, or deprived backgrounds into ladies of worth that any gentleman, even a lord, would be proud to wed. Perhaps her reason for singling Jamie Morgan out as a favorite was because the young woman had presented Edwina with her greatest challenge as well as her most prideful accomplishment.

Edwina remembered staring in dismay at the waif Captain Bonner presented in her parlor that gay spring morning in 1694. A formidable figure in a loose white blouse and sagging blue britches had glared out at the headmistress from beneath an oversize black tri-corner hat with a ridiculous bottle-green feather sticking up out of the hatband.

"This is a *girl's* school!" Lady Edwina had immediately protested. "We can't accept boys!"

"She be a girl." The captain took the girl's hat off, thrusting it into the lap of the slouching creature sitting on Edwina's parlor sofa. A cascade of soft black curls fell down over the young woman's face and the girl shoved the ebony mass back behind her ears with an angry glare that encompassed them both.

"All our young women have already had a basic education," Edwina presented as her next argument.

"She's had that," the captain responded. "She can cipher, and read and write and the like. And she can speak a mite of French too, I reckon."

"Parlez-vous français?" Lady Edwina addressed her dubiously. The girl's answer was a hate-filled stare.

"Do you know you look like a court jester with that smudge of soot on your nose?" Edwina asked the girl in French. After a moment's pause in which the girl seemed to ponder if a trick might be involved, her hand shot up to rub the tip of her nose, hard, just in case.

"Ah, but she's too old," Lady Edwina sighed. Most of their girls graduated at seventeen.

"She's eighteen and that's a fact, but if you don't take her, I reckon I don't know nobody what will."

Edwina took another look at her, at the exceptionally pretty face beneath the wild curls of ebony hair, the boy's garments, the rebellious stance of the creature who might have good possibilities if her assets could be made to outweigh her flaws, and decided to accept the task.

Even under the boy's clothing, Edwina had recognized that the girl was pretty, but when the boy's garments were exchanged for raiment more becoming to her sex, the headmistress was pleasantly surprised by the transformation. She was exceptionally lovely, a fact not missed by

156

the other beauties in Lady Edwina's school, and one that was held against her to one degree or another by her fellow students. Jamie admittedly had never had much experience with other women, especially with those of her own age group, and refused to join in many of the gossip and giggling sessions so often engaged in by women her age. Adding resentment over her beauty to her aloofness did not help her cause with her peers and many months had passed in social solitude before she made any friends among her schoolmates.

Over the next few weeks, Edwina discovered her charge to be somewhat surly but intelligent and quick to absorb the subjects offered in the curriculum, as though she had some strong reason for completing the course of study as quickly, and as thoroughly as she could manage. She applied herself to her lessons with a passion that seemed to imply she would not only master but must excel at every subject offered before she was satisfied. She already knew French, but continued to study the language until she spoke and read it like a native. Spanish was not offered in the curriculum, but Italian was, and she tackled mastering that language as well until she became fluent in it. Since she had never before had occasion to learn an instrument, and all ladies of the time were expected to play or to sing, Mistress Morgan took up the piano and harpsichord, making up for the time she had lost in childhood by practicing until her fingers were blistered and Lady Edwina had to admonish her to quit to let the others sleep. Eventually, she became fairly proficient in spite of her late start.

Unfortunately, the girl knew more than was considered acceptable in young women of subjects like mathematics and geography. Edwina was appalled when Jamie, having been assigned the duty of greeting any guests who came to the door, was found deeply steeped in conversation

157

with their benefactor, Lord Peregrine Osbourne, who was also an admiral in His Majesty's Navy. They were engrossed in a discussion of navigation and ship designs, impressing the admiral but quite horrifying the headmistress that a lady, especially one of Mistress Morgan's tender years, should talk confidently and knowledgeably on such subjects with a man.

After two years here, Mistress Morgan remained an enigma to the headmistress. There were some things she couldn't cull out of her, like her open, sometimes even ribald, manner of speaking regardless of the audience. She said what she thought and refused to hide her extensively growing knowledge behind an insipid, vacant smile and an upraised fan, as women of her era were supposed to do.

Her father had sent funds sufficient to pay her tuition costs with enough left over to see that she could want for nothing. Her wardrobe, under Lady Edwina's tutelage, was tasteful and fashionable. The new gown she was wearing today was of light pink taffeta, sloping off her shoulders, decorated at bodice and sleeves with expensive Viennese lace. Red velvet ribbons were entwined in the web of lace eyelets and matching red ribbons were fastened in her hair. After hours of practice, Jamie had learned to talk, walk, stand, and sit correctly. She was shown how to throw her shoulders back and stand erect, to hold her arms gracefully at her sides or in front of her and not ever to stand with them petulantly stuck on her hips.

Though the child refused to explain what the object meant to her, she would not surrender the gold pocket watch she carried and would not allow the object out of her sight. At night she slept with the watch tucked underneath her pillow, and during daylight hours insisted on carrying it in her muff or in a pocket or attached by a delicate chain to the skirt of her gowns. Since Edwina had been told that she had no relatives except her father, the headmistress assumed the piece of jewelry had some sentimental attachment and gave up her efforts to convince her that it was not a very ladylike adornment.

In spite of the faults she stubbornly held on to, since her first public presentation in London society young men called on her with amazing regularity and almost obsessive interest, though the girl, thus far, had not encouraged any of their advances. True, Jamie Morgan was one of the most beautiful women Edwina had ever passed through her school, and had come a long way from the ruffian Captain Bonner presented, but the men who called on her never seemed even slightly deterred by the fact that the girl was colonial born, titleless, and hadn't the remotest idea what dowry her father intended to send with her when she wed. In any case, with today's scheduled affair before them, Lady Westcott was extremely pleased with the success of her efforts. Mistress Morgan was certain to make a good impression on so momentous an occasion.

"I suggest that all of you remember we are to be emissaries of goodwill for our king and, as such, His Majesty depends on us to present ourselves accordingly." Lady Westcott walked down the line of girls like a drill sergeant reviewing the troops, her scrutiny taking in every detail of each girl's appearance and finding them all faultless.

"You will be meeting the king of a foreign land who has come here to visit," Lady Edwina explained to her charges, "and I expect you to appear at your best . . ."

"But Lady Westcott," Sarah Linden interrupted, catching the headmistress's attention by waving a plump white hand in the air. "Lady Westcott, how do we pretend that the king is not the king and yet remember that he is?"

159

Lady Edwina paused, wondering how to answer the girl. The benefactor of their school, Lord Osbourne, Marquis of Carmarthen, the same man Lady Edwina had made her pact with to open the school, had asked her to do this as a special favor to him that he, in turn, was presenting to their king. Tsar Peter of Russia was visiting England with a large contingent of his fellow countrymen, traveling, supposedly, incognito among them, though it was difficult to understand how the twenty-one-year old monarch who was known to stand six feet and seven inches tall could possibly be disguised as an ordinary man. Yet it was his plan to see all of Europe's capitals, not traveling in state as a visiting monarch, but informally, as a student of world affairs, learning the ways of the west as he would have his people learn them when he returned home again. To England, as to most of Europe, Russia was a land steeped in mystery. Until the reign of Tsar Peter's father, Tsar Alexis, the country had been closed to the west. Furthering his father's policy of opening their doors to Europe, Tsar Peter wanted to see for himself such wonders as his emissaries and retainers had described to him, but did not want his tour encumbered by the rite and ritual of each country greeting and entertaining a visiting monarch. To satisfy this kingly whim, no formal receptions were to be held in his honor. His hosts might offer balls and entertainments for the group of emissaries journeying with him, but they were not to greet him as any but another Russian in the delegation.

At the behest of King William, Sir John Evelyn, owner of a magnificent estate in Deptford, vacated his elegant home outside London, offering it to the Russians for the duration of their stay. Yet because Tsar Peter was "unrecognized", earls, dukes, and other nobles could not easily call on them, leaving the Russians devoid of English welcome and company. Lord Osbourne, therefore, prevailed upon Lady Edwina to accept an invitation on behalf of her girls to come to a picnic being held at the estate. The girls had been told they were not to see the tsar as the tsar but only as a nobleman in the delegation.

"I suppose," Lady Edwina began, "we would greet him as you would any of the nobles . . . except, perhaps," she thought aloud, "you might curtsy lower . . ."

"And how low is that?" Lacey Bell quipped, starting a short round of giggles among the girls. Several years ago, Lacey had come from the streets of London with a Cockney dialect so thick that only one in perhaps every three words was understandable to the cultured ear. She was fourteen before her father's business sense made a merchant and then a rich man of him. Lady Westcott's tutelage had removed the accent but had not managed to eliminate the quick and sarcastic wit Lacey had learned to use in her early years. Perhaps because both had come from similar backgrounds, Jamie from a shipload of rough-talking men and Lacey from the lower-class areas of London, the two had the most in common. Where Jamie was a raven-haired beauty, Lacey was similarly lovely, but with locks of daffodil yellow. Until Jamie arrived, Lacey had been the school's undisputed queen and Mistress Bell at first had not taken kindly to the competition from this "colonial waif." Lacey declared war and Jamie reciprocated, complete to the hurling of cutting comments and juvenile pranks exchanged by both sides. If a gentleman displayed particular notice of Jamie, Lacey immediately tried to take him away from her. Since Jamie seemed disinterested in them all, such plots were not difficult for the almost-as-pretty Lacey to accomplish.

Edwina thought it was because both girls were so often left alone at the school during weekends and holidays that they eventually learned there was more to be gained in befriending each other than in continuing their small-scale warfare. Jamie had no relatives but her father living far away and Lacey's parents were often abroad on buying trips for his import-export business. While the others went home to visit their families, Mistresses Morgan and Bell were often the only residents. Surely they were bound to have noticed their similarities of background and interests that slowly overcame their differences. At times, their friendship now seemed a bit too close for Lady Edwina's complete peace of mind. Both were independently minded and could see no reason to obey rules if they did not see logic in them or agree with them. Just so were they likely to take unscheduled departures from the school and from outings, leaving the company of their chaperones to wander off, exploring on their own. Edwina and the staff might be frantic with worry until they turned up again with apologies but little genuine regret for the furor their adventures caused. For that reason, Headmistress Westcott chose to ignore Lacey's last remark, herding her charges into the waiting carriages, careful to place Jamie in one containing Sarah, Jenny LeClair and Rose Standish, and seating Mistress Bell three coaches behind them.

"Jamie, aren't you just terribly excited," Sarah burst in as the coach driver coaxed the horses into motion.

"I don't know what all the fuss is about," Jamie answered casually. "A king is just a man, after all, and takes his britches off a leg at a time like any other."

"Ohh, Jamie." Rose Standish blushed, raising her gloved hand to her lips as she giggled. "You do say the awfulest things."

"Why? 'Tis true, isn't it?"

All three of her companions burst into schoolgirlish laughter. Jamie felt her cheeks flush, wondering if again

162

she had said something wrong, though her companions would not call her down for it. Over the two years she had been here, Jamie had discovered that she couldn't understand London society and that she would never come to feel at home in this environment. From the moment Captain Bonner's ship docked, she had wished immediately that he might turn the ship around to sail home again.

Port Royale might be rough and ragtag, but, in comparison, it was a haven of cleanliness next to the Old World port that met her first gaze.

She had been appalled by the squalor and filth. The docks she saw upon landing had been crowded with the masts of tall ships quartered along the marshy, muddy banks of the Thames. At the end of the seventeenth century, this vital, busy city of seven hundred fifty thousand inhabitants lay mostly on the northern bank of the river, stretching from Tower Hill to the Houses of Parliament. In autumn and winter, great mists rose up off the river to shroud the narrow, dark streets in thick brown vapors of swirling fog made foul by the smoke from thousands of chimneys. The smoke and soot laying over the streets and houses stung her eyes and singed her nostrils, the acrid odor mixing freely with the stink of offal and garbage that lay, neglected, in the gutters.

Overhanging windows of upper stories projected out over the lanes and the residents of these apartments simply tossed their garbage out of these apertures without a care for the people walking below who strolled through the refuse as naturally as if they were walking a garden path.

Main avenues were dark, airless, and congested with traffic. In damp weather carriages and hackney cabs cut deep ruts in the streets to make a ride through the teeming city a bumpy, nauseating affair in which passengers were often discharged at their destinations both mussed and bruised from the jostling.

Even the rich profusion of cultural refinements—the opera, the theater, both of which Lady Westcott treated her charges to several times a month, the market stalls and shops where anything imaginable could be purchased, could not dispel Jamie's longing for the fresh, clean air of home.

As those same two years passed she had often worried over Franco's well-being. When the months went by and word never came from him, she feared for his safety and health. Then again, another part of her mind would whisper, he's safe and well but has forgotten you. At times she hoped the latter was true and that he was well and happy, yet thinking of him, perhaps in the arms of another woman, perhaps married by now to someone else, filled her with both anger and sadness. Which was the truth? She realized she might never know. All she did know was that she loved him still, as unwaveringly as if he was here beside her, as unshakably as if he had kept his promise to send for her. Surely, had he ever returned to Port Royale, Morgan would have told him where she was or, if her father was being perverse, then Jocko, or one of the others might have given him her location. Why then, had Franco not kept his promise to come or to send for her? That he might have been killed or that he languished yet in a prison his brother might have sent him to, was too awful to contemplate. Still, she tried to live on hope that someday a messenger might appear. For that reason, she could not accept the advances made by her suitors. Of the friends she had made here in London, only Lacey knew about Franco and her dream that he would come for her.

Jamie drew herself out of her troubling thoughts, knowing that if she did not the day would be utterly ruined for her. Any break from the school's routine was welcome and a chance to leave the environs of midtown London was practically cause for celebration. Sayes Court at Deptford was close to the shipyards and, if she stretched her imagination, the smell of the sea, or the river at least, might reach her.

The girls had been talking for days about the upcoming event at Sir Evelyn's estate, many of the conversations dwelling on the tsar they were scheduled to meet. Though a few had met dukes and earls, none had ever had occasion to curtsy before a king.

Jamie felt the entire affair was much ado about nothing—an appropriate remark from the title of a Shakespeare play she had seen recently. Her father had spent too much of his time scrambling for a title out of his exploits and his reward, thus far, had been only due thanks for the Spanish and French gold he placed in English coffers. His daughter had learned the refinements and graces, but had it made a different person out of her? She thought not, to the best of her reckoning. She could speak well and dress well and understood the conversations around her, but inside she remained Jamie Morgan—older, more roundly educated, but the same girl who had left the Colonies.

The contingent of carriages left the congestion of London behind them, traveling over bumpy, pothole-spotted country roads. Fluffy white clouds drifted lazily across the blue sky and Jamie began to enjoy the autumn scenery. The foliage was just turning to beautiful shades of amber, red, and gold. The changing of the seasons was an event she had never seen at home. In the Caribbean, the seasons were divided into wet and dry, stifling hot and humid, or damp and chilly, with just enough days of comfortably warm and balmy weather to make one forget the misery the majority of the year presented. Until her

165

first season here, she had never seen snow, and watched, fascinated, as the powdery flakes fell out of the gray skies, turning the dirty streets outside her window into a glistening fairyland. No less intriguing was autumn, as the leaves of the trees, touched by the first kiss of winter cold, turned to bright patterns and colors as if a magician artist had hand-painted every leaf.

She centered her attention on the sights of nature until the carriages rounded a bend in the road and the estate came into view. Before her stood an elegant three-story manor house, with several gables and a tiled roof. Wide chimneys above the kitchens sent soft billows of fragrant smoke into the skies. Jamie could see the gardens, colorful with fall blossoms in the brightest of yellows and reds against the carpet of dark green lawn. The trees wore their fall suits of gold and crimson. Wide tables, draped in white tablecloths, were already set up under the trees, their surfaces burdened with food awaiting the appetites of the guests. The first aromas of roast goose stuffed with herbed rice and sausage and roast venison turned to a crisp golden brown began to drift past Jamie's nose, stirring her appetite.

The carriages halted and English footmen in livery appeared to open the doors and help the ladies down to the safety of the gravel driveway. Jamie took the livery man's arm, holding her skirts up as she descended, looking about, as the others were, for their first sight of their Russian hosts.

"Thank you for coming, ladies," Lord Osbourne greeted, stepping out of the shadows of the portico. Lady Westcott approached him and they spent a few moments talking as the rest of the girls were handed down from the carriages. Pastel shades of velvet, silk, and satin added their own color to the autumn scenery as the young women began to stroll about, taking in the sights the estate provided.

Jamie allowed Sarah Linden to take her arm as they strolled around aimlessly, surveying their elegant surroundings. "Oh, Jamie, isn't it marvelous?" Sarah gushed, her plump face flushed with excitement. "Just imagine, we're going to meet the monarch of a foreign land. What do you expect he'll look like?"

"Like a man, I suppose," Jamie commented, more impressed by the neat, well-kept lawns and gardens.

"Jamie, let's have a look about before introductions are made." Lacey had come up beside Jamie, taking her arm away from Sarah who looked crushed at being suddenly excluded.

"Lady Westcott said we aren't to wander off," Sarah exclaimed in a pouting tone of voice.

"Oh, posh and bother, Sarah," Lacey returned. "Having a look about is hardly wandering off. Come if you want or stay here if you're afraid," Lacey tossed over her shoulder.

Deciding she would rather face the headmistress's displeasure than be thought a coward, Sarah trotted to catch up with them. In another moment, Rose and Jenny were also trailing along on the forbidden excursion.

"Isn't this the most beautiful estate you've ever seen?" Lacey asked as they rounded a corner of the mansion toward the grounds in back. "Someday I shall have one exactly like it. If a man isn't rich enough to give it to me, then he's not the right one for me."

Jamie nodded idly at Lacey's chatter, thinking instead of the tropical foliage of home.

"What can possibly be bothering you on such a beautiful day?" Lacey asked, walking slowly by her side.

"I suppose I'm just homesick," Jamie replied. "Right now, we would be at the end of the hurricane season and the vegetation grows so fast that Sheltie, the old man who tends it, and all his helpers keep busy enough just cutting it back. Then thoughts of home make me think of Franco. I wonder how much longer before he'll come for me. You think I'm silly to be waiting, don't you?" Jamie turned to gaze at her friend.

Lacey kept her eyes down on the path in front of her. "You already know what I think."

Lacey was of the opinion that a year was long enough to wait. He had had time to sail to Spain and back with months left over for settling his business. In two years, surely, he would have been here or sent word if he was really coming. Lacey was also of the opinion that if this Franco did not have sense enough to realize the jewel he was neglecting in Jamie, then he wasn't worthy of her devotion. While jealousy had once clouded her vision, after hearing Jamie's story about Franco, she no longer harbored such resentments and felt sorry for her dearest friend. On all those long weekends in each other's company, there was not much of their past lives that the girls had not shared. Jamie had described the islands in such detail that Lacey was determined to someday convince her parents to let her go there.

They rounded another corner of the vast mansion and the back lawn came into view. Here a game appeared to be in progress though it took a few minutes to realize what was afoot.

The neat back lawn had a slightly downward slope toward a magnificent holly hedge fully four hundred feet long and nine feet high that must be the owner's special pride. A group of gentlemen who had to be their Russian hosts, not yet informed of their arrival, were gathered at the top of the hill facing the hedge. There was a great deal of laughter and conversation among the finely dressed gentlemen who were engaged, it seemed, in playing a game of races in two of the gardener's wheelbarrows. In teams of two, one man seated himself in the bucket of the wheelbarrow while the other took up the handles. At a signal, they ran straight down the hill to crash headlong into the holly hedge that was, by appearances, suffering greatly under the repeated assaults. Rounds of laughter met the emergence of the riders as they freed themselves from the entanglement of wheelbarrow and holly hedge. Everyone's suit was rumpled, which accounted for the grass stains Jamie had seen on Lord Osbourne's satin trousers.

"We'd better go back before they see us," Sarah whispered, her pert, plump face frowning worriedly.

"Nonsense, I'm sure they won't mind," Lacey returned, taking a firmer grip on Jamie's arm and starting forward.

"Lady Westcott will!" Sarah exclaimed. "She'll have our hides."

Just then, one of the gentlemen spied them. "Ladies!" he said in English. "Welcome. We didn't know you had arrived."

Lacey pulled Jamie forward since her friend seemed too engrossed in watching the game in progress to think of it for herself. Jamie's gaze was locked on the wheelbarrows crashing into the holly hedge while more guffaws erupted from the spectators.

"Might I try it?" Jamie asked suddenly.

The man stared at her in surprise but Jamie met his gaze, assuring him she was perfectly serious.

"I've tried it myself. 'Tis a rough landing, mistress. Are you certain you care to risk it? Your dress might be ruined and if you were injured . . ."

"I'd love to," Jamie burst in. "May I?" She hadn't engaged in any rough-and-tumble sport since she left the islands. This looked like a game the pirates might have invented had anyone ever thought of it or found a cleared hillside to play it on. Games of all sorts helped to

169

pass the idle hours on shipboard and chased boredom away from long days on a secluded beach waiting for the supply parties to restock the ship's provisions. Most of these pastimes were physical in nature, since the majority of able-bodied seamen couldn't read and were not especially proficient in their intellectual accomplishments. But they were imaginative. Some of the games were unbearably cruel, like the pastimes devoted to the disposal of prisoners. Those had always sickened Jamie and she avoided taking any part in them. But other games were great fun and no one was ever deliberately hurt in them. Sometimes they would have races to the top of the masts or foot-race around the deck to great hoots and jeers for the losers. Sometimes they danced spritely jigs on the deck to the tune of an accordian or a fiddle. In London, Jamie had been denied these physical activities, encouraged to spend her free hours stitching proverbs onto a piece of cloth, or reading, or playing an instrument, all of which she found relaxing or even enjoyed, but since walking or dancing were now the only exertions, the game the Russian nobles were engaged in appealed to this deprived side of her nature.

The gentleman seemed to ponder her request for a moment, then consulted the man behind him who was just getting into one of the returned wheelbarrows for his turn at a roll down the hill. "Why not?" he shrugged as he turned around to her again, apparently giving the answer the other man had decided. A gentleman in a badly rumpled violet silk suit stepped aside, offering her his place in the other wheelbarrow with an elegant bow.

"Jamie, are you out of your mind? You'll break your neck." Lacey clutched Jamie's arm for a moment.

"You're usually the first to volunteer for an adventure," Jamie chastised. "No, I won't. No one else has been injured." Jamie was determined to go through with it.

170

While her companions watched—Lacey with growing interest, Sarah in horror, and Rose and Jenny in expressions between the two—Jamie settled inside the bucket, tucking her skirts around her, careful lest any stray yardage should escape to catch in the wheels.

"In Russia, the wheelbarrow has never been invented," the man who had greeted them explained as she readied herself. "They've never seen them before and invented this game for amusement. The object is to race to the hedge and not cry out to stop before the finish line. In other words, you are meant to crash into the hedge."

"I won't cry out," Jamie assured him. "I've played games like it before."

"As you like." He smiled at her. "I'll run you down myself," he said, taking up the handles of the wheelbarrow and Jamie felt the back of the bucket lifted off the ground. The signal given, Jamie spared only a quick glance at the man she was racing against. She had only a glimpse of a handsome face with a full mustache before the wheelbarrows started their hair-raising roll down the hillside.

Jamie felt the wind of her passage against her face as the conveyance bumped ever faster over the uneven ground. She squealed in sheer delight when the bucket suddenly stopped, propelling her through the air into the hedge. She landed, tumbling, over the ground.

"Are you hurt?" The man rushed over, though not terribly concerned when he heard her laughter.

"Never better. Thank you. I haven't enjoyed myself so much in ages." She accepted his hand to let him help her to her feet.

He waited until she smoothed out the rumples in her dress, then bowed politely. "Patrick Gordon, mistress," he belatedly introduced himself. "I am a mercenary in service to the tsar and, may I say, I admire your courage."

171

"Jamie Morgan," she responded with a curtsy. " 'Tis nothing, I assure you," she added, smiling.

"I take it you've engaged in such adventures before."

"Of a similar nature. At home," she explained. "I grew up on a ship. On hot days we would swing out over the ship's yardarm, then let go to plunge into the sea. My father was always frantic, assuring us we were reckless to take such chances and would lure every shark in the sea, but his warnings never hampered our fun."

"Your father?" he queried.

"Captain Henry Morgan, out of the Caribbean colonies."

"I see." The man smiled, his gaze roaming past her to the other overturned wheelbarrow and its rider who seemed to have become helplessly ensnared in the holly hedge's clinging branches.

Jamie immediately lent herself to the task of helping Lord Gordon disentangle the other rider. While the men pulled back the branches, Jamie offered her hand to him to help him to his feet. He looked up at her, a bit startled by her gesture, but finally accepted.

To Jamie, helping out was second nature and she knew how to brace herself for his weight although he appeared fearful she might tumble over him. She helped him rise and he kept rising, higher and higher, until she had to crane her neck to look up at him. Good Lord, he was nearly as tall as Jocko!

"Mistress Morgan." Patrick Gordon appeared at her side. "May I introduce Peter Alexeivitch."

"Your Majesty." In the flash of insight as he stood before her, Jamie remembered Lady Westcott's advice to curtsy lower and also inclined her head in a graceful gesture.

He had not released her hand yet and raised her up, exchanging a few words with Lord Gordon.

"His Majesty wishes to know how you knew his identity," Gordon explained.

"Cor." Jamie forgot herself for a moment. "Who else would be so tall," she murmured, relieved to see him smile when Lord Gordon relayed her answer. She was surprised to discover she was somewhat awed and astonished after all. She had said a king was like any other man, but she had never expected to meet a man such as this one, as kingly óf form as he was of title in spite of the mussing he had received in the holly hedges.

There had been no doubt in her mind of his identity when she addressed him, even if she had not been told of his extraordinary height. He was a very handsome man, aquiline featured and sporting a full mustache. His auburn hair was shoulder-length, neatly brushed back behind his ears and fastened with a simple, thin black ribbon. His suit, though rumpled from the play, was of dark brown velvet with diamond buttons and fine lace trimming his blouse sleeves.

If ever a man looked the picture of a king, this one did. He stood erect in spite of his towering height and not stooped over as tall people often were. His shoulders were narrower than Jocko's yet seemed powerful. Certainly the large, long-fingered hand that held on to hers far longer than courtesy dictated felt strong while her fingers rested lightly in his palm. His eyes utterly fascinated her, being almost as dark as Franco's, nearly black, and intense. They seemed to hold her in their power so that she couldn't look away.

"Mistress Morgan!" a shrill voice called down from the top of the hill. Jamie's smile immediately vanished. Lady Westcott was standing at the top, her arm on Lord Osbourne's as if he would keep her from fainting, but her face was positively red and furious.

"I believe I have just ensured that I will be assigned to

173

kitchen duty for the remainder of the winter," she remarked.

Lord Gordon must have translated what she had said verbatim. The tsar laughed, a good-natured, pleasant sound, then exchanged a few more words with his retainer.

"Since you have already found him out, His Majesty says that for you he has decided he will surrender his anonymity for this occasion. He will ask your headmistress to pardon you as a special favor to him," Lord Gordon explained. "He also asks if you are Russian."

"Me?" Jamie exclaimed, her eyes wide, amazed to be so much under discussion and completely forgetting Lady Westcott's lesson on the proper use of "I" and "me." "Oh, no. My father is Welsh."

"The Welsh too are a hardy people like the Russians, are they not?" Gordon translated what the tsar said after her answer was relayed to him.

"How would one say yes in Russian?" she queried.

"Da," Lord Gordon provided.

"Da," Jamie repeated, looking up at the young and handsome tsar.

He smiled, pleased, placing her hand on his to escort her back up the hill.

Jamie wished she was an artist to capture on canvas the look on Lady Westcott's face as she realized the identity of Jamie's escort. Patrick Gordon made the introductions. "Lady Westcott, His Majesty, Peter Alexievitch, the tsar of all the Russias."

Properly overwhelmed, Lady Westcott dropped a curtsy so low Jamie wondered if she would manage to rise again. "Your Majesty."

She too, Jamie thought with an inward smile, probably

had never had occasion to kneel before a monarch. As he had promised through his translator, he requested Jamie's pardon as a favor to him as a guest in this country, claiming her rowdy adventure had been his own suggestion and taking full responsibility for it. To Jamie's further surprise, he asked Lady Westcott if Jamie might be his companion for the afternoon.

Lady Westcott stuttered and stammered and finally managed to murmur, "Yes, of course. We'd be honored."

"But I don't speak a word of Russian," Jamie nervously turned to Lord Gordon to whisper. "However will we communicate?"

"No matter, my dear," Lord Gordon saw her flustered appearance. "I or Lord Osbourne will serve as your translators."

Jamie's nerves, under these extraordinary events, would hardly let her eat a bite of the delectable luncheon that she had found so appetizing upon their arrival. She had been seated between the tsar and Lord Gordon and all afternoon, after learning of her early life aboard a sailing ship, the Russian king plied her with questions. She soon learned the reasons for his intense interest in the subject. For many years Russia had been a landlocked nation except for a single port, Archangel. Tsar Peter had plans to change all that and wanted to build an extensive navy for his country. He was fascinated by sailing and had done an exceptional amount of it along the rivers and vast lakes of his homeland. On his European journey, he had spent a year in Holland to learn shipbuilding and told her, through the translators, all about how he had worked as an ordinary apprentice learning his trade until he earned the title of master craftsman his Dutch instructors had conferred on him. Learning of Jamie's background on the *Lady Morgan*, he pressed her for every smallest detail of her adventures.

175

By the end of the afternoon, she was sorry to see the day drawing to a close. Though at first it felt awkward having a conversation through interpreters, she soon became used to it. It had been a long time since she had been able to talk to anyone knowledgeably about her favorite subject or to find someone who was as intrigued by the sea as she was. The girls often liked to hear her tales in the dormitory, but she was always stopped by dozens of questions. "Which way is aft, again? What's a hawser? Why do they call it so'west?" She found this avid listener already well informed and thus they could talk without stopping for definitions and explanations. She learned that King William had commissioned a yacht to be built as a present for the tsar and as soon as it was finished, which would be in early spring, he promised to take her on its maiden voyage. She also realized, with a sense of guilt, that she had utterly monopolized the tsar's attention and that her friends had barely had an opportunity to meet him, though they had all been entertained by the noblemen in his retinue.

The carriages were brought around and the tsar left her for a moment to bid farewell to each of his other guests.

"You've certainly had a time for yourself, flirting with the tsar all afternoon," Lacey said with a trace of pique in her voice. Lacey relished attracting male attention and still didn't quite like it if Jamie received it instead.

"I was not flirting," Jamie defended. "He was interested in my background aboard the *Lady Morgan*. That was all."

"Call it what you like, you seemed to be quite taken nonetheless, especially for a girl waiting for her true love to send for her."

"I haven't for a moment forgotten Franco!" Jamie said harshly. "I was only being polite."

"Hah!" Lacey snickered, taking it in better humor now.

176

She had learned to accept, in a way, that Jamie was prettier and, to some minds, more charming, and that she wouldn't be able to take every man who expressed an interest in her best friend away from her. She fought off the worst of her jealous impulses by reminding herself that Jamie was a year older, far more experienced, and had still adopted her as a friend. She envied Jamie's life that had been so rich and full of excitement, while she had done so little. Except for one small trip to the countryside, Lacey had never been out of London. Her parents traveled extensively but always left her behind in the care of the headmistress.

"I could never betray Franco," Jamie insisted, stamping her foot in anger, irritated, perhaps, by a feeling of shame that she really had, for the afternoon at least, managed to let him slip her mind.

"Well, I wouldn't blame you anyway," Lacey shrugged. "Two years is a long time to wait without any indication he will come . . ."

"Do be quiet, Lacey," Jamie snapped.

"As you like, but do bear one thing in mind before you think of transferring that considerable devotion of yours to another target. The tsar is a married man."

"Is he?" Jamie blurted, forgetting both her anger and her denial.

"So, the thought never entered your mind, eh?" Lacey grinned. "You needn't look at me like that. Why shouldn't it? Lord knows you've been faithful enough to this shadow of yours for ever so long . . ."

"He will send for me! You'll see! I was only curious . . ."

"Well then, for your curiosity alone, the tsar is wed. Lord Gordon told me when Lord Osbourne took over for him as translator. Your tsar has been married since he was sixteen. A political arrangement, I gather, and not

177

the happiest of unions, but there it is."

Jamie couldn't have explained why she felt disappointed. She was waiting for Franco, who would come for her someday . . .

"At any rate, I thought a warning might be in order. Although . . . I can think of worse fates than being mistress to a king."

"Lacey!" Jamie admonished sharply.

"I'd certainly give it consideration if I were in your shoes," the blond beauty admitted with candor. "I would! Truly! Good Lord, remember all we've talked about of how one loses all control over one's life after marriage? You could have your independence and the adoration of a man, like all the great courtesans have done . . ."

"Lacey," Jamie interrupted with a glare. "Do shut up!"

Lady Westcott was waiting by the last carriage. The tsar and a small contingent of his retinue were coming toward them, apparently to bid good-bye.

"Think about it," Lacey whispered in her ear with a grin, then the girl grunted as Jamie's elbow connected with her midsection.

"Mistress Morgan," Patrick Gordon addressed her. "The tsar has been asked to attend a ball this Saturday next, given by one of your countrymen, Lord Grenville. He has been unwilling to attend such functions in his honor, as you know, but if you would consent to accompany him, he would make an exception and accept."

"Do it!" Lacey squealed softly from beside her, undoubtedly hoping that if Jamie went, she might be asked along as well.

"I'm sorry, Lord Gordon, but I don't think I can . . ."

"Your headmistress has already given her consent."

"It isn't that. I am . . . I consider myself to be . . . betrothed," she explained.

"Oh?" Lord Peregrine Osbourne interrupted. "I hadn't

178

heard of this."

"I mean that I am promised to become engaged. He isn't here in England. He's to send for me." It sounded so pitiable trying to explain it, waiting for a promise that might never come true.

"Then surely your fiancé will not mind a single evening. You would be properly chaperoned, I assure you."

Jamie could think of no polite way to refuse. Would Franco really mind? 'Twas only for one evening and they wouldn't be alone.

"Do it," Lacey repeated in her ear, nudging her in the side. Jamie was sure now that Lacey expected to be asked to the event by Lord Gordon, an older but hardly an unattractive man. For Lacey's sake, Jamie nodded. "Very well. I'd be delighted."

"See now, was that so difficult?" Lacey asked after they had been handed up into the carriages and were on their way home. As she had hoped, Lord Gordon had suggested Lacey accompany Jamie to the ball and she was deliriously happy over the turn of events.

"I feel like I'm betraying Franco," Jamie complained.

"My girl," Lacey said, settling back into the seat cushions. "If you would ever open your eyes and face the facts of it, after this much time has passed, I think you may be reasonably sure that your Franco has certainly betrayed you!"

Chapter Nine

"Mistress Morgan, may I have a word with you?" Lady Westcott beckoned from the open doorway of her private office, the look on her attractive, middle-aged face one of stern disapproval. Jamie stepped out of the group of young women coming downstairs to take their breakfast before classes began.

Here it comes, she thought, feeling the gentle pressure as Sarah Linden placed a consoling hand on her forearm. At least the headmistress had put her scolding off until the following morning.

"I hope it shan't be too bad," Sarah remarked.

"Do you want me to come with you?" Lacey offered. "I can remind her she promised to withhold punishment."

"Thank you both," Jamie said turning away toward the office. "But, if punishment is to be had, I suppose I've earned it." She hadn't really expected yesterday's escapade in the wheelbarrow to be completely forgotten.

Lady Westcott waited until Jamie had closed the door and seated herself in the straight-backed chair that faced her desk. "I suppose you are well aware that I do not approve of the behavior you displayed yesterday."

"Yes, ma'am. However, if I might speak in my own defense, Lord Osbourne didn't seem to mind it, and you did say 'twas most important that the king should be made

180

to feel at home."

"I did not suppose that statement would be construed to include horseplay on a wheelbarrow. Good Lord, what must the Russian nobles be thinking of us after such an escapade?" Lady Westcott stated harshly.

"Nothing too awful, I expect, as he asked afterward if I might be Russian."

Lady Westcott glared hotly until Jamie hung her head in what she hoped was a suitably chastised manner. The headmistress did not easily accept excuses. Poor behavior was poor behavior.

"Then I'm sure I can't imagine how the nobility is allowed to behave in Moscovy, but it does seem you made quite a favorable impression on the tsar," Lady Westcott continued. "However, I want it well understood that I expect much better deportment from you in future."

"Yes, ma'am," Jamie murmured, keeping her head lowered to hide the smile that wanted to surface at the news that she wouldn't be punished. Lady Westcott had a very fertile imagination when it came to punishments, such as polishing all of the hundreds of books in the school's library or embroidering proverbs — and worst of all was kitchen duty!

It was strange how Jamie had always found it easy to backtalk Morgan yet couldn't seem to muster the courage to speak to Lady Westcott in such a manner. Her father handed out punishment that she as often as not ignored and, in a few hours, when his anger had cooled, he usually forgot he'd ever given them. At times, she had to admit that she had pushed his temper a tad over the edge, occasioning a more physical response, but she had never had trouble letting him know how she felt.

Perhaps because Lady Westcott never lost control of her temper, Jamie found it impossible to respond in the ways that had always been her habit. Lady Westcott spoke sternly but civilly on all occasions, even when angry. Her tone of authority was sufficient, and not for all the world would Jamie dream of talking disrespectfully to her. She had come to love and admire this petite, genteel woman and knew she would remember her fondly long after she graduated in the spring.

"Naturally, at the ball this Saturday, you will be properly chaperoned by Lord Osbourne and his wife, and I expect to hear glowing reports of your impeccable behavior."

"Yes, ma'am, you certainly shall, I assure you. You won't have a thing to worry about."

"Somehow I rather doubt that." Lady Westcott rose to her feet. "Meanwhile, I have called you into my office for quite another purpose and that is to tell you that you have a guest."

"A guest?" Jamie dared not let her hopes soar to Franco but could hardly help herself.

"He's only arrived this morning and is waiting for you in the library. As I am sure you will wish to spend as much time together as he can spare, you are dismissed from your morning classes."

Jamie's head was swimming. Only a very special caller would receive admittance at this hour of the morning.

Lady Westcott opened the office door that adjoined the library and Jamie hesitantly stepped inside, immediately recognizing the well-dressed man who rose to greet her and hurrying forward as fast as her legs could carry her to propel herself into his arms.

"Papa!" she cried, hugging him fiercely. Tears sprang to her eyes, not fully cognizant until now of how very deeply she had missed him.

"Here, girl, let me have a look at you." Henry Morgan pulled her away from him just far enough to cast his eyes

182

over her. "You look wonderful, pet. I see that this here London has not taken the blush from your cheeks!"

"Why didn't you tell me you were coming? Why are you here? Is everything well at home?"

"Give me a chance to answer," Morgan laughed with his deep-sounding bellow. " 'Tis a sight for these old eyes to behold lookin' at you."

"You'll never be old, Papa," Jamie said, though she too was appraising her parent in comparison to the last time she had seen him, and in spite of her words, Papa did look older. His dark hair was sprinkled more heavily with gray and wrinkles creased his face about the eyes and jowls where there had never been any lines before. He had lost weight to his tall, beefy frame and she could see that there was something troubling his mind. Jamie urged him to sit down on the settee, settling herself down next to him. "But tell me what brings you to London? Why didn't you let me know you were coming?"

"Aye, girl, 'tis a long tale I have to tell," he sighed. "Some good and some bad enough to your ears, I'm thinking. I've promised myself to tell ye all of it, lest ye hear it from other lips, not mine. Ye'll learn it soon enough on reaching home, I reckon."

"Home? We're going home? You've come to fetch me back?" Jamie could not think of anything that would please her more. Learning to be a gentlewoman was all fine, and she would miss the friends she had made here, but nothing would take the place of home.

"Aye." Morgan grinned. "We'll be going back, but not till spring. The winter is no time to be on the high seas, as you know well enough. At least I think ye remember what yer old Papa taught ye."

"Of course," she murmured, troubled as she watched her father. That was the second time he had mentioned being old. The Morgan she had left, though nearing sixty then, had never spared a thought for advancing years. What could have changed him so much? He seemed different, more subdued, than the Henry Morgan he had been.

"But first, let me have a good look at ye!" He encouraged her to stand up before him and, to please him, Jamie pirouetted to show off the fineness of the gown she was wearing. Lady Westcott insisted that unless there were chores to be done her girls dress in their best, as if they were going to go calling or expected company momentarily. That way, the headmistress said, one was never caught unawares, disheveled, and at less than their best appearance. They were allowed no breakfast until their morning toilette was completed. She was wearing a light blue gown of winter silk with pink roses embroidered across the bodice. Her hair was excellently coiffed and tiny sapphire earrings adorned her ears. For once, she was glad that the headmistress made the girls go to so much trouble before they came down for the day.

"Ye do look wonderful, pet." Her father's eyes misted, renewing the tears in her own. "I can hardly believe what I see standing before me. And ye talk so fine now, like a lady should be talkin'. Ye've done me proud, as I knew ye would.

"And now, take a look at me and tell me what be different." Her father sat up straight, as if posing for a portrait.

"I don't know," she pondered, reluctant to say what really did appear different to her—the shock of the years he was showing, his demeanor that had lost its bluster. "You are neater and cleaner than I've ever seen you before," she teased. For the first time, she noticed the fine satin suit he was wearing and that his hair and mustache had been neatly trimmed by a barber. "What should I see?"

"Why, the new me, of course! Don't it show? Ye're looking at the new *Sir* Henry Morgan! Titled so by His Majesty, King William himself!" If possible, he sat even taller than before, his back ramrod straight, his chin high.

"Papa, you don't mean it!"

"So I do, lass, Sir Henry Morgan, at ye service." He gave her a small, elegant bow. "And more," he grinned. "Ye're looking at the duly appointed governor of the island of Jamaica."

"Governor?" Jamie repeated, awed and astounded. "You have a title and governorship?"

"Indeed I do, girl!" He grinned, standing up to display his full glory, one hand tucked into the space between the silver buttons on his frockcoat.

"Oh, Papa!" Jamie threw herself into his arms, embracing him. All his life he had yearned for such recognition and now every dream had come true for him. "But tell me, how did such a thing happen? How did this come to be? What all has happened in my absence?"

"Ye do still run on like a parrot now, don't ye, girl?" He pretended sterness for a moment, then his face broke into a huge grin. "As I told ye, a great lot has happened, but first ye mind yer fine new manners and order up a refreshment for yer papa."

"I'm sorry, Papa, right away." Jamie hurried to the door that led into the foyer, spying Maggie, the downstairs maid, and ordering tea brought for two.

"Ye wouldn't have nothing stronger?" Morgan inquired.

"No, Papa, I'm afraid not. Lady Westcott doesn't allow spirits on the premises."

"Somehow, I ain't surprised," Morgan murmured, settling back on the settee. "I reckon I may as well start," he said as she sat down again beside him. "It was near a year ago now. I had me an idea about leading an expedition to Panama."

"Panama! Papa, that would take an army!"

"Indeed, pet, and an army is what I took with me. Ye know how rich those towns be. 'Twould be worth a fortune to those hardy enough to try for it. Ye know yer papa can be a glib talker when he wants to be and I convinced a dozen or more of the captains on Royale and Tortuga to join me in this venture along with their crews. We had near a thousand men. About the only one who didn't go for the idea was that Franco DeCortega of yers . . ."

"Franco? He's there?" Jamie felt her face draining to pasty white at the mere mention of his name.

"Oh, aye, ye didn't know that, did ye? Well, how would ye of learned it, being here at school and all. Aye, he's there. Come back to be a pirate after all." Morgan chuckled as if the fact gave him the greatest satisfaction. "I did warn ye about the likes of him didn't I? And ye'll be seeing, I was right. The arrogant jacka'napes! Every one of the captains wanted to join in the venture, but not him! His Worship, the great High and Mighty, told me . . . Told me, mind ye, girl, that my plan would never work! Now how would he know whether 'twould work or no, him no more'n an apprentice at pirating. Well, I mean, privateering, that is." Morgan gazed about the room as if the library shelves and the books lining them might have ears to report his slips of the tongue to His Majesty's government "That's what it is, ye know. Privateering, not pirating. Pirates is hanged."

"When did he come back?" Jamie asked in a voice that had suddenly gone weak. All this time, she had imagined him in trouble, imprisoned, ill or dead, and he had been in the Caribbean all along. Every moment she was pining for him, remaining faithful to their promises, while he had utterly forgotten her. Lacey had been right. If he was going to come, he would have long before this. She had been a fool, believing in a promise he had never intended to keep.

"He came back not six months after ye set sail for England. No sooner landed in Spain than he must've lit out again back to Royale."

"Did he ask about me? Didn't he want to know where I was?" She had to hear the answers, had to be absolutely sure.

"Not me, he never did." Morgan met her gaze evenly. There was no trace of deceit in the sapphire depths she stared into. "He might have asked one of the others, I don't know about that, but he never asked me. Said he had found his welcome home not quite what he'd expected. Something about his brother telling lies to have him thought a criminal so's he could keep all the estate. He said he had nowheres else to go but back to Jamaica. Then the scoundrel said that he was ready to take me up on my offer. He'd work for me if I'd give him his own ship to captain. Did ye ever hear the like? As if he was doing me a great favor. Well, I told him," Morgan paused as the maid entered, waiting until she delivered the tea service and went out again before continuing his narrative. "I told him that if he wanted a ship he could find his own. And what do ye think he did?"

"I'm sure I don't know, Papa," Jamie responded, feeling numbed into the center of her being. He had never even *asked* about her?

"The scoundrel went and did it!" Morgan laughed, impressed, even though he didn't particularly like "the Spaniard."

"Here's your tea, Papa." Jamie handed him a steaming cup on a delicate saucer that seemed far too fragile in his huge, work-worn hands.

"Next I know of him," Morgan continued, "he's back with a stolen frigate and a crew of mostly exiled Spaniards to sail it with him. All of them have been turned out by their own, don't ye know. Escaped convicts and sailors what jumped ship and the like. I wouldn't be surprised to learn he sprung them himself from whatever jail they was

187

rotting in. I got to say, he does all right for himself too. Takes to it sort of natural, I'd say, like he was born to it after all." Morgan chuckled. "Well, he turns in ten percent of the profits to the Buccaneer's Fund, like all the rest and has made himself a rich man, I'm thinking, but he don't spend narry a halfpenny of it. No more than it takes to feed himself and outfit his ship, I reckon. Don't know what he does with it. Stashes it away somewheres, I reckon.

"So," Morgan sighed after a disappointing sip of the steaming tea, "when I come up with this plot to take Panama, I asked him to come along and ye know what he said?"

Jamie shook her head. At the moment, a large lump had settled in her throat and she had to force herself to swallow it.

"He said my venture would ultimately fail so he wanted no part of it. Just like that, he said it. 'Twas a sound plan, damn his eyes! Right in front of the others, trying to make me look the simpleton, making me look the fool. I had to show them again how it could be done and the Spaniard agreed as to how we might succeed at taking the towns and we just might find us a great treasure, but he said 'twould be impossible to get the treasure away. Not with that many men in on the venture, and not with the reinforcements sure to come after the first alarm was sounded. He said that great a number of men would only manage to get themselves trapped and have no means of escape."

"But you proved him wrong, didn't you, Papa?" Jamie finally managed to ask, certain that was how he had succeeded in being knighted at last.

"Aye, I got away, treasure and all," Morgan answered, his broad head suddenly hanging low and sheepish.

"You're hiding something, Papa. What happened?"

"Well," he paused, reluctant, avoiding her gaze.

"You said there was something I should hear from you.

188

Tell me."

"The cursed, black-hearted Spaniard was right!" Morgan spat disgustedly. "I'm thinking mebbe he's bad luck to have around. I thought he was only saying what he did because they was Spanish towns we proposed to raid. I figured his real reason was that he didn't want to join in a raid against his own people, but, curse it all, it came to pass just like he had said it would."

"What do you mean? You're here."

"Aye, *I* am." He avoided her gaze again.

"And the others? The thousand men you took with you?"

"Captured," Morgan murmured so low she could barely hear him.

"What?"

"We did take the towns and we did find treasure but, before we knew it, there were four Spanish men-o-war blocking the harbor, leaving no means of escape except overland, the way we come. We had plans to be picked up by ship, but our ships took one look at them fighting vessels and lit out. We was stranded there, strong enough to hold the town for a while but not strong enough to fight our way out of it. I reckon ye can take a thousand men into a place in the dead o' night when nobody knows they're coming, but you can't sneak 'em out again 'cause who will stay behind to hold the town whilst the rest are leaving? I had to do it, lass," Morgan said to the stricken, angry look she gave him. "Else the whole venture would've been for naught."

"You left them to their fate," she accused, narrowing her eyes at him. "You deserted them!"

"I done no different than generals, even princes, has had to do in the past when they found themselves in a like predicament. I had to leave some behind," he said as if helpless to have done anything else. "It was just us, our

189

own crew, and a few of the other captains that got away. We took what we could carry, which was most of the treasure, and we got out overland."

"And what of the men you left to their fate?"

"It did come out right enough, pet," he assured against the anger that flashed in his daughter's glare. "Spain wanted to keep the peace with England more than they wanted revenge 'gainst those we'd left behind. Lucky for them, they didn't know yet that old King Carlos of Spain was going to up and die and leave his country to King Louis of France's nephew. They let 'em go. Anyways, most of 'em."

"Perhaps so they'll be free to take their vengeance on you," Jamie stated. " 'Twould serve you right! Papa, how could you do such a thing!" She stared at him with eyes full of disappointment.

"I know, lass, I know," Morgan looked properly chastised. "But there was no other way or everything would have been lost. And it was such a great lot of wealth."

"Then tell me, if the men you stranded are free, why didn't they report your actions in deserting them to the nearest British authority?"

"They would have, I reckon, except luck has been with your papa." He grinned and continued. "Can I help it if about the time we was taking Panama our own king gets his ire up against all of Europe? He's mad at Louis again and we're at war with France and Spain now because of the way the old king left his will. They didn't know that yet on Panama when they set the men free, but now, 'tis legal again to prey on Spanish ships and colonies so yer papa can't be arrested for taking part in a venture for the Crown, now can he?"

"So they gave you a knighthood and governorship as reward for deserting your friends," she said harshly. Many of those people he had left behind were men she had known all her life.

"Aye, well you can thank yer precious Franco for the idea that saved my hide!" Morgan grumbled, uncomfortably on the defensive.

"What does Franco have to do with it? You said he didn't join you."

" 'Twas his idea that brought me here. Don't ye think I know that now that the men are free, some of them won't be thinking of nothing else but sticking a dagger into me back? Do ye have any pity for your papa's predicament? I had no choice but to leave the islands. Least'a ways, till memories grow dim. 'Twas Franco told me to come here. He said if I turned the treasure over to the Crown, as if I had done the deed out of loyalty to the Crown, I might get pardoned if anyone did report what happened. At the least, those who are after me can't find me so easy. I didn't tell ye I was here till now because I wasn't as sure as him that this idea of his would work. After all, the one he come up with himself to have revenge on his brother didn't come out like he wanted. I didn't want ye visiting yer papa in jail. Don't think I ain't sorry for what I done, deserting the men, but I'll make it up to them. I swear to you, pet. I'm governor of Royale now, and a mighty rich man. Even after turning much of the treasure in to the king's own coffers, he let me keep a goodly portion as reward and I'll pay it back to the men I left behind when we get home again."

"Do you swear it?" Never before had she asked Morgan for his word but she felt, at this moment, as if the tables had been turned, with her the parent and her father as the wayward child.

"I do, pet. I swear it." Morgan held his hand up to gesture his vow. "Besides, ye'll be with me when we go home again, to keep me to my promise."

"Yes, I suppose I will," she said thoughtfully, remember-

191

ing that if she went home to the islands now, Franco would be there. His assurances had all been a lie. He hadn't sent for her. Hadn't even sent word that he was there. At this minute, she didn't know if she could face seeing him again. To look into his eyes and see nothing remembered of the feelings they had shared might be more than she could bear. On the other hand, her disappointment made her angry. How could he be there, living on Tortuga and Jamaica, and never once so much as inquire about her welfare? Two years of patience and for what? Waiting for a promise he had found so easy to break, or never intended to keep. The hurt at this moment cut deep. While she had worried, he had been safe. While she turned down offers from would-be suitors to attend the various balls and parties London offered, he had been doing as he pleased. She had until spring to make up her mind to stay here and make a new life for herself far away from the islands or to return with Papa, but the very first thing she would do if she did go home again, she promised herself, would be to snub Don Francisco DeCortega and, somehow, make him rue the day he ever elected to forget her!

"Something troubles you. I can see it and what's more, *he* can as well. He asks if he has offended you somehow," Patrick Gordon inquired.

They were standing in the moonlight on the terrace of Lord Grenville's estate. Behind them, music drifted out into the sweet autumn night made fragrant by the last blooms of summer on Lady Grenville's magnificent rose hedges. Through the glass doors to the ballroom, figures could be seen bowing and dipping and turning in time to the music. Jamie had tried to enjoy herself, but her troubled mind would not let her. Tsar Peter stood before her, a look of concern and query on his handsome face.

How could anyone say they were not properly chaperoned, she thought, since, without a translator, they couldn't exchange a word. It was Lord Gordon's turn to assume that duty again and he had given Lacey over to Lord Osbourne to entertain. For Lacey's sake, for Tsar Peter's, she had tried to keep a light mood and enjoy herself, but apparently she wasn't succeeding in fooling anyone.

"Please assure him, Lord Gordon, he has done nothing whatever. It isn't him at all. It's . . ." How could she say it was Franco, her almost-one-time fiancé she had mentioned at the picnic, who, she had since found out, was a faithless liar and scoundrel? "You belong to me," he had told her. Indeed! Yes, a toy he had elected to abandon, a prize he had won that had lost its value over time and distance, if she had truly ever meant anything to him at all!

The hurt was too deep to even tell Lacey about it yet. Lacey certainly knew something was amiss ever since Jamie had spoken with her father, but she seemed to sense this was one time she should refrain from pursuing her usual course of avid curiosity. She had left Jamie alone about what had happened in the interview, trying to cheer her, for a pleasant change waiting until Jamie was ready to broach the subject.

"It's . . ." Jamie tried to form the words to say it was nothing, but suddenly her torn emotions were too much for her. She had no willpower left to contain it. Tears began to fill her eyes and overflow, spilling down her cheeks to splash on the crimson velvet of her elegant gown. A huge sob burst out of her and all at once she was crying. It was everything—Franco's faithless promise, her disappointment in Morgan, her longing for home, all the anger and hurt pouring out of her in a torrent of tears.

She felt the tsar's arm come around her, drawing her into a comforting embrace as he let her cry against the soft

193

black velvet of his frockcoat. Behind her back, he signaled Lord Gordon to leave the balcony, then, alone with her on the terrace, he held her and rocked her, whispering soothing Russian words in her ear while she wept.

"It's . . . it's just everything," she confessed a short while later when Lord Gordon had been called back so that they could understand each other. "Everything in my life seems to have gone wrong now. Everything I thought I wanted to do with it has been changed."

Lord Gordon was an excellent translator, far better than Lord Osbourne who had to listen until a speaker finished, form the words into Russian, and then express them in their nearest equivalent. What took Osbourne minutes to do, Patrick Gordon accomplished instantly, translating even while she was speaking. She had found that the only time he paused between listening and relating was when he wanted to rephrase something he felt might be lost or misunderstood if he translated exactly, or if he wanted to add a word or two of his own. Just now, though, he was keeping pace with her precisely, repeating her words in Russian almost in the same instant she spoke them. With his excellent talent and speed, it was as if she was talking to the tsar directly, making it much easier for her to release her long-held-back disappointments in a flood of explanations she desperately needed to set free.

She couldn't tell Lacey these things. Lacey would sympathize and become angry herself and, thinking she was far more mature and wiser than she was, she would offer words of advice that she insisted Jamie had to follow.

Neither could Jamie bring herself to confide in Lady Westcott, not for lack of trust in the headmistress or fear that the headmistress would not understand, but simply because Jamie was still not at ease enough with members

194

of her own sex.

In every tribulation of her life, she had always gone to a man for comfort—when she was small, to Morgan and later, to Jocko, or Rory, or occasionally to Ned. Her mother had shut her out, finally and irrevocably through death. Mary had been a comforting presence, but was always busy with household bustle. Jamie hadn't even met Polly Hascombe until she was fourteen and by then her pattern of life had been established.

While her mother had stayed in bed with her disappointments, Mary had told her it was Morgan's huge hands that held her through her first steps. 'Twas Morgan who put the first spoon in her fist and told her she could damn well feed herself and that she had promptly splashed him with her porridge. 'Twas Morgan who heard the first clear word she had spoken, "No!" and the second, "Papa." Later, she had gone to Jocko with problems she couldn't take to her father, usually because the problem she needed advice about *was* her father. But it had always been the male scent, of ale and tobacco, of canvas or hemp, that offered her olfactory comfort, unyielding muscles that she leaned against for security, and deep voices that soothed her. Perhaps for that reason, she found herself telling everything to the two men on the terrace with her, the words easily tumbling out of her into their sympathetic ears.

She told them about Franco and how he had won her when her father put her up as a wager. She revealed that Franco had been her first love, her only love, and that she had waited so long only to discover he never meant to keep his vows. She explained how her father had earned his new title and her disappointment in him for what he had done. At places in her narrative, she wondered if she might be revealing too much, but one look into their sympathetic eyes told her neither of her listeners condemned her for

195

anything she had done. Tsar Peter understood, perhaps far better than most Englishmen would have with their more self-righteous attitudes and high-minded ideals regarding womanhood.

In Peter's country, the women were a lustier breed than their European counterparts—not among the nobility of old Moscovy who kept women shut away with Byzantine, male-dominating authority, but among the peasant classes where a woman worked beside her husband, slept beside him, and played beside him. Western Europeans who first ventured within Russia's borders were scandalized to find farm women taking a break from their chores to frolic naked with their husbands in the icy lakes and streams. The Russian serf classes were cleaner than western Europeans from their frequent bathing. They were hardier and far healthier than the lice-ridden, perfume-reeking, "civilized" westerners. While Peter admired many of the western customs and advances in technology and utterly despised the archaic, backward ideas and morals of his own Byzantine-structured court, he had learned rather early in life to appreciate and adopt what he liked and ignore or alter whatever did not appeal to him. The man who, in fifty years, would become known to history as "Pyotr Veliki," Peter the Great, had already selected the manners and customs he adopted for himself and would, on his return to Moscow, insist that his people learn as well if he had to ram such new and advanced ideas straight down their throats. He approved of the western custom of bringing women into male society and sharing their company. He did *not* accept the western concept that ladies should be set up on pedestals and insisted they behave with a different set of standards than those expected of men.

Peter had assumed the throne under the regency of his half sister, Sophia, as a boy of ten, co-ruling with a half-brother, Ivan, who was too ill and weak to take on any of the duties of state. When Ivan died and Peter reached his majority, he had to forcefully oust his ambitious sister from power and had ruled since then with the iron hand of the absolute monarch. In Moscow there was a saying that "God rules in Heaven, the Tsar rules on Earth."

During the course of the European tour thus far, foreign courts had been amazed by his avid curiosity and intelligence, pleased by his willingness to adopt western culture, and appalled in the very next moment when he would berate one of his own retainers who displeased him with the equivalent of "off with his head."

While he frightened some of her countrymen, Jamie thought Tsar Peter was not particularly difficult to become used to. In many ways he was very like Morgan, large, boisterous, quick to become enraged, and terrifying while he was in that state. But when his dark mood passed it was easy to get back into his good graces. She saw retainers in his group practically sentenced to death one day and laughing and joking with the tsar the very next.

After she confessed all her tribulations that evening at Lord Grenville's ball, she found her burden somewhat lighter for having shared it. Tsar Peter asked her not to be too harsh in her judgments of both Franco and her father's actions. Perhaps Franco had other reasons for not coming for her as they had planned. After all, he explained, he had not succeeded in redeeming himself and might fear feeling ashamed in her eyes. She told him he didn't know Franco, as she couldn't imagine him feeling shame over anything, but eventually agreed with Peter that there might be reasons she didn't know about. Still, she informed him, she would never forgive him for breaking his promise. About Morgan's actions in Panama, Peter said there were times when a leader was forced to desert his army so that he was preserved as head of state and would be free to fight another day. Jamie had gazed into Tsar

Peter's eyes and asked him openly, "Would you have done it?" After a moment's reflection while he seemed to examine his conscience, he admitted, no, he would not have.

Feeling she had lost one argument and won the next, they returned to the festivities and Jamie found the gay party a shade easier to bear. Over the next few weeks, she spent increasingly more time in Tsar Peter's company, invited to balls and weekend excursions held in his honor in the guise of entertaining their Russian guests visiting their country. Sometimes he played his anonymity game with his hosts — sometimes not. When he was in the mood for it, he might make one of his tallest nobles dress in elegant clothes, seat him in the place of honor, and have him introduced as the tsar while Peter himself stood behind the false tsar's place pretending to be one of the retainers, letting Jamie realize that was just what it was for him, a game, and all of the pomp and circumstance surrounding royalty, only nonsense he enjoyed making fun of. On other occasions, when he felt Jamie might profit from the attention, he allowed himself to be formally introduced as her escort. And, in fact, the word had gotten around through London society that she was favored by the visiting monarch. Rather than dampening her prospects among the eligible bachelors, her reputation was enhanced instead, with gentlemen vying for her hand on the dance floor on the few occasions she was not partnered by the handsome tsar.

Though Lacey was taking second place to Jamie's spreading fame, her friend was enjoying her own new prospects offered in being Jamie's constant companion.

Due to his new title and position, her father was also being invited to homes where doors would have been closed to him before. The newly appointed governor of Jamaica insisted that his beautiful young daughter accompany him to every function whenever the tsar did not request her attendance, leaving Jamie in a whirlwind of suppers, balls, teas, and receptions throughout the winter. Though she still resided at the school, she seldom had time any longer for classes.

By spring, the ship Lord Osbourne had been commissioned to build was completed and they took the new yacht sailing along the Thames when weather permitted. Once, just the two of them took a rowboat out to explore a tributary and a sudden storm came up, overturning their craft. The frantic searchers found them an hour later, sitting atop the overturned hull, drenched and shivering but laughing about the adventure. Along the way to becoming acquainted, he had asked her to call him Peter Alexeivitch, as his retainers did, and she soon shortened it to just "Peter." He never seemed to tire of her stories of growing up at sea and mentioned his envy of the life she had enjoyed. She was with him when he called on Sir Isaac Newton and was impressed by the way Peter seemed to comprehend all that the elderly scientist imparted to him, facts that left her dizzy trying to understand them, about the earth, and gravity, and how it held us all in place from being hurled off the planet into infinity. For Jamie, her friendship with the tsar had become a very special thing that she would cherish long after he left England to continue his European tour. But never, in her wildest imaginings, had she expected to hear the question Lord Gordon posed to her one sunny April morning in 1696 as the tsar stood gravely behind his interpreter, with a formality she had thought they had long ago dispensed with. Even Lord Gordon was not his usual, conversational self.

"I . . . I don't know what to say," she stammered, aghast at the implications the question presented.

"His Majesty realizes this must be unexpected. You may think it over for a few days if you wish, but we will need an answer by week's end. The tsar sails for Vienna on

199

Saturday next."

"I know." Her head was swimming, her thoughts unable to form clearly. "When he asked if he might see me today, I had no idea it could be about something like this . . ."

"I understand." Lord Gordon smiled sympathetically. "It is a surprise to us all," he said confidentially. "His Majesty can be impulsive and headstrong, as you've no doubt learned from your friendship, but be assured by me, who has known him longer, that he is indeed in earnest."

"Lord Gordon, please." She clutched his velvet sleeve to steady herself. "Explain to me, if you will, how this is possible? He is a king," she said, awed even as she related her puzzlement. "I'm not of the nobility."

Lord Gordon, who was Swiss and retained a slight accent, smiled at her. "Lady Morgan, as you must know by now, in Moscovy, if it is the tsar's wish, it is enough. Russia is not so democratically minded as your English parliament."

"But . . ." Jamie gazed at the tall, attractive man standing before her who had not previously given her so much as a hint that such a thing could have crossed his mind. They were just friends, companions during his stay here, or at least she had always thought so. "But he's married, isn't he?" It was for that very reason that she had promised herself not to become overly attached to him. She liked him enormously, and found him most appealing, but his marriage had stood like a wall between them as far as she was concerned. She had promised herself to put Franco out of her head and open her mind to new romantic entanglements, since he had so obviously deserted her and she would have no choice but to make new plans for her future.

"It is quite true, my lady, that he is wed. However, it was a marriage arranged by their parents and has never been a happy one. He has already made up his mind to

200

divorce the tsarevna. This will be done the moment we return to Moscow."

"For me? Oh, no, I won't hear of it!" Her reaction immediately alerted Peter to her distress and he interrupted to demand Lord Gordon explain her upset. When he had finished, Gordon immediately turned his attention back to her. "I can assure you, Lady Morgan, even without his request that I do so, that he is not divorcing the queen for your sake. It is a decision that was long in the making, reached before you ever became acquainted with His Majesty. Whichever way you choose will not influence matters as they now stand."

"Can he do that?" she queried, recalling the tempest in England's history when Henry VIII divorced Catherine of Aragon for Anne Boleyn.

"The tsar may do as he chooses, my lady," he explained. "Again I remind you, Russia is not England."

"And you do swear to me that I am not the cause of it?"

"I swear it." Gordon smiled and added, "If you knew the queen as I do, you would have no doubt of it either. Believe me, they are very ill suited to one another and it was bound to happen eventually."

"What am I to do, Lord Gordon? In all these months, I never knew he felt like that. I never suspected . . ."

"I suggest only that you give the matter grave thought, my lady. His Majesty has already told me to convey to you that he will wait for your answer until the very last moment before his departure."

Still amazed, Jamie could do no more than drop a brief curtsy as she prepared to depart, but as she turned away, Peter took her hand and turned her around to face him.

"One moment," he said haltingly in words that were uncomfortably foreign to him. During the time they had spent together, he had learned a little of her language and she of his. They could converse together without the aid of

201

the interpreters, if the thoughts expressed were simple enough, in a mixture of his language, hers, and pantomine when all else failed them. He spoke briefly, rapidly, in Russian to Lord Gordon, who then turned to her.

"His Majesty has something he wishes to say to you in private." Gordon bowed, excusing himself as he retreated from the room.

Jamie looked up expectantly at the face she had found attractive from the first time she saw it and she now considered to be that of a very dear and special friend.

"I want to say to you myself," he said slowly, "I have very deep feeling for you," he said, the unfamiliar words thick with accent. "You have been friend and . . . most treasured companion. I wish for you to return to Russia with me and become my wife."

"Peter, I don't know how to answer you." She gazed at him, touched to the point of tears. "I care for you as well. You're my friend. You always will be. But I don't know what to say."

"You will consider this, yes?" he asked.

"I will. Most deeply, I promise you."

Though there had never before been a moment of intimacy between them, Peter suddenly drew her into his arms and kissed her. The kiss was warm, sweet, lasting long enough to convey his passion. His lips were soft yet eager and she found herself responding, kissing him back with an intensity she hadn't known she could feel for him. When he released her, she almost wasn't ready to leave his arms, yet to continue might give him false hope for an affirmative answer she wasn't prepared yet to decide.

"Tomorrow, perhaps, you may answer?" he asked hopefully.

"I shall try," she promised as she detached herself from his arms. She looked back only once, wondering why in the world she couldn't just say yes to him. Franco didn't want her anymore. She owed nothing to the promises they had made and she had no other suitors she cared about. She could be a queen. All she had to do was turn about and run back to him as fast as her feet could fly. Then why couldn't she do it? Yet the reason was not difficult to understand. While her head told her she was a fool, her heart still belonged to another man. Until he was disposed of, out of mind and heart as well, she couldn't, in good conscience, promise her love to anyone else. She would have to see Franco again, even just once, to know that she could put him out of her life forever.

"What am I going to do? Peter has just asked me to become his wife," Jamie confided to Lacey. She had returned to the Westcott School, grabbed Lacey by the arm and practically jerked the girl to her feet, pulling her into an unoccupied sitting room before she told her what had happened.

"What?" Lacey looked shocked, her blue eyes opening wide enough to pop. "What did you say? You've accepted, of course! Tell me that you've accepted."

"I haven't. I couldn't. I can't," Jamie groaned. "I can't wed him, Lacey. It's impossible."

"Whycver not? Are you mad? He's asking you, isn't he? Then he must know it will be acceptable to his people. How can you not accept?"

"It wouldn't be fair to him."

"Why not? You like him, don't you? You've spent so much time together, you can't tell me you don't."

"Of course I like him, but I'm not in love with him."

"Whatever difference does that make?" Lacey blurted with an offhand wave. "To wed a king, I could learn to love him if he was as short as a dwarf and as homely as Barney, our chimney sweep, who is the homeliest man I know, poor soul. And here this one is tall, handsome, as magnificent as any man I've ever seen and you can't bring yourself to accept him? What are you waiting for? Do you still mistakenly think your Franco is going to come?"

"No, I don't believe that anymore but it doesn't matter. I like Peter enormously. He's good and kind and deserves a wife who loves him without reservation. If I can't offer him that, then it would never be fair."

Exasperated, Lacey settled down into the nearest chair with a huge sigh. "Then tell me, pray, just what you are going to do with the rest of your life?"

"I don't know. These past two years, all I've longed for is home. I miss the islands. I miss the sea. It would be foolish of me to contemplate a life that would take me away from all I love best. I know we share a love of sailing and other interests as well, but it takes more than that for a good marriage. I don't think I could live in Russia."

"You couldn't live in a palace?" Lacey squealed in disbelief. "You couldn't be happy with a gorgeous, generous man who adores you and would make you a queen?"

"Peter deserves someone who loves him for himself, not for what he can give her," Jamie said sharply. Peter had tried to lavish presents on her, but Jamie had sent them all back, telling him that Lady Westcott would not allow the girls to accept gifts from gentlemen who were not relatives or a fiancé. "I've made up my mind to it, Lacey. There is no other way for me. I'm going home."

"Are ye daft, girl? Is this why I sent ye here to London to learn ladying, so's ye could go back to the islands and wed some piss poor pirate?"

Jamie had been listening to her father's tirade for some time now as the coach jostled and bounced over the rutted London roads and, in content, it was not one jot different from the one Lacey had subjected her to for the past three days. As she had promised him she would, she wanted to give Peter's proposal serious consideration and had waited to see if a little time might make her think differently, but her mind seemed made up. The more thought she gave it, the more determined she became that Russia wasn't her land and could never be. She liked Peter, she didn't love him, and could never marry at all until she was sure Franco DeCortega was thoroughly out of her system. "I thought you wanted me to come home with you," she said when she could get a word in.

"Aye, if ye've not found a title yet to marry. There are fine lords' sons in the Colonies for ye to choose from, but to have no less than a king himself ask for yer hand and say nay to him, ye must have lost yer senses is all I can say!"

"And you've said it enough!" Jamie returned, her gaze fastened on the countryside outside her window. "I will not marry for position. When I wed, it shall be for love."

"Is that what yer fine girl's school taught ye? To harbor naught but romantic notions in yer head without an ounce of practicality?"

"I've had them myself all along. I never intended to marry without it."

"Aye, ye never intended to whilst ye had no chance for a gentleman's courtship, when ye didn't know no better than the way I raised ye. That's why I sent ye to school! To learn the ladying that would land ye a fine gentleman for a husband! And here ye have the king of a foreign land begging for yer hand and ye turn him away?"

"Doesn't it bother you, Papa, that if I did accept Peter's proposal, I'd like as not never lay eyes on you again?" She turned to gaze at her sire.

Henry Morgan looked as if that thought had not yet occurred to him. He had to search a bit for an answer.

"But it wouldn't mean, would it, that I couldn't visit ye now and again?"

"Russia is very far away," she reminded.

"Aye, so are the So' Seas, yet I been there."

"Once, in forty years," she retorted.

"Then think of how I could rest easy knowing my girl was well taken care of for the rest of her life."

"Would you be so sure, Papa? He's divorcing the present queen. He could divorce me." She didn't really believe Peter would be so fickle, but it did leave Henry briefly silent to ponder a suitable riposte. "But ye'd never give him cause," he finally shouted, gaining volume, as usual, when he felt he might be losing an argument. Jamie had grown quite used to her father's volume and no longer flinched when he started to yell, knowing he did not possess the control over her to strike her now for her disobedience. "Ye'd make him a fine queen!"

"I don't love him, Papa," she said, wishing wistfully for a moment that she could feel differently. Moscovy had been described to her in detail and was a cold land, steeped for many months in winter. As the Russian delegation spoke of their homeland, she realized that, though very frigid for much of the year, the country possessed a rugged beauty that endeared her to her countrymen, but it wasn't her land. She was partial to the warm, sea-scented islands she so sorely missed. With the exception of one hard-won port to the sea, Russia was a landlocked nation. She would gladly relinquish a throne for the salt wind in her face and a rocking deck beneath her feet again. Surely Peter, with his own love of both the sea and his homeland, would understand her reasons. "I'm very fond of Peter, Papa, but I can't marry him," she tried once more to explain to him as she had been trying in vain to explain to Lacey. "He deserves a wife who loves him for himself and not what he can give her or make out of her, and I'm sure that in time

206

he will find one with just those qualifications. It's just not me."

"And who, then, are ye saving yerself for?" Henry returned. "That Spaniard? I told ye that he never onc't asked about ye. Do you think it will be any different once ye're home?"

"I don't care a whit about Franco," she stated angrily. "He's long ago been forgotten by me as well."

"Is that true?" Morgan fixed her with a quizzical stare.

"Of course it's true!" she insisted as the coach pulled to a stop before the manor house of Sayes Court at Deptford. "Now if you will excuse me, I prefer to tell Peter my reasons in person, and alone," she added to stop her father from descending. All along Jamie had kept them from meeting, though both had requested introductions to the other. She realized with a pang of guilt and shame that she was embarrassed to have Peter meet her father. They might share certain traits and physical characteristics in common, but her father could be a genuine pain in the posterior anatomy and she didn't want Peter to know that about him since it was one thing she felt the two did not share. "I shan't be long."

"I still say ye're daft, girl." Her father's words followed her as she was admitted into the house.

"I'm sorry, Peter, and I pray you'll understand," she said, wishing her refusal did not have to be related through a third party, even if it was Lord Gordon. She would have preferred telling Peter what she had to say in complete privacy. She had explained her reasons and her hope that he might understand that she could never accept living anywhere else, just as he could not relinquish his throne or desert his people for her sake.

"I am sorry too," Peter said through his interpreter. "I

wish I could stay longer to change your mind but we've received word from home that there is trouble and we must go back at once."

"And cut short your tour? What's happened?" she asked in concern. With Lord Gordon's excellent ability it was as if they spoke to each other without an interpreter between them and they sometimes forgot his presence.

"It's only my sister again, stirring up trouble against me," Lord Gordon said for Peter. "She has the Streltsy convinced I am never coming back to Moscow." Jamie knew the Streltsy were the standing army of the nation, the Russian palace guard, sworn to obey and defend the tsar and his family. "She has told them I will not return and my wife has joined her in this plot to have my son declared tsar in my place. He's only a boy and not responsible for these acts of his mother and his aunt. I must go back to show them I am still a force to be reckoned with."

"Won't you be in terrible danger?"

"No." He shook his head, smiling to reassure her. "I have my own regiments that I left in charge who are, beyond question, loyal to me. They may quell the rebellion before I even reach home, but then only I can deal with those who moved against me. You must not fear for me. I only regret that I cannot extend my stay here in England if it might change your mind."

"I'm afraid it can't," she said sorrowfully. "I'm leaving, myself, next week, for home." Jamie fought back a choking sob, hating to part from the friend she had made. "I know you'll restore order and then find great happiness someday with someone who will cherish you as you deserve to be cherished. I shall never forget you." Her voice quivered as she stepped forward, on tiptoe, to embrace him. Peter hugged her back briefly, closely, then pushed her away from him, averting his face, yet she managed to see the regret in his eyes as he spoke a final word to her without his interpreter.

"If ever there is anything you need from me . . . anything I can do for you, you have only to ask. If I cannot change your mind, then it is my hope that you find this great love of yours and," he consulted Gordon for a moment, "discover . . . it was not lack of love for you that kept you apart. You also deserve great happiness." He took both her hands in his for a moment. "Remember you always have friend in Moscow."

"And you will always have one in Jamaica." She drew away from him, wondering as she fled if she had just made the biggest mistake of her life.

Chapter Ten

Franco DeCortega stepped off the gangplank onto the busy dockside bustle of Port Royale. The sun shone brightly in a clear sky, the summer heat causing shimmering vapors to rise from the hot cobblestones of the city streets. Sweat-drenched deckhands bore heavy cargoes on their backs while black-frocked merchants kept a watchful eye on their wares as they were loaded or carried off the several ships tied at the docks. A gaggle of passengers were bidding tearful farewells to relatives and friends they were leaving behind while other groups joyously greeted those who were disembarking. Franco made his way past the crowds, ducking into the cool shade of the first tavern doorway offering a haven. He ordered ale, then sat down to drink it at a table in a darkened corner.

For a man who had not been to sea until after his twenty-fifth birthday, he was fast learning both the ways of nature and those of men. The sea was a fickle mistress who smiled good fortune and brisk winds at your back then turned on you without warning in a burst of murderous fury. She was a mistress a man could never trust — treacherous and loving, gentle and harsh, yielding and beautiful, hard and ugly. You hated her and you loved her, frequently knowing both emotions in the course of a single day. Yet she had instilled herself into his blood and he knew he would never be able to leave her now.

Though he had not thought so then, perhaps his had been a sheltered life in Spain. Certainly he was no longer the same as when he left his father's house as a youth of eclectic tastes and high ideals. The sea had made more than a man of him, hardening his body as she had altered his mind.

Nearing thirty now, his frame had filled out, his muscles more sinewy and bulging where they had been only firm before. The glare of the sun on the water had added distinctive lines to the corners of his eyes and mouth. His hair, once burnished ebony, had faded to a slight reddish tinge, burned by the harsh tropical sunlight, and the fair skin of the DeCortega ancestors was permanently tanned to bronze.

Francisco Alonzo Montenegro DeCortega, the youngest son of Conde Carlos DeCortega and his gentle wife, Isabella Montenegro, was feeling the effects of having just ordered a man flogged, then having stood on the deck of his ship hearing the man's cries of agony, watching unwincingly as the lash was applied, counting the strokes until the last one fell and the unfortunate victim was at last taken down to be tended. At sea, there were no prison terms to be served, no courts, no justices, no magistrates. There was only the captain's law and it had to be obeyed.

Over the past two years, Franco had learned that a captain was a man set apart from his fellows. He had no one to turn to for counsel or advice. Unlike a naval vessel or merchant ship where the courses she sailed were determined by the owners, the buccaneers often voted on where they would go or the risks they were willing to take for a venture, but the final decisions in all petty squabbles or major disagreements eventually rested with their leader. He had to be a fair man but a taskmaster. He had to walk a tight rope between being the man they could turn to for a loan to tide them over and being able to instill the fear of God in their breasts. They might laugh with him, but never at him. He had to push them without ever driving them to the limits of their endurance.

Franco disliked punishing a man with the lash, having him trussed up and whipped until the flesh peeled off his back, but if he refused to show them that he would punish infractions severely, he would lose the respect of the crew who followed him and then he would lose command. If he failed to employ harsh measures, if he failed to choose their ventures wisely, if he failed to lead, they would quickly desert him to seek out another man to follow.

As captain of the *Isabella,* he was fair and the sailor had earned his punishment, but the late count's once democratically minded son found the injustice of relying on a single despot's judgment galling. Franco had ordered the offender relieved of duty until his wounds healed. It was his one visible weakness, that no man would suffer unduly aboard his ship. This was not the first time he had ordered punishment, nor would it be the last, but each time he employed such measures, he found he had to quiet his conscience with enough ale or rum to take the recurring scene away from him and give him peace.

As he sipped the bitter brew in his quiet corner of the tavern, his mind drifted back to the first time he set foot on Royale, when he bid the tearful Jamie farewell and found passage for Spain on a homebound ship. What an innocent fool he had been then. Jocko had tried to warn him, and Ned Shanks had seconded his opinion that Lorenzo, having gone as far as he did, would not be easily stopped. How well they had understood the larcenous mind as Franco had not.

Franco had come home again only to find the gates of his house barred against him. After his father's death, his mother had retired to a convent and both his sisters had been quickly married off to the first men who would take them at half their dowry each. Learning that his brother had come back, Lorenzo had worked rapidly to protect all that he had usurped. How, he suggested to the elderly and sick King Carlos, could Franco have been freed from his captivity unless he had joined the pirates, willingly accompanied them on ventures against the Spanish Crown, had, indeed, turned pirate himself to have left their clutches alive? Franco learned the full extent of Lorenzo's treachery when soldiers arrived at the inn where he was staying, presenting a warrant for his arrest. His expertise with his saber helped him to escape, but he soon discovered he could not expect to find aid or shelter anywhere in the country. Staying just ahead of the king's soldiers, he wrote a long and detailed letter to the king, explaining the circumstances he had been facing and how he had come to be released, but either the king's mind had been closed on the subject or King Carlos personally never read the missive. He sought out old friends of the family in hope of finding allies, but Lorenzo had reached them all first. Even those who were inclined to believe him feared offending Conde Lorenzo DeCortega, now one of the richest men in Spain.

Franco found himself with no other option but to leave his homeland, defeated in his goal of reclaiming his legacy, condemned as a pirate and hounded by the soldiers of the king trailing his every move. Narrowly escaping capture several times, he finally bought passage on a ship bound for the Caribbean.

Morgan had once offered him a ship of his own. Condemned as a pirate, he might as well be one and bide his time until someday, somehow, fate might turn the tables and put Lorenzo in his grasp.

Although uncertain that Morgan would take him, Franco was welcomed by Shanks and Chalks and several of the pirate captains he had once gone to such trouble to win over in friendship. Morgan was more reticent, but decided, eventually, to let him try. "If ye want a ship of yer own," Morgan had told him, "then steal it like the rest of us." He had thrown back his massive head and laughed. Later, Jocko took him aside and told him how such a theft might be accomplished.

In the dead of a moonless night, ten pirates promised a percentage out of the venture, took a raft alongside a sleeping Spanish frigate anchored in Havana Harbor. With the ship guarded by sleepy watchmen, the pirates crept over the side, overpowered the sentries, and awakened the crew with cutlasses against their throats. Franco promised them their lives if they remained silent until the ship was safely out of the harbor, then later gave them the lifeboats to sail back to the colony. Five of them, there and then, signed on with him to make their fortunes as buccaneers. The ship he had stolen had a cargo of spices and tobacco stored in her hull and Franco used his portion of the profits to hire more sailors to fill out his crew. He had a mixed bag of ruffians under his command. Spaniards, English, Dutch, and one Frenchman who spoke hardly a word of English or Spanish when he came.

Since then, Franco had learned a good number of the tricks and ruses employed by the pirates in search of prey and had invented a few of his own. In his cabin, he had a flag from every nation that could be hoisted as the occasion might call for it, signaling a supposed ally ship closer with distress flags, not letting them see the Jolly Roger until they were too near to escape. Other times, a small band might pretend to be stranded on a deserted isle and lure a ship into sending a lifeboat out to rescue them. Overpowering the lifeboat's crew, they then sailed back to the ship with a dozen pirates hidden beneath a tarp in the bottom of the boat. The truth was only revealed when the startled seamen found themselves overpowered by the swarm of pirates scrambling over the sides. Since his return, Franco's ventures had been successful and profitable, giving him a crew that was bound to him by the loyalty of greed. His cunning had earned him the respect of the buccaneers and eventually won him a place on the Brethren's Counsel. His opinions were heeded, and though he hadn't been able to convince many of the buccaneers that Morgan's plan to take Panama was foolhardy, he had been proven right.

"Well, well, Cap'n DeCortega. It's been a while since I've seen ye, man. Where have ye been keeping yerself?"

Franco looked up to see Jocko Chalks coming toward him. Shortly after Morgan left for England, Jocko had purchased this tavern on Royale to test out the life of a landsman. Since he, Ned, and most of the *Lady Morgan* crew had escaped Panama with their captain, and since they had shared in the treasure, Jocko was not one of those who bore ill will toward his absent leader.

"I've been here and there." Franco was pleased to see the dark giant. The better he came to know Chalks, the more he liked the man. Being preoccupied with his thoughts, he hadn't noticed it was Jocko's tavern he entered. "Sit down and share a pint with me," he offered.

"I believe I will." Jocko lowered his beefy frame into the cane chair across from him, signaling the barmaid to bring him a tankard.

"It appears as if you're doing well here, Jocko."

"Well enough, I reckon. I'm turning a nice profit but there ain't much excitement in it," he confessed. "A few fights, now and again, t'wixt the customers and a few heads to break, but it ain't like the old days, and I miss it, I do."

"You could buy your own ship," Franco suggested.

"Aye, but 'twould never be the same. I'm a first mate,

not a cap'n. Now, when we sailed on the *Lady,* those were the times," he said wistfully. "But I'll not see them again, with Cap'n Morgan now all respectable."

"Perhaps he'll be back," Franco offered. Knowing Morgan, he wouldn't stay away forever.

"He is back." Jocko gazed at him. "Didn't ye hear?"

"Hear what?"

"Morgan's been back near a month already. First thing he done on landing was come to look me up. It pleased me, it did, him being a fine gentleman now and not forgetting any of us what used to sail with him. Ye mean to say, ye haven't heard a word about it?"

"We just came in to port."

"Oh, well then, ye don't know." Jocko seemed pleased to be the newsbearer. "Cap'n Morgan is back, and he's been made governor now of this whole blessed island." The first mate roared with laughter. "I reckon they figured there wasn't nobody else who could govern it anyways, as Morgan founded it and it was his town to start. So now, we're all legal-like, a colony of His Majesty's government, don't ye know." Again, the hulk bellowed with laughter. "We all had a good chuckle over it, him and me and most of the old crew what sailed with us. Had us a welcome-home party right here in this tavern of mine. He's the duly appointed governor with papers and all and he has that title he was always pining for as well. He's Sir Henry now, don't ye know."

So, out of his scoundrel's deed, Morgan had returned well rewarded, Franco thought as he listened. "What of the men who were after him for the fiasco on Panama?"

Jocko grinned. "Most have done forgive him as he came back a rich man and he paid 'em off just about what was their due. For the rest, I don't much think they'll try anything now. 'Tis one thing to murder a pirate and another to kill yerself a governor, ain't it? He's safe enough, I expect. Least he has been since he come. He bought hisself the old Addison mansion, at the top of the hill. The one that looks down on the whole town. Ye remember it. Now, it's the governor's mansion."

"And he still receives his old comrades?" Franco asked, amused by the turn of events. Unbelievably, Morgan always somehow came out on top.

"Aye, he's not much changed when ye come right down to it. We're still his mates like we always was. Ye ought to drop in on him. He'd see ye for certain."

"Perhaps I'll do that," Franco pondered aloud. "Indeed, perhaps I will."

Announcing himself to the liveried servant who answered the door, Franco found it ironic that Morgan had managed to save himself and at the same time earn a governorship out of such a misbegotten adventure. He could well imagine how the ruffian Welshman had appeared at court, but Jocko was undoubtedly right that they gave him Jamaica because no one else could hope to hold the colony for the Crown. Probably he would maintain discipline and dispense justice for the colony the same way he had as captain of the *Lady Morgan*, with a swift kick in the pants for all offenders.

"If you will follow me, sir." The servant escorted him into the wide, sun-drenched library. There were leather-bound books lining the shelves, and behind a massive, dark oak desk, an expanse of windows and a patio door by which one could walk out into the flower-decked garden beyond. "I will see if the governor can receive you." The man bowed elegantly and departed, leaving Franco alone in the handsomely furnished room.

While he was looking over the book titles, a burst of feminine laughter caught his ear. The sound certainly

217

wasn't Polly's coarse chuckle, but delicate, refined, the lilting laughter of a lady. Had Morgan married? he wondered as he followed voices coming in through the open door. His curiosity aroused, he peered out at two men and a woman standing in the garden several yards away. The gentlemen, both dressed in fine suits of gay-colored summer silk, were obviously vying for the attention of the young lady. Her back was toward him but he saw a slender figure in a becoming gown of white taffeta, embroidered at hem and sleeves in bottle-green silken threads, the pattern intricate and delicate. Her black hair was unswept. Emeralds fastened in the tresses caught the sunlight in flashing sparks. One of her swains said something that caused her to turn slightly toward the gentleman. First he placed the sound of her voice and then the profile. Jamie. It couldn't be, yet it was. He hadn't given thought to it when Jocko told him Morgan had returned but, of course, Jamie had come back with him.

He had always known her possibilities—even then, the girl was stunningly beautiful—but the woman she had become left him breathless so that all he could do was stand and stare at the elegant vision before him. She was the epitome of feminine grace in her every fluid motion. Was it that she had filled out from a more girlish figure of two years past or were the seeming changes only wrought by the gown she wore that flattered the same shapely form she had always possessed?

One of the men noticed his presence and stopped talking to gaze at him expectantly.

"Forgive me, I didn't mean to intrude," Franco said, walking out into the garden to join them.

"You aren't intruding at all, sir," the young man said politely, but the look he extended to Franco revealed clearly that the suitor wished he might disappear back into the shadows he had come from. Apparently the other

218

young man flanking her was sufficient competition in his mind for one afternoon.

"Franco DeCortega at your service, sir." Franco bowed as he introduced himself.

"Edward Harcourt," the young swain returned. "This is Lord Arthur Easton," he indicated the other gentleman. "And may I present . . ."

"We've met, Edward," Jamie said abruptly, glaring at Franco with cold disdain. "Captain DeCortega is a very old friend of my father's." She stressed just the right words to point out the difference between Franco's age and that of her courtiers, who were barely into their twenties—in Franco's estimation, still wet behind the ears. "How nice to see you again, Captain." She offered her hand and Franco took it, kissing the back of it a bit more passionately than courtesy dictated. When he failed to release her fingers, she jerked her hand free of his grasp.

"I didn't know you were back," he said, finding her icy reception amusing. She was giving herself away as clearly as if she was greeting him by running into his arms instead. She hadn't forgotten him. Quite the contrary, to be so openly hostile. "May I say, mistress, you're more beautiful than ever," he remarked. Maturity had increased her comeliness and tutoring in England had only applied polish to her attributes.

"I thank you for the flattery, sir, but I believe Johnson is awaiting you. Father must be ready to receive you." She indicated the library doorway where the servant stood looking out at them.

"Of course. Perhaps we will meet again to talk over old times." He smiled at her and was rewarded with a deep scowl.

"Perhaps," she replied haughtily. "Good day, sir."

"Who is he, Jamie?" he could hear one of her courtiers asking as he left them.

219

"As I told you, simply an old friend of Father's . . ."

Jocko was correct that Morgan was the same blustering oaf he had been when he left. His clothes were finer but his manners had hardly been improved by the transition. He seemed honestly pleased to see Franco, probably for the opportunity to brag about all he had accomplished since Panama, and seemed to have forgiven him for being right about the venture. As Morgan talked on through the afternoon, Franco gazed past the governor's desk, looking for any sign of Jamie on the sun-drenched lawn beyond the gleaming windows, but she never appeared. When Morgan finally extended an invitation to stay and sup with them, Franco graciously accepted.

Unfortunately, the two swains as well were invited and took seats on either side of her at the long dining-room table. Apparently not having expected him to stay, Jamie blanched for a moment when she saw him, then studiously ignored his presence, focusing all her considerable charm on her guests. Though he had always believed in her ability if ever she had the opportunity, Franco was amazed at the progress she had made in so short a time. She seemed as if she had been born to elegance and grace. He also saw other new traits he didn't approve of as, where once she had been direct and honest, she had learned to be coy and flirtatious for her captivated audience. That she was probably stretching her newfound wiles for his benefit had not been missed by him, but he still didn't like it.

Presiding over the elegantly set table, Morgan had picked up a few manners along the way, carefully employing both his utensils and his napkin with respectable skill. Throughout the dinner served in several courses, he noticed Jamie taking great pains to center her attention on her friends at the far end of the table, leaving him to

Morgan to entertain.

"Aye, she's changed a bit, ain't she?" Morgan leaned toward him, speaking in a conspiratorial tone so that he couldn't be overheard by the young people. "I've noticed yer eye on her all of this evening and ye can forget whatever it is ye have in mind."

"Morgan, for pity's sake," Franco sighed.

"Ye can't fool an old devil like me," the governor said with a wink. "I'm just letting ye know up ahead, fair warning, ye might say, that ye've lost any chance you once might of had with her. Sorry to say it, Bucko, but since ye've lost yer land and yer wealth and position, ye have naught to offer her now."

"I'm well aware of that," Franco snapped crossly to the delight of the old scoundrel, who took great pleasure out of managing to crawl beneath Franco's skin.

"Aye, well, I'd just rather not see ye wind up broken-hearted. The tables has sort of been turned, ain't they?" Morgan chuckled. "Once she wasn't good enough and now look, ye're nothing to even dream of courting her," he cackled unmercifully. "There's justice in this here world after all, ain't there?"

Franco scowled but remained silent. Morgan would believe what he chose to believe in spite of any argument Franco might offer. He had never thought Jamie not "good enough." His concern had been for her welfare. But circumstances had indeed changed from what they had been.

"Of course, yer captain of yer own ship and probably a fairly rich man by now. There's that to be said for ye, but me Jamie is more particular than she was. Why, she turned down the hand of a king 'cause she didn't want to live in the country he come from." Morgan sat back, patting his full stomach and emitting a low belch. "She did, ye know," he stated. "Smart that was of her too, I'll tell ye. Kings is always at risk of losing their crowns in some venture or another and that ain't for me Jamie. She wants her security out of the man she weds. Besides, 'twas a land-locked nation he come from and she has too much of me in her and needs to be near the sea. She told him no, flat, and sent the poor man home with a broken heart, I'm afeared. Jamie will pick her a man with a solid family name behind him and not one who could lose it all some-day." He stressed the pertinent words for Franco's benefit. The old pirate had forgotten only one thing and that was that Franco knew Jamie too well to believe what he was imparting. She would adore the man she married before she ever undertook such vows, and money and position, even future security, would not matter. He couldn't believe she could have changed that much from the girl he had known.

"Now ye take those two there," Morgan furthered, gaz-ing down the table at Jamie's pair of eager swains. "One belongs to the house of Marlborough, and the other is as rich as Midas. Now which do ye think she'll be choosing?"

"Probably neither one," Franco replied. "As she doesn't appear overly impressed by either."

Morgan bellowed with hearty laughter, catching the at-tention of the young people for a moment. "Ye may be right on that."

After dessert was served, the company retired to the drawing room and Franco remained, hoping for an oppor-tunity to speak to Jamie alone but soon more friends dropped in and it appeared that it might be a long evening. He was about to give up and try to see her an-other day when Edward, the one "rich as Midas," escorted her out onto the patio. This would be his chance that might not easily come again. Explaining that it was grow-ing late and he should be off, he bid Morgan and the others good night, then strolled out to the terrace to bid farewell to Jamie. The patio led to a garden path that would bring him around to the driveway in front of the mansion without having to go through the house. The couple stood side by side at the balustrade, gazing out onto the moon-drenched lawn. Even though he believed she still cared for him and the interest in Harcourt was an act for his benefit, he couldn't keep down the wave of jealousy that swept over him seeing the pair together. Now if he could only find a way to rid himself of Jamie's suitor.

"Good evening," he said, smiling as he approached them.

"Are you leaving, Captain DeCortega?" Edward Harcourt asked him. "'Tis early yet."

"Indeed, but I have a busy day on the morrow. I only came to bid you both a good night. It is rather chilly out here though, isn't it? And, Mistress Morgan, your shoulders are bare?" He pretended great concern. "Perhaps I should leave you my frockcoat . . ."

"That will not be necessary, Captain," she said brusquely. "Edward?"

"Yes?" He turned to her, obviously well smitten, for which Franco did not blame him. "Oh, oh yes, I'll fetch your shawl for you."

Edward was off at a fast clip, crossing the drawing room and straight up the stairs. Franco couldn't resist a chuckle. A well-trained dog could not have responded faster to do her bidding. All she need have added was the command to "fetch" and, slaveringly, Edward would have obeyed.

"I trust that upon his return you will at least toss the poor lad a bone," he remarked, coming up to take Edward's place at her side. She only glared at him, then turned to look at the moonlit scenery.

"You can't seriously be considering him as a worthy suitor," he remarked.

"And why not?"

"He wouldn't suit you. Not at all."

She turned a flashing gaze upon him, bristling with instant anger. "And I suppose you can be the judge of what suits me?"

He moved slightly closer, only inches away. "Tell me, who knows you better than I do?"

Jamie spun away from him, cross and indignant. "You do not know me at all, Captain DeCortega! And I find it presumptuous of you to suppose that you do." Her vocabulary had certainly improved, but her training had not managed to dampen the fire of her temper. He remembered the anger she had expressed on the first night they shared together, the blazing rage shining in her eyes, the quiver of her lips, the stubborn set of her chin. He had learned then that Jamie was hardly the shy mouse he had thought she was.

"Perhaps." He smiled, refusing to be perturbed by her anger. "But before you convince yourself you despise me, I should think the least you could do is hear me out."

"On what subject?" she snapped. "Anything you might have to say could not possibly have the slightest interest for me."

"Even if I explained why I broke my promises to you? Why I never came for you, or sent word to you that I had returned?"

Jamie looked away, but not before he had seen the expression on her face that betrayed her. She would give anything to know just that. After all this time, she still loved him and he was heartened to realize it.

"I couldn't possibly care less. I was a child then," she said, turning back to him in better control. "I assure you I am quite over any silly infatuations of youth."

"Are you?" he asked, watching the lighthearted look she gave him fade before his eyes. "If so, I will not trouble you again, but I will have you know it was not for the reasons you think."

"Oh? And what could they be then?" she queried sni-

224

ACCEPT YOUR **FREE GIFT** AND EXPERIENCE MORE OF THE PASSION AND ADVENTURE YOU LIKE IN A HISTORICAL ROMANCE

Zebra Romances are the finest novels of their kind and are written with the adult woman in mind. All of our books are written by authors who really know how to weave tales of romantic adventure in the historical settings you love.

Because our readers tell us these books sell out very fast in the stores, Zebra has made arrangements for you to receive at home the four newest titles published each month. You'll never miss a title and home delivery is so convenient. With your first shipment we'll even send you a FREE Zebra Historical Romance as our gift just for trying our home subscription service. No obligation.

BIG SAVINGS AND **FREE** HOME DELIVERY

Each month, the Zebra Home Subscription Service will send you the four newest titles as soon as they are published. (We ship these books to our subscribers even before we send them to the stores.) You may preview them *Free* for 10 days. If you like them as much as we think you will, you'll pay just $3.50 each and *save $1.80 each month* off the cover price. *AND you'll also get FREE HOME DELIVERY.* There is never a charge for shipping, handling or postage and there is no minimum you must buy. If you decide not to keep any shipment, simply return it within 10 days, no questions asked, and owe nothing.

dely. "Will you tell me again 'twas for my own good?"

"It was," he stated.

"Or was it for Don Francisco DeCortega's sake that you couldn't be bothered to even inquire about my welfare?"

"What?" he asked, perplexed.

"You didn't even *ask!*" she accused. "You didn't care if I was dead or alive."

"Of course I asked!"

"My father would not lie to me about it!"

"I never asked your father," he returned. "I asked Jocko. He told me where you were. Ask him. He won't deny it." The content of his speech seemed to reach through her anger, bringing her up short. "He told me you were at school in England. Under the circumstances, I thought it the best place for you to be. At last your father had done something right for you and I shouldn't interfere. Not then. And not now when I can no longer offer you marriage."

Jamie looked up abruptly, her frown of anger turning into a troubled stare. "You've married?"

"Certainly not." He smiled, amused that that was the first thought that entered her beautiful head. "And I can't hope to until I've settled other problems first. How then could I have sent for you and taken you away from all you were accomplishing. You've fulfilled every promise of your youth and more. You had to stay where you were. I could not have you leave it for me."

"What problems?" Jamie asked, seeming to have heard only that and nothing more.

"Not here." He could hear Edward returning. "If you decide you would know the answer, my ship is the *Isabella*. She is moored at the docks."

"I trust you will not hold your breath," she replied icily, her anger intact again.

"I can but live on hope," he replied, raising her hand to

225

his lips just as Edward walked out onto the patio, Jamie's shawl draped over his arm. "I bid you good evening, then, Mistress Morgan." He bowed to Harcourt, then walked away, using the garden path.

"He seems a decent chap," Edward assessed, watching Franco depart. He held the shawl up to Jamie's shoulders but she swung away from him.

"Oh, what would you know about it!" she snapped in sudden foul humor, then glared at the shawl in his hands. "Keep it! I have no need of it!" She stormed inside the house, leaving the perplexed young man on the terrace with the shawl slung between his hands.

Sitting alone in the window seat in her bedroom, Jamie wondered if she had really been so transparent. She had known since she came back to the island that sooner or later she would cross his path. Her joy at being home again, at seeing old friends from the *Lady Morgan* crew, and meeting new ones, had been marred every moment by the fear of running into Franco at some unexpected moment. How would she react? How would he seem once she laid eyes on him again? Would she feel as she once did about him or wonder what she had ever seen in him from the start? In the two months she had been home, every time she walked through the streets of Port Royale, shopping in the many stores that lined the avenues, she hadn't been able to resist peering closely at every tall stranger, looking for his face. Any form that even casually resembled his, she couldn't keep from staring at until the man turned about or came closer and she could see it wasn't him. In the taverns when she would dine with the young friends she had made since her return, she continually chose a seat facing the door so she could look up each time someone entered.

The one place, though, where she had never expected to run into him had been in her own home, the house Morgan had bought in Royale in keeping with his governor's standing. She had turned around and there he was. Looking at him again, seeing the ghost she had sought on every street corner and in every tavern, suddenly there in flesh and blood before her, her head had reeled, leaving her dizzy for a moment. He looked the same, no, better, than she remembered. Still so handsome he left her knees weak. He was dressed impeccably, as always, in the neat black and white he seemed to prefer. He never wore satin, silk, or velvet. No ruffles of lace adorned his chest or sleeves. His jewels consisted only of the signet ring he had been given by his father. His saber was ever present, tucked into the scabbard at his side and hidden beneath the austere black frockcoat.

My God, she had thought upon seeing him again, had her feelings not changed at all in the years of their separation? Hadn't she outgrown this schoolgirl flush that came to her cheeks? Her heart still pounded wildly. Her breath had caught in her throat. Had Edward not been present to begin the conversation, she would have been uncovered for a stammering fool. The few seconds of introduction had given her time to compose herself and to harden her feelings.

She had thought she was successful in playing the role of the past lover who couldn't care less any longer for the fancies of youth. Let him see that she wasn't in the least affected by his presence, that she hadn't pined for him for a minute, that she was popular and adored and that he couldn't possibly impress her now. But he had seen through her ruse. How else had he been encouraged enough to say what he had to her? Did he have an excuse he could offer for his two years of neglect? Why would he have broached the subject anyway unless some trace of

227

affection for her remained?

Why think about him? she scolded herself, when the islands were full of bachelors with excellent futures: the younger sons of gentry sent here to make a living, the offspring of wealthy merchants who had secure places in their father's businesses, the sons of plantation owners who could live out their lives off the family revenues. There were dozens to choose from and very little competition since the men far outnumbered the available women. Often, fathers intent on finding wives for their sons, and widowers in search of a bride for themselves, had to send to England for a likely fiancé, exchanging letters with the girls and their families until an agreement was reached to bring her here to be married. These arrangements often had unsatisfactory results, as only portraits might have been exchanged or written descriptions rendered from the point of view of someone who had everything to gain out of elaborating grandly on the truth. A man waited anxiously for the beautiful bride he'd been promised and found a homely spinster had been palmed off on him instead. More times than not, the brides were forced into the voyage because the family needed the wealth or the prestige the union offered. The girls were as much as sold to a man they had never seen. Jamie had seen them aplenty, before she left and after she came back. Pretty young maidens who broke down in tears at the first sight of the fat, ancient, or ugly man presented to them as a future husband. Marriages of willing consent by both parties were rare and the bachelors congregated like flies about the honey jar around every likely female who set her dainty foot down on the island. Any one of them could be hers just for the choosing.

She gazed down on the sleeping town below, her troubled mind too uneasy to let her sleep. Lanterns lit some of the windows, winking in the darkness, and beyond them she could see the red nightwatch lamps aboard the ships in the harbor. Which of those ruby lights belonged to Franco's ship? she wondered.

He had told her she could have an answer to why he had not come for her. She had but to ask. What was he prepared to tell her? Why did he offer to tell her anything at all? Why ever did he have to bring it up? She had hoped in vain to find her feelings for him altered but she loved him as much as she ever had. In truth, she didn't think she cared anymore why he had never come if only they could find each other again. Her playact had been a disaster. She loved him and he knew it. What difference did it make to them from this night on if they were meant to be together? He had, after all, inquired about her. She didn't need to ask Jocko as Franco would never have told her such a visible lie with Jocko so close at hand to ask. He had known where she was and known that, as soon as her education was over, she would come back here. But what had he meant when he said he could no longer offer her marriage? Why not? What had changed to alter that?

With a desperate sense of urgency impelled by that thought, she rushed to her clothes chest, selecting the first gown that came to hand and dressing hurriedly but with the aggravation of having to dress herself alone. Her corset couldn't be pulled tight with no one to draw the laces so she discarded it. She donned her petticoats, then her gown, struggling like a contortionist to fasten the laces alone. She set a few pins into her hair, fastening the mass loosely into place, found her stockings and slippers underneath the bed where she had left them, then pulled her heavy-hooded cloak around her shoulders, drawing the cowl up to preserve what little she had done with her hair.

The clock in the downstairs hall was striking midnight as she crept noiselessly down the stairs, but she could never wait until morning. She had to know the reason he couldn't marry her now and that was all she could think about as she fled into the night.

Franco's cabin seemed too stuffy to allow him to sleep, yet the night was cool, with a soft westerly breeze. He had left his coat below and lounged in open blouse and trousers against a short stack of rolled canvas stored on the open deck. His arms pillowing his head, he studied the patterns of the stars in the dark sky.

The members of his crew were either asleep in their quarters or still out carousing through Royale. In singles, pairs, and trios, they periodically staggered back aboard, boisterous and drunk, shared a joke or two with their captain, then stumbled down the stairs to their bunks.

Marcel, the Frenchman, had drawn the watch, and after trying several times to spark a conversation with Franco, he finally gave it up to return to his post by the gangplank.

Franco had no desire to engage in idle chatter. He truly had not expected the sight of Jamie to affect him so profoundly. He had never put her out of his mind entirely, but when Ned and Jocko told him where she was and why she had gone, he had known it was in her best interests to remain. Franco did have nothing to offer her. He was a fugitive, fleeing accusations that had been wrong when made but were accurate enough now. He was a pirate, preying on his own kind as he preyed on any other. A richly loaded ship from any country was fair game, those belonging to Spain included. What did he owe his country for forcing him into exile without a trial? Trusted friends had proven false. Fear outweighed honor when the taking of risks was involved.

The tables had indeed turned and he could not ask of Jamie that which she had never asked of him. He had broken her heart when he left without her, but not once had she begged him to stay. She was better off where she was, he told himself time and time again when she would come to mind. If his resolve swayed, he had only to picture Jamie, the lad, remarking that there was nothing to look forward to but a hangman's rope someday. Perhaps those had been her only prospects then but they weren't now, and he would not be the cause of her facing such a dim future again. They hung a woman for piracy as easily as any man.

"*Capitaine.* . . ." Marcel roused him from his thoughts. "A young lady is here to see you," the Frenchman said in passable English. "I would tell her you cannot be disturbed at such an hour but she is . . . how you say? . . . a genteel woman. I could not turn her away."

Franco sat up abruptly, knowing who his guest had to be. He should not have taunted her into coming here. "Bring her aboard, Marcel."

He watched as his crewman returned to the gangplank to gallantly escort the young lady on deck. Marcel hovered about her, warning her to take care with her footing on the slightly swaying deck riding the gentle waves of dockside. Jamie could manage a slippery deck in a gale better than Marcel could ever hope to, but Marcel didn't know that, Franco thought with an amused smile at the concern with which his crewman performed his task.

"Thank you, Marcel, that is all." Franco dismissed the man who seemed anxious to remain instead. Franco couldn't blame him. She was covered from head to toe in her hooded cloak, but the face of exquisite beauty peering out from the cowl could not be missed. "Jamie, you should not have come," he said when Marcel left them, regretting more than ever that his words had brought her out at such an hour.

"You asked me to come," she returned, a flash of anger

231

in her gaze as she looked up at him. "You said I should know the reason and it's that I've come for."

"Then you shall have it, but not here." He glanced at Marcel, who was watching them, trying to overhear so he could gossip about it with the crew. Three more of his men were coming toward the gangplank, singing a drunken sailor's song in off-key, loud voices. "Come." He took her by the arm and led her down to his cabin on the lower deck. Whatever Marcel might make of it could not be helped. Franco locked the door to be certain of remaining undisturbed. When he turned around she was facing him, the cowl drawn back off her head, her eyes large and luminous in the lanternlight. Try as he might, he had not managed to forget her either.

"Jamie, I'm so sorry I couldn't come for you as I promised. I lost my gamble. I wanted vengeance on my brother and it has not happened. I have nothing but this ship, a ruined reputation, and the money I've been saving to someday challenge Lorenzo for what is rightfully mine. Until that day comes, I can offer you nothing. Not a home or marriage. I've made a vow that I will not rest until I have succeeded in it all."

"Is revenge so important to you?"

"Seeing that my father's will is carried out is," he stated, stalking across the cabin, his anger growing at the memory of his homecoming. "It was my mother's choice to retire to a convent upon my father's death, so I have no fears for her welfare, but I cannot say the same for my sisters. Lorenzo married them off against their will. Maria was wed to a drunkard who beats her when his temper turns foul. Theresa, the youngest, is now the wife of a man who breaks his wedding vows and displays his infidelities for all to see. How can I allow their suffering to go on? They have no one to turn to. They dare not tell our mother of their unhappiness because it would break her heart, perhaps even kill her after all she has already been through. She believes me dead. I thought it best to leave her in ignorance until I can rightfully claim my place as her son. To know I'm a fugitive, a pirate, perhaps a man who will never clear his name and may end his life at the end of a rope, would be too much for her to bear."

"Oh, Franco," she murmured, tears blurring her vision as she ran to him. "I'm so sorry," she said, holding him to her.

Franco responded to her touch, his resolve to stay away from her for her sake crumbling into dust.

"You deserved to know the truth. And now you must go," he said, but her head was shaking as she clung to him.

"My sweet darling, will you never let me do right by you?"

"What do you mean?" Jamie backed away to touch his smooth-shaven cheek. How long she had yearned to touch him so again. Her fingers brushed through the dark waves of his hair, lingering in the soft curls.

Franco took her hand away, turned it over, and kissed the palm. "I'm a wanted man in Spain now and in several of the colonies as well. Even here on Royale, I could be in danger of arrest. An order went out to all the British holdings in the New World, granting amnesty to any pirates who will swear an oath to give up their business and lead honest lives. Since they can't catch and punish all of us, I suppose they hoped it might make a few of us change our professions while pardons were being offered. Jocko, Ned, most of the men you knew, have agreed and been granted amnesty. They're free men."

"Then you must too."

"I can't. Jamie, don't you see? I have no other means of reaching my goal. I must help my sisters and stop my brother from squandering any more of our inheritance. He can't be allowed to get away with what he's done."

"What can you do?" Jamie asked worriedly.

"When I have enough wealth of my own, I can challenge Lorenzo," he said harshly. "A rich man can be forgiven his sins. A poor one never is. No one will pay heed to a penniless younger brother who was known for his mercurial temperament and his vices. Lorenzo's fortune, which is partly my fortune and that of my sisters, speaks louder, my darling, than my poverty. People remember what is comfortable for them to remember better than they can recall the truth. They know that Francisco DeCortega fought more than his share of duels. Those who do not believe me dead know of my capture but will not believe how I won my freedom."

"And when you have enough to challenge him?"

"I'll place bribes in the proper places to reach the ear of the new king. In a fair trial I can prove I was wronged. Father made a copy of his will that he put in a hidden place that only I know about. I suspect even then he did not really trust Lorenzo to honor the one he gave him. If it's still there, if he hasn't found and destroyed it as well, I can prove that our father intended the estate to be divided and that Lorenzo wanted all along to keep everything for himself."

"When will you have enough?"

"Soon, if our hunting continues to reap excellent rewards." He smiled to reassure her.

Jamie thought for a moment. "Does Father know about all of this?"

"He's well aware, I'm sure, that I am an active pirate, but he wouldn't dare move against me. Your father, sweet, has too much in his own past that he would prefer forgotten. And I prefer it for you as well. That's why you must leave and never see me again . . ."

"Franco, no . . ."

"You must! By your father's new title and appointment, your name is cleared. Associating with me could only bring you ruin."

"I don't care . . ."

"I do. I won't have you ruining your life for my sake. You have every opportunity before you."

"I won't hear of it. I won't have it. You need me now and you never did before. It's a pleasant change for me," she said, smiling. "Besides, you don't have anyone else."

"Jamie, I made a mistake coming to the mansion today. I should have left well enough alone."

"But you did come. And you've explained. I understand and I promise I'll never pressure you away from your goals. I'll help you."

"No . . ."

"I won't let you chase me away again. If you want me to leave you, then you have only to look into my eyes and tell me truthfully that you never want to see me again. Can you do that?"

"You know I can't."

"Then by your admission you have trapped yourself, Captain DeCortega, for you will never be free of me until you can."

Chapter Eleven

She knew no one could ignite the fires he lit within
her. His touch drove her mad with wanting him. His
mouth on hers was warm and inviting, his lips tender yet
ardent with desire. At last they were together again and
nothing else mattered. She understood, and there was
nothing to forgive him for. He had said he would come
for her when his problems at home were settled and that
hadn't happened yet. She should have held steady to the
faith in him that had sustained her during their absence
and known that Lacey and her father were wrong. But
none of that had importance now. She was back, he was
here, and she was in his arms again.

After she warned him he would never be rid of her, he
had lowered the lamp in his cabin and checked the door
to be certain it was locked. He came to her then and
took the cloak from her shoulders. Her loosely bound
hair came unfastened of its own accord and tumbled
riotously down her back.

"I'm so glad you haven't cut it," Franco said, entwining
his fingers in the ebony mass, then drew her head toward
him and kissed her. With experienced, gentle hands he
untied the laces she had struggled to fasten. The top of
her gown free, he drew the garment off her shoulders,
freeing her arms, pulling the material down to her waist.

Her breasts revealed, he stroked each one in turn, the pink nipples hardening with his touch, awakening the passion that had lain dormant so long.

Working deftly, and with her aid, he removed each article of the clothing she had fought to put on. The gown came off, falling to her ankles, then the petticoat followed it to the floor around her feet. When at last she was revealed to his gaze, he removed his own clothing, his eyes never leaving her, drinking in the sight of her bare, luscious flesh. Naked, he lifted her up in his arms and carried her to his bed to lay her down upon the mattress. Kneeling between her feet, he lifted her leg and kissed her ankle, then ran his tongue slowly up the inside of her calf until Jamie moaned with pleasure. As his hands and eager lips explored every inch of her trembling flesh, her legs parted almost of their own accord, her knees coming up, welcoming the talented fingers that found the core of her passion and invaded it.

When he was certain she was ready for him, he lowered himself on top of her, pressing himself into the hot, throbbing center of her womanhood. Jamie arched her back to meet his first thrust, wild with aching need. Her hands dug into the hollow of his back, letting her passion dictate her responses, following his rhythm, urging him to drive ever deeper and faster inside her, until her world finally exploded into fragments of stars and reeling planets. When at last both of them were spent, Franco remained motionless on top of her, letting her recover while he caught his own breath. "You are marvelous," he murmured, kissing her ear. Finally, reluctant to leave her warmth but fearing his weight would soon be too much for her, Franco moved away to stretch out beside her, pulling her closely against him and nuzzling her neck.

"I've decided that I am going to help you," she stated. "Whether you want to accept my help or not."

Franco smiled. "And how could you do that, my love?"

He settled comfortably on the bed beside her.

"Spain's new king is the nephew of Louis of France, isn't he? I might know someone who could reach the ear of Louis, and Louis most certainly can reach the ear of his nephew."

"Darling," Franco said, bemused. "That someone would have to possess a great deal of influence indeed to have either one even listen to his petition. I do not mean some minor envoy you might have met in a London ballroom."

"Neither do I!" Jamie returned in a huff.

Franco laughed out loud. "I don't mean to offend you, sweet. Truly, I don't. I know that you mean well and I appreciate your offer, but I seriously doubt that anyone you know could help me."

"Oh?" she queried, sitting up in the bed to glare at him. "Then you doubt if I convinced him you had been served an injustice that Tsar Peter of Russia would take up your case? Is it that you doubt Louis might listen to him? Or that Peter might listen to me?"

Franco's smile faded into a brow-furrowing front. "Then what Morgan told me was true? You were proposed to by a monarch?"

"I presume, then, you mean the latter! You doubt that Peter would petition a cause for me!"

"I didn't believe him!" Franco murmured. "When Morgan said it, I was sure he was only trying to provoke me."

"If my father told you that Peter proposed marriage, then he did not lie to you. Whether or not you believe *me* is entirely your own affair!" she threw out at him, angry and struggling to get past him to reach the floor but he was blocking her way. She couldn't get up from the bed without crawling over him, a thing she was loath, at the moment, to try.

"I wish you would get up and get out of my way!"

"Why?" he queried, deliberately turning on his side so that she couldn't pass him. She was imprisoned between him and the vast space of windows comprising the outer wall.

"I'm too angry to remain!" Her voice rose with her ire. "I don't know how I ever convinced myself I still loved you! You're a conceited bore!"

"And you're even more beautiful when you're angry." He effectively cut off an attempt to escape over his feet by sitting up, holding his arm across her path.

"Let me out of here!"

"As you wish." He leaned back, gallantly sweeping his arm out to let her pass. Jamie started across him but saw the ruse too late. He grabbed her by the shoulders and, turning over, took her with him, tossing her down onto the bed again, holding her immobile with her arms pinned to her sides.

"The tsar of Russia, then, has excellent taste. It well agrees with my own. I apologize if I seemed to be making fun of you."

"*Seemed* to be!" she raged. "You were!"

"Then I'm sorry. I would disbelieve anything your father might tell me but I would never question your word."

Mollified by his apology, Jamie stopped struggling, but her anger was not yet fully abated. "I only offered to help if my efforts might accomplish something," she said as he planted light kisses down her throat.

"I know that, sweetheart," he murmured, nibbling the lobe of her ear.

"You're heavy," she complained, his body, lying on top of hers, painfully flattening her breasts.

"Then I shall remedy the situation."

Jamie gasped as he suddenly turned onto his back, taking her with him, his arms locked around her so she couldn't squirm free. "I don't mind your weight at all."

He smiled and kissed her, then his expression grew serious. "Unlike your king, I cannot promise you marriage yet, until DeCortega lands are once again safe from Lorenzo's infamy. Only then will I be free of the promise I spoke over my father's grave. Can you possibly accept that?" Without waiting for an answer, he added. "It might be a very long engagement."

"Are you asking me to . . ."

Franco stopped her with a finger held against her lips. "I am asking you only to be mine. For now, it's the only way we can be together. I am asking you to wait until I can ask you more."

"It doesn't matter to me . . ."

"It matters to me!" he interrupted. "I will not ask you to be the wife of a man who is wanted in nearly every country but this island and a few more where none but pirates dwell. Until you can hold your head up proudly and proclaim in any port that you are the wife of Francisco DeCortega, I will not dishonor you with bearing that name."

"But my own is . . ."

"Cleared!" he interjected sternly. "By your father's new title and appointment, it is now an honorable name and will remain that way!" Since he no longer had to keep her from escaping, he lifted his fingers to her face to lightly touch her cheek. "I'm a selfish man. I can't send you away from me, though for your safety, I should. I should send you back to your father's house and never see you again, but I can't bring myself to do it. If I married you now, while still a wanted man, and if I was caught and hung for piracy, you could never live down the reputation brought upon you by bearing my name. Our children could not either, for a dead man is a silent one and can say nothing in his own defense. Until I can give you my name, clean beyond all question, I can only ask you to accept my terms and wait."

240

Jamie realized how little would be availed by argument. He was determined. "You know I'll accept any terms I must. I'm sure that I don't know why sometimes, but I love you."

"I've never known why either." He smiled and added, "But I'm glad of it. I only hope you never realize you are far too good for me."

Jamie couldn't resist smiling. "Don't criticize my taste, sir."

"I'd be a fool to argue with it."

"Where the devil have you been?" Morgan demanded of Jamie almost the moment she stepped into the house. It was almost noontime and since her father awoke between eight and nine, he must know she had not been down to breakfast.

"Out," she replied, setting her cloak down over an armchair.

"I can see that!" Morgan stormed. "I ain't blind! I'm asking ye where you've been all the blessed night. Lizzie tells me you didn't sleep in yer bed last night."

"That's right." Jamie wished he might lower his voice. Did the entire household have to overhear?

"Then where the blasted hell were ye?" he shouted, his face turning red with anger.

"If you'll stop shouting, I'll tell you where I was! I was with Franco. I spent the night aboard his ship."

Morgan's ham fists clenched whitely at his sides, his face turning dangerously crimson. "You what?" he said in a low, threatening voice that quaked with anger.

"You heard me," Jamie returned. "What right do you have to be upset? There were a good many nights I lay awake wondering where you were! And usually to learn you were in the arms of some dockside harlot and couldn't be bothered to send me word," she threw out at him, her temper roused by his attitude. She couldn't stand the way he was staring at her as if she had committed an unpardonable offense. "Besides, you lost your right to play the role of the indignant father when you put me up as a wager on a gaming table. You have no right to look at me like that. You, who never married the first time, have no right to question my morals or behavior. You can hardly hold me accountable for following in your own footsteps!"

"You dare talk to me this way?" he glared.

"I do, and I will until you stop looking at me as if I've done something wrong. I was with the man I love. And he loves me. When his business is settled in Spain, we're going to be married."

"Over my dead body," Morgan growled.

"I'm sorry you feel that way, Papa." She resumed a more normal tone. "I truly am. But it's going to happen, whether you like it or not."

"You're not marrying him!" Morgan's voice raised several decibels. He marched across the room to stand over her, trembling with rage.

"I am," she retorted, staring back at him.

Morgan raised his hand to slap her.

"Don't you *dare!*" Jamie told him, her eyes narrowing. "If you do, I promise you, you'll never see me again."

For a moment he seemed uncertain, his arm waving in the air above his head, then his massive hand dropped to his side. "I'm telling ye, ye're not marrying a no-account Spaniard. I done all this for you, girl, to see to yer future."

"You did not. You did it for yourself. It's what you've always wanted. Even sending me to school was so that you could have a respectable daughter to display."

"That ain't true."

"Isn't it, Papa?" she asked evenly. "Isn't it?"

Jamie turned away, starting to leave, but his voice

stopped her.

"I won't let you marry him!"

"You can't stop me, Papa," she said, walking away.

"Say it once more, I never tire of hearing it."

"You're beautiful, you're wonderful, I adore you," Franco whispered near her ear. "I love your ears I love your eyes. I love your nose and your lips." Each attribute mentioned was kissed in its turn until his lips lingered on the last one, kissing her deeply.

Being in his arms was the greatest joy she had ever known, hearing from his lips the endearments she had for so long prayed to hear from him. The past three weeks had been almost heaven for her. If only she could stop her father's harping over the issue of Franco, she would know utter contentment. They dared not meet more often than twice a week lest their liaisons become too well known to one and all. Franco rented a room on a weekly basis, choosing this particular tavern because access was to be had by a back door that led directly to the upper story. Designed more for escapes than entrances, the passage was only locked at night, giving a young woman in a hooded cloak free access during the day to surreptitiously meet her "secret husband." Franco had offered the landlord a princely sum for his silence, weaving an involved tale of parents who unreasonably objected to his courtship of their daughter, forcing a forbidden elopement. It wasn't far from the truth, since Morgan insisted daily that he would never allow them to marry.

"And what if he clears his name?" Jamie had asked during his tirade only this morning. "Then would we have your blessing?"

"He'll never accomplish it!" Morgan sloughed off her query.

"But what if he does?"

"You'll not marry him and that's the end of it."

Her father's answers, however, told her that it was a personal dislike and had nothing to do with Franco's lack of title or fortune, no matter how badly Morgan wanted her to marry into both. Franco's advice to go to England and turn the Panama treasure over to the Crown had saved Morgan's neck as well as winning him the recognition he had sought for so long in vain. Instead of being grateful for that, Henry was still holding it against him that he had been right about the Panama venture in the first place.

Her father did not like to be contradicted, especially in public, and that was exactly how Henry had taken Franco's comments made during the Brethren's Council meeting that had debated the plan. Nor could he accept as a friend any man who challenged his leadership of the buccaneers. No matter that Morgan had been promoted to the king's appointed governor now, he no longer reigned as undisputed leader of the Caribbean-based pirates—it seemed her beloved held sway in Morgan's old place and for that, Morgan would never forgive him.

Her father also didn't like Franco's "changing things" as they had always been in the islands. On his return, Morgan had found alterations that had taken place that were not to his liking. The amnesty order had arrived and a good number of the men he had known as able-bodied buccaneers had come in on the pardon. Instead of signing the papers and ignoring them, as Henry had done with similar amnesty orders in the past, the fellows were retiring for a life of ease on shore to enjoy the fruits of their dastardly labors. Those who now prowled the sea lanes, disdaining pardons and foiling Navy patrols, were younger men, bold, independent, and hungry for the quick, vast wealth the pirate's life offered. They had taken over the ships the old-timers sold or surrendered as they retired.

These youngsters remembered the name of Henry Morgan with the proper touch of awe, but thought of him as one of the old tars who had seen, and passed, his prime. His name no longer sent a chill down their spines. They moved out of his way on the sidewalks only in deference to an older man. They were a different breed than the ones Morgan had known and trained by his own hand. These were "gentlemen pirates." Morgan said the word with a sneer; civilized men who had new rules of conduct they played by.

They no longer attacked a gold-laden ship like a swarm of ants looting a Sunday picnic then sank the vessels with all hands aboard. They consulted ships' logs and had crews hand the goods over. They told prisoners they would be spared if they cooperated and, what was more, kept to their word. Ships were disabled so that it might take several hours to repair the damage before they could sail again, giving the pirates all the time they needed to make good their escape.

To Morgan's mind this was a damn fool dangerous way of doing business, since live crewmen made excellent witnesses in court, but the new breed of buccaneers would not suffer a man to lose his life without excellent cause for having to take it.

As a result of these new conditions, many ships threw down their arms and surrendered at the first sight of a Jolly Roger approaching. They had no fear for their own lives in letting the ship be taken, thus turned over the cargoes without resistance. Let the merchants and bankers weep over their losses, no seaman was willing to die to protect it.

Some captives were taken and held for ransom, but the gentleman pirates insisted the hostages be treated kindly and with respect. There was a death penalty now, proclaimed by the council, for any pirate who raped a woman prisoner. One of these new captains had a whole islandful of women waiting for ransoms to arrive from their husbands or fathers, and not one of them had ever had her virtue compromised. Justice was swift and unmerciful if these new rules of conduct were broken.

These new pirates still had respect for a man who could lead them, and they had elected Franco as the one they would follow. He sat in Morgan's old seat at the head of the table during council meetings and no one ever disputed his place there. He was the one they consulted about the forthcoming plans. He was the one they heeded. Since his skill with his saber was legendary, he was the one they avoided offending. Morgan could not come to terms with Franco having taken his place.

How strange it all seemed now, looking backward, she thought as she studied her lover's profile while he rested in the bed beside her. She had once defended him as too noble to stoop to piracy whatever Morgan offered him and now he led the pirates, having changed their standards to his.

"I love you so much," Jamie told him, playing with a lock of his hair that fell down across his forehead. "Even more than I used to and that, I thought, would have been impossible."

"Are you sure, though, that you want to be married?" he asked with his eyes still closed.

"Why not?" she asked, slightly troubled.

"It seems to me marriage was only invented for simpletons and fools, intended to make wayward lovers feel guilty for straying."

"Is that so?" she queried, watching him already wincing in anticipation of the blow she finally bestowed on him, giving him a short jab in the ribs with her elbow.

His eyes flew open and he grunted. "Ow! Even for a joke, love, you have a wicked elbow," he complained, smiling yet rubbing the sore spot.

"And you have a wicked mind," she returned. "Does this mean sir, that you would rather not make an honest woman of me?" she teased.

"I wouldn't dare deceive you. You'd kill me if I failed you, or mash me into pulp with your elbow." He pretended great distress over the place where she had jabbed him. "I'd sooner cross your father than you, dear."

"Oh, does it hurt?" Playfully, she kissed the spot she had jabbed a moment before.

"Um, that's better. Now that you mention it, it's a bit sore here as well." He referred to a place where she had poked him earlier to stop him from tickling her unmercifully, then he pointed a few inches over to another place on his chest where she hadn't touched him at all. "And here," he furthered when she complied by kissing that spot too. "And here."

"And what of here?" She touched a finger to his lips and Franco nodded, closing his eyes as she kissed him.

"You make me want you all over again. 'Tis worth the price of marriage, I expect," he said, drawing her tightly into his embrace. "I can never have enough of you, yet we must talk." He turned serious.

"You said so before." Jamie stretched out beside him. "What of?" When she first appeared this afternoon, he had seemed troubled as he greeted her, answering her concern with the statement that they would speak of it later.

"Darling, we've been in port for three weeks now and my men are becoming weary." He sat up against the pillows so that, holding her, he couldn't be swayed from what he must say. "I have no choice unless I would leave them to their own devices but to set sail for the sea lanes and seek out a venture or two. What's more, my lovely witch, you've cast your spell on me and I've thus far forgotten my vow to my father that I would right the wrongs done to the people and things he loved most in

247

this world. I've come no closer to reaching my goal."

"I'm sorry," she murmured, gazing at him sadly. "It is my fault, isn't it? I've kept you here and forgotten that you have other obligations."

"Then you understand?" he asked, gazing at her.

"Of course I do," she answered languidly, stretching to kiss him briefly.

"And Edward Harcourt will not wile his way into your affections while I'm gone, will he?" One brow arched as he peered at her sternly.

"He's no threat to you." She smiled.

"Nor Lord Arthur What's-his-name?"

"No one, my darling. No one at all. How can there be if I am with you?"

Franco stiffened immediately, as if she had jabbed him again. He released his hold on her and sat up abruptly. "You most certainly will not be with me!"

"Why not?" She answered his cross look lightly. "I sailed with my father. I can sail with you. I haven't forgotten how to lend a hand as a seaman."

"You're not coming!" he interjected sternly.

"Franco . . ."

"I said absolutely not!" His aroused temper would not allow him to remain idle in the bed. He got up and stalked across the floor, wrapping a towel around his middle before he came back to her. "Do you think I've gone through all this only to put you in danger? Why have we been meeting in secret all this time? Why haven't I taken you openly on my ship? To protect your name and reputation!" he scolded. "Am I to throw it away now to satisfy a childish whim?"

"Childish whim!" she repeated indignantly. "I only want to be with you. I thought you felt the same. What is wrong with that?"

"You'll ruin everything!"

"Such as?" she returned, hot at his anger. "I want to

248

help you clear you name, not stand idly by and do nothing."

"If you are that eager for matrimony and it is all that will reassure you, then perhaps we should be secretly wed."

"You needn't grant me such favors, Captain DeCortega!" she bristled. "I've only agreed to matrimony because it is what I thought I craved before, when it was, indeed, a childish whim and I didn't know anything more about it than marriage is what a woman is supposed to hope for. I've kept to it because I believed it was what *you* wanted, even though the thought of it now terrifies me . . ."

"Wait! Wait a moment. What are you saying?" He appeared perplexed, wearing a troubled frown.

"Marriage, the way it frightens me."

"You never told me that before?"

"Because I do want to marry you . . . and yet, I don't." Jamie paused, trying to think of the proper words to explain her feelings. "I'm afraid of it," she finally admitted.

"Why?" he asked, utterly bewildered by her confession. It was true Jamie never pressured him for matrimony. He had always been the one to bring the subject up, yet he had imagined it was because she understood his problems and not out of any reservations she felt about the state itself.

"I do love you, Franco," she said tightly. "And I want to be yours forever but . . . the ceremony. I don't know. I feel of two minds each time I think of it. When I knew you before, when I first fell in love with you, of course I wanted marriage. It was a dream I had never believed possible for me. I hadn't seen many married folk and knew so little about it. I knew Papa had never married, nor had Jocko or even Mary. She's lived with Tully all these years but I've never heard them speak of it. I knew

249

Ned Shanks left his wife behind in Liverpool. So had many of the other men who've joined us. They don't speak very highly of it but I thought perhaps that was just their way and had little to do with the way the majority of the world regarded it.

"Then, while I was at school, our entire education was geared toward becoming wives and mothers. We learned what would be expected of us in that capacity. We were given the virtues of a good and proper wife, told to be obedient, loyal, and silent—most of all, silent. Before marriage vows were exchanged, we were encouraged to be gay, vibrant, and bright to catch a man's fancy. After marriage, it seemed that to be just the same way was a terrible crime and would cause a husband to think his wife unfaithful and flirtatious. The day after a wedding, he can carry on the same as he always has, but she has to be something entirely different. She can't dress the same or talk to men alone. If he dies, God forbid, she must wear mourning until she follows him to the grave or remarries. If she doesn't follow these rules of conduct, she's a loose woman. At the very best her conduct is constantly scrutinized. I saw girls who left the school before I did become wives and it was as if, in the space of a few months, someone had taken their personalities away from them. Marriage had changed them so much. Girls who had been pretty and charming and witty were suddenly drab and faded and dull. Not all of them surely. Some seemed very happy and the same as they had always been, as if marriage heartily agreed with them, but there is so much a woman risks when she pledges her life to a man."

"Such as what, darling?" Franco came over to her side and sat down next to her, placing his hand over hers in her lap.

"Everything. it seems. Her independence if she ever had any, her control over her own destiny, even her

250

ability to rely on herself for the simplest decisions. If she owned property before, by the laws regarding marriage it's suddenly his. He controls the purse strings and she has no say in how he spends their fortune. He can hold land in his name while she cannot, though she holds the very same name. He can make contracts without consulting her, while one she signs isn't even legal without his name on the document. If he chooses, even though the wealth might have been hers to begin with, he can die and leave everything to someone else instead, making her beg, perhaps, from her own children, for the food she eats and the bed she sleeps in and she can do nothing to remedy her situation.

"I suppose because I was raised differently from the other girls at the school, this knowledge appalled me while the others seemed to take it in stride. Papa always let me have my own portion of any treasure taken and I was free to do with it as I liked. It was my own so that I never had to ask anyone for so much as a farthing, nor did I have to account for how I spent it. At school, Lady Westcott took charge of our funds and we had to ask her for the cost of a simple hair ribbon. We were treated as if we couldn't be trusted with a few coins in our pockets without having to account for how we spent them. It wasn't that she was mean about it, or ever deprived us of our funds. It was simply the way things were done and most of the girls were used to it. I wasn't.

"Even if he did take his hand to me a few times, Papa always let me speak my mind and never trained me to hide my thoughts. I always felt I was allowed my own mind. Now, to think of losing all my rights even to possession of my own body, makes me terrified."

"I could never do that to you," Franco said earnestly.

"I know, my darling," Jamie put her arms around his neck and hugged him. "I know you wouldn't and it's part of why I love you so. It's just the idea of it that makes

251

me unsure."

"Jamie, I give you my promise that your rights will never suffer under my domination. I swear it to you."

"And I believe you," she said earnestly. "I know it and that's why I can talk to you about it. It's only that, from what I've learned, you could break your pledge to me and I would have no recourse."

" 'Tis the way it has always been," Franco told her with centuries of tradition to back him up.

"Yes, and likely may always be, though I hope not. But do you see now why I'm afraid?"

"I do," he said, holding her and patting her shoulder for comfort. "And it makes me feel humble to realize you love me enough to risk it."

"Johnson, is Father at home this afternoon?" Jamie asked as she stepped inside the foyer.

"No, mistress, the governor is out for the day," the butler replied, closing the door behind her and taking her cloak and muff.

"Smile, Johnson, there aren't any funerals today," she couldn't resist quipping while the solemn little man folded her cloak across his arm. Morgan had hired William Johnson in England and brought him back to the island with them. Her father liked the butler's crisp efficiency. The man positively squeaked with duty and propriety.

"Yes, mistress," Johnson acknowledged, his face as dour as ever. Most probably he couldn't use his face muscles for smiling anymore, since they had apparently atrophied from lack of use. Jamie sighed. At least she was spared another round with Morgan. She had just left Franco's bed at the inn and, after her confession of this afternoon, they had made long slow love together. She didn't want the afterglow of that ruined by more of her father's badgering. While she had managed to explain her insecurities

252

to Franco, she hadn't been able to tell him all of how she still felt relief that any marriage plans, for the present, remained in the far future. She was content enough just to be with him, to see him several times a week, to know she could look forward to the next time they were together. It would suit her well if they never had to be apart at all, as long as marriage vows remained in the distant future. Each time she thought of promising herself away, body and soul, to another living person, she couldn't contain the trace of fear that ran straight up her spine.

She and Lacey had shared the uncertainty and talked about it in the whispering darkness of after-lamps-out conversation in the room the two girls shared. A man could take his wife against her will and she had no recourse under the law. Even her own parents might not support her for a husband beating her severely if they felt he had "just cause" to take such steps with her. Only the law could lay down how and when and in what manner a man could be punished. Nowhere did a man's wife have recourse to punish him. At least the law of the land now prevented him from killing her or shutting her away forever if he felt so inclined, but Jamie couldn't help her reluctance to surrender herself so deeply into anyone else's custody, even Franco's.

She and Lacey Bell had decided that courtesans must be the wisest women in the world. Much smarter than wives. They were loved by men, worshipped and pampered, and yet never lost a single freedom by the advantage of their status as single women. "Besides," Lacey had said, "it does sound like ever so much more fun!" Jamie missed Lacey's company in these months they had been parted and hoped her friend might soon convince her parents to let her come here for a visit.

"Mistress, there is a gentleman caller awaiting you in the drawing room. Shall I tell him you've arrived?" John-

253

son asked.

"If it's Edward, I'm too tired to receive him this afternoon."

"It is not Mr. Harcourt, mistress. The gentleman introduced himself as the duc de Gavrilac."

"A duke?" Jamie said, puzzled. "I know no such person. And you said he's waiting for me? Not for Father?"

"His Grace asked for you by name. If you wish, I'll tell him you cannot receive visitors."

"No, Johnson, I'll see him." Curiosity quickly outweighed her fatigue. She had wanted to lie down for a short while before dinner to replay in her mind every moment of intimacy shared with her lover, but it could wait. She dismissed Johnson and changed her direction to the drawing room. Opening the door, she gazed at the man who rose to greet her. He didn't look at all familiar, though the broad smile on his face seemed to recognize her.

"Mistress Morgan?" he asked, rushing forward to bow over her hand. He was a short man of late middle age and had undoubtedly been quite handsome in his youth. His hair was a golden shade of blond that had just begun to turn a snowy silver. His eyes were a light shade of periwinkle blue and looked extremely happy to see her.

"Yes, Your Grace," Jamie curtsied. "I'm Mistress Morgan. How may I help you?"

"You don't know me," he explained with a trace of a French accent. "Allow me to introduce myself. I am Bertrand Claude Duvalier, duc de Gavrilac."

"Sir." Jamie nodded politely before it struck her like a bolt of lighting. Duvalier! Had he said his name was Duvalier?

"I see the name means something to you," he said, seemingly delighted.

"Yes," Jamie murmured, astounded and uncertain. " 'Twas my mother's name."

254

"Forgive me, I have startled you. Please, you must sit." He escorted her to an armchair, then took one himself near her, sitting as close as he could place himself without appearing rude. "Now . . . I am indeed, as you must be asking yourself, your uncle," he smiled. "Your mother, Antoinette Duvalier, was my sister."

"Of course," she stammered, stunned that he would be here, looking for her.

"I should have written to you first and told you of my desire to see you, but when I learned your whereabouts, I rushed straight to you without thought for the proprieties. I pray you forgive my impetuous intrusion."

"Sir," Jamie managed, " 'tis no intrusion whatever to accept family whenever they can visit," she said pleasantly, but her thoughts were racing. Perhaps he was here to seek satisfaction from Morgan over the misfortune that had befallen his sister. As angry as she was at Morgan, she wouldn't allow anyone to challenge him to a duel. Bertrand Duvalier was at least fifteen years younger than her father and was undoubtedly trained in the uses of pistol and foil. "May I ask, Your Grace, why you have come?"

"But to meet you, naturally." The smile on his face never wavered from the moment she had stepped inside the room. "You are my sister's child and my only living relative."

"Your Grace," she began uncertainly. "I feel I must tell you, your sister, my mother . . ." She left off, not knowing how to say it. Maybe he never knew the circumstances of Jamie's birth and those surrounding his sister's death. How could he know that his sister despised the daughter she bore as much as she hated the father, perhaps more, since Jamie looked so much like Morgan instead.

"I thank the Good Lord that you do not look like her," the duke interrupted at her pause, almost as if he had

255

read her mind. "I feared you might be the image of Antoinette, but then I saw your portrait and was greatly relieved."

"My portrait?" Jamie felt bewilderment swimming in her head. "What portrait?"

"Ah, of course you do not know. Once again, my excitement overcomes all other considerations and all I am accomplishing is your utter confusion. Allow me to begin again at the beginning. I am, as I said, your uncle, Bertrand Claude, and, as fate would have it, your mother was my only sibling. My parents died a few years after we learned of Antoinette's demise, you see, so since then I have been without any family at all."

"I see," Jamie murmured sympathetically.

"My parents knew of Antonette's child many years ago, but I myself never learned of it until much later when I found some of my father's letters. They spoke of the daughter she gave birth to and of the . . . circumstances, shall we say?" He grinned broadly, puzzling Jamie thoroughly. How could he speak so lightly of what must have been the family tragedy?

"You must understand that to learn so late in life, and after so much loneliness, that I did, after all, have a living relation . . . I can only excuse my behavior by saying I am overcome." Tears misted in his eyes and Jamie looked away to lessen his embarrassment until he could bring his emotions under control.

"You have no family of your own, sir? No wife? No children?"

Bertrand Duvalier shook his head. "I always planned to wed, but my career came first. I have served my king and my country all my life and traveled extensively, but it left little time to court and win a lady. Now I find it is too late for me."

"But, sir, you're barely over forty."

"I am, my dear, fifty-three."

256

"Hardly an old man yet," Jamie smiled at him, liking this duc de Gavrilac already.

"I thank you for saying so. You're very kind."

" 'Tis perfectly true," she insisted. He didn't look his age. "Surely there is still time."

"Perhaps." Bertrand shrugged his shoulders lightly. He was wearing a light blue satin suit with lace cuffs and cravat but refrained from the gestures that would have labeled him a dandy. "I have not surrendered all hope, but then, I hope to have you to lift my burden of loneliness. That is, if you will permit it to be so."

"I don't understand. Certainly, as you are my uncle, you're always welcome in this house." As long as Morgan knew his past transgressions were forgiven, he would never turn out a duke.

"That is all I will ask for at present." He rose and came toward her, then lifted her hand to kiss the back of it. "I cannot tell you how greatly pleased I am to find you nothing like my sister."

"You said so before, sir. May I ask why?"

"I'm sorry. Again, I must apologize. I forget it is your mother of whom I speak and you must have a different vision of her than my own." He returned to his chair and sat, facing her.

Jamie's face reddened, as it always seemed to when she spoke of something she didn't like to talk about. "My mother is not well remembered at all. She died when I was four."

"Yes, the letters I found revealed that tragic occurrence. How awful it must have been for you. You must have been bereft . . ."

"No." Jamie gripped the arms of her chair. " 'Tis only fair you know the truth, Your Grace. My mother despised me. She hated my father and refused his pleas to become his wife. She was not satisfied that he was good enough for her. She bore me out of wedlock, sir, and

257

thereafter refused to have anything more to do with me."

"Ah . . ." Unaccountably, he smiled. "How very like Antoinette that sounds."

"Pardon?" she asked, sure that she hadn't heard right. All her life Jamie had feared the Duvalier family would despise her as her mother had.

"Your mother, my sister, was not known as one of the gentlest of women. A kind heart was never one of her assets. Great beauty, yes, as even you yourself possess, but, thank God, you are nothing like her." He watched Jamie's reactions and when she showed no great distress, went on with it. "Antoinette was always spoiled, willful, and selfish. My parents married late in life. I was their firstborn and Antoinette came at a time when they did not expect to be blessed with any more children. For me, life was different. I was sent away to school. My father expected it to make a man of me, and I have no bitterness for the way I was brought to adulthood. I was my father's heir and in his own way he loved me. But Antoinette? She was his flower, his gem. She could do no wrong in his eyes. Everything she wanted was hers merely for the asking. Instead of appreciating such boundless love and affection, Antoinette, as I remember her, was always spiteful, cruel. I remember once, when Mama scolded her, she retaliated by cutting off the blossoms on our mother's prized rosebushes. Rather than admit she was the culprit, she told our parents Suzanne had done it. Suzanne was the daughter of my mother's seamstress—a sweet, delightful child with no mischief in her. Suzanne was accused and then beaten for lying when she would not admit to the deed. I watched Antoinette's reaction to this child being punished in her place and that's when I knew she was the guilty party. With every stroke of the switch my father applied, Antoinette was smiling. This was not the first incident of its kind in our childhood, nor the last, but from that day on, God forgive me, I despised Antoinette. Now, do you see, my dear, why I am glad to find you nothing like her? However your father stood her is beyond my understanding. She would have married a very rich marquis had your father not stopped her journey. I suppose for her, nothing less than that was acceptable, but the man doesn't know how fortunate he is that she never arrived. She was marrying him solely for his money and cared nothing about him. She was incapable of caring about anyone but herself."

Jamie shuddered, thinking of the servant girl's unjust punishment. She had always thought it was Morgan who caused her mother's illness. The horror, the defilement, the insult to a refined young woman's sensibilities. But here, her uncle was presenting an entirely different portrait of her mother, from long before Morgan ever saw her.

"Please, I hope I have not distressed you." Her uncle reached out to pat her hand where it rested on the armrest.

"No." Jamie turned to gaze at him. "I'm glad you told me. But you said you had seen my portrait?"

"Yes, in England." He looked relieved that he hadn't upset her. "I had the honor of escorting it to France."

"I don't understand how that is possible. I've never sat for my portrait."

"Again, I jump ahead of myself," Bertrand Duvalier said pleasantly. "I have served King Louis as an emissary to foreign courts. It is true, I believe, that you only recently returned from England?"

"Yes, only a few months past."

"I only just missed you then. You set sail the week before my arrival. Your fame, during your time in London, has been more widespread than you think, my dear. It traveled across the channel to France and to Louis's court."

259

Jamie's eyes widened. "They know of me there?"

"Indeed, it was there that I learned the famous young woman in constant company with the touring tsar of Russia was none other than my own niece. Louis himself asked me if I had ever had the pleasure of meeting you. Regretfully, I had to say that I had not. As gossip will spread at court, it is rumored the tsar asked you to marry him."

"How could they know that?" she exclaimed.

"Gossip is the prime sport of the aristocracy, my dear," he winked, "especially when it involves a beautiful young woman and a foreign monarch. The gossip piqued Louis's curiosity and he commissioned a London artist to paint a portrait of you so that he might see for himself this beauty who had captured the heart of a king." Bertrand watched in amusement as Jamie's cheeks flushed to scarlet. "I asked him if I might have the honor of picking it up and then delivering it."

"But I've never posed for a portrait."

"The artist he commissioned has a reputation for executing an excellent likeness from memory. He saw you at various gatherings and outings, sketched you in ink, then captured your image on canvas. I must say, it is an accurate rendering and does full justice to you. Louis was greatly impressed. So was I. It is why I decided that I must come here to see you for myself. I am pleased to discover the artist did not exaggerate your beauty in the least. You are truly as lovely as your picture that, I might add, now hangs in the king's own drawing room in the palace at Versailles."

Jamie was so embarrassed her cheeks burned to realize she had been discussed in foreign courts and that an unauthorized portrait of her hung in a prominent place for all to see.

"While I was at my task of collecting the portrait, I asked the artist if he would not also do one for me.

Since I was pressed for time, he could only complete a couple of miniatures. This one," Bertrand opened his gold pocket watch to reveal an excellent likeness of Jamie inside, "and another you may have if you like. I have it in safekeeping at the inn."

"Thank you, I should very much like to have it," Jamie responded, the stunning news slowly sinking into her numbed brain. "But, really, Your Grace, I won't hear of you staying at the inn. You must have your things moved here. I shall have Lizzy prepare a room for you at once." Jamie jumped to her feet to ring the bell for the servant.

"Thank you for your hospitality, my dear, but are you sure your father will not mind?"

"Not at all," Jamie said with assurance. "He will be most pleased to have you."

"Then I wonder if you will grant me one small favor?"

"If I can, of course."

"Would you mind terribly calling me Uncle Bertrand? I should so like to hear it from your sweet lips."

Jamie met his gaze and saw the uncertainty in his eyes. Rejection would truly crush this lonely man and her heart went out to him. "Of course I will, Uncle Bertrand," she replied.

Chapter Twelve

"Ohh, that sneaking devil! I'll be damned if he won't hear a word or two from me when he returns!" Jamie slammed her muff onto the settee, her temper not in the least abated by the violence.

"Is something wrong, my dear?" Uncle Bertrand leaned forward in the wingback armchair that had hidden him from view when Jamie entered the sitting room.

"Uncle Bertrand, I didn't know you were in here."

"Who, if I may ask, is the sneaking devil who will face such wrath?" Her uncle smiled, amused by the flashing anger in his niece's eyes. Every day that had passed in the week since his arrival, Jamie had come to like Bertrand more. She had been right that Morgan, upon discovering there was no revenge in Bertrand Duvalier's heart, would open his home to him and even called him his brother-in-law. "I presume it is the captain you told me about?" her uncle asked.

"It most certainly is!" Jamie grumbled, her mind on the note Franco had left at the inn. The brief letter was tucked inside her muff but she didn't need to read it again to know every word on it:

"My love,

As I've come to know you all too well since the day

we first met, it has not escaped my attention that when once you set your mind to a thing, it is yours and you will not easily release it. Therefore, by the time you read this, you will find I have already set sail in the *Isabella*. As I told you, one more profitable venture will see me to my goal. When it is accomplished, I will return to you and face your wrath. Undoubtedly, it will be considerable.

I know that if I stayed to bid you farewell, we would argue. You would insist on coming, and I cannot allow you to risk your reputation and safety for my sake. Rather than part from you on such a note, I will leave you with the remembrance of our last time together and pray your memory of it remains as sweet as mine.

When your temper cools, my darling, remember also that missing you will make me all the more anxious to complete my task and return to your arms.

Yours faithfully,
Franco"

After reading the message several times, Jamie still didn't know whether she wanted to scream, or cry, or both. Unfortunately, even while she felt disappointed for having missed seeing him before he left, she realized she probably would have given him a devil of a time before she ever let him leave without her. Perhaps it was best this way.

Since her uncle had noticed and was concerned about the hard feelings that seemed to exist between Jamie and her father, she had felt it only right to explain to him the reason for the cool animosity beneath the governor's roof. She told him about Franco and their intention to marry after he cleared his name.

To her surprise, Uncle Bertrand recalled meeting a Franco DeCortega many years before, when Franco was little more than a boy, and had given him instructions in fencing with the épée, since the Spanish school Franco attended at the time taught mainly the values of saber. Uncle Bertrand was pleased to hear from her how proficient his one-time pupil had become. He was anxious to see the kind of man Franco DeCortega had grown into, but the introduction now would have to be put off until her wily sea captain returned. Even more disheartening was the knowledge that she would have to wait to tell him the wonderful news. Uncle Bertrand, upon hearing Jamie's confession about the difficulties Franco had encountered, was willing, even anxious, to help them. "What a small world it is," her uncle had exclaimed, "that my niece should meet and come to fall in love with a young man who so impressed me years before, that, if asked for such advice, I would surely give my highest recommendation to the union."

She had felt impelled to explain why Morgan disapproved, and Uncle Bertrand made the suggestion that perhaps it would be best to keep their own plans a secret from him. He was certain that once the difficulties were overcome Morgan would surely come around.

When she would see the gleam in his eye, Jamie thought that Bertrand rather enjoyed the intrigue he was becoming involved in. It was his plan she wanted to tell Franco about. As it was, however, she hadn't had the opportunity to even tell him of her uncle's arrival. Everything would have to wait now, until Franco returned from what, hopefully, might be his last adventure in piracy.

"Cut all the rigging," Franco ordered from the deck of the captured ship. "That should take them hours to repair yet they'll be seaworthy before nightfall."

"Aye, aye, Captain," Marks, one of Franco's English sailors responded, briskly setting off to accomplish the task of disabling the British passenger vessel that had given over a rich cargo of textile and teas bound for the Colonies. Franco would be able to sell it in Royale for a tidy profit that, even after splitting with the crew, would set him well over the goal he had set. This was one promise to Jamie he would be able to keep that one more venture would be enough.

"All the crates are aboard, *capitán*," Garcia reported. "However, two of the newest men we signed on in Tortuga have not returned from the cabins below."

"The passengers?" Franco queried with a frown. All of those who had paid for passage had been confined to the lower decks while the ship's crew was guarded on deck where they could be watched. No one in Franco's crew was permitted to tamper with the passengers.

"Aye, *capitán,* I suspect that is what they are about," Garcia responded.

"I'll look into it, Garcia. You see to disabling the ship."

"Aye, *capitán.*"

Franco was very particular about what he would and would not allow his pirates to steal. Cargoes of goods for profit were fair game since merchants usually had them overinsured and as well added an estimate for expected losses to shipwreck or theft to the profits on goods that did reach their destinations. Since consumers paid the same whether shipping was interfered with or not, Franco's conscience didn't trouble him over taking some of those profits for himself and his men. Food, medicines, and supplies needed for the survival of colonists in the New World, however, were not to be touched. Just the same, rich passengers could be robbed down to their stockings, but those who could not afford losses were spared. The two men Garcia had told him about had just joined the crew, ship jumpers fleeing a tyrannical captain, and might not know how the rules applied. They would soon find out, Franco decided as he disappeared into the darkness of the lower decks.

Lacey Bell had never felt such outright terror in her life. She had always longed for adventure and excitement but this was more than her courage could bear. The two scruffy-looking pirates that had broken down her door were going through her things, pulling her dresses out of her carefully packed trunks and tossing them aside, scrabbling for the bottom of the chests and the jewelry they hoped to find.

"I've told you, I haven't any more jewels," Lacey cried, watching them throw her belongings all over the cabin. She had only a handful of earbobs and necklaces collected over eighteen years of Christmases and birthdays and she had already given them that. "Please, don't do this," she pleaded.

One pirate, a bearded, rough-looking fellow, emptied the last of her chests while the other started to tear up her mattress, looking for what she hadn't hidden there in the first place. "Maybe the wench has it on her," the bearded one glared at her with a lecherous eye that took in all of Lacey's shapely form in a glance as he smiled at the prospect of searching her.

"No! I don't have anything! I gave you all I have . . ." She backed away from him as he started toward her.

"Leave her alone." Dorthea, Lacey's maid and traveling companion, tried to stop the man by clutching at him but he roughly shoved the woman aside.

"Out of my way, you old baggage." He pushed her so hard Dorthea fell to the floor and lay there stunned for a moment. His leering gaze returned to Lacey.

Oh, God, Lacey's frantic thoughts raced. Jamie had told her the pirates were a rough breed of men but Lacey

266

had nevertheless romanticized the tales her friend had related. Now, was this punishment she was facing for harboring such fanciful images in her head? She had been anxious to meet Morgan and the other pirates, envisioning handsome rogues with just the touch of the devil about them. Surely her imagination had never conjured someone like this burly, filthy ruffian coming toward her. Lacey backed all the way to the wall.

"The girl is telling you the truth." Dorthea had regained her feet and attacked the man, pounding on him. "She has nothing! Leave her be!"

"Mick, get this witch off me! I'll have reward enough out of the search whether she's hiding goods or no."

Dorthea was grabbed by the other one and held while the bearded man boxed Lacey into the corner. All Lacey could see was his grinning, ugly face coming closer, her nostrils filling with the stench of stale sweat, tobacco, and rum that came from him. What would Jamie do in her place? She didn't know and couldn't think beyond the sight of those huge, dirty hands coming closer to her.

"Let's see your goods, lassie." The brute reached for the bodice of Lacey's gown and she cringed, filled with terror and revulsion.

"No!" Lacey heard Dorthea shout, struggling against the other pirate holding her and laughing at Lacey's helpless predicament.

Just as Lacey closed her eyes to block out the sight of her attacker, she heard bootsteps crossing the floor, then felt the rush of air as the man was yanked forcefully away from her.

"Damn your eyes! Haven't I told you women are not to be molested?" a harsh male voice uttered in a low threat that portrayed ice-cold anger.

She opened her eyes again to find that another man had entered the room, this one tall and well dressed in black and white. A silver-handled saber was in his hand

and held across her attacker's throat. The pirate who had looked so horrible and all powerful only seconds before was now plastered stiffly against the wall beside her, his eyes wide with fright, his neck stiff to avoid the sharp edge of the blade held against his flesh.

"You dare disobey my laws?" the tall man asked, looking as if his next move might be to slit the offender's throat.

"No, Captain, no!" the one called Mick protested. "He didn't know! Neither of us did!" Mick had already released Dorthea who rushed to Lacey's side.

"Then you will be well served to learn my laws and quickly." The tall man kept his gaze and his weapon fastened on Lacey's tormentor. Lacey thought she had never seen a man so handsome or so gallant as her savior appeared at this moment.

"What did they steal from you?" the man asked Lacey, his eyes wavering to her for only a moment.

"Just these trinkets, Captain." Mick produced them from his pocket. "The ladies had no more. Honest!"

By now Lacey saw several more pirates appear in the doorway to her cabin, all of them watching the proceedings in silence.

"Give them back to her! Now!" the pirate captain barked and Mick immediately put the pieces on the dressing table.

"Now you!" He returned his attention to Lacey's tormentor, but the swordpoint at the man's throat hadn't wavered, its edge cutting the pirate's skin as the man dug in his pockets to retrieve the few pieces of jewelry he had taken. A small trickle of blood seeped slowly out of the wound and dribbled down the length of the blade to splash against the silver hilt. Her jewelry was produced and offered to the captain who took it then handed it to Lacey.

"Never, ever, forget my rules again," the captain said to

Lacey's attacker. "The women are to be left alone. You stay away from the cabins unless you have my permission to search. Do you understand me?"

The man tried to nod but it only made the blade dig into his own throat. He winced in pain as the blade cut deeper.

"Only this once a warning will suffice, but if it happens again, you will feel the full brunt of my wrath. Is that understood?"

"Aye," the man stammered. "Aye, Captain."

The blade moved so quickly it seemed a blur to Lacey's eyes. Suddenly it wasn't at her attacker's throat but at the edge of his collarbone, its gleaming tip beginning a very slow, very painful, descent down the bare skin of the man's chest where his shirt was left open. Dorthea gasped, looking away, but Lacey watched, fascinated as the sharp weapon trailed with infinite slowness toward the pirate's abdomen, leaving behind a red trail of scratched skin.

"Perhaps this scar you'll bear will serve to remind you. I promise you I will remember it and if I ever again see you breaking the rules of my ship, the next time I'll kill you on the spot." The bloody trail finally stopped at the man's sash and her attacker gazed down at his wound with open mouthed shock. His throat still oozed blood where the blade had bitten him, and now a pool of it was quickly soaking his sash and pants. The swordpoint had done no more than scratch the skin open and the wound would quickly heal but it would, most definitely leave a scar the man would bear for the rest of his life. "While you serve on my ship, you will never act under your own impulses again. You will do only as I tell you to do and nothing more. Is that perfectly clear?"

"Aye, Captain," Mick responded, glad it wasn't him who had been caught by the captain's anger. He grabbed his stunned friend's arm and yanked him away when the sword was removed. "We'll both remember, sir. Aye, sir, that we will . . ."

"Th . . . thank you, Captain," Lacey murmured when the pair disappeared into the gangway, following the other pirates who were leaving now that the entertainment was ended. "I owe you my life."

"You owe me nothing." The man wiped the blood off his sword with a handkerchief he had drawn from his pocket. "I do not tolerate disobedience from my crew," he said as if the man's only infamy was ignoring his captain's rules. "My apologies, ladies, for the inconvenience we've caused you." He bowed, then sheathed his sword again and walked out, pulling Lacey's broken cabin door closed behind him.

"I wonder who he is?" Lacey said her thought aloud. Her parents had allowed her to go to the New World to visit an aunt in Virginia for the winter, then she had their permission to stop in at Jamaica to see Jamie. She hadn't written Jamie to tell her she was coming yet, intending to do so from her aunt's plantation, but as soon as she saw her old school chum she was certainly going to tell her all about this encounter and learn if she had any idea who this magnificent savior could be.

"Well, what do you think of our plan?" Jamie asked Franco excitedly, sitting down on the edge of his bed in his cabin aboard the *Isabella*. She had been watching for his ship from her bedroom window as often as possible and spied it coming into port, then crept out of the house to avoid Morgan and ran straight to the docks to wait while the ship weighed anchor. Franco forgot all about his propriety and his fears for the safety of her reputation as soon as she appeared, swinging her up into his arms and carrying her, laughing, down to his cabin. It had taken all the willpower she possessed to hold him

270

back from making love to her until she told him what had transpired in his absence.

"I don't think I can find the slightest fault with it," Franco told her. "Your uncle doesn't mind doing this for us?"

"It was his own idea." She jumped off the bed, propelling herself into his arms. "Everything is working out perfectly. After all this time, finally things are going to come out right for us," she exclaimed. "He has to return to France anyway and then he fully expects to be sent to Spain. He really wants me to come with him, at least for a little while. And, since you'll be with us, your brother won't dare move against you while you're under Louis's protection through the office of the duc de Gavrilac as ambassador to Spain. King Philip will have to listen to your petition for justice."

"If I can find the copy of Father's will," Franco reminded her.

"Is there no one else who knows of its existence?"

"Father's solicitor knew, of course, but I learned that he died four months before Father. I'm afraid much of proving my claim rests on the copy of the will being where Father left it."

"Then it must be there. We'll just have to hope that it is." Jamie laced her fingers behind his neck. "Have I told you how very much I missed you?"

"I'd rather you show me." Franco smiled and let her squeal as he picked her up in his arms and dropped her across his bed.

"Oh, sir," Jamie pretended distress, "what of my reputation?"

"Never worry, lass." Franco sounded like an English courtier. "Would I seduce such a sweet, gentle flower, then leave her to wilt while I pluck another?"

"You'd better not!" she warned. "A woman scorned is a fearful apparition."

"One I should never care to face," he returned as he kissed her cheek, then let his lips travel down over her neck. "Why should I ever seek out the affections of another when I have you to come home to? 'Twould be like settling for a crust of bread to fill me while a banquet is being laid out before me." He nibbled the lobe of her ear while one hand explored for the fastenings of her gown, expertly loosening her bodice and exposing her luscious breasts to his view.

"I shall never ask how you became so proficient at removing female clothing," she commented as his kisses trailed down from her throat to the vee between her breasts.

"Don't," he whispered against her skin, "for they were not fit to hold your train, my lady, and even their memory dims to an insignificant light when I'm with you." He stretched out beside her, his busy hands removing her clothing and searching every curve of her body as it was exposed. He followed his hands' exploration with his mouth, kissing her everywhere until Jamie was afire with wanting him. She trembled with anticipation when he left her to remove his own clothing and then he was back in her eager arms, caressing her, kissing her, teasing her with his tongue and lips. She was more than ready for him when at last he drew himself on top of her and entered her willing flesh, gently at first and then at a faster rhythm as she responded, arching her hips to meet his powerful thrusts, their souls straining together for ever greater heights of ecstasy until they merged as one into unrestrained rapture. Then exhausted and content, they relaxed in each other's arms.

Nestled in his arms, Jamie let her fingers entwine in the sparse matting of ebony hair on his chest. "I have something for you," she remembered. "A gift."

"There can be no greater welcome-home present than those you've already given me, your news of your uncle

272

and then your sweet self . . ."

"Ah, but this one is more tangible." She smiled, wiggling out of his arms.

"More tangible than this?" He grabbed for her waist but she was already gone, kneeling beside the bed, searching for her muff among the articles of her clothing abandoned on the floor. She found the muff and reached inside it, drawing out an object that shimmered and glittered in the afternoon sunlight spilling through the curtained windows. "This, I believe, once belonged to you." She held it out to him.

"My grandfather's watch . . . But I gave it to you, long ago."

"And now I'm giving it back. I said I would only keep it until you were free. 'Twas only spite that made me keep it when you left me. If I could not have you, I wanted something of yours to hold. Open it. There's something inside." She watched him worriedly, hoping he would not object to the liberty she had taken. The pocket watch contained a place for a miniature portrait but none had been there when she received it from him. Franco opened the case, seeing the miniature Uncle Bertrand had given her, and his face lit with a broad, pleased smile, dispelling her fear that he might disapprove.

"My love, I treasured this once before as a remembrance of my grandfather. I shall value it twice as much now." He pulled Jamie into his arms. "When will your uncle be ready to depart?" he asked as he held her. "You make me all the more anxious to settle this and make you my own forever."

"He's ready whenever you are," Jamie told him. "As soon as the *Isabella* is ready to sail."

"Then I'll make her ready today." He started to rise from the bed but Jamie pulled him down to her again.

"It can wait just a little longer, can't it?"

* * *

"Papa, I wish you wouldn't take it this way."

"And how, then, am I to take it when me only daughter tells me she's running off with a man I'll never approve of."

"We are not 'running off.' If we were, would I be standing in front of you telling you about it? Franco is taking us to France and then to Spain for Uncle Bertrand to take up his duties there as envoy. While we're there, he's going to straighten out this entire affair with his brother. Then you won't have a thing to worry about, as your daughter will be marrying wealth and position, just as you've wanted."

"It's the man I don't like!" Henry Morgan shouted, losing his temper as he was losing having his own way. They were in her father's office with the door shut, but Jamie had no doubt the entire household could overhear the argument.

"Then tell me why, Papa." Jamie sighed wearily. "Give me one good reason to object to Franco."

"He's a Spaniard, curse it all, girl! Don't ye know we'll be at war with Spain in the not distant future?"

"If it comes, it won't last any longer than it takes for King William to come out of the snit he's in over Philip getting the Spanish throne."

"That's treason ye're talking, woman!"

"It's the truth and you know it!" she returned. "England and Spain have been at war a dozen times for one cause or another. What has that to do with us?"

"The Colonies is part of the British Empire," he blustered. "Ye'd be siding against yer own countrymen."

"Then, so be it!" Jamie stomped her foot in anger. "I am siding with the man I love! If that makes a traitor of me that I will not give him up for the whims of those in power, then it's a traitor I shall be!"

"Hush, girl, do ye want the entire staff to know the

274

traitorous mouth ye've got?"

"Let them hear it! They've heard everything else!"

"The man is going to leave you flat." Morgan tried a new tactic. "Ye mark me word, girl, he will. I know him better than you do. I've watched him here those months whilst you were away . . ."

"That isn't true, Papa . . ."

"Ye watch and see. First chance he gets ye'll find him in some other lass's arms. Men of his kind can't stay true to nobody. It's in his blood. No one woman is enough for him . . ."

"Papa, I am going with him and as soon as his name is cleared, we'll be married. I would like for that to happen here in Jamaica in front of my father and friends, but if you won't have it, then it will happen elsewhere. He's going to be the father of your grandchildren someday, Papa, and I'd like for you to be part of that, but if you insist on remaining obstinate, you'll find I'm every bit as adamant as you are!"

"Yer just like yer mother, ye are . . ." he began, but Jamie wouldn't have it.

"No! Don't ever accuse me of that again! Now that I know the truth about her that even you were never aware of, I'll not accept that I'm anything like her. If anything, it's your own bull-headedness I've inherited. What I am is what you've raised me to be, so you can blame yourself if you don't care for it now."

"That devil of a Spaniard has turned ye against me!"

"No, he hasn't, Papa." Jamie shook her head, tired of the argument. This was not the way she wanted to say good-bye. "No one is against you. Whether you choose to believe it or not, I do love you and I wish with all my heart you would try to be happy for me, but if you won't, then it's your own doing, not mine or Franco's." She turned away from him sadly, her anger lost somewhere in the moment of parting. She should have known

Uncle Bertrand's advice had been right. They should have left and settled accounts with Morgan on their return. He had tried himself to sound her father out on the subject and was surprised to find Morgan's mind so firmly set against it. He had warned her she would only face his rage and obstinacy in telling him she was leaving.

"I'll turn out the militia to stop ye!" her father threatened. "I'll have ye blocked in the harbor!"

"By the time you can do all that, we'll be gone," she said over her shoulder. The hopeless argument was making her head throb. "That's why I waited until the last moment to tell you, so you won't have time to use your powers as governor to stop us. I've left you Uncle Bertrand's address in Paris where I can be reached. They'll forward a letter if need be."

"After all this time, ye're going to desert me." Morgan's voice sounded like an old man's, but she dared not waver in her resolution, else she would be trapped forever under his thumb.

"Good-bye, Papa. Take care of yourself." Jamie walked away from him, passing through the doorway into the entry with a firm step. Her things were already packed and aboard the ship where Uncle Bertrand and Franco were waiting for her, ready to set sail the minute she arrived. She had insisted on seeing Morgan alone for this last interview, realizing it probably wouldn't be a pleasant one. She was closing a chapter on her life in walking away from Papa and she wished fervently that it could have ended in some other way.

"Good night, children. Sleep well, both of you."

"Good night, Uncle Bertrand," Jamie offered him a smile.

"Good night, Your Grace," Franco responded, then

turned his attention on Jamie when the duke left them alone together. They had dined together in Franco's cabin, the *Isabella* safely out to sea, but Jamie couldn't help the morose mood she was in though she had tried to lighten it for their sakes. "What is it, darling?" Franco moved his chair closer so he could put his arm around her.

"Oh, it's just Papa. I keep thinking of his voice when I left him, when he realized I was really going. He sounded so sad and forlorn."

"Sweetheart, your father can sound any way he wants to if it will get him what he wants. He's a wily old actor when he chooses to be."

"No, Franco, this sounded real. I truly hurt him."

"Did he leave you any other choice?" Franco asked.

Jamie shook her head. "It's just that I hate parting from him on such a note."

"I expect your uncle is right, my love. Give him time and when he realizes he can do nothing about it, he'll come around. Meanwhile, smile for me." Franco cupped her chin in his hand. "We have our own future to see to."

Jamie complied, putting her arms around his neck. "I love you so," she murmured. "I could never live without you."

"Nor I without you." Franco held her closely against him and kissed her hair. "You're mine, for today and for always. Nothing will ever come between us, not time, or distance, or anything else."

Chapter Thirteen

Franco was stunned, staring at the vision before him. He hadn't felt such outright awe since the day Jamie was first revealed to him as a woman.

"Well, do you like it?" She turned about in front of him, pleased by the look on his face.

"You need not ask such a question." He found his voice at last. "Look at you. You're exquisite. More than that—divine."

"You flatter me unmercifully, sir." Jamie spread her white lace fan and curtsied coyly. She had had the gown made especially for this occasion and the seamstresses had worked overtime to have it ready for today's event. The skirt was row upon row of white lace over satin, the scalloped edges of each tier of lace decorated with seed pearls and diamond chips that caught the light, reflecting sparks like captured fireflies. The bodice and sleeves were of the same lace over satin, sloping off her shoulders and exposing the uppermost portion of her full, firm breasts. Jamie wouldn't wear a wig that was the latest rage in French fashion, having her own ebony tresses fastened into an upswept style and instructing the hairdresser to entwine ropes of pearls in the black waves of her curls. The gown had cost her most of the funds she had taken with her from Jamaica but was worth the expense to see such admiration in his eyes. She wanted to pay for it herself to keep its purchase a secret and surprise the men in her life. Uncle Bertrand had already given her several

278

of the family heirlooms and Franco had been generous in presenting her with whatever she liked out of the chests of jewelry, thus her ears and throat sparkled with diamonds that matched her costume.

Her happiness over the last two months had to be reflected in her face and posture as well. The sea voyage had been heaven for her, to be in Franco's company day and night, to lie in his arms while the ship's motion rocked them to sleep, to revel in his undivided attention, to experience such passion as they had shared together. Jamie had her own cabin aboard the *Isabella,* but the fact that she hardly, or never, used it, went chivalrously unmentioned by her gracious and understanding relative. Part of her wished her trip might never end, while the other half anxiously looked forward to seeing all their problems solved.

"Madame de Montespan will pale beside you, my sweet," Franco prophesied. As the custom of the court dictated all white, he was dressed in a splendid suit of that color that looked marvelous against his darkly tanned skin.

"And you, darling, will outshine the Sun King himself," Jamie commented, making Franco laugh to hide his embarrassment over donning such a richly elaborate garment. Franco hated laces and frills but had to wear both to appear properly attired to meet the king. "It does make you look less like a Protestant minister than your somber black and white."

"A Protestant minister?" he queried with an upraised brow. "I? If we were not expected to meet your uncle in a few minutes, I would show you a few things you'd never learn from a minister."

"I don't know. I hear they're a deceptive breed, pure passion away from their pulpits," she tossed back. "Perhaps I should try one and find out."

"I'll give you . . ." Franco grabbed her into his arms.

"Not now. We'll be late," she laughed, pulling free of his arms. "Uncle Bertrand is waiting."

"Then your lesson in passion will have to hold until we return."

"You'll fall asleep on me as you did last night."

"I had too much brandy with your uncle," he defended.

"Excuses, excuses," she giggled lightly, fleeing for the door before he could catch her.

"Your Majesty, may I present my niece, Jamie Morgan, and her fiancé, Don Francisco DeCortega."

"Well, well, what an exquisite creature you are." Louis of France hardly noticed Franco beside her, raising Jamie's hand to his lips and immediately placing it over his arm with a proprietary air. "Your portrait in my salon hardly does you justice, my dear," Louis began to walk away with her and Franco frowned, preparing to follow them.

Bertrand Duvalier stopped him, holding back on Franco's arm. "Jamie knows what to say to him to get what we need," he warned. "Leave it be. Your jealousy will only put a fly in the ointment."

"I won't let him take her off somewhere alone," Franco said, looking after them as they strode away across the lawn where an afternoon party was in progress.

"I've given her all the advice she needs to handle Louis. Trust her."

"It's *him* I don't trust!" Franco turned away reluctantly.

"You've already competed against one king and won and you weren't even there," Bertrand reminded him. "Calm yourself, my friend, her heart is yours."

"It's her body I'm worried about at present. Didn't you see the way he looked at her?"

"I've seen the way every man has looked at her since your arrival." Bertrand smiled. "Such is the price one pays for possessing a beautiful woman. It's just Louis's way to flirt with every young lovely that visits his court. Besides, I think it shan't be long before Madame de Montespan makes her move to step in," Bertrand indicated the king's long-time mistress standing by the fountain, surrounded by handsomely dressed men and women but positively glaring after Jamie and the king. "I had better head her off before she interferes too soon and my niece never gets the chance to ask for our favor." Bertrand moved toward the woman anxiously tapping her fan against her palm, leaving Franco to stew in his jealousy.

Jamie, he had learned, was far more than he had even predicted she was capable of becoming. Not a soul here would believe she was the same girl he had met three and a half years before. He was still discovering assets he hadn't known she possessed. He never knew she spoke French until she greeted her uncle's friends with full mastery of the language. He was left in shock after he asked her if she had studied it at the school and heard her reply that Mary Lambert had taught her many years before. Italian was the tongue she studied at Lady Westcott's, she told him, then proceeded to utterly charm an Italian count and his countess in that language as well.

How petty he felt for ever fearing she might not fit in had he been able to take her home with him three years ago. His father would have instantly fallen under her spell, just as the Spanish ambassador to France had succumbed to her charm. She spoke well to every guest she met, men and women alike and Franco's chest swelled with pride, but at the same time he realized Bertrand was correct that there was a heavy price on loving a beautiful woman and that was the monster of jealousy presently consuming him, especially when he noticed he could find neither Jamie nor the king among the milling guests.

* * *

281

"He was only showing me my portrait in his drawing room," Jamie explained, sitting beside Franco and across from her uncle in the enclosed carriage that was taking them back to Uncle Bertrand's estate near the king's palace at Versailles.

"You were gone long enough for him to have shown you every room in the palace!" Franco complained. The afternoon lawn party had lasted until late into the night, having gone indoors at sunset and continuing through a many-coursed dinner, then dancing and festivities that followed until the small hours of the morning. Louis seemed intent on spending much of the evening in Jamie's company, as did many of his guests and retainers. Franco barely had the opportunity to speak to her, much less to catch her for a dance, and his temper was well up.

"Well, he was kind enough to show me around a bit," Jamie admitted. "But I did get the safe passage for you. His secretary will write it out and have it delivered to you tomorrow."

"And what did you have to give him in return for it?" Franco grumbled.

Bertrand suddenly choked, coughing, then took an intense interest in the darkness passing by his window.

Jamie's back stiffened with instant anger as she turned her head to glare at Franco. "I should slap your face for such a question, but I'll answer it. I gave him my thanks, if you must know, in *verbal* form. Louis was a perfect gentleman, which is more than I can say for you!"

Just then, the coach rolled to a stop in front of the Duvalier mansion and Jamie was out and away from the vehicle before the startled coachman could descend.

"It's not my affair, I know, but that was not the wisest

thing to have said," Bertrand commented with upraised brows, ignoring Franco's glare. "Take care, *mon ami*," he warned. "Jealousy can undo the greatest affection."

"I don't understand it." Franco shook his head a minute later as they walked inside the house. "I can't believe what I said to her. I've never felt like this before. No woman has ever done this to me."

"Perhaps it is that you are not yet used to dealing with her as a woman," Bertrand suggested. "The Jamie you knew before was a girl who was madly in love with you, so much so that you knew you had no rivals. Now she is a woman who, in turn, is capable of being adored by many men. If you will keep her, you will have to come to terms with that."

"I know you're right, Bertrand. Meanwhile, I owe her an apology."

Franco started up the stairs to her room and rapped on the door. When she didn't answer or acknowledge, he pushed it open to find her sitting in the window seat in her shift, looking out into the darkness of the night. Her beautiful gown was discarded across an armchair as if she had immediately dismissed her maid, insisting on being left alone.

"Jamie," he called, but she didn't turn. "I'm sorry, darling. I had no right to say what I did to you. None at all. Please forgive me." Franco came up and sat behind her so that he could put his arms around her and urged her to lean back against him. She came without protest, saying nothing, her gaze remaining fixed on the blackness outside.

"Sweetheart . . ." He turned her so that he could see her tear-streaked face and felt the utter cad for having hurt her so. "I didn't mean a word of it. It's just that I hardly had a moment to be with you and I envied the others for each second you spent in their company. If I could, I expect I would keep you locked inside my cabin and allow no one but myself near you."

"Truly?" she murmured, her lower lip trembling as she gazed at him.

"Truly, my love." He smiled, then kissed her gently. "If I ever again become so boorishly possessive, you have my permission, no, my demand, that you strike me alongside the head with a brick, if need be, to bring me to my senses."

"I promise you, then, I shall." She turned about to nestle against him and, a few minutes later, he picked her up in his arms to carry her to her bed where he made long, agonizingly slow, love to her until dawn.

Franco had sent word ahead that he was coming. He had already received his audience with Philip who agreed to honor the safe conduct Jamie obtained from his uncle, Louis of France, long enough to hear him out, especially when Franco made him aware that a goodly portion of the treasure he had collected over the past three years would go to the Crown as the spoils of privateering ventures against Spain's enemies. That a portion of the gold and jewels came from Spanish ships would remain forever undisclosed and unquestioned.

It was Jamie's own suggestion that she wait outside the chambers until Franco's audience with King Philip was concluded, not out of fear of a repetition of what had happened at Louis's court but rather to allow him the opportunity to savor this victory alone. His name was cleared by the king's command, all charges pending against him dropped, and there was nothing Lorenzo could do now about his younger brother's homecoming.

Since they were expecting him, Franco's sisters and their families and the entire staff of the DeCortega household were on the steps to meet his carriage as it rolled into the driveway.

Franco had described Maria as the eldest sister, having been born between Lorenzo and Franco, thus Jamie assumed she was the taller woman with sable brown hair lightly salted with gray. Around her skirts three children, two boys and a shy little girl, were gathered. The younger woman with a toddler at her skirt and another in her arms was the first to step forward as Franco descended from the carriage, hardly giving her brother time to hand Jamie down to the driveway before hugging him fiercely, weeping in her happiness at seeing him again. Obviously Franco was the favorite of all as the other woman took her turn greeting him, then the servants and staff. In spite of all Jamie had heard about Spanish stiffness and formality, it was a boisterous reunion with many happy tears and smiles, except for two men who stood slightly apart on the steps of the magnificent, ancient manor house watching the proceedings without any emotion. One of them must be Lorenzo, but which, Jamie wondered while she stood all but forgotten in the happy welcome.

She had already made up her mind to despise Lorenzo DeCortega, but had thought he might at least slightly resemble Franco, yet neither of the men on the steps looked anything like her preconceived notions. One was short and paunchy, already losing his wisps of light brown hair though she doubted he had yet reached forty. The other man was tall, though not as tall as Franco, and very lean, with a sharp beaklike appearance. He looked by his bearing like someone who might be suited to an accountant's trade or a banker. She had expected to see some trace of villainy in the countenance of the eldest brother, but could find nothing in either face that reflected such an evil soul as she had decided he must possess.

"Sisters, friends, you must permit me to introduce my companion," Franco broke into her assessment of the men, reaching for Jamie's arm to draw her forward. "Maria, Theresa," he announced, "my fiancée, Mistress Jamie Morgan."

"Franco, you're going to be married?" Maria exclaimed delightedly, coming forward to kiss Jamie's cheek.

"Indeed, as soon as we return to the islands," Franco beamed.

"Then you'll be leaving us again?" Theresa looked immediately bereft.

"Not immediately, dear one," Franco assured the baby of the family. "But I'm afraid Jamaica has become my home now."

Jamie could have shouted with joy to hear him say it. It was one thing they never spoke of, the future and where they would live after they were married. She wondered if he was afraid to make any plans until this matter in Spain was settled, as if speaking of them and planning a future together might tempt the fates to turn against them.

In the next few minutes, they were ushered inside the house and Maria finally remembered to introduce the pair of men who had stood idly by all the while. Neither, it turned out, was the infamous Lorenzo. One was the husband of Maria DeCortega Garcelón and the other was Theresa's husband. Jamie's knowledge of Italian helped her to understand much of the rapid-fire Spanish being spoken and she soon figured out that the tall one who looked like an accountant was, unbelievably, the rake who could not remain faithful to Theresa. When the man excused himself a few minutes later to attend to "pressing business" the truth came out that Theresa had left him, taking shelter in her ancestral home. Only out of courtesy to the DeCortega family had he made a brief appearance today. He had become enamored of some flaxen-haired beauty he had set up as his mistress and would not fight Theresa for custody of the two children.

The other man, of course, was Maria's husband, Esteban Garcelón, the one who, by reports Franco received the last time he was in Spain, drank too much and lost his temper, taking out his drunken rages on his helpless wife. Esteban, however, stayed through dinner, remaining fairly sober, cognizant every moment of Franco's watchful eye on him and well aware of the younger brother's past successes in duels over far less serious matters than his sister's happiness.

Supper was over and the company had retired to the salon for coffee and brandy before the subject of Lorenzo came up.

"You all have done an excellent job of dancing around it, but now it is time for me to know." Franco faced his sisters and brother-in-law from his armchair beside the blazing fireplace. For the first time since she had known him, he looked comfortably at ease and at home in the dark, polished surroundings of the house he had grown up in. "Where is Lorenzo and why isn't he here?"

For several seconds there was nothing but silence and Jamie stared curiously from one face to another.

"Francisco, God is punishing him." Theresa broke the unnatural quiet, her eyes misting with tears that she dabbed at with a white lace handkerchief.

Franco leaned forward. "What do you mean?"

Maria glanced nervously toward Jamie.

"She is going to be my wife," Franco said harshly. "There is nothing that can take place in this family that she should not know about."

"He's ill, Franco," Maria finally provided. "The doctors say it is a cancer."

"He's dying?" Franco's brows lowered as he stared at Maria who nodded solemnly.

"He confessed the truth, Franco. First, to his confessor and then to Esteban and our mother. She knows now that you're alive and she's anxious to see you, but, of

287

course, she cannot leave the convent. We can go to see her tomorrow, if you like," Theresa explained rapidly.

"He confessed . . . what?" Franco's gaze fell on Esteban Garcelón.

"Everything," Esteban said. "The note he sent to the pirates, the burning of the will. He wishes to cleanse his soul before he meets his Maker. He said he lied to Isabella when he told her you were dead."

"And our father. Did he lie to him as well?"

Esteban lowered his gaze to the carpet.

"He didn't know it would happen, Francisco," Theresa burst in, tears now streaming freely down her cheeks. "Father's heart . . . He loved you and to think he had lost you, that he had sent you to your death by sending you away."

"Damn him!" Franco exploded out of the chair to stalk across the room. Jamie flinched at the unexpectedness of his outburst. "Curse his soul to eternal damnation! He killed him! The same as if he had murdered him!"

"He didn't think Father would take it so hard," Theresa interjected. "He swears he didn't expect it. You know how strong Father always was, a rock. Lorenzo is suffering for it now. He's so ill . . . He's paying for the sins he committed. If you could but see him . . ."

"He deserves to pay!" Franco slammed his fist against the wall, rattling several pictures in their frames. "Where is he?"

"Upstairs," Maria answered quietly. "In his room. Waiting for you."

"He wants to beg you to forgive him, Francisco," Theresa added, wringing her hands.

"Let God forgive him," Franco said in cold contempt, "for I never will!" He turned and stormed out the door, slamming it behind him.

* * *

"Come, dear, I'll show you to your room," Maria said into the silence that followed Franco's departure. Theresa was weeping quietly while Esteban filled his glass with brandy and took it with him into the next room. Franco's sister lit a candle to escort Jamie upstairs.

"I'm sorry that your introduction to our family had to be under such trying conditions," she said as they ascended the thickly carpeted stairs.

"You needn't apologize," Jamie told her. "Franco has seen my family at our worst. My father was the privateer who held him for ransom." If Maria was going to be her sister-in-law, she might as well know the truth.

Maria stopped on the stairway to gaze at her. "No . . ."

Jamie nodded. "I'm afraid so."

" 'Tis a strange world we live in, is it not?" she commented, starting up the steps again. "Tell me, is it true as I've heard that Franco won his freedom in a game of dice?"

"His freedom, and me," Jamie said. "In the same throw."

To Jamie's relief, Maria Garcelón laughed. "What strange customs you English have." Jamie had noticed a resemblance between the sisters and Franco in similar patrician noses, heavy-lidded eyes, and expressions that were frequently alike. Theresa was the prettier, but appeared high-strung while Maria had a motherly air about her that made Jamie feel comfortable in her presence. Franco had told her that Maria had often taken care of him when they were children, though she was only two years older. She had been late to wed because she had taken care of an ailing grandmother until the woman died six years ago. She was thirty when Lorenzo arranged her marriage to Esteban and had borne three children in quick succession. Perhaps that accounted for her looking so much older than the others.

"At any rate," Maria continued. "I am glad to learn

Franco has found someone to settle down with. At times, I wondered if he ever would."

"How so, señora?" Jamie asked, following Maria down a long, damp corridor. Franco's home was huge, three times the size of the Tortuga mansion, but its stone walls emitted a moist chill that made Jamie wish she had taken a shawl to wrap around her shoulders. The furniture in every room she had seen was of dark wood and very heavy. Medieval arms and ornaments hung from the walls between portraits of long-deceased ancestors. There were few windows, and most of them had panes of stained glass that even on the brightest day would fail to permit much light to enter. She was extremely relieved that he had said they would not be making their home here. Though it held an Old World charm of elegance and vast wealth and power, she was sure if she gave her imagination any rein at all she would begin to see ghosts in every dark corner.

"Franco was always the wild one," Maria explained. "He courted a number of women but never with any real intentions. Father was furious with him over it. I'm afraid he was a bit of a heartless scoundrel, courting two and even three at a time." Maria smiled to make light of it. "But, don't worry, my dear," Maria saw Jamie's disheartened expression, "none were so pretty as you and I have never known my brother to make promises he does not intend to keep. Those others were nothing but the flirtations of youth." She opened a door in the middle of the corridor. "Here is your room. I hope it is satisfactory."

Jamie saw a warmly glowing fire that dispelled the gloom of the tapestried, weighty furniture immeasurably. It was cozily warm and inviting as she stepped inside. "It's lovely. Thank you."

"Eduardo has already brought up your trunks." She pointed them out where they had been placed on the floor. "I'll send one of the maids up to help you unpack and undress. If you're fatigued, feel free to retire and let the maid see to the unpacking."

"Thank you, señora. You've been very kind."

"I hope you will feel free to call me Maria. After all, we shall be relatives soon, shall we not? If you need anything, at any hour, simply pull the bell cord and someone will come." Maria gave her an affectionate hug that went a long way toward making Jamie feel welcome in these new, strange surroundings.

A little while after Maria left, a maid appeared to help her out of her clothes and tucked her into bed with a glass of warm milk while she unpacked Jamie's trunks and put everything neatly away. After she had gone, Jamie waited in vain for Franco to appear while the candles burned low and the blazing logs died down in the fireplace. They had spent every night together for two months on board his ship and in Uncle Bertrand's house, making this time alone seem unbearably lonely. How she wished Uncle Bertrand was with them but he had stayed on at Philip's court. This was a new place, strange to her, and she needed company with whom she was familiar. She knew he was upset but why, then, didn't he need her even more now, after learning what he had about his father and brother?

In his place, she would have wanted comfort in his presence, to find solace in his arms. Why didn't he need the same?

She had no idea how to find him in this vast, many-roomed castle. She didn't dare ring for someone to ask about him. His family was Catholic and might frown on the closeness of their relationship. Uncle Bertrand was French. He was used to the free love and intrigues of Louis's court, but Franco's relatives might not be so open-minded. Still, in so large a place, couldn't he sneak into her room as they had done for the first few days on

Franco's ship before they realized Uncle Bertrand was willing to look the other way?

Jamie tried to settle down to sleep but the bed was so empty without him and she couldn't help being hurt that he was staying away. Finally, still thinking of Franco and worried about him, she drifted off into uneasy, toss-filled slumber.

A different maid than the one who had waited on her last night awoke Jamie to a cup of steaming hot chocolate placed beside her bed. The drapes had been pulled back from the windows and clear panes of glass let in a bright burst of cheery sunlight.

"Good morning, señorita," the woman said in fairly precise English. "I am Lucinda. Doña Garcelón sent me to serve you. If you will tell me which gown you wish to wear today, I will fetch it for you."

"If you wouldn't mind, Lucinda, I should prefer to bathe first."

"A bath, señorita?" Lucinda appeared shocked. "At this time of the year? You would surely catch your death."

"I bathe daily, Lucinda, when I can, at any time of year."

Lucinda clucked her disapproval. "A bath is terribly unhealthy, señorita."

"Is it too difficult to arrange?" Jamie interrupted her. She had gone through similar judgments that she was sure to die from so much bathing at Lady Westcott's, yet she continued to fill the tub in the washroom with heated water through the winter as well as the summer.

"It is no trouble, if you insist."

"I would appreciate it," Jamie told her, and Lucinda finally left to fetch the hot water for the tub, leaving Jamie to sip her cocoa and wonder when she might ever see her fiancé again. That he had not come to her at all last night weighed heavily on her mind. She was worried about him and about what was suddenly happening to their relationship.

They had been so happy aboard the ship, growing closer with each passing day, but then the possessiveness he had displayed at Louis's court had come between them and the cruelty of that unnecessary remark. Was it simply jealousy that had made him so unreasonable when he knew she was only courting Louis's favor for his sake? And now this, totally ignoring her since last night, staying away, keeping his grief and his anger locked inside him and not sharing his thoughts with her, not allowing her to enter that part of himself. Was it because he was home again that his attitudes were changing? Was he regretting that he had promised her so much or was it only her imagination taking flight after what Maria had told her about Franco's fickle youth? Was she being unfair in taking his absence from her personally when, in truth, she had nothing to fear?

She knew she wouldn't find her answer lying in bed all day and finished her cocoa, then got up to search her closets herself for what she would wear.

Jamie knew the minute she saw the woman that she had once been Franco's lover. She was tall, with a regal bearing that swept into the dining hall where breakfast was being served as if she owned it. She was wearing a riding habit of dove gray trimmed in crimson and a jaunty riding hat with a crimson feather in the hatband. She was undeniably beautiful with her flaxen hair done up in a French knot that stretched the faultless skin taut over high, perfectly formed cheekbones. The simple yellow frock Jamie had chosen to wear today seemed paltry beside the woman's elegant costume. Jamie could feel the woman's animosity when Maria introduced her as Franco's fiancée. A glare of pure hatred suddenly emanated out of her dark green eyes. Doña Elena Vega was married, as her wedding band testified, but the fact did not keep her from displaying her hostility behind a veneer of pleasant smiles and remarks.

"Franco went out early this morning," Maria answered Elena Vega's query on where the happy prospective bridegroom might be. "He didn't say when he might return." Maria had told Jamie the same story, but Jamie thought she was covering for his absence and didn't know where he had gone, or when.

"Ah, it's too bad then, that I've missed him." Doña Vega accepted Maria's polite invitation to join them for coffee, taking a seat at the table as if she had every intention of waiting there until Franco did return. "I intended to call to see how poor Lorenzo is faring."

Jamie easily read Maria's glance. Probably the woman had not called in all these many months since Lorenzo first fell ill.

"The doctors say it is only a matter of time," Maria told her, pouring hot coffee into a cup then setting it before Doña Vega.

"Such a pity," the woman exclaimed without sympathy. "At least Franco has returned in time to see him before . . . Well, before . . ." She stirred sugar and cream into the aromatically steaming cup.

Jamie was pleased to learn that obviously Doña Vega was not privy to the family secrets since she knew nothing about the rift between the brothers. She had appeared today for one purpose only, having heard of Franco's return and rushing right over, making Jamie curious about whether the affair she was sure had taken place had been before or after Doña Vega's marriage. While Maria carried on most of the conversation with the guest, Jamie noticed how often she caught Elena Vega glancing at her, assessing her, sizing her up as a rival, quite possibly hoping Franco's impending wedding plans would not present any serious obstacle to a renewal of a relationship with Franco. Jamie wanted to scratch her eyes out just for entertaining the thought she was so openly harboring.

"When do you and Franco intend to wed, my dear?" Elena finally asked her, talking down to Jamie as the younger, and, of course, far less experienced woman. When Maria called her "my dear" it sounded warm and affectionate, but Elena's use of the term simply seemed patronizing.

"As soon as we return to Jamaica," Jamie took great pleasure in replying and watching the older woman's face fall. For the space of several seconds, Elena Vega didn't seem to know what to say.

"Franco is going back then, to that awful place? Why would he when he had so much trouble there. This is his home."

"He considers the islands his home now," Jamie explained. "You underestimate him, Doña Vega. He has long ago resolved any problems he had encountered there, and the islands are really quite lovely. You should visit them sometime."

Elena visibly bristled.

"If ever you do visit, you must stop in to see us," Jamie offered pleasantly. "I know Franco would be pleased to receive you and your husband whenever you might care to call."

Jamie thoroughly enjoyed her victory as the woman glared. "Thank you, dear," she said with ill-concealed hostility that made Jamie want to gloat.

Changing the subject, an hour passed before Doña Vega gave up her vigil and left, leaving a message that she would call again in the near future — to look in on poor Lorenzo, naturally.

"The abominable witch!" Maria said when the woman

finally made her exit. "She's been chasing after Franco since the day she first saw him, and she a wife and mother. Your presence must have truly set her back on her heels. You handled her very well, I must say," Maria said with a smile.

"Has she ever managed to catch him?" Jamie felt impelled to ask.

"I'm sure only in her own mind," Maria replied, ringing the bell for the servants to come and clear the table. "There was a time when I thought . . . But, oh, it doesn't matter. It was so long ago."

Not long enough to set Jamie's mind at rest. Not with the woman so anxious to see him after four years had passed. She was discovering that much of what Franco had told her about himself was true. He had built a bad reputation before he left, not only for his mercurial temperament but also for the romantic swath he had cut before his father sent him away. Had Carlos known something about Franco and Elena Vega that encouraged him to send his youngest son away from temptation? Jamie couldn't quite accept that a mere mild flirtation would have brought the woman here so quickly after learning of Franco's return. And where was he? Why had he forgotten her so easily to go off, God only knew where, in his distress? While the voyage here had been a loving and passionate interlude, Jamie felt like everything was quickly falling apart since they left the ship, first in France and now here. Just as she had been afraid four years ago when he left her to return home that she might lose him to his old way of life, the insecurity was resurrecting itself, making her feel he was, indeed, slipping away from her.

Perhaps she didn't know him as well as she had believed. He had told her he once courted women with less than honorable intentions, but two, even three at a time? Youthful wild oats could only cause some of it and she had to wonder if there was something deeper and more sinister at the root of the casual relationships. Were there more Elena Vegas waiting in the wings? Was he not, after all, the kind of man she had thought he was and fallen in love with?

If only he was here to ease her mind. If only he would come to her and share his pain, but she had been shut out, deserted, and was forced to question why—why was this happening between them?

"If you will excuse me, I'll look in on Lorenzo and then we can tour the house." Maria intruded into Jamie's troubled thoughts.

She didn't want to stay down here alone with nothing to do but dwell on Franco. "Would it be all right if I came with you?" she asked. She still hadn't met him and her curiosity was stirred.

Maria seemed to weigh the decision uncertainly. "It isn't a pleasant sight," she warned. "Are you certain you feel up to it?"

"He is Franco's brother," Jamie explained. "I should like to meet him while I still can."

"Very well, then," Maria smiled. "Come along."

In the upstairs hall of a different wing from where her own room was located, Jamie smelled the unpleasant medicinal odor emanating from the sickroom even before Maria opened the door. She was about to meet the man her imagination had conjured into the form of a demon, a monster of selfishness and deceit. She had prepared herself for anything but the sight that met her eyes as she followed Maria into the dying man's bedroom.

The heavy velvet drapes were partially closed, giving the wide room a stuffiness that was oppressive. Theresa sat vigil by the bedside, sewing on a piece of embroidery. The overpowering stench of camphor and sulphur and the waste products of the illness, made Jamie nauseous and she had to hold down an impulse to gag on the stifling scents. But most shocking of all was the ogre her mind had created who was nothing but a weak, sick man, frail in his infirmity, surely no more than a few days away from death. She couldn't imagine what he might have been like when he was robust with health. It looked like a skeleton was posed in the bed, dressed in a pale green dressing gown and propped up against the pillows. His transparent skin was stretched taut as a drum over his face, his cheeks ruddy with fever, contrasting sharply with the pallor of his complexion that was fish-belly white. Jamie had come prepared to hate him and now she couldn't. Nothing but pity welled up in her. If this was God's punishment, surely it was too much to atone for with this ghastly suffering. His breathing was ragged and raspy, as if each breath he drew was a struggle. Intense pain registered in his face though she knew they must be giving him heavy doses of morphine. Theresa reached out and touched his shoulder to wake him and the sunken eyes opened. Jamie saw they were the same shade of intense black as Franco's, and a lump of pity swelled in her throat.

"Lorenzo, this is Jamie Morgan." Maria leaned over him. "She is Francisco's fiancée and has come to see you."

Lorenzo's head turned toward his sister, the dark eyes glazed with pain, questioning. "Franco?" his lips mouthed the word but the sound that came out was no more than a harsh whisper.

"No," Maria explained gently. "He will not come. Not yet." She patted the thin, gnarled hand that rested on top of the bedcover.

Lorenzo turned back to Jamie, gazing at her for a moment and she would swear he tried to smile, then he began to struggle to remove a large gold ring from over the swollen knuckle of his wasted hand. Theresa put down her sewing to help him. When the ring was free, he held it out to Jamie, insisting with his gaze that she take it.

Uncertain, Jamie looked from one sister to the other for what she should do.

"Take it," Maria urged her.

Jamie complied, letting him drop the ring into her palm. He seemed satisfied and sank back against the pillow, the brief activity utterly draining him.

"What is it?" Jamie clutched her fingers over the large gold ring in her hand. Franco already had a signet ring that had been a present from his father. Besides the watch it was the only jewelry he ever wore.

"It's the seal of the Conde DeCortega," Maria explained. "It belongs to Franco now, and to his son, and to his son's sons after him . . . come, he's fallen asleep."

Jamie took one last look at the gravely suffering man in the bed then followed Maria from the room.

"Franco, if you would just see him for only a minute," Jamie pleaded.

"Now they've enlisted even you to work on me?" Franco strode across the room away from her. He had returned by midday with no explanation offered for his long absence. Jamie didn't know where he had slept last night, if he had, or where he had been all morning. Theresa was still upstairs with Lorenzo, and Maria had excused herself to look in on the children, leaving them alone in the library. "Is everyone conspiring against me?"

"No one is conspiring against you."

"How easily everyone forgets," he continued as if he hadn't heard her. "I was the one he betrayed! He killed my father, put my mother through unnecessary grief, lied about me, had me hounded out of the country, and yet you all can so easily say, 'Forgive him, Franco, he wants to beg your pardon.' Why should I forgive him? Why should I be the one to show mercy when he had none for me?"

"I'm not asking you to do this for his sake, Franco, but for your own. He's still your brother and what he did is, perhaps, unforgivable. Then don't forgive him, but at least let him see you. Let him say what he wants to say to you before it's too late."

"To let him say what?" Franco's voice rose to a terrible shout. "That he's sorry? Sorry our father is dead? Sorry that our mother looks like an old woman before her time? Does he want to say he's sorry he left me to my fate, hoping your father would kill me?"

So that was where he had been, Jamie thought as she listened to his rage. He had gone to the convent to see his mother.

"Mother tells me to forgive him. Maria and Theresa. And now you as well."

"Because we can see what this is doing to you," Jamie argued. "This hatred you are trying to sustain is eating you alive. Don't make the same mistake Lorenzo did in turning against your own flesh and blood."

"He is the one who turned against me!" Franco said so fiercely that Jamie unconsciously flinched.

"Then let him say he's sorry!" she returned. "What else can he do when it's impossible to take back what he's done? What else can he offer? Let him say it to you."

Franco spun around on her, his anger burning. "If I go up those stairs, it will only be to end his miserable life!"

Jamie stared at him. "Have you absolutely no mercy in you?" she finally asked him. "When we came here, I hated him as much as you. But he's confessed to having wronged you, not only to his priest but to Esteban and the family. There is nothing else he can do to undo it, except apologize. If you can't find it in your heart to at least hear his plea, then you leave me to wonder if you

300

will be so hardhearted against me someday as well if I should ever disappoint you. If I weren't able to reach you to say I'm sorry, then you would leave no recourse to make amends."

"I can't do it, Jamie. Don't ask me," he said, his mind firmly shut on the subject.

"Very well then." She rose from the settee to pass him on her way to the door. "But if the words 'I'm sorry' have no meaning to you, what then is it to mean to me when *you* say them? Are they just empty words to you?" Jamie walked out, leaving him to settle with his conscience.

Theresa's face was as white as a sheet as she joined Maria and Jamie in the sitting room.

"What is it?" Maria started in alarm. "Lorenzo?"

Theresa shook her head to answer the question. "Franco just walked in," she murmured as though unable to believe what had just transpired. "He asked me to leave them alone together."

"Is he angry?" Maria prompted, looking past her sister toward the stairway.

"I don't think so. He didn't seem so. He just walked in and asked me to leave them, then sat down in the chair by the bed."

"Oh, thank God!" Maria made a quick sign of the cross in front of herself.

Later that night, Lorenzo DeCortega died quietly in his sleep. Jamie never asked Franco what had happened in the sickroom and he didn't offer the information, but by his peace of mind at his brother's funeral, she assumed he had found the mercy to forgive him.

Chapter Fourteen

"Franco, I was going to ask Lorenzo, but he was so sick since the day we came, I never had the chance."

"I know," Franco said matter-of-factly. "You have made a mess of your finances and presently find yourself in an embarrassing predicament. A loan will tide you over until you can redeem yourself."

"Well, yes," Esteban stammered, "but how did you know?"

"What else would have brought you here to remain faithfully by Lorenzo's bedside," Franco replied, ignoring the flush that had spread over Esteban Garcelón's features. Esteban had asked Franco if he might speak to him in private on the evening of Lorenzo's funeral and Franco suggested the walk in the garden to give them privacy from the guests inside. Night had fallen and a full moon lit their path.

Esteban had no option but to swallow the remark, since it was the truth and he needed the money badly. Creditors were breathing down his neck. It was primarily for the access to the DeCortega fortune that he had married Maria. "Then, will you?" he asked. It was degrading to have to ask favors of a younger man, especially one he had heard so much about but knew so superficially. Lorenzo had been a man of the world, with a gentleman's faults and vices. He would have understood Esteban's dilemma, but Franco DeCortega was cut of a different fabric and Esteban didn't know yet what kind of man he was dealing with. He had heard all the rumors about him, that being left to his fate and penniless, Franco had fought back against the odds and won a considerable fortune of his own. The crown had granted him full pardon as a Spanish privateer, but tales were already circulating that some of the treasure turned over to the throne had come from Spanish coffers in the first place. What sort of man turned such adversity to such advantage?

They walked several yards in silence while Franco pondered Esteban's request. "No," he said finally. "I will not make you a loan since you will only spend it to quiet your creditors then be in the same position a few months hence. What I will do is strike a bargain with you."

"What kind of bargain?" Esteban was puzzled. Did he have hope, or not, of getting his hands on any money?

"I will pay off your creditors immediately. In turn, you will agree to sell the house in Barcelona, the apartment in Madrid, and you will liquidate all of your assets." Franco held up his hand to forestall Esteban's protest. "You will then use these funds to go into partnership with me."

"Partnership?"

"There are opportunities in the New World for people to make a new start. I know a man there who thinks a superior grade of coffee could be produced in the high elevations of Jamaica. I want to hire him to test out his theory, but I do not have the time or inclination to run a plantation. I have other plans. I hear your family has made a living off the land for many generations."

"That's true, Francisco, but . . ."

"The choice is simple," Franco went on over him. "You go into partnership with me and run the plantation, or

303

you can face debtor's prison for all I care. Theresa and her children are coming to Jamaica with me. There is no need for her to stay here with a husband who is busy playing musical beds with his mistresses. I advised Maria to leave you behind as well, but she insists you have good qualities in spite of your faults. She believes if you set your mind to it, you can make a success out of such a venture. Is she right?" Franco looked down at the shorter man.

"I can run a plantation. I've done so before. But this setback, I assure you, is only temporary."

"I'm certain it is." Franco started walking again. "As it will be settled one way or the other by coming with me or facing a term in prison for your debts. Which is it to be?"

Esteban drew himself to his full height, which still fell considerably short of Franco's. "I would be honored to go into business with you," he stated, since his back was to the wall.

"There are a few conditions that must be agreed to," Franco continued. "You must agree to stop drinking and no gambling."

Esteban almost protested, then thought better of the idea, visualizing what debtor's prison might be like. "Very well, I agree."

"Good, then it's settled. You and your family will sail with us when we return to Jamaica. Only one more thing . . ." Franco paused in his step. "This is not a condition but, rather, a warning."

"What is it?" Esteban asked concernedly.

"If I ever hear of you striking my sister again, drunk or sober, you will deal with me for it. I won't whip you, I'll kill you. Do we understand each other?"

"Most assuredly, Conde DeCortega," Esteban replied.

* * *

Jamie was startled awake by the hand that quickly smothered her impending scream.

"Shh! These stone walls will echo to rouse the entire household," Franco whispered near her ear.

"You scared me half to death!" she scolded when he took his hand away, though her anger was slight in comparison to her relief that he was here.

"Well, I did think of waking you by jumping straight upon your delicious body." He gave her a lecherous smile as he pulled down the covers to reveal her shapely form beneath the light material of her nightdress. "But then, I remembered you have a terrifically wicked elbow and thought you might strike first and ask who it is later."

"I assure you, I would have." She laughed, delighted to see him much his old self again. "Franco, I'm so glad you're back."

"I was never away."

"Yes, you were," Jamie touched his cheek lovingly. "Farther away from me than you've ever been before." She pulled his face down to hers and kissed him long and deeply.

"I can't wait any longer for you," he said huskily.

"Nor I for you," Jamie murmured, already feeling a warm rush of desire sweeping over her. Franco moved away to take his clothes off and left blouse, britches, and boots in a pile on the floor beside the bed, then pulled back the covers to get in beside her.

"Your feet are cold," Jamie squealed when he put them against her warm ankles.

"You'll let me warm them on you, won't you?" He held her still, laughing when she started to struggle, her squirming lifting the hem of her nightdress until he felt her naked skin against his. "This must go." He pulled the nightgown up and away, over her head, then cast it aside letting the garment drift like a white cloud onto the pile of his clothing. "That's better," he remarked. "I'll not let

305

even that come between us again. Nor anything else."

Jamie understood what he meant and nodded, feeling so much love for him swelling inside her that she thought she might burst.

"You are the best thing that has ever happened to me," he said, gazing deeply into her eyes. "I don't know what I would do without you."

"I feel just the same," Jamie said softly, stroking her fingers through the dark curls at the back of his neck. "I adore you," she whispered. "I always will."

"And I, you, my love," he returned, beginning to stroke her fine curves with the palm of his hand. "I think we should be quietly married before we leave for home. Since my sisters will be coming with us, we don't need to face Maria's clucking and moaning that our premarital union is a shade premature of the fact, and I will not face three weeks aboard ship with you in your cabin and me in mine. Will you do that, my love?" he asked, brushing a wisp of her hair away from her cheek with his finger. "Will you marry me?"

Jamie's eyes filled with tears of happiness that wouldn't allow her to speak.

"Don't cry," he teased, smiling. "Now is not the time for tears. I told you I would ask you the moment my name was clear to give to you. I know you aren't terribly fond of the terms in the contract, but I give you my oath, you'll never have a complaint if I can help it."

"Would you be still long enough to let me accept," she chided. "I would marry you if the terms were slavery."

"They never will be, darling. Not for you." He reassured her, kissing her forehead. "I'll never take your independence from you, as it is part of you that I have come to cherish most. I only ask that when you need me, you will never hesitate to come to me with any request."

"I promise," she murmured, pulling him down to her. She opened her mouth to meet his lips, urging his eager

306

tongue to explore the deepest recesses of her mouth while she let her hands move over the smooth contours of his back, the curve of his hips, then down over the swell of his buttocks. This time they merged together as never before, secure in their promises to each other. Their mouths and bodies met in a searing union that was frantic with haste to be united and wild with the release of pent-up passions as if this time was both the first and the last they would ever be together. Their hands explored each other in a frenzy. His mouth roamed over her body and Jamie shuddered with the pleasure his lips provided, her nerve endings afire from the touch of his demanding hands and, in turn, Franco seemed to want to fill her with the very essence of his being until, enfused, they might be as one—one body, one soul, one love for all eternity.

"Señorita Jamie Morgan?" A small boy accosted her on the street while she waited for Maria to emerge from the shop. Her soon-to-be sister-in-law had gone inside to purchase a pair of gloves she saw in the window and Jamie decided to stay outside, enjoying the warmth of the late autumn day. She had already learned that the best way to keep Maria from dawdling over the shopping was to let her think she was making her uncomfortable standing around and waiting. While Theresa tended the children busily exploring their uncle's ship, and while Franco and his crew outfitted the vessel for their homebound voyage, Maria had asked Jamie to accompany her for some last-minute shopping. Jamie and Franco were going to be wed this evening in a candlelight ceremony in a small chapel near the seaport so that his crew as well as his family could attend. She planned to wear the white lace gown Franco liked so well for the occasion, and she already wore a large ruby surrounded by diamonds that was her engagement ring. She had met Franco's mother in her severe black-and-white habit, cloistered with the Sisters of a Jesuit order, and the woman had given them her blessings, kissed Jamie's cheek, and welcomed her to the family. Isabella DeCortega now Sister Maria Dominica, was relieved that her immediate family was leaving Spain before the rumors of the outbreak of war in Europe became a reality. She would miss them but had found peace and serenity within the order where she could pray for the souls of her husband and her son.

Franco left the estate and its holdings in the capable hands of an uncle he was sure he could trust. For now, the dark gloomy house with its treasury of soured memories, was closed up to wait for better days when the DeCortegas might return under happier circumstances. Esteban had stopped drinking the same night he had his discussion with Franco and already seemed to look and feel better with each day that passed while Theresa's mate had made no more than a perfunctory call on them to bid farewell to his children.

Jamie smiled at the boy who had pronounced her name in the Spanish manner, with an *h* instead of a *j*.

"I am Señorita Morgan," she responded.

"For you," the child said in English, presenting a folded slip of paper. Jamie dug inside her muff for a coin to give him, but the boy scampered off, ignoring Jamie's call to him to wait. Puzzled over who would be sending her a note and why, Jamie opened the message and read it, her face paling more visibly on every word. It was signed "Garcia," Franco's first mate, and briefly said that there had been an accident and that Franco was severely injured.

Refusing to let herself panic, Jamie threw open the door of the shop and called out to Maria. "Franco's been hurt. An accident on the docks. I'm going to him. Finish up and join me," she said quickly, noticing that Maria was in the middle of making her purchase. Maria blanched, but nodded, hurrying the shopkeeper along. She would be only a minute behind her but every second felt critical as Jamie started walking fast toward the dock only a block away.

"Where is she? How could she have vanished in so short a distance?" Franco paced up and down in front of the gangway, occasionally searching the faces of those below as if she might suddenly appear there.

"I don't understand it," Maria said disconsolately. "I know I was less than a minute behind her. She should have reached the ship before me. Had there been an accident, I would have seen it."

"You should never have left her!" Franco barked, making his distraught sister weep.

"It isn't Maria's fault." Esteban placed a protective hand on his wife's shoulder.

Franco paused in his pacing, rubbing his fingertips across his brow. "I know that. I'm sorry, Maria. It's just that something is happening here that makes no sense. How did she come to think I was injured? Who recognized her to tell her such a lie?"

"All I know is what she told me when she hurried into the shop, frantic with worry. I saw no one with her. She left alone, coming here."

"Elena Vega?" Esteban suggested.

"To what purpose?" Franco riposted. "Elena would have nothing to gain. Our brief affair was over long before I sailed from Spain."

"Perhaps not in her mind."

"Still nothing could be won in acting against Jamie. She would risk her marriage, her son, everything. Elena enjoys her lovers but for none of them would she put so much at risk."

"Then who?" Esteban posed. "And why?"

"For ransom is the only thing I can think of," Franco replied, but just then he saw Garcia, who was heading the search party, coming back to the ship in a great hurry.

"Capitán," he said, out of breath from his exertion. "I talked to everyone on the dock. No one saw her. However, I learned from one of the merchant vessels that an English ship was in the harbor this morning. They claimed to be fixing damage done during a storm but stayed only a few hours, then left."

"What ship?" Franco grabbed the first mate's arm. "Does he know the name? Can he describe it?"

"Sí, capitán. He knows the name. The *Sea Wind.* Its home port was Jamaica. Royale."

"Clyde Bonner," Franco said aloud. The captain of the *Sea Wind* owed a great deal to Henry Morgan for favors over the years. At least he knew now that Jamie was safe. Bonner would take great care to protect his precious cargo until he returned her to her father.

"Whatever my father is paying you, I'll double it. Triple it."

Clyde Bonner shook his burly head. "It will do ye no good, lassie," he told her adamantly. "Yer father said to take ye home and it's that I'm doing. You, nor your Franco, either one, can offer me the pardon papers to sign. Only yer papa can do that."

"He's blackmailing you!" Jamie shouted into his face, standing before his desk in the captain's cabin of the *Sea Wind.* On her way to Franco, two burly mates had grabbed her into an alley, thrown her into a gunny sack and the next thing she knew, she was aboard the Jamaica-bound ship.

"Aye, it's blackmail, I reckon, but he's paying me well

310

enough. Even if ye offer me more, there's not a safe port where I can spend it, so I'll settle for less to have me a haven. I spent three years on that barren split o' land called Tortuga, avoiding the navy patrols each time I lifted me sails. With no place to lay anchor, me treasure serves no purpose laying buried away on a deserted island. Hardly nobody honors a letter o' marque these days and none but blind fools believe there's a difference 'tween a privateer and a pirate. I've had me day and I'm ready to retire for a life o' ease, but I can't take pleasure in me riches till I have me a place to come home to. Can ye offer me that, lassie?"

"No." Jamie shook her head, realizing she could offer Bonner nothing against the bribe Morgan held out to him. But Papa was sorely mistaken if he thought this would be the end of it.

The only bright spot in Jamie's homecoming was finding Lacey on the docks to greet her. Morgan didn't have the nerve to show up, sending his secretary instead to escort Lacey to meet the ship.

"My poor darling." Lacey said, embracing her friend on the Port Royale dock. "How awful it all must have been for you."

"The coward doesn't have the nerve to face me." Jamie sought out her father in vain, seeing only Stuart Cunningham standing beside the governor's carriage. "It's good to see you, Lacey. You don't know how much so right now. Perhaps your presence may stay my hand from committing patricide when I see him."

"Who?" Lacey looked at her, her lovely brows perplexed.

"Why, Morgan, of course! Who else?"

"Whatever has he done?"

"You mean you don't know?"

"He's been very pleasant to me. A nicer gentleman I've never met. I only arrived two days ago, and when he told me the awful thing that befell you, I was horrified to think of it. Especially after the close call I had myself . . ."

"What has he told you, Lacey?"

"About the pirate, of course. That villain who kidnapped you and spirited you away."

Jamie's fists clenched at her sides. "Now I'm sure I will kill him," she swore venomously. "The only villain in this affair is named Henry Morgan! Did he happen to tell you the pirate's name?"

"No, not that I remember. He seemed too distressed to speak it."

"His name, Lacey, was Franco. That's who I was with, and we'd have been married by now if my interfering father had kept out of it!"

"Oh," Lacey murmured, seeing the whole picture now.

"If he thinks he can hide from my wrath, he's wrong!" Jamie stalked past Lacey to the waiting carriage. "The governor is going to hear a very good piece of my mind before this day is out!"

The lookout Franco had posted in the crow's nest spotted them first and shouted the news down to the deck.

"*Capitán,*" Garcia entered Franco's cabin, stopping in front of the table scattered with sea charts, "there is a whole armada of English Navy vessels in the harbor."

"The scoundrel! I expected as much. He'll have us all arrested as pirates if we dare dock in Royale. Then we'll go on to Tortuga, Garcia. Set course right away. He can't hold the ships in port forever and as soon as they're gone, we'll be back."

"*Sí, capitán.*"

* * *

"Ye're not leaving this house without an escort!" Morgan stood adamant behind his desk, shouting. "I'll not let ye slip off to be with that no-account scoundrel again, no matter how much ye pout and throw a temper! I say he's not the man for ye and it's my last word!"

Jamie glared at him in silence. There was no point in pursuing the argument they had been through so many times before. For the past two weeks she had been a virtual prisoner in her home. If Morgan did allow her out with Lacey, it was under the "protection" of several guards of the governor's militia, ordered to keep her under strictest supervision. The remainder of the time she was confined inside the house, with security personnel posted, and upon trying her door one night, she discovered her father locked her in her bedroom after she retired.

"It's time ye started seeing Edward Harcourt again," Morgan continued in a voice only slightly lower in volume. "He's been to call on ye several times and ye won't give the lad the time of day."

"Nor will I," she stated emphatically. "There is no point in leading Edward on, or anyone else for that matter. I'll have Franco and no other."

"Ye're going to damn well do as I think best!"

"I damn well won't!" she returned in a normal but vehement tone.

"I'll make ye marry Harcourt! I'm yer papa and it's my right to see ye wed to the man I choose."

"If you do that, Papa, I will explain to Edward that I've lived with my lover these three months past and that it is damaged goods he'll be getting. What's more, I will assure him that I have every intention of renewing my liaison at the earliest opportunity and continuing it ever after. If it's an adulterous wife he wants, it's that he'll be getting."

313

"Damn it all, woman! Have ye no sense of decency?"

"No more than your own, Papa," she replied, meeting his hard stare.

"I'll find a way to stop ye!" her father swore. "Ye'll marry a proper English name and money or ye'll never wed at all!"

"Then it shall be the latter."

"We'll see about that," Morgan promised her. "We shall just see."

Franco had often thought that Morgan's mansion on Tortuga seemed rather peaceful without the old pirate's presence. Even when filled with captains and mates it was, over all, quieter than when Morgan had been around. The large house remained as it had always been, available to the Brethren of the Coast to reside in whenever they were ashore. Franco was staying here, in the same room Mary Lambert always gave him, for the past three weeks of waiting for word that the navy patrol ships had moved out of the harbor.

Many of his crewmen had wives, legal or common law, and children, who resided in the pirate port, and his crew had begun their visit with glad hearts to see their loved ones again, but most could not abide for long the joys and responsibilities of their attachments. For seafaring men, the life of the father and husband became boring in a week. Two of his crew were arguing and fighting with their spouses, three were more than anxious to set out again for the open sea, just as their wives had become eager by then to be rid of them and have control of the households back in their capable hands without interference by the "man of the house." Five of his crewmen had already called on him to beg him to order them back to the ship before they killed their wives or their wives killed them.

For Franco, this time away from Jamie was nearly unbearable. He had never found himself missing a woman before, but then, he had never been so deeply in love. When he left her the first time, it had been a near child he deserted and he had consoled himself with the certainty that their separation was the best arrangement for all concerned.

But she had returned to Royale with every promise of her youth fulfilled and more. She had not forgotten him with time and new experiences. Absence had only changed deep infatuation into the deepest and truest love he had ever imagined. He was anxious to be back with her, holding her in his arms once more, and couldn't imagine a day would ever come when he might want to part from her.

He had sent Esteban and the family on to Royale by another ship without him. Morgan had no way of knowing the man was Franco's brother-in-law, and thus, Esteban could start looking for the property to build the plantation on and begin their new home in their new land. Maria had strictest orders to keep her identity a secret and not to call on Jamie under any conditions. Pirates who had called at Tortuga had told him of Jamie's confinement under guard and it would be best, at present, to let Morgan wonder when Franco might return and make his strike against him.

"Captain DeCortega?"

Franco looked up from his ruminating by the fire in the dining hall of Morgan's Tortuga mansion to see Mary Lambert curtseying in front of him. She had never quite forgiven him for deserting "her girl" four years ago and remained formally stiff and proper in his presence. Only the direst need could bring her here to address him.

"Captain, it has come to my ears that that rascal, Morgan, has been keeping my Jamie a virtual prisoner in her own home . . ." Mary began. "I know . . . I know

315

I haven't been exactly friendly toward you, sir, but it was because I thought you were doing my girl wrong. And, well, I'm sorry for it. I was mistaken, as I've come to learn, and I apologize most heartily for it."

"That's quite all right, Mary." Franco smiled at the old woman who was growing gray now.

"Well, sir, I've been thinking that my girl might be needing her old Mary now and . . . and . . ."

"And you know that I am sailing for Royale soon and you would like to ask me to take you along?"

Mary frowned at him worriedly. "I suppose I've little right to ask you for favors after the way I've treated you all these years, but I do so want to see my girl again."

"As I am certain your girl would love to see you. Rest easy, Mary," Franco assured her. "Of course you may come along. I should have asked you myself had I thought of it."

"Merci . . . thank you." Mary beamed, relieved and happy.

"Go and pack your things. You shall have Garcia's cabin for the voyage."

The woman rushed out, her skirts rustling over the floorboards. She had barely gone when he was once again interrupted. "Captain, did I hear you say you sail for Royale in the near future?"

"You did, Polly." Franco rose to his feet to greet the woman. He didn't know quite why she was here. She was on Tortuga when he arrived with no explanation for her presence in the pirate haven rather than on Royale with Morgan. She had resumed her place as Morgan's mistress soon after the pirate's return as governor, and though he refused to let her move into the mansion, he kept a set of rooms for her in the town. Franco presumed some kind of disagreement between them had propelled her here, and perhaps now she was regretting the haste of her actions.

316

Nearing thirty, Polly was still a most becoming woman. Her gowns were as ever, flamboyant and garish but seductive just the same. Her golden blond hair was upswept, leaving a provocative curl or two loose to frame her heart-shaped face. "I wonder if I might beg you to accept one more passenger." She peered at him around the edge of her lace fan.

"Have you decided Morgan has suffered enough in your absence?"

"I don't know if he has or not," she pouted prettily, "but Tortuga bores me near to death when there's naught to do here the livelong day. Since them damn pardons came, all the good old tars is gone from here. And these new seamen, such proper, stiff gentlemen they are. A working girl could hardly make herself a living any more depending on them for her daily bread." Franco stifled a chuckle as the woman talked. The younger men in the islands now preferred to keep a mistress of some intelligence and refinement, not ex-tavern wenches like Polly. Companionship was at least as important to them as the sexual favors offered, and no intellectual stimulation would be offered by Polly's ilk. Still, the woman deserved the courtesy of his refraining from laughter at her complaint. "If I'm going to be angry with him, I suppose I can do so as easy on Royale and make my displeasure even more deeply felt," she finished.

"I imagine you can," Franco commented.

"What the devil is that supposed to mean?" A spark of anger flashed, wondering if she had been insulted.

"Nothing, dear lady," he answered lifting her hand to his lips. "Only that if your scorn would not move him, nothing could."

Polly seemed delighted with the comment. "Then you would not mind taking me with you?"

"I would not, but I have promised the only possible cabin to Mrs. Lambert."

317

"I'm sure Mary won't mind if I share it. If she will, then may I come?"

"As you wish," Franco could think of no reason to refuse her.

"Good morning, Jamie." Lacey yawned sleepily as she sat down at the breakfast table, eyeing all but the coffee with complete indifference. Jamie had poured a cup for her when she heard her coming.

"You should better say good afternoon," Jamie chided with amusement at her friend, still groggy with sleep.

"What o'clock is it?" Lacey stifled another yawn.

"Near midday."

"So late? Oh, dear, I must have been more fatigued than I realized. I had a marvelous time. It was a wonderful ball, wasn't it?"

"Yes, it was," Jamie said, continuing with the list she was writing. The governor had decided that his inaugural ball was long overdue and invitations had gone out to all the neighboring islands as well as to fine families on the hillside who had made the colony their home. His insistence that Jamie attend the ball had only been complied with out of consideration for Lacey. She knew her father had spent most of the night letting all the bachelors know he had a marriageable daughter who could expect a generous dowry. Jamie had remained just barely polite to them all.

The festivities last night had gone on until nearly dawn, accounting for Lacey's bleary-eyed condition this morning.

"I'm sorry it wasn't much fun for you." Lacey suddenly remembered Jamie's forced attendance and embarrassment at being displayed by her father much like a fine work of art might be shown off in a shop window. The price around her neck had been the frequent mentions of

318

her dowry that went along with the prize. The rumors circulating about through Royale high society that she had run off with a man, or been abducted, as Morgan claimed, couldn't seriously tarnish a reputation that carried such a rich reward for overlooking the slight defect of a somewhat soiled chastity. "How long have you been up and about?" Lacey asked.

"I haven't been to bed." Jamie looked up from the menus she was writing for the cook. Since Sir Henry had no wife, all of the tasks generally associated with a governor's lady had fallen to her and she performed them for the sake of the guests, not for him. She and her father had fallen into barely speaking during the course of a day, since if they did exchange words, it only led to another argument. Though she despised what he had done in kidnapping her away from Franco, and hated the way he was trying to marry her off, she still loved him as her father, and missed the companionship they once shared. The bad times, the hard times, had dimmed in her memory and only the good remained of when she had only her father for affection and attention. If only he would come around to realizing his refusal of accepting Franco was based on jealousy and spite.

The mansion was filled with off-island guests staying with them for a few days, and each of them had to be fed and made comfortable. "I only splashed water on my face and changed my gown this morning. Most of our company came down to breakfast already and have gone off here or there, to look about."

"Then why don't you finish that and go to bed. I'll take over for you while you rest."

"Thank you, Lacey. I believe I will." Jamie was feeling dreadfully tired and discouraged after last night's affair. She was beginning to doubt Morgan would ever come around. She was sure Franco was back by now, but the patrols covering the harbor would keep him from reaching her. The impending war with Spain was more than sufficient to keep a Spaniard's ship at bay, and, as well, there was Franco's known reputation as a privateer. "You can trust me to see to today's affairs while you sleep," Lacey insisted. "If you don't get some rest, you'll nod off at super tonight and drown in your soup!" Both girls laughed merrily. "I may know some news that might help you sleep." Lacey smiled at her craftily. "I looked out my window this morning and the patrol ships are gone."

"Gone?" Jamie parroted in the happiest voice she had used in weeks.

"They must have moved out of the harbor this morning. He couldn't keep them here in port forever. Not to fend off one single ship when there are so many pirates still preying on vessels along the coast. I wish I knew who that one was who saved me," Lacey said wistfully. "I should think I'd have run off with him in a minute had he asked me. You really don't know who he could be?"

"As I told you, Lacey, there are a lot of new pirates about. I don't know them all anymore. Perhaps it was William Kidd, or Stede Bonet, or even Bart Roberts from your description. You'd have ill luck winning Roberts, though," Jamie giggled. "He won't let a woman near his ship. He thinks we'll contaminate his vessel and corrupt his crew."

Lacey joined her in laughter. "Whoever my dashing knight was, I shouldn't mind corrupting him, I can tell you. I was terrified at the time, but it's the most exciting thing that's ever happened to me when I look back on it. Thanks to the one who kept it from becoming a horrible memory. Well, now perhaps your Franco will be able to reach you, with a message at least. I hope so for your sake," Lacey said, noticing that the place reserved for the governor at the head of the table was still set out with his plate, napkin, and silver. "Hasn't Sir Henry been down to breakfast yet?"

Jamie looked up from finishing her marketing list, startled by Lacey's question and gazing at her father's untouched place. Throughout the busy morning of greeting guests as they came down and seeing to their comfort, she hadn't noticed his absence. "No, he hasn't been," she remarked with a frown. Never in her life could she remember Morgan sleeping this late. Even after a full night of drinking and carousing, he slept no more than a few hours, then was up and about with a day's work to be tended. Whether at sea or in London or here in Tortuga, he had continued the schedule and only took brief naps to refresh himself throughout the day. "That's curious," she said, vaguely uneasy with his absence.

"Well, it's hardly surprising," Lacey chimed in lightly. "He was dancing almost the whole night long. I don't think he missed a single lady's dance card."

"Certainly he did, every time he was cornering a bachelor as a likely prospect for me," Jamie grumbled.

"Even so, I'm sure I've never seen Sir Henry happier than he was last night."

"Yes." Jamie agreed smiling. "He was that. And you're probably right, he must have overextended himself. I suppose I had better wake him or he'll never sleep tonight. On my way up to bed, I'll look in on him. Will you see to his breakfast?" Jamie straightened her papers and rose from the chair.

"I'll have Lizzie heat the serving trays. Everything has gone cold and I'm sure he'll be hungry. Take a good long rest and don't worry about anything. I shan't wake you unless the house is afire or a certain sea captain makes a clandestine appearance." Lacey winked playfully.

Giving it over into Lacey's capable hands, Jamie trod wearily up to her room. At her father's door, she gave a light rap against the wood. "Papa?" she called, rapping again a bit louder.

Hearing no reply, she turned the handle and pushed

321

the door open. "Papa, it's after noontime." Jamie listened for the sound of his snoring, but there was only stillness from the bulk underneath the covers. She crossed to the windows, drawing the drapes back to flood the room with sunlight. Normally that action would rouse him from his bed roaring that a man had a right to his rest and his privacy without cursed, female interference. The shape beneath the covers never moved as she watched it. Apprehension began to wrap icy fingers around her heart. She approached the bed to shake his shoulder. "Papa? Papa, please wake up . . ."

Knowing already beyond the shadow of a doubt, Jamie pulled the covers back to expose her father's resting form. His eyes were closed, as if he was soundly asleep, but the steady, heavy breath that should rustle the hairs of his bushy mustache was still. Morgan was dead.

Jamie sank down onto the bed beside him. "Oh, Papa," she sighed, then let the tears come.

"Captain, we'll be making a pilot of you yet," Sneed, Franco's chief navigator and pilot, clapped him on the back for his efforts at bringing the ship safely into port. The crew was busily engaged in throwing the lines over to dock her. Port Royale was still asleep at this grey predawn hour of the morning. Soon, the sun would rise and the city would come alive, and by then Franco intended to have Jamie spirited away from here, beyond Morgan's reach. Franco surrendered the wheel to his pilot to secure and hurried below to his cabin. He would wash himself, shave, and change his clothing, then send Jamie a message that he was back. She need only make up an excuse to be out and meet him at their secret rendezvous, the inn where they had spent so many secret hours together. There he would take care of any guards the governor had sent with her and they would be away and married before Morgan could interfere again.

He closed his cabin door before he realized he was not alone, spying a shapely form sprawled out in his bed underneath the covers.

"Good morning," Polly greeted him, smiling. She was naked beneath the sheet. "I hope you aren't too very angry, but Mary snores something awful and you were up at the wheel all night. I hoped you wouldn't mind my borrowing your quarters."

"I don't mind, but it's morning now and I'll expect you to return to your own." He tossed his frockcoat over a chair and started to roll up his sleeves.

"You needn't be so unfriendly about it," she pouted. "I thought we was friends."

"Acquaintances would be more accurate," Franco said curtly, well on to her game and not liking it. "I doubt Morgan would appreciate learning of this. Hadn't you best take care?"

"Oh, he wouldn't be jealous." She shrugged. "We have us an understanding that way."

"Well, I'm afraid I don't. I will give you three minutes to be out of my bed and back in your own cabin or I shall yank you out and take you there myself."

"There's at least an hour yet before dawn." She continued to lounge beneath the sheets, felinely graceful in her posing. "Absolutely no one is about yet. And I'd never tell a soul . . ."

"There will be naught to tell," Franco snarled starting toward her. Seeing the threatening look on his face, Polly clutched the sheet against her, backing against the windows. "I can't spare the time for your games. You will get out of my bed and out of my cabin at once else I will pluck you out and set you on the docks of Royale as you are!" By the time he finished his speech, he had reached the bedside and Polly flinched, expecting him to follow through on his threat immediately.

323

"All right! All right!" Polly said when he had backed up sufficiently to let her realize she had a reprieve, albeit a brief one. "This was never my idea to start." She angrily gripped the sheet as she came out of the bed, wrapping the material, toga-like, around her. "I admit I had no objection to it, but I'll not take the blame . . ."

"What did you say?" Franco caught her wrist. "If it wasn't your idea, whose was it?"

"Why, Morgan's, of course! Who else? You're a handsome one and I've had my eye on you since you came, but I wouldn't have tried this one, I can tell you, lest he told me to!"

"Morgan sent you to Tortuga to wait for me, didn't he?"

"He did. He said there would be a pretty present or two for me out of it, depending on how well his plan succeeds."

"What's the rest of it?" Franco demanded, his grip on her wrist tightening. "There's no point to seducing me unless he can be certain Jamie hears of it. What does he have in mind?"

"Ow, I don't need torturing. I'm talking, ain't I?" Polly squirmed.

Franco let go of her wrist but stood between Polly and the door to be sure the woman realized she would not escape before she told him the rest.

Polly rubbed her arm, wincing. "He wanted me to lure you into my bed so's he could convince Jamie you weren't no good for her. He has a fellow up to the house ready to spill the tale to Jamie that your ship is back the minute it's seen. That way, she'll come here straight away, of course, and see it all for herself."

"Get out of here," Franco seethed, as close as he had ever come in his life to striking a woman. Polly saw the blind rage and started to circle around him toward the door, her eyes suddenly wide with terror. "If I ever hear

324

that you've lied to her, I promise you I'll find you and wring your pretty neck!"

Reaching the door, Polly pulled it open and scrambled through it, closing it firmly behind her. "Oh, Lord!" He heard Polly wail from the gangway a moment later. He threw open the door again to hear Polly babbling hysterically. "It isn't my fault," Polly stammered, gazing, terror-stricken, from him to Jamie and back again. "I didn't tell her nothing! I'll keep my promise. I swear it." Her head shook violently. "It ain't my fault! I said nothing at all!"

Jamie stood stock-still, her face so pale Franco feared she might swoon. Tears filled her eyes as she looked from Polly's sheet-draped form to Franco in trousers and disheveled shirt sleeves. "I apologize for coming unannounced," she said stiffly, her back ramrod straight with the effort it took to force the words out. "I came to tell you . . . to say . . ." Her voice broke with a pent up sob.

Franco walked toward her and reached for her arm, but she jerked violently away from him. "No!" she glared. "Don't ever touch me again!"

"Jamie it's a trick. Morgan meant for you to see this. He planned it. It's all a lie."

"You're the liar!" She trembled in hurt rage. "How easy it is for you to blame your deceit on another."

"I am telling you the truth!"

"I know what I've seen," she said, tears spilling freely down her cheeks.

"Morgan wanted you to see this. He arranged it . . ."

"Morgan is dead!" she returned, shouting the words into his face. Polly gasped in startled disbelief.

"Jamie . . ." Franco tried again to go to her and make her listen through her grief. More than ever, she needed him now.

"I said, don't touch me!" Her voice turned cold, hard with hatred. "Your reputation as a ladies' man is very much intact, Captain. It seems you haven't changed at all from your youth. How many more do you have dangling from your string? And how clever to blame your falsity on a dead man, since he can neither verify your claim or deny it."

"I didn't know that," Franco murmured.

"Didn't you?" Her eyes narrowed just as her father's used to when beyond listening to reason or argument.

"How could I? You know we only just came in."

"And I know what I saw! What else should I have expected. From either of you." Her glare turned on Polly as well.

"What Franco's telling you is the truth," Polly stammered, her shock turning into grief and regret.

"Do you think I'd believe you? While he lived you weren't faithful. Why should you be now? Save your breath, both of you!"

Franco knew it was futile to try to stop her as she turned away and fled up the ladder to the open deck. Polly was openly sobbing into the loose folds of the sheet she was wrapped in.

"Get dressed!" he said brusquely, shoving Polly toward Garcia's loaned cabin. Perhaps when Jamie's shock and grief subsided, she might listen to reason, perhaps not. For now he could only wait and hope.

"Damn your soul to eternal hellfire, Morgan!" he muttered under his breath sure that he could hear the blustering pirate's ghost laughing at him in victory.

Chapter Fifteen

"You're sure, then, that there is nothing to be done for it?"

"Quite sure, mistress," the solicitor, Mr. Penrose, said in sympathy. "I tried to tell him such a course was unwise, but he was utterly set on it and would not listen to reason."

"I understand." Jamie forced a smile to her lips. "It isn't your fault and I thank you for your efforts on my behalf."

They were in Mr. Penrose's office and Henry Morgan's will had just been read. Lacey sat on one side of Jamie and Mary Lambert on the other. The room seemed claustrophobic, cluttered with law books, the stuffiness of the enclosed space making it seem difficult to breathe.

"I'm afraid the Royale mansion was purchased with government funds," Mr. Penrose furthered the bad news. "Therefore, it must be surrendered to the next governor. You do, however, have the home on Tortuga to fall back on as a residence."

"But not the funds to maintain it," Jamie finished.

"No, I'm afraid not," Mr. Penrose answered morosely, then threw his hands up in the air in despair. "Until the terms of the will are met, my hands are tied. I have no choice but to abide by its provisions."

"There is, then, no problem, *chérie*." Mary Lambert intruded. "You will, of course, come back to Tortuga with me."

"And live on what, Mary? On the goodwill and charity of the Brethren of the Coast? It was their home before it was mine. I would not take it away from them. Nor could I even hope to pay its upkeep unless I began to charge them rent and I shall never do that."

"She'll come back to London with me," Lacey inserted.

"Lacey," Jamie reminded her. "We haven't sufficient funds to obtain passage for one of us, much less two . . ."

"I can sell my jewels. There aren't very many, but I'm sure they'll bring enough."

"No, Lacey dear, but thank you for offering."

"What else will you do, pet?" Mary queried.

"She'll come home with me," Lacey stated, only to be immediately countered by Mary's insistence that Jamie return to Tortuga. Both began chattering at once, arguing for their own course of action. "Please," Jamie said loudly to be heard above their babble. "I am not helpless yet." She gestured them both to silence. "Mr. Penrose, as I understand it, my father bequeathed all of his liquid assets to the man I marry."

"If the union meets the required terms of the will, yes."

"The scoundrel! How could he?" Mary began to weep.

"But his personal possessions are mine to do with as I choose?"

"Most of your father's assets are in cash, gold, and jewels and those are all left to the man you will wed someday. There's very little else. Well, there are his clothing and personal effects. Those might bring in some income if they were sold."

"And what of the *Lady Morgan?*"

"The what?" The solicitor gazed at her blankly.

"My father's ship. She is personal property, is she not? His personal property that now belongs to me?"

"Well, I would suppose so," Mr. Penrose stated. "The ship was not mentioned one way or another so I suppose it would be a personal effect. However, while I realize it would have sentimental attachment for you, it is quite old. Practically derelict, I understand. You may have difficulty selling it . . ."

"I don't plan to sell her, Mr. Penrose." Jamie rose to her feet. "I just want to know that she is, beyond question, my ship now."

"Indeed so, Mistress Morgan, but if you don't sell it, whatever else can you possibly do with it?"

"We'll see, Mr. Penrose. We shall see." Jamie nodded good day to him.

"Jamie, what can you possibly be thinking?" Lacey asked. The governor's mansion was still theirs for the remainder of the week until the acting governor took possession. Mary had found the day too emotionally taxing and had gone to her bedroom in the mansion to lie down. Jamie and Lacey were in Jamie's bedroom, sitting by the window seat that looked down on the town. "I've seen your father's boat when he had it brought here and I am afraid Mr. Penrose is right. It won't bring very much, even if someone would purchase it."

"I've told you, I don't intend to sell it."

"Well, what else is there to be done with it? You can't be thinking sensibly." Jamie had told Lacey of Franco's betrayal and that, coming so soon after Morgan's funeral, had fired the younger girl with the desire to look after her friend's welfare in her double grief. "Now you must let me decide what our course of action shall be, and as I see it, we get the most we can out of the old boat."

"It's a ship, not a boat," Jamie corrected sternly. "And I know exactly what I will do with it. I will do precisely what Morgan once meant I should, though he may not have known it when he saw to it that it was all I should know. For seventeen years my father raised me as the son

329

he never had. If a son was left penniless and homeless, he would take matters into his own hands. Papa thought that leaving me in this predicament would force me to choose a husband he would have approved of, but he's left one other option open to me."

"What can that be?" Lacey gazed at her, puzzled.

"There is only one thing I know besides 'ladying,' as he called it, and it is what I shall turn to now."

Lacey continued to stare at her in bewilderment, then, slowly, realization and awareness. "Jamie," she murmured. "You can't be serious."

"What else would you suggest? That I marry Edward or Arthur out of need?"

"There is Captain DeCortega . . ." Lacey suggested cautiously.

"Never!" Jamie blasted back at her.

"Perhaps, as he said, it was a mistake . . ."

"Yes, the one he made when he proved he's a faithless snake!"

"Jamie, you don't know that for certain."

"I know what I saw!" she threw back. "Polly, I know well enough, has no conscience whatever regarding who she will share her favors with, but to know his morals are no better . . . no, worse than hers. At least she does it for profit. Don't you see? It's obvious that it means nothing to him. He'll take a woman's affections wherever he can find it as easily as changing his shirt. I'm glad I learned it now about him." Jamie shook her head, willing herself not to cry. She had shed enough tears over the last week. First with Morgan's death and funeral, then discovering Franco with Polly, and now this on top of it all, learning she was penniless unless she submitted to Morgan's will regarding marriage. "No." She steeled herself. "I trusted Franco and I was wrong both times I let myself believe in him. I'll never marry anyone. I've learned my lesson and I'll never let love cloud my vision

330

again. Maybe I should wed someday and be certain my husband meets the requirements, then when I have what is rightfully mine, I'll slit the bastard's throat to leave myself a wealthy widow!"

"You're only angry and hurt," Lacey inserted. "You don't mean a word of it." She watched Jamie storm across the room.

"Perhaps, perhaps not, but I will not sit idly by and let fate determine my fortune. No man, ever, father or husband, will control my future."

"But what do you want to do with the boat?"

"Ship, Lacey! It's a ship!" Jamie had pulled out her trunks and began to throw balled-up gowns and petticoats into the bottom, packing in willy-nilly fashion. "Morgan always wanted a son. Now he shall have one. The entire world shall see that James Allison Morgan has taken up where Henry Morgan stopped. If ever the owners of merchant ships quaked to hear his name, now they will quake to hear mine."

"Surely you don't mean to turn pirate?" Lacey squealed.

Jamie stopped throwing her garments into the bottom of the trunk to gaze up at Lacey. "Do you think anyone will offer me a letter of marque to make me a legal privateer? Of course I'll turn pirate!" All at once she was in motion again, emptying the contents of her clothes chest onto the floor and sorting through them. "Don't worry. I shall see that you have passage home . . ."

"Jamie . . ."

"Don't try to talk me out of it. It's my life, I shall do as I please with it, and it does *not* please me to sell myself into marriage just to have a roof over my head and food in my belly. I would rather take up Polly's profession and realize the profit for myself!"

"I shan't try to talk you out of it. I want to go with you."

Jamie stopped her packing to gaze up at Lacey where she now sat on Jamie's bed.

"I mean it! I do!" Lacey said excitedly. "I know I shall be a burden at first, but I'll learn. Oh, please, let me come with you."

"Lacey, they hang pirates. Man or woman makes little difference."

"Then we shan't let them catch us." Lacey refused to be daunted. "Please, you must let me come with you."

"This is not a game of charades or a masque. It's serious, deadly business."

"Jamie, you just outlined your prospects for my benefit and only reminded me that mine are no brighter. A dull husband. A dull life. Droll children and a full but unbearably boring social calendar until I die, quite probably of boredom. My entire life I've dreamed of having even one adventure. Your life has been full of them. You've seen places that I could never hope to, until now. Men have the opportunity to do something exciting before they tie themselves up in marriage and family life. Perhaps I might not mind doing the same when I have memories, at least, to look back on. Even ones I might not dare tell my grandchildren about." Lacey smiled, prompting a smothered laugh from her friend.

"There would be no more laces and satins." Jamie turned serious to warn. "You'll have to dress as a man."

"I can do that. I'll even cut my hair."

"It's more than dressing in a man's clothing. It's doing a man's job as well. The sea is a rough life and there's no giving up when you tire of it. You can't call a carriage to take you home."

"Is that how you think of me? That I could give in so easily?" Lacey's blue eyes gazed at her mournfully.

"I only want you to be absolutely certain of this because once you've begun there is no going back to the life you knew before. You may don a dress again, but

332

you'll never again be the same. It's a difficult path once you've chosen. The storm you experienced on your passage over was nothing to compare with a hurricane, and you'll see one or two of those in a season. And you won't be allowed the comfort of your cabin. You'll be out on deck, furling sails and trying to keep the ship afloat and the waves from washing you off the deck. You'll have to work as hard as the men work, in heat that will fry your skin to copper. You'll have to climb rigging and swab saltwater off the deck. You will have to learn to use a pistol and a cutlass, and you'd best not come if you fear you couldn't."

"If you're trying to frighten me, you're succeeding, but you haven't changed my mind. If you won't agree to take me with you, why then, I shall stow away if I must."

Finally, seeing she was unable to dissuade her, Jamie nodded. "Very well. I only pray you never regret this course you've chosen. Pack your things and we'll store them against the day we ever decide we should become ladies again."

"She's what?" Franco's voice rose to a terrible bellow.

"You've heard me quite correctly, Captain DeCortega. She's taken the *Lady Morgan* to sea."

"And you allowed it?"

"I had no power to stop her," the lawyer returned, facing the irate captain glaring down at him from across the expanse of his desk. "The ship is hers to do with as she pleases."

"And what damn fools did she find to sail it for her?" Franco demanded.

"Why, Jocko Chalks, I believe. And Mr. Shanks," Mr. Penrose answered, unperturbed by the captain's anger. It wasn't his fault the young lady proved to be intractable in the matter. He had done his part in attempting to

333

dissuade her. "In fact, I believe most of the old crew signed on. I heard she was asking about for the old tars to come back and many did, I'd well imagine."

"Have you no sense, man, to allow her to do such a thing? Don't you know what she'll do with it?"

"She said she would be running cargo about the islands," the lawyer explained. "I understand there is a living to be made in it. I don't know what else she could do, considering her father's will has left her penniless."

Franco stared at the man, his rage dispelled by shock. "He left her nothing?"

"Only his personal property and the ship. I wouldn't be telling you this much, as a man's last will and testament is a private matter, but you said you are a close friend of the family and I hoped you might be able to persuade her to simply fulfill the will's provisions so I may release the funds to her. There is quite a fortune to be had and . . ."

"How might she fulfill this obligation?" Franco interrupted, unable to believe Morgan would do this to her.

"Why, by marrying, of course. The man must be a gentleman of title and independent means. When those facts are proven to me and a certificate of marriage is presented, I may release the funds."

"And until then, what was she to live on?"

Mr. Penrose shook his head sadly. "As I had to inform her, Captain, nothing. Not one farthing am I empowered to release. It was his hope to force her to act quickly in this matter. I tried to talk him out of it but . . ." Penrose shrugged. "I suppose that is why she took the ship to sea as she did. She will try to make her living with it, contracting to transport cargo for the various merchants and planters, but that's no life for a woman. I quite agree with you, sir. I do hope you can persuade her to give it up. I'm certain she could sell the ship and realize some profit to live on for a while."

"She'd never do that, Mr. Penrose. She would sell her right arm before she would give up that old wreck."

Franco left the solicitor's office, walking back toward the docks. He had hoped that a few days would give her time to realize that what she had seen had been in error. He had written her to explain, but the letters were returned to him unopened. The boy who tried to deliver the last one swore that the people living in the big house on the hill insisted she no longer resided there. Refusing to believe it, he went himself, forcing his way past the servants to find her and make her listen to reason but she was gone. Upon bullying his way to the new master of the house, a man named Stallings now made temporary governor in Henry Morgan's stead, Franco was told that though he had offered to let her stay on as long as she wished, she refused, having her trunks taken down, and disappeared. Stallings had no idea where she had gone or what she planned to do. He had suggested Franco try to gain the information from Morgan's solicitor, Mr. Penrose.

Of all the evil deeds Morgan had accomplished in his lifetime, to Franco's mind this had to be the worst of them. Even in death, the old bastard was not finished with trying to run his daughter's life.

Regardless of what she had told Penrose, Franco knew the true reason she took the *Lady Morgan* to sea. The crew that had signed on with her were the proof—those men would no more turn to ferrying cargo than fish could learn to fly. Traveling in and out of the same ports, sailing the same sea lanes, Franco was bound to catch up to her someday. He could only pray that when that time came he could convince her to give up this dangerous course she had chosen to follow.

Chapter Sixteen

Elizabeth Ferris realized too late that she had made a strategic miscalculation, as her father, Colonel Edmund Ferris, would have called it. She had no means of escape that would not call attention to herself and attention was what she wished to avoid at all costs. Her feet and hands felt as cold as if she had plunged them into ice water and her flesh quivered noticeably. She had to bite down on her lower lip to keep it from trembling. She had donned boy's clothing and shorn off her long, copper-colored locks, tucking the remaining wild curls beneath a stocking cap, but she knew if she stood to walk across the room, she would be immediately unmasked and, God, she didn't want to contemplate what might happen next.

Though the establishment had been practically empty when she arrived, allowing her to be deceived into thinking it might be a safe haven, the tavern had gradually filled with customers. The smell of rancid smoke burned her nostrils, the odorous screen slightly obscuring her vision of six loud, burly men playing a game of cards at the very next table. Other games and boisterous conversations progressed around the other tables in the now crowded room. Most fearful of those closest to her, she watched them swill cups of ale and rum in sloppy abandon that left liquid dribbling down their bearded chins. At another table nearby, two men pawed the same tavern wench while the woman giggled drunkenly between them, her mirth even further heightened when the mood of the rivals turned ugly, changing their expressions into masks of jealous rage. The innkeeper, a hulk of a black man with a clean-shaven head and a single, glittering gold hoop earring in the lobe of one ear, stepped between them, promising to "crack their heads like coconuts" if they continued to press the issue, then roughly shoved the woman out into the center of the room. "Get to yer duties, girl," he growled. The wench whimpered loudly, "It ain't me fault," but, realizing she elicited no pity from her employer, she trounced off to the bar, her hiked-up skirt swaying provocatively with each practiced step.

Elizabeth remained in her dark corner, sitting as close to the well of the stairs as possible. She didn't know what she had been thinking to believe she might escape like this. At the time of her decision, almost any fate had seemed preferable to wedding that fat old man her father had chosen for her. True, she was almost nineteen and nearly too old to catch a husband in her mother's estimate, therefore should be happy with what she could get under such desperate circumstances. And true as well that Lord Bramwell, her intended, was very rich and well connected, but her parents would be receiving most of the benefits of linking their name to his. What would she have out of the arrangement but an ugly, ancient husband to cater and tend to?

During the long sea voyage that brought her here to this island shore, she had consoled herself over not knowing what her intended husband might look like by imagining, even knowing his age, that he might at least be dignified and attractive. If not that, then praying she could uncover a gentle heart that might win, if not her love, at least her respect and affection. But the ship docked and Lord Bramwell called on his promised bride, shattering her illusions completely. He was three inches shorter than she and as grossly round as a gourd. He possessed no neck at all,

337

just rolls of fat that slid their way inside the collar of his cravat. He reeked, as only the grossly overweight can stink from an unwashed body, and attempted to overpower that acrid scent with the masking odor of a strong sweet-smelling cologne that made her stomach churn.

Even if she could overlook such shortcomings in search of the gentle, kind heart, she was destined to be disappointed. He was disgusting! Utterly and completely as gross of character as he was of form. His mannerisms were effeminate, overly polite, disagreeably stuffy, as if he considered himself so far above the society of the kindly ship's captain who took her here that he could afford to be condescending. He kissed Elizabeth's hand and her flesh recoiled. No, absolutely not! She would rather die than marry this aging fop her parents had chosen for her. They had never seen him. They knew him only through the letters he wrote that had seemed to be gracious enough. Now she wondered if his secretary had written them. Surely he could not have penned such pleasant missives that had made him seem to be a decent enough sort. How could they ever have dreamed they would be sending her to this?

She was one of five daughters and her parents did have a certain desperation to find eligible husbands for them all, but this—this was too much to expect her to endure.

Her first thought on being left alone in her cabin to pack had been to write to her parents at once and tell them what she had found at her journey's end. Surely, learning how Lord Bramwell repulsed her, they would never insist she go through with it. But a small, nagging fear had clutched at her chest as she sat down at her small table aboard ship to write the letter. What if they did insist she marry him? Her mother had not loved her father and he had not loved her when they were married. The contract had been arranged during the reign of King Charles II to satisfy a whim of the Crown. Charles himself had wed his queen out of political necessity rather than romance, and if he could sacrifice, why not his subjects? Charles had used dissatisfaction with his homely bride as his excuse to keep fascinating mistresses, like the unforgettable Moll Flanders.

In her present state of mind, Elizabeth would far prefer being mistress to a man of her choosing that she found devastatingly interesting and attractive to being forcefully, honorably wed to an effeminate, boring pig!

The fear that her parents might reply with orders to marry Lord Bramwell prompted the panic that resulted in her cutting her hair and stealing boy's clothes from the crew cabins then sneaking off the ship in the middle of the night. At least it had seemed to her to be the middle of night when nine bells tolled as she slipped down the gangway into the dockside streets of Port Royale. The nearly empty tavern in which she had sought refuge from the hue and cry sure to be initiated upon discovery of her absence was now teeming with customers, all rowdy, burly, frightening-countenanced men.

Elizabeth hoped her pursuers would look for a young lady of her description at the inns or trying to book passage on one of the other ships in the harbor. She thought they might not notice a copper-haired boy, slender of form, hiding inside the rough and filthy dockside taverns.

"Here, lad, will ye be nursing that tankard all night?" The tavern girl who had enjoyed provoking the fight earlier stopped at Elizabeth's table, her sky-blue eyes staring straight into Elizabeth's green ones. "This place ain't meant to rest yer weary backside, luv. We serve ale an' spirits and if ye have a taste fer neither, ye best move on to make room for a real man."

Elizabeth lifted the pewter mug to her lips and sipped. The tavern wench laughed, throwing her head back in mirth. "Ye call that drinkin'? Me five-year-old can swig good ale faster'n that."

Elizabeth forced herself to down half the tankard in a few swallows. The dark ale was smooth but bitter, burning

339

her throat. The fermented bubbles churned in her stomach and she jerked spasmodically with the strength of the loud belch that escaped her startled lips. Her face flushing with embarrassment, she almost apologized but realized the mistake it would be in time.

The barmaid cackled, her hands on her hips. "That's better, bucko! I'll fetch ye another."

Elizabeth did not want another but knew of no way to refuse it. Nor could she yet muster the courage to rise from her seat and make her way to the door. Captain Wells might have discovered her absence by now and have his crew combing the streets in search of her.

The barmaid returned with another dew-laden mug, setting it down on the rough-hewn wooden table. "Here ye are, luv. Eh? I see ye haven't yet finished yer first." The woman eyed her suspiciously, apparently thinking there was something terribly awry with a seaman who didn't swig his ale as if he was dying of thirst.

Quickly, Elizabeth drained the tankard, stifling another belch beneath an upraised palm that wiped the foam from her lips.

"Ye know, ye ain't half bad, luv." The tavern wench looked her over, up and down, appraising with the eye of a connoisseur. "Bit young, but then, I don't mind bringin' em up meself. Break 'em in right that way," she cackled, slapping Elizabeth's back and nearly choking her when she tried to sip from the fresh tankard. "Me name's Maddy. Maddy is for Madelaine. What's yers, luv?" To Elizabeth's distress, Maddy made herself comfortable on the stool next to hers.

"It's Edward . . . Ned," Elizabeth stuttered, trying to make her voice low enough to sound passably masculine, but it came out broken, lilting to a high-pitched squeal, then down to ridiculously faulty baritone.

"It's awright, luv. Ye needn't be afraid of ole Maddy." The woman moved closer and Elizabeth could smell the reek of the overly sweet-scented perfume she was wearing. Maddy was probably considered quite attractive by this crowd, a bit on the plump side with an ample bosom displayed by a low cut, off-the-shoulder blouse that was tucked into a full, ankle-length skirt. Her stomacher was a bright, eye-blinding red. "Well, ain't ye goin' to offer yer Maddy a drink?"

"Certainly," Elizabeth replied, again attempting to sound male. "Won't you join me?"

"Aye, that I will!" Maddy signaled to the man tending the bar, then hitched her stool nearer to Elizabeth. The tavern's owner must be more interested in the extra shillings for drinks than his tavern girl's efficiency, as he shuffled over with a brimming tankard of ale and set it in front of the woman, collecting his payment from the coins Elizabeth had scattered on the table as she had seen the other customers do.

"Ye talk kind of funny," Maddy commented. "Like ye have a bone stuck in yer throat."

"I . . . I've had a case of the grippe," Elizabeth explained hurriedly, changing octaves. "I'm only now recovering." For good measure she coughed lightly into her hand.

"Are ye now? I thought ye lookcd a bit puny and pale. Weakened ye some, I'll wager." Maddy gripped Elizabeth's upper arm so tightly it hurt. "Ye could use some fattenin'. Why don't ye let me take ye upstairs to me room and order us up a fine supper?"

Elizabeth felt the blood rushing to her cheeks again. "No! No, thank you. You're kind, I'm sure, but," she met Maddy's suddenly daggered stare, "well, you see, I don't quite have sufficient funds. All I have is my pay and most of it went to the doctor."

Maddy appeared to consider this for a moment. "Tell ye what, luv. I like ye, I do, and to prove it, I'll stake ye tonight. Ye kin owe me till the next time ye're in port."

Elizabeth had a fleeting glimpse of Maddy searching her

341

pockets for every valuable she possessed while she slept, then tossing her out into the streets. She may have led a sheltered existence in Devon, but wasn't entirely stupid!

"I couldn't possibly let you do that." Elizabeth realized she was treading on dangerous ground. "It wouldn't be right to accept money from a lady."

"Why not? Don't ye like me?" Maddy snuggled closer, having appreciated Elizabeth's referring to her as a lady. Probably few who knew her would employ such a term in describing her.

"Of course I do!" Elizabeth's voice broke into another high-pitched squeal. "Certainly, but . . ."

"Leave the lad be, Maddy," a voice that was low-pitched though not deep, said from the table just behind Maddy's stool.

Maddy's face hardened into a look of disappointed disgust for only an instant before she pasted on a false smile, turning toward the intruder. "We was just gettin' acquainted," she said in as bright a tone as she seemed capable of mustering.

"Aye, and I know the misfortune that befalls those who make your acquaintance. Shove off!"

Elizabeth looked past Maddy to see a surprisingly young man slouched in a straight-back cane chair, his boots propped on the table. From his tone of authority, she had thought to find a much older man.

"You heard me, Maddy. Off with you, now, or I'll fill Jocko's ear with what you and your mates are up to."

"I'm sure I don't know what ye mean," Maddy said with an innocent air.

"Shall we go up to your room and see if it's empty?" the young man challenged.

Frowning and muttering, Maddy picked up her skirts and left in a huff of indignation.

"You'd best take care, lad," the young man warned her. "That kind will have at least two accomplices awaiting you

342

upstairs. They'll pick your carcass clean, then sell you to the highest bidder."

"Sell me?" Elizabeth echoed, appalled.

"That's right. To a slaver or to some ship's captain too mean and cheap to hire his labor. You won't wake up till you're far at sea and thus can't do much to remedy your situation but work for free."

"Thank you . . . mate." Elizabeth tried to match the tones and expressions she had heard around her. "Can I buy you a drink?"

"I've got one." The man lifted a tankard to his lips. He was slight of build, probably only in his early twenties, dressed in ordinary seaman's garb, a baggy lawn shirt, and trousers. Much of a clean shaven face that appeared as if it might be very handsome was concealed beneath a large, black tri-corner hat. Whoever her savior was, he was alone and Elizabeth wondered if she might be safer joining him.

"Would you mind if I . . ." Elizabeth coughed, realizing that was not the way to phrase it. "Mind if I slip over, mate?" she asked him.

The man simply nodded toward the other cane-backed chair.

She tried to appear suitably swaggering as she crossed to the other table and plunked heavily into her seat. "I'm new in the port," she explained.

"I can see that." The tri-corner hat lifted just a trifle to peer at her from beneath the brim. "And if you don't employ more care in choosing your companions, you won't live long enough to become an old resident."

Elizabeth gulped audibly, swallowing the lump that had formed in her throat.

"Whatever you're running from, son, it can't be as bad as what you could end up facing. Go home while you still can," the man advised.

"I . . . I can't possibly." Elizabeth thought of Lord Bramwell, a fate that seemed worse than death.

343

"Royale's no place for a gentle lad. How old are you, boy?"

"Fifteen." She tried to present a believable age to her concerned companion. At least one person in the ghastly seaport possessed a kind heart. Elizabeth was already somewhat taken by the fineness of the face her companion presented. Curls of black poked out from beneath the tricorner, and when he turned just so, where the lanternlight struck him, he was exceptionally pleasant to gaze upon. His eyes were large and of a strange violet hue, long-lashed and attractive. He seemed almost the same age or only slightly older than Elizabeth's own, though from his manner in dealing with the barmaid, she had taken him for a much older man. He wasn't at all like these others. No one could possess a face of such sweetness and have less than the noblest of hearts.

"And what brings you out to a place like this and at this time of night?" her savior asked.

"I thought to find work as a cabin boy." Elizabeth offered a fleeting plan that had occurred to her, though she didn't know if she could manage to pull it off.

"From here that's an unlikely goal to be realized." The man leaned on his elbows against the table. "Most of the ships calling here have a full complement already and cabin boys are the most unessential of the lot. Do you know what kind of life it is you're seeking? 'Tis hard work, lad, and gets harder as you grow."

Teddy and Paul, the two cabin boys aboard the *Sea Star* had seemed to enjoy their work well enough. All they had to do was fetch and carry and deliver messages between passengers and crew.

"From this port," her companion continued, "at your best you'll find work on a merchantman and they'll give you every dirty job the lowest seaman won't handle. At the worst, you'll end on a slaver and that's a job you won't forget till your dying day."

344

"Well, I thought, perhaps, a ship like the *Sea Star*," she ventured, but the man just grinned, revealing teeth that were small and pearly white.

"Cabin boys on the passenger ships are apprenticed. Their fathers have signed them on to a captain they know and trust. You'd need references to be considered and the waiting lists can be a year or two long."

"Oh," Elizabeth murmured, sipping from her tankard. The ale she had already imbibed had made her so light-headed she had actually begun to believe she might have found the means of her escape until the young man she was sitting with introduced reality into the discussion.

"So what will you do, lad?" the man inquired gently.

"I . . . I don't know." Elizabeth's chin trembled as an irresistible urge to cry overcame her. She buried her face in her hands to hide her tears.

"You won't consider going home?"

"I . . . I can't."

"Very well then, boy, gain control of yourself." The very kind man handed her a handkerchief, crisp and clean, from a trouser pocket. "Come along with me. I have your answer and a job for you." The fellow rose, expecting Elizabeth to follow him and not looking back to see if she did or not. He presented a very slight, slender figure maneuvering through the tables. "I'm off, Jocko," he called out to the black man behind the barman's counter.

The huge fellow looked up and waved. "I'll be along a'fore the tide turns, Cap'n," he shouted. "Soon as I've checked these here books."

"Captain?" Elizabeth questioned under her breath, trotting to keep up with his brisk pace. "You're captain of your own ship?" she said as they reached the street, forgetting in her amazement to use a deeper tone. She realized her error when the man suddenly stopped in midstride to turn around and stare at her. He was only an inch or two taller than she. "What did you say your name was?" he de-

345

manded.

"Ah, Ted . . . Teddy," she replied, too shaken to remember just what name she had given before.

The violet eyes studied him intently. "You seem tall for your age, Teddy."

"I . . . I am. My father always said I was tall for my age." For a moment, Elizabeth was terrified he would change his mind and leave her. In the next, she was frightened that he would take her to sea, and then what? How could she possibly keep her sex secret on a shipful of men? However, the prospects seemed thread-slender of being able to ever escape this cursed island and Lord Bramwell, by any other means. He set out again down the long line of ships tied at dockside and Elizabeth meekly followed, walking behind him until they came to a medium-sized ship that appeared, even in darkness, to be dreadfully old and dilapidated. The man climbed the gangplank and "Teddy" scurried after him. Without a word to the crewman on watch, the captain led the way down to the lower level of the ship.

"Mike!" He rapped on a door in passing, then entered what appeared to be the captain's quarters. "Sit down, boy," the captain ordered. He took off his tri-corner to reveal a bandanna tied around his head much as many of the sailors aboard the *Sea Star* wore to keep the fierce sun off their heads. "Well, did you hear me, lad? Sit!"

Elizabeth promptly sat in the chair opposite his at the small, rickety table, bare except for a single lantern burning. The cabin door that she had softly closed behind her when she entered was suddenly thrown open again with a bang that made her jump. "Captain," a loud male voice boomed. "Are we still to sail at high tide?" Elizabeth saw a tall, scruffy man with a full beard come into her line of vision. He sported a gold earring and several rows of chains about his neck that glittered against the stripes of his dirty seaman's shirt.

"We sail as soon as Jocko's aboard, Dawson. Have the rest of the crew reported?" the captain asked him.

"All but Hatch. He's gone and got himself into the jail-house again. Drunk and disorderly."

With a scowl, the captain reached into a drawer of the small vanity behind him and took out a handful of coins giving them to Dawson. "Bail him out, then."

"Aye, Captain," the mate responded, then departed.

Elizabeth nervously coughed to find her voice. "Is this by any chance, a pirate ship?"

The captain stared straight into her eyes. "It is," he replied evenly. "Are you ready to run for home again?"

Elizabeth shook her head firmly, deciding on no account would she return to Bramwell. "Captain, I have a confession to make that I fear you will have to know before our departure," she began, unable to meet his gaze. He was, after all, so young and handsome. Never would she have believed she would say what she was about to. " 'Tis true, I am a runaway. I entered the tavern where you found me to hide from my pursuers. I didn't know where else to go," she explained, surprised that she was able to do so dry-eyed. "If you hadn't come to my aid, I don't know what might have become of me. You've already proven to me that you have a kind and generous heart and I would only ask that you continue to be merciful. I think that I could easily come to love you in time . . ."

"Love me?" The captain leaned forward. Elizabeth dared only a glimpse of the furrowed frown that had appeared on the fine features of the captain's face.

"You . . . you see," she stammered, trying to force the words out. "I . . . I'm not a boy at all. I'm a woman." She removed her cap to release the short crop of curls. "I believe, sir, that you are a kind man and will not take cruel advantage." She bravely lifted her chin, determined to meet her fate, whatever it was to be, without cowardice.

A short burst of laughter behind her caused Elizabeth to

spin around in surprise. She had neither seen nor heard the young man enter and was mortified to realize her confession had had an audience. He was the captain's age, or thereabouts, clean shaven and slender, wearing the same kind of bandanna wrapped, turban-style, about his head, and was presently stomping the floor with his booted feet in uncontrollable mirth that jarred Elizabeth's already sadly frayed nerves Every guffaw made her want to cringe with embarrassment.

"Mike, this is no way to greet our guest," the captain chided while Elizabeth's face flushed to crimson to realize her declaration of love had been overheard. "Stop it now," the captain said, but began to smile, then to snicker, finally joining the crewman in rousing laughter.

"I never thought you could be so cruel," she threw out at him, her body trembling to hold back her tears.

"It's not you we're laughing at," the captain gained sufficient control to say between bursts of mirth, but chuckles continued to punctuate his words. "It isn't directly you, at any rate. I mean, it's not your fault."

"I fail to see what is so amusing about an honestly stated emotion, sir. You deride me unmercifully for confessing that I love you."

At this, the crewman behind her lost his ability to stand, laughing so hard he sat directly on the floor, rolling in laughter. The captain, watching his crewman fall, broke into renewed peals of laughter too, until tears rolled down his face.

"I'm sorry, but you can't possibly love me." The captain shook his head, clutching his side. "You see, I am a woman too." Removing the red bandanna, a swirl of long black hair tumbled out to fall about her shoulders.

Elizabeth stared, dumbfounded.

"And Mike there, who can't control himself, is also of the female persuasion." They both broke into renewed peals of laughter.

Gazing from one to the other, watching their mirth and rethinking its cause, Elizabeth's face first cracked with a smile, then a grin, then a giggle escaped, and finally she too burst into hysterical laughter.

"So, now that you know our story and we know yours, are you still of a mind to join us?" Jamie Morgan asked.

"I can't believe I didn't realize," Elizabeth said smiling.

"Neither did I until you gave yourself away outside the tavern. Even so, I wasn't certain until you confessed." The trio began to break up into giggles again. They sat about the table in the captain's cabin, drinking wine by lanternlight. Dawson had entered a short time ago to tell them Jocko and Hatch were aboard and Jamie told him to cast off. Only then did he notice that three females now sat around the captain's table. He gazed at the newcomer curiously for a moment, then shrugged as if it shouldn't surprise him and went out.

"Do the crew all know you're women?" Elizabeth asked.

"They know, but we don't make much out of it," Jamie replied.

"She means that we don't remind them," the one introduced to her as Lacey Bell provided. "Jamie's name, of course, really is James Morgan. Her father's idea of how to ensure fate will give you a girl child when it's a boy you've put in your order for."

"It could have been worse had I come a boy and gotten a name like Margaret or Cecilia," Jamie added, chuckling at such a thought.

"At any rate," Lacey furthered. "I'm called Mike and the crew all call her Captain or Captain Jamie. It's simpler that way so they think of us as fellow crewmen and not as women. It's too bad you cut off your lovely locks. You needn't have as Jamie could have shown you how to conceal them. You must have had beautiful hair."

349

Elizabeth fingered a close-cropped lock, twirling it about her finger. "It will grow back," she sighed.

"Seriously," Jamie inserted. "If you've decided you want to go back to England, we can put you safely ashore in a port where you can make your way home again."

"I'm afraid that if I go home they'll only send me back to Lord Bramwell. Or they'll find someone equally repulsive to marry me off to. If you'll have me, I'd rather take my chances here as one of you. Jail, or even hanging, might be preferable to a lifelong marriage to a man I can't abide."

"Our sentiments precisely." Lacey raised her cup in salute. "So then, here's to the Ladies of the Spanish Main!"

"And welcome aboard, Teddy!" Jamie inserted as all three clicked their cups together.

Tossed by a giant wave, the ship pitched beneath her feet and Jamie tightened her grip on the wheel, fighting to retain control against the wildly rolling sea that was a cauldron of white-capped, violent waves. Gale force winds threatened to sweep her slight weight overboard, and if not for the safety of the lifelines lashing her in her place, she would easily be washed off the deck. Sleeting rain pelted her face, its salt-laden fingers stinging her skin through her drenched clothing. The sky had darkened until she could barely see the outline of the *Lady Morgan*'s bow. Thank God it was not a hurricane she was fighting but only a summer tropical storm, common enough from June through November, and sufficiently terrifying for those unfamiliar with its brutal and unexpected ferocity. Lightning crashed against the black clouds in brilliant displays of blazing white. Thunder rolling out of the skies vibrated the deck with a rumbling drumroll that cadenced the storm's violence.

"Go below, Captain," Dawson, the third mate, shouted to be heard above the roar of crashing waves. " 'Tis my turn at the wheel."

Jamie's teeth chattered from the chill wind, muffling her reply. "She's my ship and my responsibility and I'll see her through," she managed to answer from between lips that shivered uncontrollably.

Ned, on the other side of her, shook his grizzled head. "Let Dawson take her, ye stubborn wench, else we'll have us no captain at all when ye drown right here at yer post. Go below."

The door to the lower cabins sprang open, spilling feeble lamplight on the deck and silhouetting an enormous shadow that crowded the entry. Jocko heaved himself onto the slanting deck, fighting the wind and rain as he crossed the sodden, slippery planking. "I thought ye'd be giving 'em trouble about leaving the wheel," he scolded as he reached them. "Let Dawson take it. Ye've had enough. Ye'll come below now or, cap'n or no, I'll tote ye away on me shoulder."

Jamie realized she couldn't fight all three of them.

"Ye've proved yerself enough times over," Jocko advised near her ear so she could hear him. "Give it up, lass. Ye've had enough."

Ned seemed to see it as already settled, unfastening the ropes that held her steady at the wheel, tying Dawson into her place while Jocko gripped Jamie about the waist to keep the waves and wind from washing her overboard. A bolt of lightning dazzled the sky in a blinding display that lit the deck, and Jamie felt every hair on her body prickle.

"Down!" Jocko shouted, taking her with him as he fell to the deck, throwing his body over hers as a shield. The explosive shockwave of the lightning bolt pummeled them both as an ear-shattering crack of thunder roared through their ears. The deck heaved dangerously to starboard before the ship righted herself again, and only Jocko's grip on her kept Jamie from sliding into the sea. As the ship came upright, there was a loud creaking snap behind them, and

Jocko turned around in time to see one of the three main-masts, split by the lightning bolt, slowly, almost casually, tipping toward them.

"Roll!" he shouted, pushing Jamie in one direction while he took the other. Ned saw the beam coming and pitched himself to the side just before the towering mast crashed onto the deck.

" . . . we commit his body to the sea." Jamie finished reading the rites, then watched as the plank was upended, sending Dawson's shroud wrapped body into the softly lapping waves. The storm that had taken Dawson had passed, leaving a calm, clear, azure day behind. The crew had gathered to hear last rites and, the simple service ended, slowly and sadly walked away. Dawson had been a good friend to many of them and a dependable liaison between the seamen and the ship's leaders.

"It should have been me," Jamie murmured, gazing at the place where her third mate's body had vanished into the depths. She had known him since she was a child. Dawson had once made a doll for her out of straw and bits of rags. She had never played with it but had kept it. She still had it somewhere in the sea chests stored in the attic on Tortuga.

"You mustn't think that way, Jamie. It isn't your fault." Lacey placed a consoling arm about her waist.

"Lacey's right," Elizabeth added. " 'Twas only chance that it was him and not you at the wheel. I didn't know Dawson well, but I liked him. I'm sorry he's gone, yet it terrifies me to think that it could have been you instead, had it happened only a minute sooner."

Jamie turned to gaze at her. "Will that comfort his wife and children?" she asked.

"I'm sure it won't," Lacey answered. "But the Buccaneer's Fund will take care of them. You know that."

"Yes," Jamie stated, walking off from them. "And so will I."

"Curse it all!" Jamie swore, kicking the offending hunk of wood with the heel of her boot. The charred beam lay across the broken planks of the *Lady Morgan's* deck. The rail was split, the wheel smashed to splinters. "She'll take weeks to fix," she grumbled, thinking herself alone on the stricken ship that had limped back to port on the remaining sails after Dawson's sea burial. As if fate had decreed the man's time was up, the only damage had been caused by the mast falling across the very place where the third mate was tied to a post that was intended to preserve his life.

"I doubt she's worth repairing," a smooth, soft voice said from behind her.

Jamie was already angry before she spun around. "I suppose you find this a pleasant sight!" she snapped, her hands raising to her hips as she glared at him.

"You know better," Franco replied, leaning against a sturdier remnant of the broken deck rail, his arms folded across his chest, his long legs locking at the crossed ankles. His black broadcloth frockcoat was flawlessly neat and impeccable, the light ruffles on his white shirt casually stirred by the slight breeze. The storm's passage had raised a strong salt sea scent into the wind that cooled the summer heat.

"She'll cost more than she's worth to fix, and even then will be barely seaworthy," he said, surveying the damage with an appraising eye.

Jamie stiffened. "I have already had enough trouble without adding the sight of you to my misfortunes." She stalked toward him and stopped just in front of him. "I need no advice from you, Captain DeCortega. I will have the ship repaired and she'll be as good as she ever was."

Franco smiled at her as if she was a child who had to be

humored. "I'll gladly loan you the money if you're short," he offered.

"I'll take nothing from you, in money or advice!"

"Repairing this wreckage is bound to cost you as much as you've put aside these past months . . ."

"See to your own troubles, Captain and leave me to mine!"

"I'm afraid I can't do that." The arms folded across the chest came down to his sides.

"And why not?"

"I have a strong interest in your welfare, my love, whether you accept that interest or not," he replied, nonplussed by her anger.

"Save your breath," she bit out harshly, her eyes narrowed to slits as she glared at him. "Save it for Polly and the rest."

"As I've told you a dozen times before, nothing happened!" The first flash of anger appeared in his eyes.

"And I don't believe you, so where does that leave us?"

"I suppose that is up to you," he answered. "You're set on believing the worst of me. Nothing I can say or do will change your mind."

"In any case," Jamie shrugged indifference, "it wouldn't matter. Morgan's action with the will has taught me one lesson I won't be forgetting again. In this world, men hold all the power and no man, ever, will hold such power over me again. I trusted Morgan and you can see where it took me. Part of the money I can't put my hands on was mine to begin with. He promised to keep it safe for me. Now I can't touch it unless I abide by his wishes."

"Not all men would do the same."

"No? Then pardon me if I prefer not to risk it," she threw back venomously.

"You're only hurt and angry. When you've stopped long enough to think things through, you'll see the future in a different light."

354

"Why does everyone insist I don't know my own mind?" she nearly shouted in exasperation. "First Mary and Lacey and now I must listen to you."

"Because you don't," Franco replied to her question. "From the very beginning, you've never trusted me. You speak of broken faith, Jamie, when you've never held that faith to start. You set me beside Morgan as the example, as you set all men."

"And they never disappoint me," she returned nastily. "Look what I got out of trusting you."

"Did you? I doubt it. You would rather believe the worst of me than listen to what truly happened that night. It's easier than giving yourself over to a commitment. Perhaps I can't blame you for your fears with the example your father set on the merits of love and devotion, but neither can I break down this wall you're erecting around your emotions!"

"That's not true!" she countered loudly. "There is no wall. I loved you."

"Yes, you'll love, but you won't trust, Jamie, and one is useless without the other." Before she could reply, he turned and walked off the ship, leaving her to stare after him.

"What are we to do, Jamie? Fixing the ship has cost us every bit of the money we've saved." Since she came, several months past now, Elizabeth Ferris had taken over the accounts and disbursement of funds for the ship's company. She had an excellent head for figures and kept neat, well-ordered books no one could contest.

"We'll do just as we've done before in a like predicament," Jamie stated. "We'll prowl the sea lanes until we've matched what we spent."

"But you said not a week ago that we were going to head into port until it's safer than it is now. The Navy has all those patrol vessels prowling the sea lanes in search of the likes of us, and the new governor of Royale has sworn he'll hang each and every pirate they bring him."

"Do you see another option open to us?" Jamie asked crossly, snapping at the younger woman.

Lacey had seen the fouler sides of Jamie's moods before, but Elizabeth never had. "No, I don't," Elizabeth replied sheepishly, taking her friend's anger personally.

"If you haven't the stomach for it, then stay in port!" Jamie said, then stormed out of the cabin, slamming the door behind her.

Elizabeth looked over at Lacey. "What did I do?" she asked her.

"Nothing," Lacey replied. "It's nothing either of us has done. It's just losing Dawson, the broken mast, and the damage costing us so much to fix. She holds herself responsible for all of us and it's too large a burden for any one person to carry. I think she would prefer you and I did stay in port, at least for this next voyage. If we don't come along, we can't be taken if the ship is captured. She's not angry at you or at me. She's just angry."

"I wish there was something we could do to help."

"So do I, Liz, but she'll have to work it out on her own."

"Do we really dare take the *Lady* to sea again?"

"Jocko and Ned agree that we've little choice. She's seaworthy enough after the repairs."

"But the patrols," Elizabeth said worriedly.

"We all know it, Liz. Jamie more than any of us, but we haven't much choice. You can stay behind if you want. No one will think less of you if you don't want to come."

"No." Elizabeth shook her head firmly. "I'll come."

Chapter Seventeen

Over the past months, John Terry Junior had discovered that he hated the sea and the Royal Navy every bit as much as he thought he would back when he had vehemently protested his upcoming fate into his father's will-deafened ear. He despised salt spray in his face, found no pleasure in standing on a rocking deck, and wished with every fiber of his being to be home again, enjoying every pleasure and vice the Bermuda isle afforded to the spoiled and pampered son of the governor. John Junior didn't like the captain of His Majesty's ship, the *Rochester*, because Captain Young made so obvious his open resentment of John's appointed position as his first lieutenant. Young had worked his way up through the ranks to attain his captaincy after years of dedicated service. It rankled the old man that his lieutenant had gotten his commission out of the contacts and string-pulling of a wealthy and influential father.

John had found the best defense against the old man's ire was to remain out of his sight and this he had been fairly successful in accomplishing all the way from Bermuda to the Virginia Colony and back into the Caribbean on their scheduled round of duty.

He was presently hiding in the cabin he shared with Lieutenant Brady O'Rourke, where he could safely remain until at least suppertime. Lieutenant O'Rourke, who did not have a governor father, attended the daytime watch while John took over after the captain retired for the night.

Lying on his bunk with pillows supporting his head, he was trying to read by the light streaming in through the portal, but *Famous Sea Battles* was boring him silly, and his mind was wandering to how he might convince the older Terry to release him from this torturous shipboard existence. He had been sent to sea in his father's efforts to make a man of him before he spent all of his youth, and all of the elder Terry's money, on the pursuits of a wastrel. In John Junior's estimation, the elder Terry had exiled him here without mercy to die of ennui.

Of course, he could simply refuse to sail when the *Rochester* left John's home port in a few weeks, but then he would have his father's wrath to deal with, not to mention the ire of the Royal Navy. Such an action would also leave him devoid of funds, as John Senior would most assuredly disinherit him as he threatened to when his son tried to refuse his commission.

John slammed the book shut and sighed deeply. A few minutes passed before he realized the ship was slowing down. Curious, because nothing *ever* happened on this ship, he sat up to look out the portal. Nothing could be seen but a clear blue sky and endless ocean, devoid even of clouds to break its monotony.

"What the devil . . ." he said aloud, deciding there was no help for it but to go out on deck to see what the unusual occurrence was all about.

A flurry of activity met his emergence into daylight. Deck hands were scattering about in all directions. John saw a small, uninhabited island a few hundred yards away off the port bow but couldn't imagine why they would be stopping. Lieutenant O'Rourke hurried past him and John gripped him by the arm. "Brady, what is it?"

Brady answered by extending his arm, pointing across the water to a small lifeboat John had clearly missed in his initial survey. A flutter of frilly white material inside it hinted at the presence of an unconscious female passenger.

"Good Lord," John muttered. "Is she alive?"

"We think so. Bates, he was the one on lookout, swears he saw her arm wave briefly before she fainted."

"Did she come from the island, do you think?" John began walking beside O'Rourke toward the ladder from which they hoped to reach the lifeboat and its passenger.

"Doubt it," O'Rourke replied. "The current here heads toward the reefs. Probably she is the only survivor of a mishap at sea and has been floating toward the island. There was that strong squall we avoided yesterday. Perhaps they didn't, and sailed right into it. It's fortunate we came along before the pirates found her. They're thick as fleas on a hound in these waters."

John had been praying for just such an event ever since he boarded the ship, looking for a break in the dull routine. The *Rochester* was commissioned to sail the sea lanes in search of pirates and bring them to justice. The closer they came to the Caribbean, the nearer he hoped he might be to seeing some action. A good fight would give his fencing muscles fine exercise, but that would not seem to be forthcoming today as he helped Brady use long-handled hooks to snag the lifeboat and draw it closer to the *Rochester*'s ladder.

"Poor thing," O'Rourke remarked, gazing at the lovely young blonde in the bottom of the boat. She was pretty and slender, her forearm stretched over her eyes as though to protect them from the fierce tropical sun. Disheveled tresses floated in a pool of slimy seawater beneath her head. "She must have been adrift for days," Brady said. "Will you go down or shall I?"

John heard her moan, prodding him into action. "Hold the ladder steady. I'll fetch her." He started down, hearing Brady answer Captain Young's query with a shout of, "She's alive!", then the deckhands raising a rousing cheer. They had all come as close to the rail as they could

359

manage, intent on the welfare of the hapless creature they were saving.

Reaching her, John checked her neck for a pulse, finding a strong, steady beat, then gently lifted her into his arms. He heard commotion on the deck above and assumed it was caused by the excitement of the rescue.

"Brady, you'll have to help lift her aboard." He gazed up the ladder with his burden in his arms, startled to find no one above to answer his summons. There was a terrible din of shouting and metal clanging above. "Brady, damn your eyes! Where are you?"

John felt something sharp prick his skin just over his jugular vein and froze.

"Set me down ever so gently, Lieutenant, else my hand may slip and cut your throat."

Oh, blast, Terry thought, but didn't dare give the curse utterance with the point of the dagger so close to its mark. He gently set her down on her feet while the dagger remained at his throat. Now he knew what the trouble was on deck. While the crew was engrossed in the rescue of the fair young maid, pirates had used dinghys and lifeboats to row to the far side of the ship, scramble over the rail with grappling hooks, and had caught the crew of the *Rochester* by surprise. The fight was well over before John's lively captor signaled him to climb the ladder ahead of her back to the deck of his ship. From the look on her beautiful, slightly sunburned face, he didn't care to test whether or not she would use the small weapon she held, quite expertly, in her dainty hand.

"Well, this is an adventure I won't care to write home about," Brady remarked, standing with the other ship's officers on one side of the *Rochester*'s deck while the common seamen were herded into an open hatch to be confined on the lower deck. "Imagine trying to explain that a

360

navy patrol vessel has been bested by the very pirates she was sent to subdue and all without a single shot fired. I wouldn't care to be in Captain Young's place when he tries to explain this before the Admiralty."

"Oh, shut up!" John barked in foul humor. He was watching the progress of the pirate ship which had appeared from behind an outcrop of rocks when signaled that all was clear by a single shot fired from the *Rochester*'s cannon. He was galled that when the opportunity had come, he had been deprived of even the slightest resistance. Surely there had to be some means of turning the odds to the *Rochester*'s favor before the rest of the pirates arrived. As it was, it had taken only seven crewmen from two small dinghys to best the entire ship's complement. Overwhelmed by the surprise of the attack, most had not even had time to arm themselves, thinking themselves engaged in a simple rescue. The sailors were locked in below before the pirates turned their attention to the well-guarded officers and started to tie them, back to back, in preparation of their captain's arrival. A desperate plan was quickly forming as the pirates came nearer to pairing him up with O'Rourke.

"Brady, be ready," he murmured just before the pirates reached him. With a sudden lunge, he propelled himself into the closest pirate, knocking the man off balance, depending on Brady to take care of the other one. He smashed his fist, hard, into the bearded face below him, then prepared to launch himself at the next target, when a pistol shot cracked the air with a loud report.

"Next one's in yer gut, bucko," a calm, deep voice boomed. John stopped, realizing only Brady had followed him into the fray and, like it or not, the *Rochester* was beaten.

"Well then, lad," the voice said in a friendly fashion. "Do ye think to take us all on by yerself?" A hulking presence of a man approached. The encircling pirates opened their ranks to admit him. " 'Tis foolish to fight by yerselves, lads, when these cowards here don't have the guts to back ye." The black man glared down the line of John's fellow officers, reserving a special sneer of contempt for Captain Young who had been spared the indignity of being tied up but had not aided his two officers in their last desperate effort. " 'Twill do ye no good to be food for the fishes, laddie-bucks. Ye best back down now," he advised, coming closer to where John still sat on the unconscious pirate.

"Careful, Jocko," a pirate warned with a grin. "He's a mean 'un. I kin see it in his eyes." A few of the pirates chuckled while the one called Jocko continued his steady, approach.

"Well, lad, do ye give it up to be tied with the rest or do I blow a hole in that fine suit of yers?"

With a defiant motion, John stood up, then marched over to stand beside Brady. "I surrender," he stated, "but I refuse to be trussed up like an animal. You have my word, sir, upon my honor, that I will conduct myself accordingly as your prisoner and that will have to suffice."

"Well, la-dee-dah!" a pirate mocked him, provoking laughter from the crew. John noticed that the pirate ship had come alongside and more pirates were added to the audience.

"I'm a'feared that ain't good enuf, boy," the massive pirate stated.

"It will have to be, sir, as I will not be bound." John clenched his fists, ready to fight to the death to retain his freedom.

"Ye're a daft fool, bucko." Jocko reached out with a hamlike fist to grip John's lapels. A sharp whistle from the deck of the pirate ship stopped the hulk's motion, making him turn toward the sound. John's gaze followed the pirate's, spying a surprisingly small figure dressed all in black, standing on the bridge and beckoning to the monster with a waving arm. To John's further astonishment, the ogre-sized presence responded, bounding like a puppy to his master's side, crossing the two-foot span between vessels with accomplished ease of footing. Their initial purpose forgotten for the moment, John was left free to watch the two figures on the other deck. The small one—who seemed woefully short of stature standing next to the giant—seemed to be upbraiding the bigger man, the wild gestures of his black-clad arms betraying his anger, while the big one mutely hung his head under the admonishment.

Finally the small one stormed away, leaving the giant to follow, stomped across the pirate ship's deck, then leaped the span to the deck of the *Rochester*. John would have expected Jocko to be the captain of this lot, yet it was apparent that it was the slender one who was their leader. He must be a bloodthirsty bastard to command this band, John thought, watching the figure in black approach.

"Hatch!" the figure shouted in fury, storming over to one of John's tormentors, who immediately backed off from the captain's anger. "I'm going to nail your hide to mainmast for a decoration!" The slender figure was half the size of the pirate being upbraided. "Are you still suffering from your last bout with the bottle or have you completely lost track of your senses? Don't you know a patrol ship from a passenger vessel by now? This is a Navy ship, you big stupid ox! There's no treasure to be found on her! What did you think we were to gain out of this? Trouble, that's what we've gained out of it. And what the devil has gotten into the rest of you as well?" The fury strode down the line of the original attackers. "I said to wait for an unescorted merchantman or a passenger ship, not to attack the first vessel you laid your stupid eyes on!" The little figure stopped just in front of Hatch again. "Now, just what are we supposed to do with a British patrol ship and a shipload of Royal Navy officers and crew?"

The pint-sized captain of the scruffy, burly crew tapped

a booted foot impatiently. "Hold 'em fer ransom?" Hatch offered with a weak, sickly grin.

The slim figure looked like it just might scream, throwing up its hands and storming again down the line of abashed crewmen, muttering, "Damn-fool-jackass idiots!"

"Well, Brady, I can see we aren't the only ones facing an embarrassing predicament," John commented as the figure passed him. "It" was even shorter than he was.

The figure paused long enough to snap, "Oh, shut up!" then spun about and stormed off.

"I'm sorry, Jamie. It's all my fault." Lacey hung her head in abject despair. She was still dressed in the soggy gown she had worn to lure the ship closer and her wet hair hung limply on her shoulders. "It wasn't bad enough and now look what I've done."

"It isn't your fault. It's Hatch's! And Jocko's, who should have stopped him! Good Lord, what were they thinking of! The Navy won't let this pass. They'll remember this ship and every one of our faces and there can be no better witnesses for the Crown than officers of His Majesty's own Navy. We won't even be safe in Royale now. Our only option is to lie low until memories fade."

"With what?" Elizabeth queried overloudly in her excitement. "This is our first venture since fixing the mast. We haven't any money left."

"Oh, criminy. I've really done it," Lacey wailed disconsolately.

"You haven't done anything but what the others told you to do!" Jamie scolded her for her sniveling. "Now stop that at once. You're still new at this and I don't expect you to know better. I do expect it of them!" She cocked a thumb toward the closed door to the gangway. The three women were in the captain's quarters aboard the *Lady Morgan* where Jamie had retired to think the problem through.

Ultimately, she felt the fault rested with her. She should have known better than to leave any important decisions to Hatch. He was the lookout of the group they had left on the island with Lacey to await a ship's passing. He was to wait for a rich, unescorted passenger ship or cargo vessel and should certainly know them from a heavily armed patrol ship. Had they tried one of their ruses on the high seas, they should all have been blown clean out of the water.

As 1698 approached, preying on the shipping lanes had become so prevalent throughout the Caribbean that His Majesty's government appointed a task force of navy ships to patrol the waters, their purpose to escort honest shipping out to midocean where danger of attack was minimal and to run down and bring in every pirate vessel they came across. Some were trying the same tricks the pirates had used in the past, pretending to be a stranded merchant to lure them close, then opening fire with the heavy guns as soon as they were certain it was pirates who had fallen for the trap. The letter of marque had become an item from an illustrious past, as had the definitions of privateer or pirate. The lines had been crossed too many times. Just as the pirates had not found it practical to see what flag a ship was waving before opening an attack, the patrol vessels fired first, without asking to see a privateer's license, which, at any rate, were not being issued any longer. Europe had turned its interests to colonizing, rather than raping the lands across the water and the buccaneers, once so vital to holding these islands for the glory and wealth of the crowns, were now thorns in the sides of the governments who preferred them removed to make room for settlers.

Port Royale, Morgan's original pirate colony, was now a fairly respectable, teeming, and busy city, with shops and markets and tree-lined avenues, where the gentry built stately homes on the hillsides and the poor were segregated to the older, dilapidated portions of the town. The docks remained rough, with brigands roaming the alleys, but much of the remainder of the city's streets were safe, protected by the governor's militia.

Thieves were thickest near the docks, and usually a fugitive could hide there if he called no attention to himself, but law and order prevailed most often now in Henry Morgan's old City of Sin. The Sodom and Gomorrah of the islands was becoming much like any other portside town of the new world. All the Brethren of the Coast had left to them was Tortuga and a few other small havens in which civilization hadn't yet intruded.

"Perhaps Hatch's plan might not be inconceivable," Elizabeth offered. "We might realize a profit out of ransoming the captured crew."

"Are you daft, Liz?" Jamie snapped crossly. "And just how are we to hold them? There are as many of them as there are of us."

"Well, just the officers then."

"Elizabeth, the matter is serious enough that we have taken one of the very patrol vessels assigned to bringing us to justice. If we hold them ransom, or harm one silly hair on their heads, His Majesty's government will never cease trying to have each and every one of our necks in a noose."

"They'll want our necks stretched anyway," Lacey inserted, in better control now that Jamie had convinced her she was not to blame. After all, she had only been the bait in the trap and hadn't selected the target. It could as easily have been Liz in the lifeboat since the two of them took turns luring ships to the rescue of a damsel in distress that gave the pirates time to position for a sneak attack. As she had once longed for adventure, she was having more than her share of it and usually loving every moment.

The trio worked well together as a three-way partnership, though Lacey and Elizabeth had adopted the cardinal rule of the sea that the captain's will was law and looked to

Jamie as their leader, just as did the men. So far, she had not lost a single seaman to a faulty plan of attack and few captains anywhere could claim a like remarkable score. For that, and for good judgment that had taken them through several profitable ventures, the male complement of the crew followed their female captain loyally while a few had even boasted of broken noses and blackened eyes won out of defending their female leader's honor and abilities.

"We're already wanted for hanging anyway," Lacey pursued the subject.

"Yes, James and Mike and Teddy," James argued. "But it isn't general knowledge that we're women. It will be when we let this bunch go."

"Perhaps we can hide the patrol ship and strand the crew . . ."

"Sink the damned thing." Liz added her opinion. "And maroon the crew on the island."

"Oh hush, both of you, and let me think!" Jamie snapped. She stood up and began to pace the brief length of the cabin. "We need money to tide us over, but we daren't try to take another ship now." She uttered her thoughts aloud. "And hiding on Royale is out of the question now."

"But if we maroon the crew . . ."

"And what if another patrol comes along right after we leave to pick them up? How would you like to be strolling along, dressed in your finest, only to run straight into one of them with the entire militia behind him?"

"Oh," Elizabeth murmured, abashed.

"Maybe I do know where we can get our hands on the money to tide us over till memories grow dim. We need to pay the men off to return to their families until we can call them back again, or to hide, if their faces are too well known, and still have some left to hold the three of us over easily as well. Mr. Penrose has that much and more," Jamie stated.

"Penrose!" Lacey squealed. "But he only holds your inheritance. You can't get your hands on it unless you think to hold him up for it."

"I can if I present myself with a legal husband. One who fulfills that damn will's provisions."

"Jamie, you can't be serious," Lacey murmured in astonishment.

"It's time I claimed what is rightfully mine anyway. Lord knows, I earned my share of it."

"But you have to marry to get it," Elizabeth inserted in the same awed surprise as Lacey. The girls had all shared stories on their past. "You'd need a husband."

"I'll have one."

"Where are you going to get one?" Lacey broke in. "You haven't seen Edward Harcourt in a year. He's likely married by now."

"Not Edward, goose! I don't want a husband who'll be hanging about my neck for the rest of my life! I need him for one function and one function only, and that is to display for Mr. Penrose's benefit."

"Then what?"

"Then I send him on his way with my thanks and enough gold in his pocket to have made it worth his while. The will only states that I must present legal documents to prove the marriage has taken place. It doesn't state that I must stay wed to anybody!"

"Wherever can you find someone with the right rank and title to fulfill the will's provisions and who will be willing to strike such a bargain?"

Jamie propped her booted foot up on the seat of the stool and leaned on it to peer down at Lacey. "Someone who might have something to gain and nothing to lose out of the bargain."

"Who? Where would you look?"

Jamie let her eyes roll upward, then cocked a thumb in the same direction. "Who, Lacey dear, is most often

368

handed a commission in His Majesty's Navy thanks to his father's influence?"

"A lord's son, perhaps. And earl's, or a duke's, or . . . Oh, no," she murmured. "You can't be thinking of one of them."

"If just one of them comes from the proper background and has the right connections . . ."

"Jamie, this is insane!" Elizabeth blurted. "Even if he's there, he's a Royal Navy officer!"

"So much the better. Above reproach," Jamie riposted.

"But whyever would he agree?"

"For his life, to start with, and for the lives of his mates . . ."

"You'd never kill a man in cold blood," Lacey sneered.

"Aye," Jamie smiled, "but he won't know that, will he?"

Those not engaged in watching the prisoners were swarming about the ship, throwing hatches up, crashing through cabins on the lower decks, dragging crates and chests out into the open to be searched with careless abandon. A patrol vessel carried no cargo of value, only provisions and the crew's own personal effects. Their supplies, arms, and ammunition quickly disappeared over the side of the pirate ship while clothes chests and the crew's belongings were investigated with more diligent care. Items vanished into pockets or were tossed aside for the next pirate to rummage through. John watched a swarthy, bearded fellow hold up *Famous Sea Battles* and, with a bare glance at the title, toss the book overboard. The same thought had struck John several times.

Jocko seemed to be in charge while the captain was absent. The huge man-mountain stood on the bridge observing that the division of property proceeded without incident, just the look of him assuring that differences of opinion over ownership would be amicably settled. John had eventually lost the argument about remaining free, with his hands untied. Two pirates had held him while a third bound his wrists. Still, his legs were unshackled leaving him free to stroll toward the giant first mate, dragging Brady with him.

"What do you plan to do with us?" John asked, being observed every moment by a sharp-eyed pirate with a scar on his cheek.

"That ain't up to me, laddy-buck. It's for the cap'n to decide."

"Then where is the captain?"

Jocko gazed down at him with a curious half smile. "Now I don't see just how that concerns ye, mate. If the cap'n ain't here, ye have nothing to worry about."

Deciding there was little to be learned from the close-mouthed mate, John edged nearer to one of the pirates digging through Captain Young's clothes chest. "Who captains your vessel?" he demanded. He had thought sounding brusque would command more attention. It did. All the pirates within earshot of him chuckled, including the one he had addressed.

"Captain Morgan, Your Worship." The pirate gave him a mocking, low bow, accompanied by more deriding laughter.

"Henry Morgan is dead. Do you mean Morgan's son?" he queried. This time the laughter was loud and uproarious. John gazed from face to face, perplexed.

"Aye." The nearest pirate grinned. "We sail under Morgan's offspring awright, and ye'll be finding it out soon enuf."

In the year that had passed since Henry Morgan's death, his legend had grown. The suspicions once roused about the late governor of Jamaica seemed to have been confirmed by the publication of a book in England that had

370

eventually reached the Colonies. Written by a man who claimed to have sailed with Henry Morgan on his early adventures, the book gave explicit details of acts of piracy mingled in with privateering ventures. Morgan had fought the publication of the book in the courts and had won his suit since the Panama victory hailed him as a hero, but after Morgan's death, the book went to print unhampered.

Morgan's daughter had vanished after her father's death and when Morgan's old ship began to appear again to threaten the sea lanes, rumor had it that Morgan's ghost was her master. Those more realistically minded decided that perhaps as well as a daughter, the wily captain might have left a son behind that no one had ever heard of until he took up his father's old profession. As had been stated in Exquemelin's book, Morgan's penchant for disposing of all witnesses had not gone unnoted by the crew of the *Rochester*, who had little doubt, after what John had learned, that the son might be similarly inclined.

Morgan, like Jocko, had been a big man, strong enough to break a saber near the hilt, snapping the steel like tinderwood. The one-time pirate had had a habit of fingering the hilt of his cutlass as if ready to draw it from the scabbard; an impatient gesture of stifled energy that looked like death waiting for an excuse to strike. John saw, even from this distance, the same gesture in the younger Morgan. He continued to wonder how the infamous pirate had managed to sire such a puny son and, indeed, how such a son kept command over a scurvy lot of pirates. The captain had reappeared on the deck of the pirate ship and strolled casually toward the captives, sharing a few words with the first mate along the way. Upon reaching the lineup of officers tied in pairs, it was the burly first mate who spoke.

"What be yer captain's name, son?" He addressed Brady O'Rourke, standing just behind John Terry.

O'Rourke, favoring a shoulder wounded in the fight, answered. "He's Captain Nathan Young of His Majesty's

371

Navy, and let me tell you, you shan't get away with this."

"Aye, and who asked ye for yer opinion?" Jocko strode up to Brady, glaring down at him like a great, fierce bear. The young lieutenant's courage began to falter. "Then what be yer name, boy?" the pirate asked him.

"My name be . . . *is*, O'Rourke, sir. Lieutenant Brady O'Rourke."

"Right, then, Lieutenant Brady O'Rourke. Ye'll please be keepin' yer crab trap shut now, ye hear?"

"Yes, sir."

Jocko turned to John. "And what be yer name, lad?"

"John Terry."

Jocko's face registered a flicker of interest, then he just as quickly stifled it. "Ye be a lieutenant in His Majesty's Navy as well, then, don't ye?"

"I am."

"Any treasure aboard we ain't discovered?"

"If there was, I'm certain you would not have missed it." John sneered, refusing to be intimidated.

"Maybe we oughta be sure of that, eh?" Jocko lifted Captain Young by the lapels of his coat until the man's feet dangled inches off the deck.

"Leave him alone." John pried himself between the captain and the pirate, making the man put him down. "Can't you see he's already frightened nearly to death? He can't tell you anything. There is no treasure."

The one they called Jocko stared from the quaking captain to the bold young officer, the remainder of his grip loosening until he finally dropped the captain altogether, discarding him as so much quivering rubbish. "Awright, mates, get the rest o' the supplies aboard the *Lady* and make ready to cast off."

"What are you going to do with us?" John asked the pirate the same question he had posed earlier.

"Well now, lad," Jocko smiled ominously. "I reckon that might depend on you. Tell me, do ye be the same John

372

Terry as is related to the governor, John Terry of Bermuda Colony?"

John paused. To admit his relationship was as well as asking to be held for a large ransom. He laughed. "No, I'm often asked that, but I'm no relation whatever."

Jocko glared at him, then turned to O'Rourke. "Does he speak true? If ye're lyin' I'll cut yer tongue out."

O'Rourke paled, but answered, "No, he's no relation."

Jocko was still eyeing them both suspiciously, as well as casting an eye at Captain Young who hadn't offered a word since the pirates boarded. Finally, his gaze settled on John again. "Somehow, lad, I don't believe ye. Mates, take 'im aboard the *Lady*."

Being given a helping hand across the void between ships by the first mate was a bit like being lobbed over the net at a tennis tournament. Jocko either did not know his own strength, or didn't take it into account when dealing with naval officers. The pirate jumped over first, then grabbed John's shoulder and heaved. John had to scramble to keep his footing until his motion stopped.

"Take some care, will you, man?" John griped in a fury. "I presume you want me alive for whatever purpose you have in mind for me."

"Not me, Bucko," Jocko returned, unperturbed. "Don't give narry a damn meself, but ye're right that it might displeasure the cap'n some."

The massive black paw reached out for him again to turn John toward the doorway to the cabins below deck, but John jerked free of it. "Thanks, but I do not need to be shoved the entire distance," he barked, starting out under his own power.

He was escorted into a room that must serve as the captain's cabin. Rolled-up charts stuck out of every conceivable nook and cranny in the Spartanly furnished abode. There were heavy purple velvet drapes over the many-paned window and beneath them a fair-sized bed neatly covered with a dark green spread. John noted that the bed was built into the wall. The night table beside it was French in design with a single brass lantern perched upon it. The small wardrobe in the corner was of Spanish decor and the table at which the captain sat was made of sturdy English oak. All the pieces had been nailed down to the floorboards. John had a practiced eye for all such things as furnishings, styles, and designs, the more extravagant the better he knew them, and decided this cabin's interior could only be labeled Provincial Plunder.

His disapproving gaze finally settled on the captain of this crew of misfits and thieves. A better look convinced him that Morgan's son seemed even more ludicrous than his first appraisal.

The slender figure seated at the table, booted feet propped on its scarred surface, couldn't weigh more than a hundred twenty pounds, if that much, even taking the knee-high boots into the accounting. The black stockings over the calves had a decidedly female turn. John's gaze strayed upward to a slim waist wrapped in a red silk sash with two silver pistols tucked into it. Delicate tapering fingers touched the handle of one weapon, fidgeting there just as John had heard described as a Morgan gesture. A balloon-sleeved loose black blouse was open at the neck, and as far down as the shirt revealed, which was not too far, there was a clear, clean ivory-hued chest. If John Terry Senior had thought his son was a disappointment, what a trick life had played on Henry Morgan.

The captain's gaze was taking John's assessment too, looking him over from his boots to the top of his head much as a housewife might ponder the purchase of a cabbage for the family dinner table until John wondered if this effeminate captain remembered what sex he was. The appraisal made him almost recoil physically from the scrutiny.

"This be the one, Cap'n?" Jocko inquired.

With another quick survey that took in all of John's form, the captain nodded. "He'll do as well as any."

John stared as the booted feet came down from the table and the captain leaned forward. He couldn't have said just how he knew, whether it was the voice in its own pitch and not angrily berating the crew, or the shape, or the movement, but suddenly he did know. "It", "he", the captain, was a woman! A beautiful one from the look of her without the tri-corner hat to shade her face. Her hair was concealed in the folds of a red bandanna which she finally removed, letting the wavy, raven tresses fall down her back and shaking them free with a toss of her head.

"Close your mouth, lieutenant, and sit down. We have much to discuss and little time to indulge in it," the female captain said in a brusque, no-nonsense tone. She indicated the chair directly across from her own.

John suddenly realized that he was gaping and closed his mouth, easing himself down onto the seat, then finding that he couldn't sit back comfortably with his hands bound behind his back.

"Might I have these off at least?" he inquired, lifting his arms as far as his bonds would allow to display his discomfort.

She gazed at his problem, then nodded to Jocko, who slit through the ropes with a single upward slice, releasing John's wrists.

"Thank you," he muttered, unwilling to be grateful for any small favor she might allow as he rubbed his arms to restore circulation.

"You can go, Jocko," the captain said.

"And leave ye alone wi' him?" the first mate protested.

"I think the lieutenant is wise enough to realize that thirty of us stand between him and the deck of his ship. He won't try anything foolish, will you, Lieutenant Terry?"

"Thirty to one odds, under these circumstances, are the kind that I find unacceptable."

"There, you see?" She looked up at the hovering pirate. "That's all, Jocko," she repeated when the hulk failed to move. "Get!" she ordered crisply, starting the man finally into motion.

"Aye, Cap'n," Jocko grumbled, opening the cabin door, then closing it again quietly behind him.

"I'm Jamie Morgan," she stated as soon as they were alone.

"I'd heard Morgan's daughter was the belle of the season in London a year or so back, as well as the most eligible young woman on the islands."

Obviously, the comment did not sit well with Mistress Morgan, as she took a small dagger out of her sash and began to plunge it recklessly, point first, into the tabletop while focusing an irritated glare on John. "What I was a year ago has nothing to do with me now."

"From lady to pirate?" he queried with a smirk that made the dagger plunge just a little deeper into the marred wood. "I suppose I'm expected to say, then, that it is a pleasure to meet you."

"You'll find no pleasure in knowing me," she replied.

"I didn't say that I would." John bore the glare she bestowed and gave it right back.

"I shall ask you once more, are you Governor John Terry's son?" she inquired harshly.

"No," he stated, staring straight into her eyes, which he might have found excessively beautiful under other circumstances. "We simply bear the same name. Merely coincidence."

"Is it?" she smiled like the cat cornering the canary. "Perhaps I can get a more truthful answer out of that quivering mass of flesh you call your captain."

"He can tell you nothing that I have not already said. There is no treasure aboard a naval patrol ship, as you

376

should well know, and trying to ransom me to Governor Terry will avail you nothing as we are not related."

"You'd better be, Lieutenant Terry," her tone almost purred provocatively, "or you'd better be able to pretend that you are."

"What are you talking about?"

"I have a problem, Lieutenant, and I've selected you to solve it. I need your good name and at least a pretense that you are indeed the son of the governor. I need a husband of good reputation. I've picked you."

John stared, unable to believe he had heard right. "You're mad! Is this a jest of some kind?"

"Only the one my father created. I'm simply fulfilling what I must to retrieve what rightfully belongs to me. Morgan wanted to ensure that even upon his death, I would afterward marry a man he would have approved of. He's left all of my inheritance to my husband, not to me. To get it, I have to present a mate with a good name. Yours being at least the same as the governor's should serve that purpose."

"But I'm . . . not the governor's son." John still suspected ransom might be on her mind, or surely some trick. In any case, he was determined to stand on his story.

"That doesn't matter," she replied with a shrug. "The name is the same and that will suffice. I only have to present *you*, not your pedigree."

"You can't possibly be serious . . ."

"Morgan was, therefore *I* am. If you'll do it, I'll see you handsomely rewarded and sent on your way. We should never have to cross paths again."

"And if I won't?"

"If you enjoy living, you'd better." She gave him a warning smile.

"You'd kill me for refusing?"

The dagger dug into the tabletop again playfully. "Now if you won't offer your cooperation, I would have little reason

377

to keep you counted among the living."

"And what is going to happen to the crew of the *Rochester?*"

"That is entirely in your hands, Lieutenant. My crew is right this minute marooning your shipmates on that island in the distance, then the *Rochester* will be sunk. Now another ship might not happen to sail near this island for several months, or years, or for purposes that would aid them, ever, in their lifetimes."

"Or one might happen along this very afternoon," he returned.

"True, if you are willing to gamble their lives on it. I've been to that island, Lieutenant Terry. Unless your friends can drink saltwater and eat scrub palm, there is little else to sustain them. On the other hand, give me your word that I will have your cooperation and I'll leave provisions for them until you are set free in a port where you may reveal their whereabouts to the proper authorities to initiate their rescue. You may explain your escape with any tale you like, except the truth. In any case, I doubt you would want to reveal the real circumstances of your release, since having a wife who's a known pirate would do little for either your reputation or your career." She smiled, a smile that would be lovely if he hadn't already decided he despised this cold, heartless caricature of a female.

"I don't believe you," John stated in icy contempt. "You wouldn't condemn twenty-eight men to death for a reason like that. You won't kill me for refusing this insane demand."

"No?" she asked tauntingly, fully aware that she possessed all the high cards. "Shall we, then, just see about that?"

Morgan's only offspring decided to give John the opportunity to consider her proposal. While he pondered the state of matrimony, he could stay shackled in irons to a

378

cross beam in the ship's lower hold. The old ship, Morgan's original, leaked seawater at least six inches deep in the hull and John's trousers were soaked from being forced to sit in it. The hold stank with the smell of saltwater and rotting boards, doing nothing whatever to lighten his despondency.

He had convinced himself, during the last two hours of sitting in the semidarkness soaking in brine water, that absolutely nothing would coerce him into wedding anyone, much less that creature upstairs. Wed Morgan's daughter? Hah! Never! I'll not be forced into such a— At that moment, one of the ship's rats decided to taste John's boot heel. The nibble couldn't possibly be felt through the leather, but John shouted a loud "ugh!", jerking his foot away. The repulsive little animal squeaked back furiously, then scurried into the darkness.

"What did ye say, mate?" A question floated down from the stairway.

"There's a rat down here." John's face registered abject disgust. During the course of his twenty-six years, spent almost entirely in the islands and far away from the docks and the seamier establishments, he had hardly ever seen one, much less been close enough to see its beady black eyes glaring at him.

"Aye," said the disembodied voice from the top step. "Only one? Well, ye'll have lots more comp'ny afore long. They comes out bolder at night."

"You'll let me be eaten alive by these creatures?"

"Not me, mate. It's the cap'n what wants ye to stay put till ye agree to her terms or rot, whichever comes to ye first. Meself, I hope ye agree, on account of it's me gets stuck seeing that the worstest chores is done and me stomach can't hardly take the smell no more . . ."

At that moment, the loathsome beast peeked its head out of the darkness again. Assessing his chances, John presumed. "Very well!" he yelled up the stairs. "I'll do it. Let me out!"

379

The second mate, Ned by name, who had been awaiting just such a reply, now came scurrying down the nearly vertical steps much like the little rodent that had taken its refuge again at the sound of bootsteps on the ladder. Ned too had whiskers, but a full face of them and two beady eyes that were periwinkle blue instead of black. There, but for size, for Ned too was a rather small and squat one, the similarity between man and rat ended. "Yer ready to corroperate then, are ye?" The periwinkle blues twinkled merrily. He was probably grinning, but in all that hair, who could tell? John contented himself with a glare up at the second mate. "I needs yer word, lad," the pirate said. "On yer honor, if ye got any."

"I do! I pledge on my honor! Let me out of here."

"Aye, well, it ain't as bad as all that now, is it?" the mate searched a large key ring. " 'Tis only till the cap'n has what's rightfully hers and then ye're free." The second mate leaned down behind John, unfastening the rusty lock with a key that John prayed might still work. "Right then, lad, up ye go." Ned lent him an arm that was surprisingly iron-muscled to help him to his feet.

John stretched his muscles, cramped from the dampness and confinement. He fleetingly toyed with the idea of pouncing on Ned, but just as quickly discarded the notion. He had felt the motion of the ship underway and since they were probably miles from shore by now all he would succeed in doing in a bid for freedom would be to save them the trouble of throwing him overboard.

"Come with me then, mate." Ned seemed not the least concerned about turning his back on the captive and leading the way up the ladder.

The seat of John's pants was soaked as were the insides of his boots that made an audible squishing sound as he followed the mate to the upper deck. Pirates busily engaged in several tasks took time out to snicker and whisper at the Navy lieutenant's passing, as if every last one of them knew of John's plight and found it amusing. Ned took him to a cabin that was slightly smaller than the one John had shared with Lieutenant O'Rourke aboard the *Rochester.* He hadn't quite expected such consideration in return for his cooperation. The room, though tiny, was comfortably furnished in the same provincial plunder as the captain's cabin. The room contained a small table and two chairs, nailed to the floor, and a cot-sized bed against the far wall covered in a velvet spread. A large sea chest had been deposited in the center of the room.

"Cap'n figured ye might want to change yer clothes. There's some in here that might fit ye." Ned pointed at the chest. "We'll come to fetch ye later." The second mate turned briskly about and strode out of the cabin. A moment afterward, a key turned in the lock.

This was absolute insanity that could not be happening to him, John thought as he sat down on the bed, then just as quickly sprang to his feet again, remembering his soaked-pants condition. John Terry had eclectic tastes and a high regard for expensive things, even if they were stolen. He opened the chest and began to rummage through it for something that might fit him. Like the cabins, the chest was a collage of articles of clothing that ranged from a size that might fit Jocko's enormous frame right down to squirrely Ned's, including one rather elegantly tailored suit of Spanish design with a long slash in the sleeve. John pulled that out and frowned, wondering by the bloodstain on the sleeve if its owner might have turned down the captain's proposal and thus been tossed to the fishes, minus his clothing. Finding a pair of trousers that would fit him, as well as a blouse and frockcoat, he spent the remainder of the time before they came for him, trying to dry his boots and shine them back to the high gloss with which they had begun this adventure.

John Terry Junior wasn't quite the fop his father accused him of being, but he did like his clothing neat and his appearance meticulous. His tastes, before being stuck in Royal Navy blue, had run to bright colors, silk shirts, satin waistcoats, not too much lace or ornamentation but stylish. His wavy brown hair was always neatly fastened behind his neck, and he preferred his face clean-shaven. John wasn't quite a peacock, but he did spend more than the usual amount of time taking pains with his presentation. Right now, as he rubbed the black leather boots with a handkerchief he had found in the chest, the brisk polishing was becoming a furious scrub.

How could I let myself be forced into this . . . this farce? Marriage? To a woman he didn't even know? Ridiculous! The toe of the boot already reflected an image of his scowling face, but he kept rubbing the leather angrily.

Word or not, I'll not be coerced into this. Bought like a cabbage in trade for my life? I've taken more care in purchasing a horse than she does in selecting a husband! What would his word mean anyway, when given to a pirate? He would simply refuse and insist she take him to shore — the boot polishing slowed. And she undoubtedly would . . . *if* he happened to be able to swim that far . . .

No one yet had met the second Captain Morgan and returned to tell the tale. The thought gave him an uncomfortable feeling about his assessment of whether or not she truly could kill him. Yet there had to be a way out of this. Where was that agile Terry brain keeping itself now when John needed it?

The key turned in the lock again, and this time it was Jocko who stepped through the doorway. "Put yer boots on, lad. Cap'n wants to see ye."

"What for?" John gazed up at the pirate, yet began to put his boots on. "She has my promise, what else does she want?"

"I expect she'll tell ye what she wants when ye get there." Jocko leaned on the doorframe, waiting.

Slowly an idea began to hatch as he watched the burly

first mate. "Jocko, when the *Rochester* was taken, it looked to me as though you were the one who led the action." He took his time with the boots. Jocko's beefy arms merely crossed over his barrel chest. "I mean, my first impression was that you must be the leader. Naturally, I'd assume it looking at such a big strapping fellow such as yourself. Why shouldn't you be?" John glanced up. The pirate's face only registered impatience.

"I know how difficult it must be for a man like yourself to take second place when leadership could so easily be yours." John gave him a friendly, conspiratorial smile.

Jocko smiled back. "Seems to me that might be mutiny ye're talking, laddy-buck. Best put yer boots on."

John had finished with the boots but still sat on the bed. "I can't help but wonder that you don't, well, rather resent taking orders from a woman. I certainly know I would."

Jocko took a single step forward that brought him right to the edge of John's cot. "Ye'd best get a move on, Bucko. The cap'n don't care for waiting." The pirate reached down, taking John's arm by the elbow. A single upward tug pulled him off the bed and propelled him, eyes wide and head first, across the room, where he hit the wall and bounced off, then staggered to keep his feet.

"Ah, now, I'm truly sorry about that, Mr. Terry. Ye will tell Cap'n Jamie I didn't mean to mess up her intended now, won't ye? It's just, I can't hardly help it. I don't know me own strength once I gets riled. And there ain't nuthin' riles me faster than talk of mutiny." Jocko gripped his elbow again, escorting him through the door. "Ye do understand what I'm saying to ye, don't ye, bucko?"

"Absolutely, Mr. Jocko." John gingerly touched his forehead where an egg-shaped lump seemed to grow beneath his fingers. "You've made yourself quite clear."

Jocko deposited him, rather roughly, in the same chair

across from Captain Morgan where he had sat earlier. John really hadn't needed the downward shove into the chair seat that was a reminder to him to behave himself. The table was set for dinner for two in a gleaming service. The captain was dressed as she had been this afternoon, only the pistols and dagger removed from the red sash. The bandanna was absent, revealing the loose waves of black hair left free to flow down over her shoulders. John gazed across the table at her. Jamie Morgan would be as remarkably beautiful as her reputation in the islands had claimed if not for her manner of dress, and her manner in general.

"How did you get that?" the lovely violet-blue gaze landed squarely on John's bruised forehead. Jocko's presence still loomed like a forbidding shadow behind John's back. "The ship rocked and I lost my footing. I struck my head on a table."

She gave him a scowl that clearly said "clumsy oaf" without having to speak it, then the gaze turned to Jocko. Without a word, the hulking presence departed, closing the door behind him.

"I'm having supper sent in here. I hope you don't get seasick as well."

"I don't." John frowned. Come to think of it, there were a good many things that detracted from Jamie Morgan's assets. "Now, Miss Morgan, surely you aren't serious about this marriage . . ."

"As I told you, it wasn't my idea. It was Morgan's, and he was." As though prepared for his comments, she drew a paper out from beneath her plate and tossed it across the table to him. He scanned through the contents that turned out to be Henry Morgan's last will and testament. Just as she had said, there was a stipulation that provided James Allison Morgan with a small fortune in gold and jewels on the day she presented her legal husband to the lawyer.

John looked up at her. "Is your name really James?"

"Have you read the will?" she sighed in exasperation.

"Yes." He tossed it back across the table. "Is that your real name?" John chuckled, producing a frown from his companion.

"You have a dangerous sense of humor, Mr. Terry."

John's smile faded, but Terry blood was not the kind to stay cowed for long. "What has happened to my shipmates?"

"I left them with supplies to last a month. By then, you should be free to rescue them. If not . . ." She left off with a meaningful shrug.

"Might I ask why it must be me? Surely, you must know someone who would be willing."

"Mr. Terry, I'll make it simple for you. I only want my money. I do not want to spend the rest of my life paying for it. You look like the type who will satisfy Penrose as a husband who fulfills the will's requirements."

"Penrose?" John interrupted. "Oh, yes, the lawyer."

"He must approve or it's no money."

"So you get your money and then what?"

"You go your way and I go mine."

"But we'd still be married."

She shrugged indifference.

"I don't want a wife!"

"And I don't want a husband," she returned smiling. "Obtain a divorce if you like. Lord knows you could find grounds enough if it means so much to you." She laughed, grinding on John's nerves. "Is it a deal then?" She poured wine into two goblets, then handed him one.

"Now wait a minute." John took the goblet and swallowed a mouthful before continuing. "Let me see if I have this correctly. You expect me to legally wed you, present myself to Penrose as your husband, then just walk away and we never see each other again."

"You're a bit slow, Mr. Terry, but you're getting it."

"And if I refuse, you'll kill me," he said more matter-of-factly than he felt at the moment. "Then how do I know you won't anyway? Once you have your funds and have no further need of me, you may decide you prefer widowhood."

"I couldn't kill my own husband," she stated in what looked like genuine shock. "You go to hell for murdering your own kin," she stated.

"Where do you think you go for murdering anybody?" His voice rose to a shout trying to fathom her logic.

"I won't kill you and you have my word on it," she shouted back.

"A lot of good that will do me. The word of a pirate!"

"I don't lie."

"Why? Because that's a sin too?"

Instead of shouting, she glared at him. "Are you going to do it or not?"

"What's in it for me if I do?"

"Your life! Isn't that enough?"

John sat back and chuckled, still irritated but feeling he might have found an upper hand after all. She did need a live husband, and he needed money if he ever wanted to see freedom from the Navy and Governor Terry's thumb on his life. "Oh, no, my dear, you'll have to sweeten the pot a bit more than that. Once I'm out of your mercenary little fingers, what's to keep me silent about our arrangement?"

The glare transformed into a suspicious stare. "What do you mean?"

"I mean, Miss Morgan, that you would still *be* my legal wife. I could claim certain benefits that no court in any land would deny me."

This time her expression was pure shock. "You wouldn't. You wouldn't want to . . ."

"I might not." He grinned in triumph. "If there was some renumeration for my trouble."

"What?"

"Renum . . . money!" he snarled.

386

"I see." She leaned back. "How much?"

"Forty percent should keep me amply rewarded."

"Forty percent!" she shouted.

"Without me you get nothing at all. It's a small price to rid yourself of one no longer required husband."

"I'll give you ten percent."

"Forty."

"Twenty but not a farthing more."

"Forty."

The daggers were back—in spades. "Forty then, but I better never see your face again."

"The feeling is mutual, Miss Morgan."

A sharp rap on the door heralded the entrance of the cook with their supper. The mate glanced from one to the other, feeling the animosity like a tangible force. He finished setting down the platters, then hurriedly went out.

"After you, Miss Morgan." John offered her the serving dish.

She glared at him. "And you call *me* a pirate!"

Chapter Eighteen

A few days later, John was standing on the port deck, leaning over the rail and gazing out at the endless expanse of water. Since his agreement to go along with Captain Morgan's plot to cheat her way into her inheritance, he had been allowed full freedom on the ship. He could come and go as he chose and his meals were brought to his room. No more invitations to dine with the captain had been forthcoming, which suited him fine.

Word given or not, he still wasn't sure he intended to go through with his end of the bargain. He wasn't, at present, interested in marriage to anyone, but the future might hold different prospects. To bind himself, even briefly, to a woman he intended never to see again in his life did not seem to be the wisest course to follow. On the other hand, it was a great deal of money, enough to tide him over in style until his father's anger cooled about resigning from the Navy, and it would — in time.

On the acceptance side of her proposal, there was the very high probability that Mistress Morgan would get herself hung for piracy one of these days. The *Lady Morgan*, though seaworthy, sturdy, and fast, was an old ship. Some gunner with good aim might sink the damn thing with all hands aboard. Prospects looked a bit brighter for going through with the bargain.

Contrary to his belief that Jocko ruled the ship for her, he soon discovered that Captain Morgan ran it fairly well by herself. Jocko was the backup muscle, to be sure, but she was far from hiding behind the first mate's swarthy back. Mistress Morgan might know more about the sea and sailing than Captain Young had known in his twenty-year career. She made out the charts, she gave the orders, and the entire crew of cutthroat pirates hopped to it. He managed to ask Ned Shanks for some of the reasons behind it.

"She's Morgan's kid," the second mate said as if that statement explained it all. On his excursions about the ship he had queried a few others on the same topic and the general opinion seemed to be that most of these men had been with Henry Morgan for years, some owing their lives to him, having been freed from trouble they had gotten into aboard their own ships and due to die for it. A chance attack by Morgan's band had set them free from shipboard life under tyrannical and sometimes sadistic captains given the full sanction of authority from the ships' owners and the maritime laws of the 1680's. Low wages and brutal conditions made sailors eager enough to be plucked right along with the cargoes and treasures that were raided, willing to trade their lives in exchange for the reward of wealth offered. In the buccaneer's life, a cruel captain, or a weak one, or one who displayed poor judgment, soon enough found himself deserted or dead. Ability alone swayed these men to follow a leader and Cap'n Jamie had won their full respect with profitable schemes and ventures. What's more, she was the ship's only pilot, a fact that made her indispensable to a ship that would be unable to function without an able navigator. The few, mostly lowliest sailors, who might harbor an idea of taking over the ship, would have to plow through the entire ship's complement of old-timers to do it—Jocko, Ned, and a few other characters among them.

Beyond that discovery, his short time at sea aboard the *Rochester* had taught him enough to know they were on a southwesterly course, one that would not take them toward Jamaica where Jamie's inheritance was so assiduously guarded.

"Why are we headed southwest?" John stepped over to Jocko, who was standing in the middle of the deck, hands on hips, breathing in and out in huge lungfuls that raised and lowered the barrel chest. "That is, if it is permissible to ask," he added, wanting no more lessons from Jocko administered the hard way.

A few more enormous gulps of air went in and out before the first mate answered. "I reckon there ain't no harm in ye knowing. We're headed home."

"Home?" John questioned. "But I thought the captain wanted to see about her inheritance."

"In time, laddy-buck." Another gulp went in and out before the first mate paused to gaze down at him. "Now ye don't think we're going to sail right into Port Royale, flying the skull and crossbones yet?" Jocko's head fell back with a hearty laugh.

"No, I don't suppose we would."

"We sail for home first. Then ye'll take other passage to Jamaica."

"She doesn't mind my learning where home is?" John inquired.

"I can tell ye where it is, lad. Yer whole Navy knows but don't dare come nigh it. Tortuga Bay. I'm sure ye've heard of it."

"That I have," John stated. The first mate was quite correct in assuming the knowledge would serve John little good. The Navy was only too well aware that, since more land bases had been closed to them, the pirates of the Caribbean had centered their forces on Tortuga, making the island and bay almost impregnable to attack without suffering heavy losses. Even gaining entry held little reward, since, just as they had done before, the buccaneers were still adept at disappearing into the marshes when the odds turned unfavorable. John's only hope for escape would be to bribe another captain, who might or might not prove trustworthy, leaving him possibly worse off than his present situation.

In curiosity, John asked if Morgan's daughter now ruled the colony in her father's place just as she had taken command of his ship.

"Naw," Jocko answered him. "Ain't nobody who actually rules the colony 'cept the Brethren's Council, but there is those who is given wider berth that some. Guess you could say that was Morgan's place while he lived—he was the one ye took care in crossing. With Cap'n Jamie, well, there ain't none quite willing to risk trying to rule her, if ye knows what I mean. But the one to look out for, if I was in yer place, lad, that would be Captain DeCortega. He's the informal ruler of the bay, ye might say, on account of there ain't many who would try to cross him either, not and hope they might live through it."

"DeCortega? A Spaniard?" John questioned.

"Not no more, he ain't. There ain't no pirate what really calls hisself a countryman of the land what gave him birth. Ain't hardly no point to it, once yer own has done given up on ye and declares ye hung if they ever lay eyes on ye again."

John imagined there was some truth in that for all of the pirates. Still, he had no reason to think the unofficial leader of the Tortuga Bay buccaneers would take any particular interest in him, but as the *Lady Morgan* sighted her home port, whispers began passing from ear to ear among the crew that "Cortega" was already here and that he surely wasn't going to like "something." Each time, glances were cast in John's direction that puzzled the lieutenant as he overheard more snatches of conversation

391

that seemed to have him already listed as a dead man when "Cortega" found out about that "something."

While the *Lady Morgan* docked at pierside, John gazed about at the ramshackle port, noticing that the only ship that appeared to be in excellent condition was a three-masted frigate christened the *Isabella.* The hushed conversations flowed continually around him with cautious glances leveled at the streamlined ship they tied up next to. As soon as the gangplank was lowered, Jocko appeared beside him.

"Cap'n says ye're to room at the mansion," he advised him.

"What mansion?"

"Ye'll see soon enough. May as well pack whatever stuff ye've managed to gather. Ye won't be back to the *Lady Morgan.* But I want ye to listen tight, lad, and mind a warning. Here there ain't no laws but who says what and has the means to enforce it. I'm telling ye for yer own good. A Brethren's Council decision that ye oughtn't to have been kill't ain't going to serve ye no good once ye are. Ye best watch yer step around here. And yer mouth!"

"I will bear your warning in mind, Mr. Jocko." John scowled, having no intention of taking care with either. After three years of college in New England and having grown up on Governor Terry's island, John had gained somewhat of a reputation as an able, aggressive fighter when the occasion called for it. Apparently Jocko held a different opinion of him, or perhaps the pirate merely viewed all honest men as weak and sissified.

John went below and gathered the few articles of clothing he called his own, mainly his old uniform which Captain Jamie had had cleaned for him to wear when they made their appearance before Penrose, then Jocko escorted him past the docks, through the ramshackle town toward the middle of the island where the hidden mansion finally came into view.

Nearly obscured by tropical foliage, the house was a rambling affair built out of white stucco. Trees and vines hid the mansion's existence from sight until one was practically inside it.

They stepped into a wide foyer where a staircase of expensively veneered wood led to the upper stories. On their way, Jocko had told him that Morgan had willed the house to the buccaneers and that all the captains shared quarters here while in port.

"This way," Jocko said steering him into a large dining hall. There was a long table with twenty chairs lined around it; only seven of those chairs were occupied. A few of the occupants turned around to see who had entered, then just as quickly turned away in disinterest. John saw the two other women who were part of Jamie's crew, one the young lady who had held a dagger against his neck, the other an attractive creature with short copper-colored hair. Both were attired in men's clothing like the captain of the *Lady Morgan*.

"Come in, Jocko." Jamie Morgan sat in the first chair to the right of the head of the table.

"I brung him like ye said, Cap'n." Jocko started to close the remaining distance to the table.

Jamie did not get the opportunity to reply as the man sitting at the head of the table chuckled lightly, turning all attention on him. He was not quite sitting, more like languishing, in the large armchair. One elbow rested on the chair arm supporting his head and he was engaged in thoroughly looking John over. What would probably be very long legs were spread out somewhere underneath the tabletop.

"Surely you must be joking, my dear," the soft, elegant voice spoke, the dark gaze turning briefly to Jamie. There was a very slight trace of a foreign accent, but the speech was impeccable, as was the man. John could only see a white cotton shirt tucked into black trousers; the neck of the shirt was open to midchest, revealing a heavy scattering of thick black hair. The man's eyes were an intense black in a medium-dark complexion, and the sable-black hair was fastened neatly at the nape of his neck with a plain black bow.

John glared back at him, which only occasioned another chuckle out of the nonchalant pirate. So, this was the Terror of Tortuga Bay, John thought, assessing the man just as he was being thoroughly looked over himself. He didn't seem so much to John, being no monster-sized superman, such as Jocko was, and as Morgan used to be. In fact, he could discover nothing about the man's appearance to account for his being considered the unofficial heir to Morgan's place as the leader of the Caribbean-based pirates.

"Our arrangement is none of your concern, Franco." Jamie scowled at the man for his baiting laughter, then turned her attention to Jocko. "Take the lieutenant upstairs and show him to his room. You do know better, I trust, than to try to escape?" The violet-blue eyes leveled on John.

John's own temper was beginning to surface at being regarded as a prisoner again. "I consider our arrangement to be one of business, Mistress Morgan. Thus, I do not require bonds or locks to hold me to my end of it. And she is correct, sir." John turned his attention on the leader of the colony. "Our arrangement is not your concern."

The black eyes flashed for only a moment, then the look vanished, replaced by amusement. "So, the pup has a tongue, has he?"

This time, John's irritation impelled him to step forward, but Jocko's arm stretching across his chest stopped his forward momentum.

"And spirit as well," Franco said laughing.

"Stop it!" Jamie interrupted, administering a kick to Franco's shin to chide him for his trouble. The pirate leader merely glanced at her before continuing to irritate Terry with his slow, mocking smile.

"Jocko, please escort Mr. Terry upstairs to his room," she said, continuing to watch DeCortega disapprovingly.

"We'll settle this another time," John promised, flashing a blazing gaze at the pirate.

"That will be my pleasure," Franco responded with a self-confident smile.

"Off with ye now, lad," Jocko took a step backward, gesturing John to follow him.

John listened to derisive male laughter as he left the dining hall, the sound of it setting his temper close to exploding.

"Leave him alone, Franco. I mean it!" he heard Jamie say over the laughter, then they were too far up the stairs to make out further conversations.

Jocko waited until they had ascended to the second floor. "Mr. Terry, it ain't no order, but if ye don't mind a word of advice, ye best stay away from DeCortega. He ain't an easy man to cross."

"You've already warned me about that, Mr. Jocko, and I can take care of myself," John returned abruptly.

"Aye," the pirate grumbled. "But I'm just telling ye that Morgan hisself gave Franco wide berth when he was riled on something. Ye watch out for that saber of his, else ye'll find yerself skewered."

"I'm well able to handle a sword myself," John stated. "But tell me, what is his interest in our arrangement?"

Jocko shrugged as they walked toward the end of the hall. "A time back, Cap'n DeCortega wanted to marry her hisself but something happened between 'em. Ever since, she won't hear nothing he has to say on the subject. They run into each other now and again, as the seas hereabouts is getting smaller all the time it seems, and she'll talk with him and all, but not on that particular subject. This scheme of hers is bound not to rest well with him, and since he can't change her mind none, well then, he's likely to take it out on you."

"I see. Well, be assured, Mr. Jocko, I am well able to defend myself."

"I ain't got no doubt of it. I knows ye can fight. I seen ye aboard the *Rochester* and I knows ye're brave enough, but taking on Franco with the swords? That's as well as asking to get yerself kill't. I ain't seen nobody better than him."

"You expect me to surrender to him like a whipped dog?" John asked heatedly, glaring up at the first mate.

"No, I reckon mebbe ye can't do that, but I know that if it was me, I'd turn belly-up right quick."

"Why do you insist on doing this, Jamie?" The pair sat alone in the now empty dining hall. The others had partaken of their suppers and left but Jamie was waiting to keep Lieutenant Terry company when he appeared for his own repast. She didn't dare leave him alone with Franco unless she knew her new fiancé would be safe with the old one.

"I've already told you. It's time I had my money. And I shall have it. What's more, your permission is not required to pursue any plan I choose to follow," Jamie replied evenly. "My life is my own. I can do with it as I please. Once I have what is rightfully mine, I will free myself of Mr. Terry."

"Are you certain that he will so easily vanish out of your life? What's to prevent his returning when he pleases?"

"I accept the lieutenant's word." She glared at him. "He has no reason to return. He'll be anxious enough to never see me again once he's received his portion. I've made certain of that."

"Have you?" Franco leaned back in the oversized chair that had once been Morgan's seat at the table. "Jamie, if it's for the money, I've told you . . ."

"And I've told you, I want nothing from you," she returned hotly. "See to your own affairs and leave me to mine."

"*You* are my affair!"

"Not any longer!" she shouted back.

"You're going to let it go this far all on the mistaken idea that I was unfaithful?"

"It has nothing to do with that," she returned. "I simply want what is rightfully due me. This is no more than a business pact. You may rest easy, if that is your concern, that Lieutenant Terry has no more interest in me than the percentage he asks for. Nor do I have any in him."

"Do you promise me that is the truth?" he asked, watching her intently.

"I do not need to promise you anything, but if you like, yes, I promise it is the truth. Now will you leave me be on the subject? And will you promise to leave the lieutenant be as well?"

"Why should I?" he grumbled.

"Because I ask you to. You owe me that much from the past. And because if anything should befall him, I am the one who will be held accountable. Unless you'd prefer to see me hang," she challenged.

"I promise you, then, that I shall not harm your precious lieutenant," Franco stated sarcastically. "If only because you would be held accountable."

"Thank you," she murmured grudgingly.

"But that promise only holds until you have your funds. The day after, if I see him again, he's mine."

Jamie sighed in exasperation, wishing she could wring the neck of whoever had told Franco about her plans. It seemed he was aware of everything before she even reached the mansion, and had been badgering her about the foolhardiness of her plan since her arrival. They had met several times since that fateful day in Port Royale when she found Polly leaving his cabin and each time the subject eventually came around to his wanting to explain and her refusing to listen. Why hear more lies? To what purpose? She had set the course for her life now and intended to abide by it. Franco had proven himself to be as faithless as Morgan and why set herself up for a lifetime of grief?

Perhaps he was right when he said she refused to trust anyone, but why should she? Everyone she had ever believed in eventually left her disappointed. Morgan had left her penniless and all because he had to have his way with her life. It wasn't fair, she thought, to have adored Franco for all those years in vain, believing in him only to be hurt by him at his earliest opportunity. What had she ever gotten out of trusting anyone but heartbreak?

"I don't like the way he looks at you," Franco muttered into his winecup.

"You are seeing things that are not there," she returned firmly, wanting to end this conversation.

"Just as you saw things that were not there once yourself," he said, casting a sideways glance at her. "If you would but listen, you might realize you were mistaken."

"Would I?" Jamie was tired of hearing it. She leaned forward to smile at him, sure that she was about to snare him into a trap. "Very well then, tell me. I'm listening."

Never before would she sit still long enough to hear his explanation, stalking off with her ears closed to any subject she did not wish to speak about, just as her father used to. Her statement caught him unprepared to answer.

"Well, I'm waiting," she said impatiently, but Franco was already staring behind her to a figure that had appeared in the entry.

"Good evening, Lieutenant Terry." Franco glared at the man who had intruded at the worst possible moment.

"Good evening, Captain . . . Mistress Morgan," John took the seat saved for him at the table just beside Jamie Morgan's chair.

"I'll ring for Louisa to bring in your supper. How was your bath?" Jamie asked pleasantly, ringing the small silver bell to summon Mary's helper.

"Quite comfortable, thank you." John looked past her to the handsome, scowling face of the pirate captain. He still recalled only too clearly the derisive male laughter he had heard that afternoon, and the memory of it made him itch to prove, once and for all, that he was not Jamie Morgan's prisoner. He wondered as well what the pair had been conversing about that came to such an abrupt conclusion when he appeared.

Now he knew where DeCortega's animosity came from and John could easily grant that Jamie Morgan was a most extraordinary woman. He had met the other two women of the *Lady Morgan* crew and both were attractive, albeit as unladylike as Captain Morgan herself, but neither possessed her qualities of capability and independence. Elizabeth, the one with the bouncing copper curls, seemed the least experienced of the trio yet displayed a spirit almost as self assured as Jamie's. Lacey, though she had capably achieved his surrender with the dagger poised at his throat, seemed the most femininely inclined, while still unsure of herself and often seeking guidance from the others as well as their approval. Any one of them presented a challenge a man couldn't help but respond to — and Jamie Morgan owned it to the greatest degree.

Beyond the fact that she was one of the loveliest creatures he had ever seen, she possessed a spirit that dared a man to breach her defenses and win her for his own.

He still held doubts that she would have killed him had he continued to refuse his cooperation, but the very idea that she left him unsure of it gave her a certain distinct, and dangerous, attraction.

No wonder DeCortega wanted her. This was a woman who could not be won by sweet words whispered in the moonlight. As he sat at the table awaiting his supper, he found himself somewhat astounded to discover that over the past few days, and then the last few hours, what had begun as grudging respect for her abilities was quickly growing into fascinated interest.

Even as she grumbled over the division of her inheritance that he had insisted upon, he had seen by the gaze in her eyes that he had won her respect. While undoubtedly stewing over his forty percent, she had treated him, ever since, more as a guest than a prisoner. He was unwilling now to lose that standing just because DeCortega didn't like the competition. Then too, he had never let any man laugh at his expense without calling him out for it.

An uncomfortable silence had ensued around the table as the serving girl entered and set a plate of food in front of him.

"As I understand it, you are to leave for Jamaica at first light tomorrow," Franco began the conversation.

"Yes," Jamie replied, watching him warily. "Captain Stoker is in port and I've arranged passage with him."

"And are you ready, then for your journey, my dear?" Franco inquired solicitously. She glared at him for using the endearment.

"Not quite," she answered.

"Then perhaps you should go up and finish your packing," Franco suggested innocently. "I'll keep your guest entertained for you."

"I've no doubt you would," Jamie replied, peering at him curiously. Franco was leaning back in his chair, his long legs stretched out underneath the table. He looked harmless, but with Franco, one could never be sure.

"Go ahead," he encouraged, smiling. "We'll be fine, won't we, Lieutenant?"

"I'm sure we shall," Terry responded, not in the least intimidated. "Please do finish, Jamie. The hour is growing late and you do need your rest for the morrow." He deliberately used her first name to obtain exactly the response he wanted from DeCortega which was the scowling frown he received for his trouble.

"I suppose I should then." Jamie watched both of them for a moment then, hesitantly, rose to her feet and went out, leaving the dining hall door wide open.

Franco allowed him to finish his meal in uncomfortable silence, and John was determined to ignore the pirate's irritating stare. The most feared man on the bay was not going to have the satisfaction of even slightly disturbing his repast. Just what, pray tell, was so impressive about DeCortega that even the hulking Jocko treated him with deferential respect? He was probably no taller than John's own six feet three inches, no wider, and he couldn't for the life of him see anything in the Spaniard to become upset about. All he had heard since they approached the colony were warnings to stay away from the man and all because DeCortega was suffering from a severe case of jealousy?

John pushed his finished plate away from him and met the Spaniard's hostile stare. DeCortega broke eye contact first, leaning forward to pour wine from a crystal carafe. He filled John's goblet and then his own. "Tell me," the pirate captain began, "surely you cannot intend to see this farce through."

"And why not, sir. We made a bargain and I intend to keep my part of it."

The pirate's smile stayed in place but hardened to malevolence. "Is it for the money?"

"I do not believe our arrangement is any of your concern."

"Jamie Morgan is my concern!"

"I do not think the lady agrees," John returned.

"Answer my question!" the pirate's smile disappeared entirely. "Is it for the money?"

John Terry had never taken well to being ordered about, by anyone. "No," he answered, grinning. "I'm madly in love with her."

"You're lying," DeCortega accused, his eyes narrowing to slits.

"Am I? Then I suggest you wait a week and see if by then I have not changed her mind about the state of matrimony." John nonchalantly drained his goblet, lying through his teeth and enjoying every moment of DeCortega's discomfort, just retribution for the way he had been treated by the captain earlier. "Now, if you will excuse me, I have my own packing to attend to before our departure."

John started to rise to his feet.

"Stay right where you are!" DeCortega's voice did not rise yet seemed to fill the room.

"I should like to remain and chat, but perhaps another time." He turned away but the flash of a saber passing within inches of his head turned him back. The sword cut into the tablecloth with a loud crack on the wood.

"I said stay!"

"Very brave of you, sir, considering that I am unarmed."

"That can easily be remedied." Franco stalked to the sideboard, taking one of a pair of crossed sabers down from its place on the wall. He tossed the weapon, hilt first, toward him and John caught it. Testing the weapon, John slashed through the air with it. It was fine tempered steel with good weight and balance.

DeCortega was already poised en garde, his free hand

tucked into the back of his belt, the saber pointed between John's eyes.

John lunged first, testing his foe's skill. Franco retreated, blocking John's thrust, then swung in an arc that John barely had time to deflect. The man was good, damned good — an excellent fencer. The clashing sabers echoed down the hallways of the mansion as the two opponents parried and blocked each other. John had won many of his matches whether in practice or in the few earnest duels he had engaged in, but he found it increasingly difficult to keep ahead of the aggressive Spaniard's attacks. He was hardly being allowed the opportunity to engage in any offensive maneuvers since he was busy enough fending off the quick thrusts and lightning lunges. He heard footsteps coming toward them from several directions, then Jamie's voice shouting for them to stop and he gladly would have but dared not lower his guard. Finally, Franco caught John's weapon with the tip of his saber, moving in and twisting his blade around John's in an envelopement, then he jerked the weapon out of his hand. John leaped backward, landing in a sprawl over the table top with Franco's saber immediately across his neck.

"I gave her my word, so I will not kill you, yet," Franco whispered into his face, now burning with embarrassment at being disarmed like a mere beginner. There was no greater shame for a fencer than losing his weapon, unless it was to also be knocked backward onto his rump. "However, I strongly suggest you discover a means of escape before you reach Jamaica," Franco finished before he removed the saber and let him up.

"Just what the devil did you think you were doing?" Jamie began berating the pirate leader in a fury. "I leave you for not even five minutes and look what I find! So much for your promises! That is the last time I shall take your word for anything!"

403

"You don't understand, my love," Franco answered nonchalantly. The man was not even perspiring in spite of the room's suddenly oppressive heat as John lifted himself up from the tabletop, brushing bread crumbs from the seat of his pants. "The lieutenant and I were only playing about. You didn't think that was in earnest, did you?" The pirate laughed. "He asked me to show him how I had disarmed an opponent in the past and I did. Isn't that right, Lieutenant?" DeCortega turned to him for confirmation.

What else could John say unless he wanted to admit he had been bested in a most embarrassing manner. "Yes, that's right." He tried to straighten his mussed appearance, running his hand through his displaced brown hair. "I asked him to show me how it was done. The captain merely obliged my curiosity."

Something in Jamie Morgan's gaze clearly questioned the believability of both their statements as she looked from one to the other. "You're both all right then?" she queried.

"I'm happy to hear you concerned over my welfare," DeCortega replied with a smile, but Jamie only "harumphed" and turned to John.

"You aren't injured, Lieutenant?"

"No, not at all," he assured her. " 'Twas as the captain said. Only a game."

"I should appreciate both of you taking any further 'games' out of doors before you wreck the furniture," she chastised them both. "Lieutenant, we do have to get an early start on the morrow."

"Quite right." John still felt uncomfortably heated, especially his cheeks that were burning, leaving him to wish for once that he had grown a beard that would have hidden the flush on his face. Not only Jamie had witnessed his disgrace but the two other women who sailed with her as well as several of the servants. "I shall be up directly." He wiped the perspiration from his forehead with his napkin.

"Well, good night then" Jamie grumbled before stalking out of the room, turning once more to look at both of them over her shoulder.

Franco had sheathed his sword and was leaning against the fireplace mantel as if nothing of importance had occurred a few minutes before. "Remember my advice, Mr. Terry," Franco called to him as John started from the room. "The next time we meet, I may not have a vow to keep."

"What do you intend to do with Lieutenant Terry once you have your money?" Lacey was stretched across Jamie's bed amid the silks, satins, and laces of several discarded gowns and petticoats, watching Jamie pack the small chest she intended to take with her tomorrow.

"Why, I've told you before, Lacey. I'll send him on his way. Unfortunately, with forty percent of my inheritance," she grumbled, selecting a silvery blue satin gown and folding it neatly into the chest.

"Then you really don't have any interest in him?"

"Interest? How do you mean?" Jamie glanced up curiously. Lacey paused for so long Jamie began to doubt she would answer and looked up again.

"I mean, romantic interest," Lacey murmured a bit shyly, making Jamie smile.

"Oh, dear." Jamie stood up and came toward her. "Don't tell me that you are smitten."

"Well," Lacey shrugged indifference. "He is rather handsome, isn't he?"

"I suppose, if you don't mind a snobbish bore," Jamie returned.

"Do you really think him snobbish?"

"You should have heard him in my cabin. The man

fancies himself a rare prize, I can tell you that much about him."

"Still," Lacey said dreamily. "I like him. I've talked with him once or twice and he seems rather nice to me. Perhaps if you knew him better . . ."

"No thank you, Mistress Bell," Jamie replied. "I have one purpose and one purpose alone intended for Lieutenant Terry and after that he can go to blazes along with the rest of the male gender."

"Then would you mind terribly if I went along to Jamaica?"

"Of course not." Jamie resumed packing. "Besides, who else would I ask to be my maid of honor, even if the wedding itself is a farce."

Lacey sat bolt upright, her eyes wide and excited. "Truly, Jamie?"

"Naturally," Jamie smiled indulgently. "I'd let you be the bride if I thought Penrose might fall for it. Believe me, once the lieutenant has served his purpose, he's all yours as far as I am concerned."

"No matter how you act toward him, you're still in love with the captain, aren't you?"

"I am not in love with anyone, Lacey." Jamie concentrated on folding another gown she had selected to take along.

"I know you too well to believe that," Lacey stated. Lacey had been surprised to discover that Jamie's Captain DeCortega was the same man who had saved her those many months before. She had known him instantly, but he didn't recognize her, even after the several times they ran across each other.

"Jamie, I've kept something to myself because you've never liked talking about Franco, but now I feel I must say it. Remember my telling you about the man who came along to rescue me from that awful fellow who wanted to paw me to search for jewels?"

"I remember." Jamie continued packing.

"It was Captain DeCortega."

"How nice," Jamie commented, working steadily at her task.

"Aren't you at all curious to hear the details again?"

"I heard them once already. Lacey, I know very well whose side you're on in this, just as I know Jocko is the one who spies on me for Franco. Even Mary now takes up his cause. I'm sure you think it's in my best interest to convince me he performed some bit of chivalry on your behalf . . ."

"But he was the one!" Lacey insisted. "I swear it! I swear it on our friendship which is dearer to me than anything else. It was him!"

"Well, what if it was." Jamie returned to her packing. "It has nothing to do with what he did to me."

"But it does," Lacey sat down on the bed, looking up at Jamie. "You didn't allow me to finish."

Jamie gazed heavenward with a weary sigh. "Then tell me whatever you feel you must, but I promise you it will make no difference." She moved the chest over to sit down next to Lacey.

"What I want to say is that I believe him."

"I believe him because of the way he acted toward me."

"Because he chastised a seaman for trying to molest you?"

"No, because he didn't try it himself!"

Jamie got up to walk across the bedroom.

"You said you'd hear me out," the younger woman chastised. "Well, don't you think it odd?"

"How could I? I said the man was a faithless cad, not a beastly fiend."

"You're missing my meaning. Jamie, if, as you say, he's a faithless cad, then why didn't he try with me? Surely if he is as you say he is and chases anything in a skirt, he wouldn't have let such an opportunity slip past him. I'm not claiming I'm irresistible, but I consider myself at least as attractive as Polly. The plain fact is that he paid so little attention to me, he didn't even recognize me when he saw me again. He still doesn't know it was me he rescued. Perhaps I am being vain about my looks, and you can think me a braggart if you want, but I know I can turn a man's head and I didn't turn his. I prefer to think that only happens when a man is blind with love for someone else."

"Lacey, you're impossible." Jamie laughed.

"But don't you see the inconsistency? If he is such a skirt chaser, why did he leave me alone? Why does he still? Why does he hardly take notice of Elizabeth? I tell you, it makes no sense to me that he would take Polly to his bed, at that time, and in that place, when it was so likely you'd discover them together, and yet not pay the slightest heed to a young woman who would easily have been swept off her feet after what he had done for her. And he didn't know I knew you. Why would he have thought he could ever have been found out? That's why when he says your father set it up for you to see, I believe him. Even if he was a womanizer, the captain is no fool."

"Is it possible I've been wrong?" Jamie posed aloud, walking to the window and looking down at the greenery below. "But you didn't hear what I heard about him and from his own sister. You never met Elena Vega."

"That was before he ever met you," Lacey countered. "Are you so utterly blameless or will you tell me you and Tsar Peter never shared a kiss in all those months?"

Jamie's face flushed to crimson, remembering. Was she, she wondered, judging him guilty on the strength of what had passed before and what could indeed have been set up for her benefit? She had been so bereft at the time, she might have jumped to any conclusion just because her mind was thinking so unclearly during those dark days and nights. Morgan had died at the worst possible moment, while they were both angry with each other. Now they never would make up their differences. The weight of regret she carried had been a heavy burden to bear and she waited anxiously for Franco to be with her. Is that what made her so unreasonably angry? Had she been blinded by her hurt into seeing only what, in truth, she wanted to see? How much easier it had been these past several weeks believing the worst of him. She didn't have to worry and wonder if she might lose him. She had made it an accomplished fact all on her own.

Ever since they met she had harbored a secret fear locked inside her that, she was not quite good enough to win Franco's love. There was something wrong with her that had made her mother hysterical just to look at her. Whatever the awful fault was, it was so horrid that her mother had put a pistol to her breast to escape it. So she had thought when she was four. She had believed she packed those fears away when Bertrand told her that her mother was entirely self devoted and slightly mad, but apparently the locks weren't as tight as they should be, for she still feared that whatever it was remained missing. The real truth was, she was still afraid.

"I'm still awaiting the answer you promised me." Jamie stood in the open doorway, leaning against the frame, her arms folded defensively across her chest.

"I didn't think you were still of a mind to hear it," Franco said, continuing to remove his shirt then draping it over a chair.

"I asked you for it, didn't I? Let's hear it then."

"Close the door and come in," Franco said harshly. "I

won't have the entire household listening."

Jamie did as he said, choosing the rocker near the window. "Well?" she prodded.

"What's the use when you'll never believe me? I can see by your stance that you've already made up your mind and any feeble effort I might give has already been disbelieved before I've even started."

"I suppose you're right," Jamie stood up, starting to stride toward the door. "I wouldn't believe you, whatever you said." She reached for the doorhandle just as Franco reached for her, grabbing her by the wrist and spinning her around to face him. "Damn it, woman! Are you going to let Morgan win after all? After all we've been through together? Is he to win by way of a foul joke he's played on us both to have his way?" Before she could struggle free of him, he pulled her into his arms, locking her tightly into his embrace. "You loved me once. I'll prove to you that you still do." His mouth came down on hers savagely, kissing her hard. Taking her with him, he turned and dropped across the bed, forcing her down onto the soft mattress, keeping her trapped there with his body over hers. "I'll never let you marry another man while I have a breath of life in me," he swore, trailing kisses down the length of her throat, stretching back the material of her blouse to cover her shoulder with his hot, demanding mouth.

"Franco, let me go," she pushed against him.

"Not until you realize we belong together. We're of a kind, you and I, as you could never be with that dandy you've chosen." He kissed her neck again, this time, softer, gentler, taking both her hands in his and lightly forcing them down against the sheets, entwining his fingers with hers. He kissed her mouth again with deeply lingering passion, until Jamie arched herself against him with a small moan.

In spite of it all, she couldn't deny to herself that she

still loved him desperately. No man's arms could hold her as his did, caress her as he did, fill her with longing desire as he could. Perhaps just for this one last time, she could give herself over to his lovemaking once more. She hadn't changed her mind about wedding John Terry to gain her inheritance. She had to. There was no choice in the matter. She saw marriage and lifelong commitment with Franco as impossible now. Without trust, how could love possibly survive and grow? But perhaps, just this once more, she could experience the sheer wonder of the pleasures they had shared with each other in the past.

Franco found the opening of her blouse and reached inside, caressing the soft flesh tenderly. Jamie briefly gripped his arm until he looked at her. "I want you to know nothing has changed. I still intend to wed Terry for my fortune."

"How can you say that?" His gaze darkened.

"I need the money," she replied, stroking the back of his neck. "That's all it is. That's all it can ever be. I want you to know that too. There can never be anything more between us than that. He needs the money and so do I and that's all we will ever share between us."

"Then why go through with it!" he seethed. "I can get you your money. I'll give it to you. All that you'll ever need . . ."

"I told you I won't take it from you."

"I won't let you do this."

"You can't stop me," she returned in the same even voice she had been using all along, a tone soft yet set with determination. "But for now, finish what you started." She began to pull his face closer to her own, meeting his lips, kissing. "Make love to me, Franco. Let me know again how it feels to be in your arms."

"You never need know what it is like without them," he promised as his lips traveled over her neck to the base of her throat.

411

At this moment, everything in the past was forgotten and forgiven. She wanted only to build a memory that would last her a long, long time. His body molded against her until she could feel the throbbing center of his manhood against her thigh. "I won't let you leave me," he promised, his voice growing husky with desire.

He started to unfasten the ties of her blouse and Jamie gently pushed his hand away, smiling a secret smile as she began to remove her clothing. At last revealed to his appreciative gaze, she turned toward him, stopping him from rising with a hand against his chest. "This time, 'tis my turn to be the seductress."

Franco's gaze questioned her and she leaned toward him, then kissed him, urging him to lie back, raising her leg and swinging it over him. Sitting astride him while their passion-filled kiss lasted, she moved her hips against him until he moaned with desire. She lowered her head to his chest, kissing and nibbling his bronzed skin.

"Jamie, *madre de Dios!*" he murmured, his eyes closing as he reveled in the ecstasy she was providing. "You've taught me well," she said as she teased him with her lips.

"And you've the inborn talents of a siren," he said, enjoying the sensations. Building her memory of this night with carefully chosen bricks, she let her imagination fly, touching, caressing, using the knowledge he himself had provided of what gave the human body the greatest pleasures, titillating until his body was as tight as a bowstring. At his urging, she moved away only long enough to allow him to remove his boots and trousers then came willingly into his outstretched arms to take her place again. Tensed and ready, she eased herself down on top of his throbbing shaft, trembling as he filled her, passion overwhelming her as she started to move on top of him, letting nature provide the rhythm. Forgotten was her desire to leave him with a lasting impression in pursuit of fulfilling only her own desires now, satiating her passion selfishly, hungrily, devouring him with her urgency. His lean hips thrust against her until, as one, the earth seemed to shatter and swallow them whole. Crying out with the culmination of her need, Jamie at last sank back against him in exhaustion, drained to an emotional edge that was held together like cracked glass that would shatter at the slightest touch. For several minutes, they lay quiescent, while Franco gently stroked her hair.

"My God, woman, is there no end to the surprises you can present?" he murmured.

Jamie answered only by pressing her lips to the hollow of his throat, her mind unchanged even by this that they had shared together.

"Have I changed your mind now?" he asked, pausing in his strokes against the soft waves of her hair.

"No," she replied, not daring to look up at him. She felt his arm tense for a long moment before it began stroking her again.

Jamie had looked for him everywhere but there was not a trace of John Terry to be found. She burst into the dining hall, finding Franco at his breakfast with two other ships' captains. "Where is he?" she demanded, standing in front of Franco, knowing full well he had the answer to the mystery.

His eyes slowly raised to hers, only innocence and mild bafflement displayed on his face. "Where is who?" he asked.

"You know damn well who!" she shouted in a fury. "Where is John Terry?"

"Whatever makes you think I would know where the lad has gotten himself to?"

"It seems a tad strange to me that you are here while the *Isabella* has gone to sea! And don't deny it. I saw her leaving from my bedchamber window."

"I wouldn't think of such a thing. Of course she's at sea. Garcia is perfectly capable of taking her out without me," he replied.

"While you sit here? Why would he?"

"I didn't feel like sailing. 'Tis only a short run to Royale and back."

"To do what with Lieutenant Terry?" she asked, her hands on her hips.

"Ah, yes, I do recall the lad saying something about wanting to leave the island. Pressing appointments at home, I believe. He must have asked Garcia for passage."

Every word he uttered was a lie and he didn't bother to conceal it. She knew Terry would not have left of his own accord. He needed that money to see freedom from his father's wishes as badly as she needed it for her own purposes. "You've kidnapped him!" she accused angrily.

He gave her a taunting smile. "Whyever would I do that to the poor boy? I did promise you, sweetheart, that I would not harm a hair on the lad's head."

"I seem to recall other promises you made me that had little meaning for the likes of you!"

For a moment, his face flickered as if she had touched a raw wound. "I have never broken my word to you, whether you believe me or not. I have not done so now. Your precious Terry is unharmed."

"But he is aboard the *Isabella*, isn't he? You forced him aboard her."

"It was hardly necessary to force him," Franco grinned broadly. "The lad was not in any condition to protest." He laughed, the two other captains chuckling with him. "There is nothing for you to concern yourself over, my sweet. Just a few drops of a concoction Garcia brews up that does no harm."

"Damn it!" she seethed, shaking with anger. The cackling snickers of the other men combined with Franco's

414

attitude fueled her rage beyond containment. "I should run you through for this!" she said tightly, glaring at the trio. "In fact, I think I will!" Before he could react to stop her, Jamie reached for Franco's saber and snatched it out of the scabbard. Instantly, he was on his feet, held at bay by his own sword. His mirth utterly fled, as did that of his companions who sat stock still, staring at her, gape mouthed, wondering what she might do next.

"Jamie, put it down."

"Not until it has tasted your blood, I think, Captain DeCortega."

"It is not a toy," he warned. His stern tone only made her angrier.

"Nor do I intend to play with it," she retorted, staying well out of his reach. Her only intention was to watch the smirks and jeers fade off the faces of all three of her tormentors and she had succeeded very well in that. "I should run you through for your interference. And the other two of you as well, just on general principles." She swung the point of the weapon toward them.

"Jamie, you won't use it. Now return it to me," he said, speaking as he would to a naughty child.

"Would you care to stake your life on whether I will or not, Captain?" She turned the sword tip toward him, determined to evoke some small glimmer of fear out of him before she put the weapon down but the other two captains decided to take the opportunity to rise from their chairs, apparently of a single mind to rush her.

She swung the saber in a horizontal arc above their heads forcing them both to duck and scatter the contents of the table. "Don't test me!" she warned. "Out! Out of here! Both of you, lest I try this steel on you instead!" With a few wild flourishes of the blade she sent the pair diving for the exit, scampering through the kitchen door-way as if a madman was on their heels.

"Now, you!" She turned the point toward Franco who

had not had a chance to rush in and disarm her. "You have tampered enough with my plans. I'll have no more of it. And you'll not make a fool of me in front of your friends again." Her arm trembled with rage, her nerves feeling close to shattered.

"Jamie, give me the sword," Franco took a step toward her.

"I shall give you exactly what you deserve." She jabbed with the weapon, knowing full well how fast his reflexes were, expecting him to step back out of reach of the saber's sharp point, but he didn't move back. Instead the weapon's tip disappeared into the folds of his white blouse sleeve. Immediately, a stain of red appeared. Startled, he gripped his bicep as if to stifle the small trickle of blood, his gaze staring at her in clear disbelief mixed with slowly rising anger.

"Ohh!" Jamie murmured under her breath, appalled by what she had done. Never for a moment had she expected to make good on her threat. She watched him, thinking only that she could easily have killed him if common sense hadn't, at the very last second, made her strike at his upper arm instead of his chest.

She wanted to say that she hadn't meant it, but her lips wouldn't form the words. She tried to read his look and failed. Her feet felt rooted, waiting for a response. For a long moment, he only stared at her. Finally, his gaze never wavering from her eyes, he spoke. "You missed, my lady. My heart is here," he pointed at his chest. "Do it, then, and be done with it."

Only then did she notice that the saber was still held up between them, pointing at him threateningly. She lowered the point away from him. "I didn't mean . . . I thought . . ." she stammered, trying dozens of ways to explain that she hadn't meant to do what she had done, but all of them seemed so feeble.

"I warned you to leave me alone!" The words finally

burst out of her unbidden. She hurled the saber to the floor where it clattered as it rolled across the polished wood, then she turned and fled, running out of the room with hot tears stinging her eyes, her palm held up to her sobbing lips.

"Jamie, is it true? You stabbed Captain DeCortega with his very own saber?" Elizabeth's green eyes were wide and incredulous.

Wasn't there anything that could happen on this cursed island that everyone soon didn't know about? The island, though it possessed a population of several hundred, was a small community and stories carried far and fast. Evening had settled over Tortuga Bay and already the tale had probably circled the island before Elizabeth heard of it.

"Yes, it's true." Jamie grumbled her answer but refused to explain that she had not meant to draw blood only to threaten him. Let them think what they like.

She had not seen Franco since she left him in the dining hall this morning. Morgan had once sliced his swordarm and now she had added her own wound to the very same arm, but he had made her outraged and furious over John Terry's disappearance, his actions smacking of Morgan's schemes and ruses to have his way. Fine then, he had managed to spoil her arrangement with Terry, but she hadn't given up yet. Any softening of the heart she had begun to feel for him had just been cured by his actions.

"Stow your gowns again and find Lacey. We're away as soon as I get the crew assembled," Jamie told her.

"Away? Away where?"

"To sea, of course, or need I remind you that without Lieutenant Terry, we're in the same predicament as before?"

"But I . . . But Lacey . . ."

"But what?" Jamie's temper was in no mood for a game of charades. "What is it? Where is Lacey anyway?"

Elizabeth hung her head, sheepish.

"Liz, where's Lacey?"

"With the lieutenant," Elizabeth finally provided. "She asked Captain DeCortega if she might go along to be there when he woke up. She fancies herself in love with him, I guess."

"Oh fine!" Jamie stalked off down the hallway with a furious stride. "Just fine! Let her fancy herself in love! We'll do it without her! Are you coming along or not?"

"Aye," Elizabeth trotted to catch up to Jamie. "I'm coming."

Chapter Nineteen

"The key word, my boy, is repentant," Governor Stallings said from behind the massive mahogany desk that Henry Morgan had purchased with government funds for the Port Royale mansion. "I fully understand what the young lady has been put through, but hardship cannot explain everything. And while I've agreed that a chance for pirates to redeem themselves is preferable to the time and expense of hunting them down, the prisoners we are presently discussing have made it quite clear that they do not seek mercy from the court."

"Sir, how will it look to posterity if we let the men go and hang only the women?" John argued.

"But it is 'only the women,' who will not offer to cooperate." Stallings reminded him.

John looked to Robert Maynard, seated beside him, for any suggestions his friend might provide. Maynard was a lawyer as well as a Navy officer, and John had known him for years. He had asked Robert to come over to Royale from Bermuda to help him present his case before Stallings. It was Robert's idea to reopen the general pardons granted just before Morgan took office and continued thereafter only at the discretion of the governor. He had argued that it would be far less expensive and reap greater rewards than the course the government had been pursuing of late. Now that England was going to war over the Spanish Succession, her Navy was needed elsewhere. John's relationship to Governor Terry had gained them admittance to Governor Stallings, and Maynard had presented the case which Stallings agreed to during the course of their last meeting. A proclamation was issued and the first released under the reopened amnesty were those presently being held in the jails, including all the male members of the *Lady Morgan* crew. Their reprieves gave assurances to those still roaming that they would be granted amnesty if they turned themselves in. Within a few days buccaneers started to appear on Royale to sign their names to documents swearing them to an oath that they would never again take up their old professions. But the pardons were only granted to those who at least offered a sham of repentance. The two women, the only prisoners left in the prison with the exception of a few pickpockets and drunks, refused to sign the agreement, saying that in all honesty they knew of no other professions they could turn to.

"I don't think you are aware, Lieutenant, of the severity of the charges pending against these . . . ladies. You forget, I knew Jamie Morgan when I served under her father as Lieutenant Governor and never would I have believed that young woman capable of crimes like these, but there they are. Read them for yourself. Attempted murder. We have the eyewitness testimony of the men who saw her fire down into the hold at her own crewmen."

'Sir, she didn't hit anyone," John inserted.

"Perhaps she's a poor shot," Stallings returned. "In any case, she did it, inciting them to fight after the crew had entered the hold of their ship to make clear their own intentions of surrendering. Her very words condemn her. Read them."

"I know them. "Stand up here and fight, you spineless cowards, or I'll shoot you myself." John repeated the statement he had read over and over again in the written reports made out by the witnesses aboard the patrol vessel that caught the *Lady Morgan* at sea and blocked the ship from any hope of escape.

"Inciting to mayhem," Stallings said. "Disorderly conduct,

420

at the very least. And that isn't mentioning the piracy charges. Theft, kidnapping, willful destruction of His Majesty's property in the form of sinking the *Rochester,* stranding the crew of that vessel . . ."

"I understand that, sir."

"I've only begun." Stallings looked up from reading the charges.

"What if I offered my personal assurances that the two women in question would never return to piracy?" John posed.

Stallings sat back in his comfortably upholstered seat. "I do not see how you can possibly guarantee their behavior, Lieutenant. The moment they were set free, they would be out of your hands entirely."

"But my own wife was one of them until recently."

Governor Stallings stared at John in appalled silence.

"We were wed only a few days after I returned, but, before that, she was in their company and I can't help but think that she could easily be with them in their predicament at this very moment. The women are her friends."

"What did your father say to this?" Stallings interjected.

"He's delighted, sir, since he thinks she'll make me face up to responsibility, and he may be right. He knows about her past, sir, and he's willing to overlook it."

"Well, that's fine for you, Lieutenant, and for your new wife, but as for her friends . . ."

"What if they were to wed as well, sir? Wouldn't their husbands then be responsible for their future conduct?"

"Well, I suppose if decent, law-abiding husbands could be found . . ." Stallings really didn't want the hanging of women on his record. It was such an unpleasant business. Bad enough to execute a man for his crimes, but women? Unthinkable. He could cite instances of it being done, but in every case it was most regrettable to have to take such a course of action. Women were the gentler breed and had to be protected from the baser facts of life. If one began executing them like men, and demanding punishment like a man's, one might be forced to begin acknowledging their rights as full citizens in every corner, with the responsibilities and privileges thereof.

"Do you, then, have any likely candidates to take responsibility for these women?"

"Lieutenant Maynard is in need of a wife." John ignored the stare Robert Maynard gave him. "Perhaps he might speak for one. Didn't you tell me, Bob, you envied me having a beautiful wife to come home to?"

"Y . . . yes," Robert stammered. "A wife, not a bloody pirate!"

"The other two are no bloodier than Lacey, and you thought her charming." Maynard was gaping, but remained silent.

"That still leaves one of the young ladies unaccounted for," Stallings stated.

"She is engaged to be wed already, sir. In fact, her fiancé only recently arrived here to claim her. He will agree to vouch for her future behavior."

"I presume the gentleman is not of the same profession . . ."

"The gentleman, sir, is Conde Francisco DeCortega. He is Spanish, but intends to make Royale his permanent home."

Stallings lowered his brows into a concerned frown. "I once met the gentleman and, as I recall, his own reputation is somewhat tarnished."

"It was, Your Excellency, but I believe you will find that he has been cleared of all charges that were pending against him in his homeland and is thus reinstated to all rights and privileges due his esteemed rank. His title has been restored and he has every reason to keep his reputation in good order. And, sir, since he chooses Jamiaca as his home now, perhaps it would be in our best interests to see that he is assured of welcome in our colonies. The DeCortegas are quite wealthy, I hear." John could well imagine what it had cost DeCortega to seek him out on Bermuda to enlist his aid. He had learned of their arrest almost immediately and set out at once to find John Terry and beg him, if necessary, to do what he could for them. The man must have felt desperate to go so far for her sake. It was a strange sort of stiff apology DeCortega had offered him for drugging John's drink, then spiriting him away in the dead of night, but, as John had found Lacey out of it, perhaps all had worked out for the best. As he had told Stallings, the senior Terry couldn't be happier at having a daughter-in-law to keep his son in line. To John Senior's mind, this was better than a Royal Navy commission by far, and he wondered why he'd never thought of it himself. There would be no more gambling and wenching and lying about in the sun with a wife to support, but the decision had not taken John long to reach that he wouldn't find a better woman than the one he had married and she was worth every bit of the freedoms he had surrendered.

John could see Stallings adding up figures on the tax rolls from what he had hinted about the DeCortega fortune, as well as considering what else might fall his way out of developing a personal friendship with a rich and influential displaced Spaniard. With the war coming, the DeCortegas couldn't easily pull up roots again.

"Very well," Stallings said after a brief consideration, tapping the feather end of his quill pen on the desk blotter. "If these gentlemen will be responsible for them, I will sign the clemency papers, but I expect your co-signatures as my assurance of their intentions. Your own as well, Lieutenant Terry, since you've offered."

"You shall have it, sir." John gazed directly at the governor, ignoring the frantically trapped look that had appeared on Maynard's face.

"John, your father really should reconsider your future." Stallings stood up to indicate that the interview was ended. "The Royal Navy is not the place for you. You should study law like your friend here."

423

"I am considering it, sir." John smiled pleasantly.

"Good day to you then, gentlemen." Stallings offered a handshake to both. "And my deepest congratulations on your marriages."

"Thank you, sir."

Escorted to the door by the butler, Maynard waited until they were outdoors before exploding. "Have you taken leave of your senses bringing me into this? I don't want to marry!"

"Calm yourself, Robert. You haven't even met the lady yet."

"And I don't wish to," Maynard stormed from beside him.

"You may change your mind when you see her at her best. Haven't you always told me you like auburn hair?"

"She has it?" Maynard looked at him dubiously.

"Russet. Like the leaves on the trees when they turn in autumn. And eyes as green as emeralds. Fair, alabaster skin as soft as a downy pillow . . ." John continued the enchanting list of Elizabeth Ferris's assets as they returned to the inn where they were to meet DeCortega to tell him of the failure or the success of their venture.

"Silence back there! Do you hear me? Quiet, I say!" The jailer rapped on the wooden cell door with the heavy nightstick he carried, but the giggling and laughing continued unabated. "This is a jailhouse, not a soiree . . ." he yelled, but they couldn't hear him. "Lord, give me men to guard from now on," he muttered under his breath, giving it up as hopeless.

"Pardon me, sir."

Two young men in Royal Navy uniforms stood before him. "Well, what do you want? Speak up or I'll never hear you over that ruckus!" He jerked his thumb toward the cells in the west wing. Giggling female laughter drifted out of the back, echoing down the stone walkway.

"We've come to see the prisoners. Here is our permission,

424

signed by Governor Stallings," John said, presenting the paper that allowed them access. The jailer barely glanced at it before taking his keys and opening the door to the cellblock. "Maybe you can shut them up," he muttered, leading them down the rows of empty cells to the last one in the line. "Lord knows, I've tried, but they don't give me a minute's peace. Have no decent respect, those two. Can't do nothing with the likes of them. If that's what you gentlemen is here to try, your time is wasted." He stopped before the barred cell, opening the cell door for the officers. "Shut up for a minute," he shouted over to the giggling trio of women. "You have more visitors."

The women were sitting on the straw-strewn floor in a circle and looked up at their entrance. Lacey gave her new husband a delighted smile of welcome. "Thanks for getting me permission to come, John. We've had ever so much fun catching up."

"You sound like it. We could hear you all the way up the corridor," he commented, smiling himself at the sight of them enjoying themselves in spite of the dismal surroundings.

"We're recounting old times we had aboard the *Lady*." Lacey beckoned to him. "Come join us."

"Call out when you're ready to go," the jailer said, then, with a final glare at the trio of women, he left them alone.

"We were just remembering when Teddy first joined us," Lacey explained, taking her place in the circle on the floor again as Terry and Maynard took seats on the prisoners' cots.

"Who is Teddy?" Maynard gazed at John.

"That's me," the one with bright auburn curls piped up from her place in the circle.

"Robert Maynard, I would like to present Mistress Elizabeth Ferris, previously of Dover, I believe?" He smiled at Maynard, who was obviously taken with the young woman's beauty.

"Good day to you, sir." Elizabeth nodded politely, remembering the proper training of youth in spite of the seaman's garb she was wearing.

"Good day, mistress," Maynard seemed thunderstruck and almost tongue-tied for the first time in his life, staring at her, his usually light banter stunned into silence.

"I believe I may have found a way out for you," he addressed Jamie.

"And what's that?" Jamie giggled. "By our promise to behave like good girls from now on?"

"Jamie, you must take this matter seriously," John chided her. "Believe me, the Royal Navy is entirely serious. They *will* hang you."

"Then shall I spend the rest of my life taking in washing for my living? Shall I ask Jocko for employment as a tavern wench? Tell me another option that is open to me!"

"There is another option," John offered. "Marriage!"

Jamie's face darkened dangerously. "Say that once more and I will throw something at you!"

"You were willing to wed for your money . . ."

"Yes, to someone who had no interest in staying about afterward. And that is the only kind of marriage I'll have."

"What about Captain DeCortega?" John posed warily, knowing full well how she felt about that. Lacey had told him.

"Now I *will* throw something at you!" she grumbled, but made no move to follow through on her threat.

"Listen to me for a moment. All that is required in this instance for you to win your freedom immediately is the promise to marry. If Franco gives his signature to the document, you are free."

"And what makes you think he would do such a thing?"

"He has already agreed."

Jamie stared at him, her lovely mouth slightly open but silent for several long seconds before she murmured. "He's here?"

"Of course he is," John replied. "How do you think I came to learn of your plight? He came to seek my help when he heard of your arrest, to see if my contacts might help arrange for your pardon. He agreed to the terms immediately."

"Very kind of him, I'm sure," Jamie grumbled.

"Jamie," Lacey urged. "You don't have any choice. Speak to him first, before you condemn him."

"Who is to promise for Liz?" She looked up at John, the thought striking her suddenly.

John was about to reply, hoping Maynard would go along with it, but Robert stood up and stepped forward. "It's me," he stated. "I'm the one." He gazed at Elizabeth. "I'll sign the paper for you, if you'll allow it."

Elizabeth smiled, pondering deeply and not finding Maynard too wanting. "It's very kind of you, sir."

"I know 'tis only on a promise to marry but, perhaps, in time, it might be considered in earnest?" Maynard asked.

"I am deeply in your debt, sir." Elizabeth's gaze revealed that she definitely was in favor of coming to know the lieutenant better.

"That leaves only you unspoken for, Jamie. So what will you have me tell Governor Stallings?"

"I suppose I haven't any choice," Jamie murmured.

Robert Maynard, when he saw the prospects dressed in attire considered becoming for her sex, was highly pleased by the result. He stood near Mistress Elizabeth Ferris, a prospective bridegroom's grin of satisfaction spread all over his handsome face.

Elizabeth gazed from the magistrate signing her pardon to the Navy lieutenant, her eyes lingering long and with pleasure on the officer. Maynard was much closer to her own age than old Bramwell and very much more pleasant to look upon. His dark brown hair had a slight curl to it where it fastened behind his neck with a wide black ribbon and he was most resplendent in his uniform. She liked the way he seemed so sure of himself when speaking to the magistrate, yet stuttered and blushed each time he addressed her. Her parents, when she wrote to them, might be disappointed that he wasn't wealthy and influential, yet would likely be pleased enough that she had a good match. He had prospects of going far.

Rather than exchanging the looks of a couple in love, the other couple standing before the magistrate avoided eye contact, but each time it became necessary, their exchange was a glare of harsh disapproval directed at the other.

Franco had only appeared a few minutes before court convened, not leaving them time to exchange conversation. His attitude seemed to convey that he felt put upon for the bother he was called on to serve in her behalf. It wasn't as if he had to go through with a bloody ceremony, she thought, anger darkening her own countenance.

"Since these gentlemen are making themselves responsible for you, I trust you ladies have learned a lesson from these past weeks in jail and will consider it in your future conduct," the magistrate sermonized, his white, powdered wig perched neatly on his head, his black robe intimidating and somber. "It is only because of the good names of your future husbands that the court will even consider your release. I trust you will conduct yourselves accordingly so as to never risk staining their sterling reputations."

If not for her foul mood, Jamie would have found the justice's comment amusing. Perhaps Maynard was all right, but Franco was as much a pirate in the past as she had been and John Terry was perfectly willing to sell his sterling reputation for a percentage only a few weeks back. Instead, she listened soberly, pretending to heed every word of the judge's good advice until, finally, he ceased his preaching, signed the documents, and released them into the custody of their prospective bridegrooms.

"What will you do now?" Franco posed the question to the other two couples standing on the steps of the courthouse in the bright sunshine. Anyone passing the couples would have taken them as just having inquired into the obtaining of marriage licenses or of making a minor complaint to the magistrates. Lacey wore a light green gown of watered silk and Elizabeth, a stunning sunshine yellow, while Jamie was gowned in sky-shaded blue, the three of them looking like a spring bouquet on the sidewalk.

"I'm taking Lacey back to Bermuda. My father has arranged a number of balls and receptions to celebrate our marriage," John answered, lightly holding the delicate hand that had once put a knife to his throat. Now, she merely wrapped her fingers about his palm, smiling up at him.

"Since I have time on my hands until my new orders arrive, Elizabeth and I are going with them," Maynard provided to Franco's questioning look.

John Terry turned to Franco. "Why don't the two of you join us?"

"I'm used to being seen about Royale and should not care to take chances on another island at present with war so close at hand," Franco replied.

"I quite understand." John Terry nodded, seeming sure that Franco spoke for Jamie as well, for which she contented herself at present with no more than a frown that Terry failed to notice. "Well, I wish the best to both of you. Our passage leaves within the hour and we must arrange accommodations for Robert and Elizabeth. You will keep in touch, I trust. You know where to find us."

"Indeed." Franco took Terry's outstretched hand, their previous animosity forgotten.

"I hope someday you will show me how you accomplished disarming me so easily," Terry laughed good-naturedly.

"A trick of the wrist, but it will be my pleasure to teach it to you when next we meet."

"Jamie, will you be all right?" Lacey asked in concern, seeing that Jamie had not smiled once during the entire exchange. "I feel as though we're deserting you."

"You aren't at all, Lacey. Be happy." Jamie rushed forward with a warm embrace and to kiss Lacey's cheek. She truly was pleased that her friends had found happiness. "And you,

Elizabeth," she hugged her firmly, "I shall miss you both, but we'll be seeing each other again soon." The parting was about to turn tearful until Terry suggested they had better hurry or they would miss their passage. Jamie watched the four of them walking away, arm in arm.

"Shall we go?" Franco asked with a cold, hard edge in his tone.

"Go where?" Jamie responded in kind, turning her face up to him. "Why are you angry with me?" she demanded.

"I think the answer to that should be obvious," he replied, taking her roughly by the arm and leading her down the street in the opposite direction.

"If you did not want to sign the bloody proclamation, then you shouldn't have!"

"What else was I to do—let them hang you?"

"How kind of you to be concerned!" Her voice raised, catching the attention of passers-by on the bustling street.

"You might consider thanking me for your life!"

"Oh? Then thank you for that as well," she retorted, but Franco only glared hotly, then started out again at a quick pace that forced her to trot to keep up since his grip on her arm was rock firm. "Where do you think you are taking me?"

"For now, to an inn. To a decent, respectable inn where no pirates have ever set foot. A place, no doubt, you've never been before."

"And do you intend to drag me the entire distance?" She pulled back as hard as she could, but only succeeded in slowing his progress slightly until he took a firmer grip and yanked her into motion again. "Let go of my arm!"

"Not on your life." Franco continued to tow her behind him, his gaze locked on the direction he was taking. "You are in my custody and I am not about to misplace my responsibility."

"Is that what I am?" she queried furiously.

"Each time I let you out of my sight, I find you in deeper trouble. What would you have done had I not come?" He

430

spun about to question her.

"Since I was not expecting you, I would have found a way," she retorted. "You'll not earn my gratitude for your oh-so-noble deed! I never asked it of you."

"No, you don't need me for anything, do you?" He stood before her, ignoring the strollers along the avenue who paused to peer at the bickering couple stopped in the very center of the sidewalk creating an obstruction.

For several seconds, Jamie only stared up at him, wondering about the slightly sad look on his face. "I don't know what you mean," she finally replied, her brow vexed.

"It would be nice to know, Mistress Morgan, that you could ever turn to me in any crisis, but you won't, will you?"

"I can't," Jamie said soberly. "I can't explain why. I just can't."

"Maybe I can tell you. You're afraid I'll let you down. You think that I'll disappoint you, and rather than risk testing me, you'll simply never put your faith there. I promised you before and I'll say it again. I won't disappoint you." Franco took her arm again and they walked the rest of the way to the inn in silence.

"I'm going out for a while to tend to some business. I expect to find you here when I return."

Jamie said nothing as he walked out the door.

She wasn't there when he came back, and several days later Jocko told him she had taken a ship to Jamestown, claiming she would start a new life there. Furious, he followed her, knowing she would be forced by necessity to meet the terms of her father's will and, on his arrival, he had searched each and every church, chapel, and magistrate's home in the driving rain, seeking some word of her until he finally threw open the door of Reverend Horvath's with a bang that threatened to break the door off its hinges.

Chapter Twenty

For days after their wedding night, Franco refused to acknowledge her existence, which suited Jamie as well, since she had no desire to speak with him either. Her heart ached for him but she couldn't tell him. She had choked down enough of her pride for his sake and couldn't swallow any more. How easily she had let him know in the past of her love for him but the only time, it seemed, he truly wanted her was when she pretended to no longer want him.

Oh, but it was such a lie, she thought as she strolled the starboard deck of Franco's ship. She did want him—desperately. She just wasn't able to come crawling back as he seemed to expect her to. He wasn't about to apologize and neither would she. For the past several days she slept alone in the cabin. She didn't know where he took his rest. Perhaps in Garcia's quarters, since his first mate took the duty when Franco was not on deck. He came in and got his clothes for the day and never said a word to her in passing. She pretended to be busy at sewing or reading to give her the excuse to ignore him. Was this the way it would end, then, with even their friendship destroyed? She supposed so, since neither would give in to the other.

When the ship finally docked at Royale, Jamie packed the few garments she had altered to fit her into the chest he had provided and walked out onto the deck.

The gangplank was lowered over the side and Jamie walked toward it, casting a long, lingering glance over her shoulder to see Franco on the upper deck, standing with Garcia. He saw her getting ready to leave and only looked. She waited, he stared. She turned and walked toward the gangplank, praying he would call out to her. Amid the shouts of seamen fastening lines and stowing rigging, the sound of his voice never came. Steeling her resolve, she forced her shoulders back and walked off the ship.

"Jocko," Jamie said to the broad, tall back in front of her. Her old first mate stopped counting bottles of liquor on the barshelf and swung around.

"Jamie, lass . . ." He came around the counter and grabbed her up in his bearlike embrace. "Ye had all of us worried sick to death, girl. We learnt ye went to Jamestown and figured ye had gone to see that lawyer fellow but, tell me, did he advance ye any of yer rightful money? Is that how ye've come back to us?"

"No." Jamie shook her head, heartsick. "I'd rather not talk about it now, Jocko. There's something I have to ask you." She swallowed the nausea building up in her stomach again as it had so often over the past month. "Jocko, I need your help. I need a place to stay. I haven't any money . . ."

"Lass, ye don't need money around me. Ye know that. My home is yers. It always was."

"I know that," she tried to smile, "but it may be for some time that I'll have to live off your generosity."

"However long, 'tis no matter to me."

"Thank you." She felt dizzy, her knees too weak to support her. The room started to spin.

"Here, lass . . ." Jocko grabbed her as she started to topple. "Sit down." He pulled a bench out and made her sit down on it. "Are ye taken ill?" He gazed at her in concern.

"No, not ill." Tears blurred her vision as the first mate sat down beside her, thinking of Franco letting her go, saying nothing to call her back, not even trying to stop her. "Jocko, I'm pregnant!" she blurted. "It's Franco's child and he doesn't want me anymore." She broke into sobs, leaning against the mate's burly chest for comfort.

"That can't be true, lass." Jocko held her close, letting her flowing tears stain his shirt. "I never knowed a man to love a woman as much as he does you."

"It isn't so," she said in short, wracking sobs. "If he did, he would never have let me walk off his ship just now."

"Why don't ye dry yer eyes, pet," he patted her shoulder, "and tell yer ole Jocko everything."

If this was the way she wanted it, Franco could think of no means to stop her. He could drag her back aboard by force, but what would it accomplish? He couldn't chain her to the walls of his cabin. He had hoped making her his wife would make a difference, but even that couldn't hold her if she truly meant to be free of him. At least she could use the marriage certificate Father Ramirez had signed to obtain her inheritance to live on. She wouldn't be desperate enough to wed herself to a stranger or to take, again, to piracy. If that was all he could do for her, it would have to be enough. She could obtain an annulment without too much difficulty because he wouldn't fight her over it.

He left Garcia on the bridge in charge of taking on the supplies to outfit the ship and went below to his cabin. Her scent still lingered in the room, the lemon verbena sachet she used, and for the first time since he stood over his father's grave, he felt like he wanted to cry. Never had he thought it might end like this, with her walking away from him. He had thought only death could ever truly part them. She loved him, even through her schemes with John Terry and Andrew Carmody. He knew those plans had to come to nothing because she loved him instead. When she saw every bit of what Morgan intended her to see with Polly, he had known, in time, he would convince her of the truth and win her back. Fate would never let it end any other way. They loved each other.

Now, except for the lingering scent, not a sign of her ever having been here remained. Her clothes, her hair combs, the hand mirror and brush she had taken from the chest to use, everything had been removed. Surveying the cabin for anything she might have overlooked, he saw the edge of a piece of folded paper poking out from beneath the teakwood catch-all tray on his dresser. He slipped it out and unfolded the paper, perusing the scrolled writing only long enough to realize it was their marriage certificate. Of all things to forget! Without it, she couldn't prove she had abided by the terms of Morgan's will.

He refolded the paper and jammed it into the inside pocket of his frockcoat, then left the cabin, slamming the door behind him.

"Lass, go back to him," Jocko advised solemnly. They had taken a table in a dim corner of Jocko's tavern to remain undisturbed as the early crew of bartenders and serving girls began to arrive to start the business day. "The man's yer husband now. 'Tis where ye belong."

"I can't go back after what I've said to him!" Jamie wrung a sodden handkerchief in her hands. It was so wet with shed tears that several droplets splashed onto the polished table.

"Tell him that ye didn't mean it. Give him the chance to tell you he didn't mean what he said neither. I swear, I've never seen such a pair as the two of ye!" Jocko berated. "Never, at no time, can both of ye tell the other what's really on yer minds. Ye know damn well Polly's a liar when it suits her purpose. And she'd do anything yer papa asked her to, especially if it was something she wouldn't mind doing any-ways, like bedding Franco if she could! Ye're no blind fool to not be knowing yer papa would have schemed up such a

435

plot. Had ye not been blind with grief then, ye'd have seen through it plain enough by yerself! Cap'n Morgan was my captain, and I loved him like I've loved no other man alive. 'Twas him gave me a home here and he gave me my name. Not Big-Un, as my massa once called me, but Jocko, a man's name, and the respect that goes with it. Took me in, he did, an overgrowed, runaway slave with nowheres to hide and he give me a future as a free man. But I still knowed him for what he was—a schemin', conniving devil when he couldn't have his own way by no other means. Ye know, deep down in yer heart, Franco never betrayed ye. 'Twas the truth he told ye that it was Morgan's plot."

"I suppose so," Jamie murmured. She had to believe it now after Franco had so often denied it, explained it, proved to her that what was seen with the eyes wasn't necessarily the truth. Why would he have taken Polly just as they were coming in to home port, when he could have done so on Tortuga, or during the voyage, and never risked being caught? It didn't make sense for him to have done so.

"Lass," Jocko put his oversize hand over her small one, "the man is yer wedded husband now and the father of the babe ye carry. Ain't it time ye settled these differences? If ye won't do it for yer own sake, then do it for the sake of the babe."

Jamie turned her hand about and squeezed Jocko's fingers, offering him a feeble smile. "You're right. I'm going right now to find my husband," she told him. "We have a lot to talk about."

"That's the girl," Jocko said as she rose. He watched her walk out the door into the bright sunshine.

The first tremor shook the entire building with an ungodly roar. A rent appeared in the plaster above Jocko's head and chunks of debris fell like rain all around him. Bridget, the barmaid, screamed as a large timber dislodged from the ceiling and fell across the bar, cracking the heavy wood. Jocko tried to rise to his feet but the floor rocked beneath him, tumbling him over onto his back. He thought he was losing his grip on reality as the room before him pitched and weaved like a ship's deck in a storm-tossed sea. It couldn't yet it was, rising and falling as if riding wild waves and fighting gale winds. The floorboards squealed in protest and cracked with loud, popping sounds. Nails came out of the bending wallboards and flew across the room like grape shot. The bottles on the bar shelf shimmied and rattled, ever nearer to the edge until they tumbled over, breaking explosively. Shards of glass burst across the room like deadly missiles, forcing Jocko to duck behind an overturned table. Bridget tried to run, screaming from the room, lost her footing and was pitched to the floor.

Jocko had to remind himself that this wasn't a rocking deck in a hurricane. It was dry land. Dear Lord God Almighty, he realized suddenly, it was an earthquake, and a big one.

Jamie knew it was the pregnancy that made her stomach feel so queasy. The last time they had been together had been their wedding night, almost two months past now, and that was the only night it could have happened. She remembered her surprise during the voyage when she experienced seasickness for the first time in her life. A few days later, when it didn't abate, she realized the truth. Counting back, she had missed her monthly cycles and she wondered then if this was nature's way of trying to tell her she was about to make a grievous mistake.

Now what would he say to learn he was going to be a father? Would he think the baby was the only reason she came back? She paused on the sidewalk and suddenly couldn't keep her balance. All the buildings in front of her started to shudder as a mighty rumble shook the earth, the ground moving as if the earth wanted to shake her off. She gripped the edge of a shop corner to steady herself, fighting to stay on her feet, grasping the building to stay upright. The ground roared angrily and people began to scream and shout. Before her horrified eyes, a building across the way crumbled under the shaking, tumbling into a heap of rubble. Then the next one went and the next, each falling over onto the other like dominoes in a line. Startled screams turned into high-pitched, terror-riddled screeches of anguish and pain and hysteria. People tried to run, wildly attempting to escape the falling timbers, plaster, and stone of the crumbling stores and shopfronts along the avenue. People staggered to their feet only to be pitched to the ground again by the rolling, rumbling earth.

In Jamie's memory Royale had experienced earthquakes before but never one of this magnitude. She knew if she could stay out of the path of falling debris and avoided the huge cracks that might suddenly appear in the earth's foundation, it would all be over in a few minutes.

She selected the huge beam supporting a portico on the shop's front and clung to it for her life. The crashing, breaking sounds were all around her, drowning her in the noise, the screams and cries and moans of despair, until she buried her head beneath her free arm and held on to the rocking pillar with all her might. Then, as suddenly as it had started, it was over. The earth stopped moving, stopped rumbling. She could smell smoke and knew fires must have broken out all over the city, but she had made it. Her baby had made it. She was safe, at least for now. Aftershocks would come but would not be nearly so violent.

Another thought slammed into her brain and made her rigid with fear. Yes, the earthquake was over, but she had survived them before and remembered the quake itself was not the greatest danger, it was the aftereffects. The earthquake was like a pebble dropped onto the surface of a pond. It produced ripples, and the ripples so near the seaside meant — tidal wave!

The last one had flooded the streets all the way to the hills where the governor's mansion stood. This quake had been so much stronger. The wave would be even larger. God in heaven, such a wave would be huge!

She looked around her wildly to see if anyone else had realized what she had. The survivors were picking themselves up off the ground, weeping, moaning, searching the rubble for loved ones they had lost, calling out for a missing child, a missing friend. Their faces were shocked, tear-streaked, bewildered, but they thought all the danger was past.

"No!" Jamie cried out to them. "It isn't over! Not yet!" She waved her arms frantically, trying to get their attention. "It isn't finished. You must reach high ground, as high as you can climb. Get into the boats, the ships. Get to deep water! Get off the island or get to high ground! Listen to me!" she screamed, but they only stared at her as if they were watching a madwoman.

Franco burst through the broken door of Jocko's tavern, taking in the wreckage in a glance. Part of the roof still stood, and the survivors were huddled beneath it. Jocko's bartender had been killed when the stairs to the upper story collapsed. The quake had caught Franco on the street and he had kept running, even over the pitching earth, trying to reach Jamie in the only place he hoped desperately she might have gone.

"Jamie!" he called out to Jocko, seeing that the first mate and his other employee were uninjured.

"She left a few minutes afore the shaking started. She went to look for you," Jocko told him.

"She went back to the ship?"

"Aye, went to find ye, she said." Jocko waved to him to be gone and Franco tore down the street the way he had come.

He had to have missed her in the crowds that had come flowing out of the shops and inns when the shaking began. He was heartened to realize she had to have been coming back to him. What other reason could there be for her to return unless she still wanted him. But with every quake-shocked face he saw and failed to recognize as hers, fright for her safety swelled higher in his chest. She had to be among the survivors. He swung women around to look at their faces, refusing as yet to search among the corpses.

"Jamie!" he called out, but his voice was lost among the tumult of other voices calling for loved ones in the litter-strewn, dusty street. Growing more frantic by the moment, he kept calling, kept searching, making his way back toward the *Isabella*, the direction Jocko had said she had taken.

He heard a voice he thought he recognized, but it was behind him. He spun about and then he saw her, moving down the middle of the street, clutching at the people she passed, talking to them with desperate urgency. "Go to high ground. Please, listen to me. You must escape! The wave! The wave is coming!"

The people pulled away from her as if she was a mad zealot screeching that the world was coming to an end. Franco pushed his way through the people to her side.

"Jamie!" He grabbed her arm and swung her around, pulling her into his arms. "Thank God! You're safe!" He held her tightly as if to pull her inside himself. "Thank God," he murmured. She was clinging to him, sobbing, clutching the material of his frockcoat to hold on tight. Then he realized what she had been saying and knew she was right. He pulled free of her, shouting into her face. "Go to the *Isabella!* I'll get Jocko and the rest."

"I'm not leaving you," she said adamantly, trying to follow him.

"No! You must tell Garcia to make ready to cast off. He may not know the danger. Hurry!"

His last shout seemed to reach her and she started off,

440

disappearing among the crowd, headed for the ship. He prayed she would reach it safely as he hurried back to the tavern. Halfway there, he ran straight into Jocko and the tavern girl.

"Jocko, the wave!" He grabbed the big man's shoulders.

"I know it. We was just coming to ask ye to take us aboard."

"No," Bridget suddenly murmured, her eyes wide with fright. "I won't be aboard a ship if a big wave comes. I won't!" She started to back away from them.

"It's the only chance ye have." Jocko reached out for her, catching the edge of her sleeve, but Bridget twisted out of his grasp to run off in the direction most of the crowd was taking. "Come back here, ye twit!" Jocko called after her but Bridget was gone.

"It's no use, Jocko. They'll never reach high ground in time, but they won't heed us," Franco told him. He'd seen the futility of Jamie's efforts and they couldn't afford to lose any more time. The wave was already on its way to them.

They reached the ship and Franco found Jamie already issuing the necessary orders to set sail. Watching her as he rushed across the gangplank with Jocko on his heels, he felt proud of her abilities, even though he hadn't always approved of the ways she employed them. She knew what had to be done now and had set the crew to doing it, the tone of certainty in her voice precluding any arguments.

He reached the bridge and ordered all sails fully unfurled to catch the brisk wind that had kicked up over the island, blowing them away from the shore. As the wind became even more violent, the mainsail's center seam split, but she held, catching the hard breeze and billowing out, the canvas stretching to its limit. Providence seemed to be helping them as their speed picked up, hurling them out to sea. The only chance they had was in deep water, meeting the wave head-on. A slight deviation to port or to starboard and the tidal wave would pick the ship up and toss it straight back to the shallows. Too far to either side and it would turn them completely over. But if the ship's prow sliced directly into the cresting wave's center, like a matchstick, it had a chance of staying afloat.

The orders issued and the work done, they tied themselves down, helping one another until everyone was lashed to something on the deck, then there was nothing left to do but wait until they met the wave.

"Ned?" Jamie shouted to Jocko. As the strongest, Jocko had volunteered to take the wheel, lashed to the pilot's post.

"He took the *Lady* to sea only yesterday," Jocko called back to her.

"Thank God," she murmured. Most of the men from her old crew would be with him, miles away by now. Even McGee, the champion mouser, would be down in the ship's hold attending to his only duty. Jamie was tied to the forecastle rail with Franco lashed to the rail beside her. She could just reach out to touch his hand and did so as she looked over to him. "Your sisters? Their families?"

"They're on high ground," he assured her. "It may just wash over them but they should be all right."

The sky was steadily darkening and she had to shout to be heard over the crashing waves and howling wind. "Franco, I want you to know I lied that night. No one could take your place."

He smiled at her. "I lied too when I said I didn't care what you do. I love you." His voice strained to be heard above the rising volume of the storm.

"Why have you never said so before?"

"I have."

"You never did," she retorted. "Not once in all the time I've known you."

"I must have," he argued, the wind catching his words and tossing them away.

"Take my word for it. You never did! I would certainly remember it if you had."

"Have I been as remiss as that?"

Giving up on her shout as a blast of wind tore across the deck, she just nodded.

"Then is it too late to remedy? I love you!" he shouted louder to be sure she heard him. "I have always loved you! I've loved you since you were a boy!"

"You big, silly oaf! Why couldn't you have said so four years ago?"

Then the sky darkened with the wall of water rushing straight at them and the tidal wave washed over the deck.

Epilogue

Seven months later.

"If you don't stop pacing, you'll never survive this day."

"I can't help it. I've never been made a great-uncle before." Bertrand Duvalier paced to the window then back across the parlor floor. "How can you stay so calm?" he asked of his nephew-in-law.

"A facade," Franco assured him. "All the calm is on the outside. Within, I'm a nervous wreck."

"You'd think the two of you were doing all the work," Maria DeCortega Garcelón remarked as she walked past them with a stack of fresh towels she carried up the stairs.

"Take my advice, both of you," Esteban inserted. "I've been through it four times now and I know whatever we do does not make the slightest difference up there!" He pointed over his head. "We wait, we worry, the baby comes." He shrugged.

Laughter eased the tension slightly. Esteban was doing well with his promise to Franco. Under his supervision, the coffee plantation was thriving, and with his new sobriety, so were Maria and the children. He touched nothing but a glass of wine now and again and he looked healthier for it. Esteban said it was the mountain air, but Franco knew it was from staying away from the whiskey and brandy.

Beyond the windows, on the lawn outside, Esteban and Maria's brood of four played with Theresa's two children. Theresa was upstairs with the rest of the women — Maria,

Mary Lambert and the midwife from town.

Port Royale had been utterly leveled by the earthquake and the tidal wave that followed it. The survivors who had escaped to high ground in time or in ships as the crew of the *Isabella* did, had returned to start over. Since Royale held too many memories of lost loved ones and of its reputation as the New World Sodom and Gomorrah, the rebuilt city had a new name to start its new life as a peaceful, vital, civilized community.

Franco was building Jamie a house there, on the hillside that overlooked the harbor. Until it was ready, they were staying with Esteban and his family. Franco had hoped the house in Kingston would be ready in time for the birth, but Jamie's labor pains came a few weeks too early.

Bertrand had arrived only a week ago, finding passage as soon as he received Jamie's letter that they had survived the quake and that he could expect a grand-niece or nephew soon. He had told Franco, but Franco wanted to wait until after the birth to tell Jamie that Bertrand was naming their child his heir. The baby would inherit all the Duvalier wealth as well as the Gavrilac title.

Franco's own title would go to his eldest, and if the baby was a son, he would be a duke of France and a count in Spain someday — a lot of title for one tiny baby to carry, but his parents had decided their children would be raised in the New World that was their homeland. Franco was starting a shipping business to be based in the new port of Kingston.

Franco heard footsteps on the stairs and looked up to see Theresa's flushed form descending.

"Francisco?" She beamed at him. "A boy! You have a son!"

He was about to rush up the stairs to see his wife when Bertrand Duvalier fainted.

"Isn't he beautiful?" Jamie touched the downy black curls on the infant's forehead.

"How could he not be? Look at his mother." Franco leaned over the baby to kiss her cheek.

"He looks like you, you know," she remarked.

"How can you tell?" Franco studied the infant's sleeping face. "He looks a bit like a red-faced monkey to me."

"Oh, you." She swatted his arm. "I wish Morgan had lived to see him," she said wistfully.

"He would have been proud of the job you've done," Franco smiled.

"I never want to go through that again!" Jamie referred to the sixteen hours of labor.

"But you will," Franco promised her. "I intend to keep you busy from now on raising babies."

"Knowing you," she teased, "I have no doubt of it. What shall we name him?"

"I already have."

"Without consulting me?" She looked up questioningly.

"I didn't think you would object, since I've named him after your father."

"Henry?" her nose wrinkled distastefully. "I loved Papa but Henry DeCortega sounds terrible to me."

"That isn't his name," Franco stated, waiting until her brows lowered into a puzzled frown. "We're calling him Morgan. Morgan James DeCortega."

Jamie thought about the name for a moment. "Morgan James *Francis* DeCortega," she decided. "And he'll grow up to be just like his father."

"Heaven forbid!" Franco exclaimed, and they both laughed.